VOICES OF THE SOUTH

Also By Walter Sullivan

Fiction
The Long, Long Love
A Time to Dance

Literary Criticism
Death by Melancholy: Essays on Modern Southern Fiction
A Requiem for the Renascence: The State of Fiction in the Modern South
In Praise of Blood Sports and Other Essays

Memoir
Allen Tate: A Recollection

As Editor
Band of Prophets (with William C. Havard)
The War the Women Lived: Voices from the Confederate South

Textbook
Writing from the Inside (with George Core)

SOJOURN OF A STRANGER

By Walter Sullivan

LOUISIANA STATE UNIVERSITY PRESS
Baton Rouge

Copyright © 1957 by Walter Sullivan
Originally published by Henry Holt and Company
LSU Press edition published 2003 by arrangement with the author
All rights reserved
Manufactured in the United States of America

12 11 10 09 08 07 06 05 04 03

5 4 3 2 1

Library of Congress Cataloging-in-Publication Data:

Sullivan, Walter, 1924–
   Sojourn of a stranger / Walter Sullivan.
     p. cm. — (Voices of the South)
   ISBN 0-8071-2917-8 (pbk. : alk. paper)
   1. Racially mixed people—Fiction. 2. Mothers and sons—Fiction.
3. Tennessee—Fiction. I. Title. II. Series.

PS3569.U3593S65 2003
813'.54—dc21

                                                      2003054343

The paper in this book meets the guidelines for permanence and durability of the Committee on Production Guidelines for Book Longevity of the Council on Library Resources. ∞

For Jane

hold not thy peace at my tears;
For I am a stranger with thee, and a sojourner, as all my fathers were.

O spare me a little, that I may recover my strength, before I go hence, and be no more seen.

—Psalms 39:12-13

SOJOURN OF A STRANGER

◆ 1 ◆

THEY MOVED ALONG the road in an established order, slowly and quietly through the heavy dust as if they were part of a funeral cortege or a wagon train for an army. Or at least that is the way he thought of them, sitting beside his father in the buggy with the old brassbound rifle unloaded across his knees and the shotpouch at his side filled with gravel. When the woods were dense—oak, hickory, hackberries with their top leaves curling and yellow in the July heat —they were a train and he would wait for the enemy to attack with his gun leveled at the turn in the road or the thicket beyond his mother's carriage. That was the hard part of the game: she had insisted on going first to avoid the dirt, just as she had compelled his father to hire the wagon that came behind them to carry the piano, the press, the slender, gilded chairs. So he had always to contend with the sight of Vernon perched like a bird on top of the carriage box, a white cotton duster buttoned tight up under his chin and a soft black hat pulled low on his head to keep the sun from his eyes. But at the moment of final danger Allen Hendrick's courage was equal to this too, to the delicate conveyance that bounced and swayed along the road in front of him. He jerked the slack trigger until the steel meshed into his flesh and at the edge of the forest Englishmen and Indians fell bleeding under the trees. Then Vernon would speak and it would all be over.

Vernon would turn around on the box and look down at Allen Hendrick with his eyes open wide and his lips parted to show his teeth so that he had a sort of wild, surprised look as if he had forgotten that Allen was riding along behind him or as if he had been asleep when the shooting began. When he talked, he let go of the reins entirely, looped them around the whip socket, and leaned over toward the buggy with the white duster wrinkled and pulled tight over his chest. "What you want to yell so for?" he said to Allen Hendrick. "You done scare the mamma squirrels away from they breakfast."

And Allen's father would speak, smiling faintly, fingering the spectacle ribbon that dangled between his buttonhole and his pocket. "No, what you heard was gunfire. He just killed twelve men and we'd better move along before their friends discover what he's done and set out after us."

Then with the rifle put aside, its barrel resting on the dashboard, he would hear the beat of the horses' hoofs, the sad creak of an axle, and he would think how the hero died in battle for his country and was carried home from the war. Allen Hendrick would look at the carriage and try to imagine himself lying there, dead and washed and shrouded, pale from the loss of blood; he attempted to mourn his own mortality, but it would never go. He could never get the right pitch, the proper tone of sadness. For the day was too bright, the air too warm, and under the summer sky birds sang in the wilderness and a breeze blew and sycamore leaves changed color in the sun. Somewhere far away a crow called and a flicker hammered against a limb, and a rabbit crossed the road in front of them, brown as the dust except for its belly and the underside of its tail. When the wagon jolted, there was the sound of his mother's piano, the faint, tinkling, senseless notes, foolish as a girl's laughter, as weak—against all the great spaces of the forest—as his own dream of death. Occasionally he caught sight of squirrels on the branch of a walnut tree or possum tracks by the weeds at the side of the trail, and his heart celebrated all the things which he could not see, but which he knew were there—the deer, the bear, the yellow-eyed cat who peered from the heavy foliage.

"Now, Father," he would say, "how far is it now?" and the answer would come, not in miles, but in the number of days they would still have to travel in order to get there. He would reach out to touch the wheel of the buggy, to let the warm iron rim turn beneath his fingers, wondering how they would know, how they could ever possibly tell exactly when the first horse walked into Middle Tennessee, or the carriage crossed the Sumner County line.

Allen Hendrick watched, in the days that followed, for some sign, a change in the land or in the scent of the air, or failing everything else a gesture from his father; and this came, at night, when they had been on the road for a week. They were out of the wilderness, past the log stores of backwoods settlements, the half-cleared, lonely farms, and his father pointed in the darkness to a fine brick house, saying, "That is where the Weavers live."

To Allen Hendrick the name meant nothing. He had heard of his grandfather, who had been a general in the War of 1812, and of his Aunt Valeria and of Captain Rutledge, but the name Weaver had never been spoken in any of the stories of war his father had told him. "Are we there, sir?" Allen Hendrick said. "Are we in Gallatin?"

"You will know Gallatin," his father said. "Gallatin is a city like Memphis. It is just not quite so big."

That afternoon they had passed through Nashville and Edgefield, but his father spoke as if there were only two cities in all of Tennessee, as if there were nothing east of Memphis but a desert or an ocean that one had to travel across to get to Gallatin. He had been drinking and his voice was heavy, not indistinct but a little slow, as if he were tired from the long passage. When he turned to speak again, Allen Hendrick caught the smell of brandy, distant, sweet as a flower, on the damp night air. "We have simply gone from one city to another," Allen's father went on. "But there is one thing that can be put down in our favor. Nobody else in the history of our nation ever came East to run away."

"Sir?" Allen said.

"Yes," his father replied. "We are unique. When you run away you are supposed to head for Texas."

He did not quite understand this. He had never thought of what they were doing as running away, but he did not question Marcus Hendrick further. He simply waited, riding in silence through the quiet streets that were smoother than those in Memphis, past the older, cleaner residences, the fenced lawns, until they stopped in front of a white frame house and Vernon descended from the carriage.

"It's Aaron," Vernon said.

Allen Hendrick saw an old colored man start down the stairs from the porch. He was white-headed, thin, with legs as skinny as wagon spokes and a stomach full and round like a baby's. The old man bent forward slightly, taking the steps one at a time with a dirty lantern held close to the planks to light his way.

"I'm surprised to see you ain't dead yet," Vernon said. "You old enough to be."

"You ain't nothing," the old man said. "You less than nothing."

All his teeth were worn down and some of them were gone; when he spoke his lower lip curled out and showed pink in the light cast by the lantern. Allen Hendrick watched him make his way to the buggy, the bent old man hobbling on his own thin legs as if after all the years he had lived he had almost forgotten how to walk. He raised the light to look at Allen Hendrick's father, held it close to the fair face, the eyes that were red from brandy, and stood for a minute silent with the pink lips puckered up into a little circle. "You altered," he said then, taking the man into his arms as if he were caressing a child, "you been gone too long, Marse Marcus."

"Perhaps," Allen's father, Marcus Hendrick, said in a slow voice. "There's a likely chance that I have." He turned to Allen, bowed slightly without raising himself off the seat. "This is my boy, Uncle Aaron."

"I seen him," the old man said. "But all the time I had it in my head wrong. I calculated he'd favor you."

Allen Hendrick went toward the house. He walked up the steps slowly, holding the sound of old Aaron's voice in his memory, trying to measure the quality of those last words, to establish whatever it was the old man had meant to say, not with the words, but by the sound itself, the strange tone of speaking as cold as a winter wind. He knew that his grandfather had arranged for the house and furnished it and that Aaron was one of the general's slaves who had waited for them with the key. There were other things he knew beyond that—things about his mother and his father and the life they had lived before they left West Tennessee. But all these he attempted to put outside his thoughts.

He walked on to the parlor, where his mother stood with the furniture she had brought from Memphis piled around her in the middle of the floor. Her hand was resting on the piano, her fingers moving slightly, feeling the varnish on its rosewood cabinet. To Allen Hendrick she looked altogether composed, not even soiled by the journey. The skirt of her black silk dress hung in full, even folds and her hair was still in place, pulled toward the back of her neck with only a little wave across the top to show where the bonnet had been worn. She regarded Allen Hendrick, pleasantly, half smiling, and her eyes seemed to him beautiful and bright.

"We are here," she said. "We are in Gallatin."

"Yes, ma'am," Allen Hendrick replied. He only half heard her, for he was tired and he wondered where he would sleep.

She turned away, walked toward the other end of the room as if she were inspecting the premises, but the light was poor and most of the furniture had been covered against the dust. "You will like it," she said after a while, speaking from the edge of darkness, from across the dark space of carpet. "Oh, you will like living in Gallatin, won't you, Allen?"

"Yes, ma'am," he repeated. "I expect so."

In the silence that followed, Allen Hendrick thought that he could not wait any longer, that he would have to leave and find his bed, even before she had told him good night. His head ached, throbbed with the beating of his pulse and his eyelids were burning and heavy. But he remained, hearing Vernon in the hallway, laughing, still deviling Uncle Aaron, and the old man's voice was grumbling, creaking with age.

She came back nearer the light and sat down on one of the little chairs that had come with them in the wagon. "You will go to see your grandfather tomorrow," his mother said, and she went on to speak of how the house stood high on a hill overlooking a garden and a lake, and of the fields that dropped away to the river.

"For your grandfather's land goes to the river," she said. "And downstream, on the other side, is General Jackson's plantation."

He looked up at the name. He caught her eye, glittering and lovely, reflecting the flame of the candle before she looked away. She looked past him without turning her head, as if she had been seized by a precipitate bashfulness born out of sorrow or shame. He did not think of it exactly like this, but he came later to remember it: her eyes and her face and the story that she told. For as they sat together, breathing the air that had grown stale in the shuttered, vacant room, she told him of New Orleans and the war.

With the candle sputtering, shadows playing over her dark hair and the smooth skin of her forehead, she told him how Jackson and Laffite had whipped the British with an army of jailbirds and pirates and bearded men from Tennessee. She talked quietly, her voice even and soft, almost as if she were discussing a shawl or a fancy bonnet; he leaned toward her in the dark room, heard her story under the strange roof, surrounded by the covered chairs, shapeless and foreign like a group of sedentary ghosts. Allen Hendrick listened to the words that were almost calm, except for the faint catch in his mother's throat when she paused to get her breath. His weariness was gone and he saw it all clearly in his mind—the breastworks, the officers on horseback, the red-coated Englishmen who crossed the swampy field.

"When it was over," his mother said, "they returned to the city." They went toward the cathedral, cheered by the citizens through the narrow, muddy streets, and all along the way ladies crowded onto balconies to look and wave their perfumed handkerchiefs. This was the grandest part of a victory, Allen Hendrick thought, to march with Andrew Jackson past all the people in the square. For the old general had ridden to the *cabildo,* straight and tall, as slender as a sponge stick, and behind him were the volunteers in fringed hunting shirts and the free men of color—*les gens de couleur libre,* his mother had called them—who had manned a battery under the moss-hung oaks.

"Oh," his mother said, "it was a grand sight, indeed. And two days later General Jackson went back to the cathedral, surrounded by his soldiers, to be crowned with laurel and hear Abbé du Bourg say Mass."

"Were you there?" Allen Hendrick said finally. "I mean, did you see them come back?"

She smiled, her lips parting to show the fine white teeth.

"Ah, no," she said. "I was not born then."

But for Allen Hendrick this would not do. "Then how do you know?" he said, for he believed most of all in that part of the hero which could be seen and touched, the flesh that stood the brutal fire.

"From my brother," she said. "My brother was with the army at Chalmette."

And Allen Hendrick thought only, I will see him tomorrow. His mother was silent, waiting, her hands clasped tight in her lap, her head tilted forward slightly, as if she were listening for what he would have to say, but Allen Hendrick did not notice this. Looking past her to the shadowed wall, he made his plan, thought how he would go down the river and stand until General Jackson rode across the field on the other side and Allen would greet him. He would say, "Good morning, sir," and the great tall man would salute from the back of his horse. His mother waited, but Allen Hendrick did not question why she had told him the story, or why she had spoken at such length of General Jackson, or why, during the time his father had talked of war, he had never heard of his uncle. His mother's kin who had commanded a fieldpiece, who had touched a spark to the fuse and heard the cannon roar.

He was fourteen years old, and he did not realize that she was trying to give him something to live by. Something out of her past that he might be proud of, a token to compensate for the taint in her family's blood. In the time that followed, he came to realize what she had been trying to say to him while the candle burned itself out and the Negroes laughed in the hall. But not now. Now he was thinking only of General Jackson.

"I must see him," Allen Hendrick said. "Tomorrow."

"See him?" She was still leaning forward, watching him, her eyes wide as if she could not believe she had heard him right. As if he had said something that no gentleman would ever say, not even to another man. "See him?"

"Yes, ma'am," he said. "If I wait long enough General Jackson will ride over his place."

"Oh." She looked down at her folded hands, at the dress still clean and unwrinkled after the journey. "Oh, he is gone, too. He has been dead for some years too."

He left her then. He told his mother good night and walked toward the doorway, the painted door that hung ajar on the dark cherry facing. He is dead, Allen Hendrick thought, and I will never know what he really looked like. There was only the word of his mother that Andrew Jackson was tall and lean and straight on his horse, but she had never seen him either.

When he was almost to the hall she said, "Your grandfather is a general," and her voice seemed weak across the room, a little husky. "You will visit him."

He did not answer. He had turned around to face her again and for a while she still would not let him go. The light hissed, flared bright behind her, blurring her features, so that her lips seemed to be shut close together. He could see that her eyes still watched him as if, he thought, there were something more to say, some fact that she had left out of its proper place. But he was wrong about this. "Good night," she said. "Good night, Allen." And he went to find his bed.

He went up to sleep, disappointed that so much greatness should have passed from the world before he had reached the age of reason. But as he climbed the steps he recalled too that his mother had spoken of his visit to General Hendrick and the sound of old Aaron's voice came back to him, strong and cold like the moving air. He slept badly and in the morning he set out with his father.

All the way to Cedarcrest Allen Hendrick surveyed the strange land around him—the green tobacco, the sloping pastures, the limestone that seemed to grow out of the earth—and as the heat of the morning came on and the horses began to lather, he searched for the driveway where they would turn off, the hill they would climb to see the house. For that was how his father had described it to him, standing in the first light of day with one foot on the mounting block, pulling on the thin gloves that he did not need in July. "You can look down over the valley," he had said, "over the trees that grow along the creek bank, and when you see the house on the next rise of ground you will think it is small." Then from the back of the gray gelding he went on. "That is because of the distance and the symmetry of its design." This had been said in a deep voice, spoken carefully, as if he thought the sound of the words might help Allen Hendrick to understand them. "It is a big house," his father said, "and they will be waiting to see you."

They will be waiting, Allen Hendrick thought, and the slick, warm leather of the saddle squeaked with the gait of his horse. His grandfather who was a general in the same war with Andrew Jackson, and his Aunt Valeria, a widow, the wife of his father's dead brother. Waiting to look at him in the broad light of day, to hold him in view of their strict eyes as old Uncle Aaron had done under the dim glow of a lantern. They would search his face for some mark, some cast of feature which would prove to them that he was at least part Hendrick and that all the force of his father's manhood had not been absorbed by his mother's doubtful flesh.

These were not the words which came to his mind as he watched the turn in the hard-packed road or the course of a fence that ran beside a pasture. Allen Hendrick could not have said what it was beyond the heat of July that made him tremble slightly, feeling the beat of his pulse in the vessels next to his skull, the weakness that came to his stomach stronger and sharper than hunger. He tried to fashion in his mind some image of the relatives that he had never seen, to decide beforehand what he would say when he had dismounted under the cedar trees. But the past seemed to rush upon him as quick as the wind in his face, and he remembered another meeting a long time ago in the store his father had run in Memphis.

He had been alone and he had waited on a man from Arkansas, a tall, lanky hunter with skinned knuckles and long hair and eyes not much bigger than blue whistlers, not much larger than buckshot and very close together. And after the swap had been made—furs for some powder and lead and coffee—the man did not leave at once, but stood for a moment by the long oak counter, looking at Allen Hendrick and biting his lower lip in thought. He had a beard that was greasy around the edges and just beginning to turn gray, and his face was very brown from the sun, and his sharp, thin nose was slightly pitted. After what seemed to Allen a long time, he said:

"Son, ai're you Major Hendrick's boy?"

"Yes, sir," Allen replied. "I'm Allen Hendrick."

"Well, son," the hunter said, his voice tinged with surprise, "you never look it." He paused and leaned forward regarding Allen's face. "You never look like a nigger. You don't look no more like a nigger boy than I do."

For an instant Allen believed that the hunter was making a joke, joshing him with a kind of crude humor that a man out of the wilderness might think was funny; but there was no smile on the man's face, no look beyond mild amazement in the buckshot, blue eyes. And slowly, spreading in Allen's breast like a stain or a blot of ink on a piece of paper, the fear and the anger came and his breath grew short.

"I'm not a nigger," Allen said. "I'm not a nigger."

"Son," the man said almost gently, "you don't look it for a fact. I reckon somewhere else you could pass for white."

The hunter took his parcel and started for the door, a big, stupid, uncouth man who could neither read nor write nor calculate figures, who even in Memphis looked strange and foreign in a fringed hunting shirt and leather trousers and a pair of buckskin moccasins, fringed too and beaded. He moved a few steps, his features looking, behind the shaggy beard and the deep tan, serious and pensive; and then he stopped and turned back to Allen and said:

"You never knowed about it, did you, son?"

And when Allen made no reply, he went on, "You never knowed about it, and about your pappy and mammy, did you?"

"Knew about what?" Allen asked. He was beginning to cry; he could feel the tightness, the painful trembling in his throat.

"Why," the man said, "about how your mammy was a nigger, or part of a nigger. A kind of a nigger they have down the waters in New Orleans. And how your pappy went plumb down there on a packet boat and brung her back here and her his wife and all. With a fancy dress and a gold ring shining on her finger."

"No," Allen said, feeling the desperation, hearing it in his voice, "no, she is white as you are."

"I ain't no nigger," the man said quickly, his eyes growing smaller still. And then, after a pause, he said more softly, "Son, the reason I spoke of it, I thought you knowed."

And he turned away once more and this time did leave, walked into the Memphis sunlight, into the narrow, dusty street, and then was gone.

He left, and Allen stood trembling behind the counter, his hands clutched together, his face hot and wet with tears. Then Allen moved too, and walked the length of the store, down the cluttered aisle, between the ax bits and the barrels of rum, the plow lines and the lanterns and the bolts of cloth, the cones of sugar and the rolls of wire and the pewter dishes. "No," he said, speaking to the empty store, but the sound of his voice was very soft, and he said again, "No," but once more without conviction, and then he sat down on a keg of nails to think.

He sat there for a long time, thinking of what the man had said, the word nigger, vibrating in his brain, ringing there with a sure rhythm like the regular blows of a hammer on a piece of iron. He saw in his mind his mother's face, the nose slender, the lips full—but not thick—the hair and the eyes dark, the skin golden. The skin lighter, the features more delicate than those of the man from Arkansas who had called her a nigger. He did not understand it. He knew next to nothing of miscegenation, of mixed blood, and he had never heard the stories of New Orleans, the tales that came up the river of quadroon and octoroon women who were almost white, and who became the mistresses of white men and who lived in ease and luxury along the rampart. Nor had he heard of the old families of color, cultivated and rich and growing lighter, but unwilling to leave their homes or change their names. If he might have seen some of them in their ruffled shirts and flowered waistcoats—the Dumases or the Legoasters or the Lacroixes—he would have agreed that they looked a little foreign and talked a little strange, but he could not have convinced himself that they were Negroes, for to him, in his simple view of the world, being a Negro was having skin that was black.

Yet he knew, in spite of his ignorance, that something about his mother's life was wrong. He knew that she was lonely, that she had no friends. She never went calling and no one called on her, and she spent her hours reading or playing the piano, or knitting in front of the parlor window, where occasionally she looked up from her work to watch the street. She did not go to church or to the stores to shop, and often when she rode in the carriage she kept the curtains drawn.

Now, as he rode through Sumner County with his father, Allen remembered thinking this, and he remembered too how suddenly on that day in Memphis he had known that it was possible. There in his father's store, he had seen half-castes, yellows they were called, and he knew that if there could be a mixture of half and half, equal parts of black and white, then there might be any other combination and a man might be one fourth or one eighth or one sixteenth Negro. The taint might be in his blood and his face would not show it.

So the knowledge of his heritage came to him, but along with it a hope, the substance of a dream. For the man from Arkansas had said, *I reckon somewhere else you could pass for white.* And Gallatin was somewhere else, and he had believed as he came through the wilderness, that in Middle Tennessee the scandal of his birth would not be known. Or rather, he had thought that only his grandfather would know of it, and General Hendrick being his own flesh and blood would never tell. But now he was aware that old Aaron knew, and if Aaron knew, every slave in the county had heard the story too, and what the slaves had heard the masters were apprised of. He realized, almost intuitively, how General Hendrick's position would be changed; for a man might accept in private what he was forced to reject in public, and he wondered how his grandfather would receive him now. . . .

"We turn here," Marcus Hendrick said, and they moved off the pike onto a narrow, gravel road.

"Is this Grandfather's land?" Allen Hendrick said, motioning toward a pasture that sloped bright and green back toward the highway.

"Yes," his father said, "this is part of Cedarcrest." He said the last word slowly, let it hang in the air between them as if the name itself held some pure value like money or an easy conscience.

They went up the last hill, past the slow, grazing cows, on beyond an ancient strawberry mule that stood idle in the sun. Then the house came in view with the valley spread out before it, the creek, the grove of sycamores, a bridge with a painted railing. The building itself was old and gray, plain in front without even a veranda; but at the end of a brick walk that led to the drive he saw them waiting. A short, slender man in a linen suit and a woman a little taller than he was with hair that was almost red. Allen Hendrick held back on the reins, slowed his horse to a walk, thinking that if he could delay, put off the meeting for yet a moment longer, there would be some way to prove that his mother was white.

They rode on, down toward the creek, toward the man and woman on the other side.

"Father," he said, and his father turned to him, not quite smiling, his look not quite steady. "Is that lady Aunt Valeria?"

Over the beat of the horses' hoofs his father said, "I don't know. I have never seen her either." Then he added, in a tone that sounded too serious for the words, "But whoever she is, she is beautiful to look at."

◊ 2 ◊

ON A DAY ten months before Allen came to Gallatin from Memphis, Valeria Hendrick had stood alone in a steamboat cabin watching for an instant her own motionless image in the looking glass. Finally, she pinned the long veil in place and put on her gloves and turned back toward the room, toward the red-upholstered chair, the red carpet, and the narrow bed pushed up close to the wall. Standing a little weak and uncomfortable in the September heat, behind the closed door, the drapery-covered window, she made sure for the last time that everything was packed: her clothing, her books, and the picture—the oil miniature in the mahogany frame. Then she sat down to wait for General Hendrick.

Valeria lowered herself into the chair, slowly, trembling slightly, tired, not from the last days she had spent in Natchez or the journey up the river, but from the effort of not remembering, of not daring to recall the final terrible hours when the febrile excitement had ended and the face had turned yellow as gall above the sheet. In her mind she took up her life when the rosewood casket was lifted onto the boat and she came on board to bring her husband's body home. She had stood in the cabin, feeling a weakness in her joints, a certain heaviness in her head, and the hem of her mourning dress had lain like a mark on the gaudy floor. The whistle had blown, the paddle wheel began to turn, and Valeria leaned on the foot of the bed and wept: against her bereavement, against the last, cold moments of John Hendrick's sickness, against all the yellow fever that had spread over the city as if it drifted like smoke on the humid, sultry air. As she sat now, listening for the general's footstep along the deck, enduring her weariness that was like an ache in the substance of her brain, Valeria thought, I must be ready when he comes.

She sat with the crepe drawn over her face, her hands perspiring inside the gloves, and tried to prepare herself for the moment when the knock would come and she would move to the closed door and turn the gilded knob. She had considered it beforehand, decided how, when they met, she would stand in front of him strong and erect, not like a woman but like a soldier; for she believed that, more than anything else, that was what he would admire. She believed this because she was seventeen and he was an old man. She was a girl and she had come from Natchez to Nashville with the burden of her journey somewhere below—the silver-mounted casket, the body packed in salt, put out of sight beneath the level of the water. She had made her trip and in all her weariness she could not see at once that the time for strength was over, that even an old man would be touched by her carefully braided hair or the shape of her breasts beneath the somber cloth. But in the end Valeria changed her mind or her resolution failed, for she did not get up out of the chair. The general found her cabin after the other passengers had left the boat, and his tap against the door frame was quiet, muffled, just audible above the distant noises that came from the landing and the street. She hesitated, smoothed the front of her dress, and asked him to come in.

She spoke softly toward the blank wall, the curtained window, and then the door opened and the general stood just inside the room. He waited a moment, looking down at her as if he were not quite sure that he had come to the right place. It was, Valeria thought, as if he knew that he could not bear up under any delay, any fumbling, mistaken meeting that would be discovered only after his grief had been exposed. He stopped for a second before he crossed to take her hand—a thin gentleman of less than medium height in a linen suit, a soft shirt, a limp blue cravat. Valeria studied his face in astonishment, recognizing each feature in its turn: the thick hair that curled around his ears, the dark eyes, the nose, marked with ruptured veins, but thin and delicate above the white mustache. It was as if sickness and death, the span of her life itself, had been abrogated by a sudden shift of time. As if like a princess in a fairy tale she had awakened still young after a long sleep, to find the world around her had altered and grown old. She stared at the handsome, wrinkled face, the hair turned gray, the slender body growing feeble in the legs; and it seemed to Valeria that she saw the figure of her husband as he would have been if he had lived for thirty years beyond the fever.

"Miss Valeria?" General Hendrick asked.

She did not answer.

She had trained herself for this meeting, held out the last force of her will against the time when General Hendrick would call her name and move toward her in the cabin. But now that he stood next to her, touching her glove with his pale, half-wasted hand, she could only nod with her lips pressed tight together. For in her mind Valeria had seen him simply as an old man, not as the broken image of his son, and she dropped her gaze away from the fantastic resemblance. Frightened, outraged, she felt for one quick instant as if she were the victim of a sort of malicious and ghostly prank. She had watched as the hot, quiet days went by and the fever made its progress: the cold, sallow skin, the easy breath, the bed soiled black with blood and stinking from the corruption of his bowels. She had seen this and under the candlelight, against the quilted cushion, she had seen the still face, dead and bathed with the mustache newly waxed. She had brought herself to believe, not in the vulgar, whispered platitude or in the promise of God, but in the dignified security of death itself, and she had thought for a while that she was almost safe—as safe from the torment of her loss as the corpse that lay on the pillow.

General Hendrick spoke again, talked to her about the boat, or his own travels, or perhaps of the bluff at Natchez. She did not know. But as the words filled the air around her, indistinct, distant, meaningless, like sounds from another room, Valeria came at last to understand that the quality of death was more final than all the living suffering she had refused to remember, and her throat ached and her eyes burned behind the veil.

They left the boat together. He held her by the arm, his hand under her elbow, and they went up the long flight of wooden stairs to the street. The day was bright, the late summer sky blue and clear with a few scattered clouds hanging still and far away above the earth. She went through the warm sunshine, through the world where men paused to stare at her mourning and turned to whisper when she had passed. She moved with the general by parked wagons, horses that stamped against the flies, and she felt a little embarrassed, awkward and conspicuous like a child who performs before his elders; but she was cheered too, in spite of her dulled senses and the lesson the general's face had taught her. For after the loneliness of her journey, the meals taken in the red cabin behind the latched door, she walked again among the living.

They came finally to the surrey and General Hendrick helped her up to the back seat. The cushions were dusty, the leather worn and cracked, but the team was shining, well fed, groomed like ladies for a ball. When he had got in himself and had sat down beside her, he pointed to a driver, an old colored man wearing a green frock coat and a handkerchief tied around his neck. "This is Aaron," General Hendrick said.

"Hello, Uncle Aaron," she said, seeing the white hair, the shrunken, sad face, the round pot belly.

He bowed, not low, but slowly. His eyes were red, a little tearful, and his voice was cracked with age. "Young Mistress," he spoke and waited by the horses.

They sat in the open surrey, under the heat of the sun, and it seemed, for a while, that the general did not realize they were standing still. He kept his gaze straight ahead, his face motionless as if he were studying a landmark on the horizon. Then suddenly he looked down at Aaron. "Well?" he said.

"We ain't hardly ready yet," Aaron replied, glancing once at Valeria and nodding his head toward the boat.

"Confound it!" General Hendrick said. "You mean you haven't got—" and his voice stopped abruptly, leaving the street quiet after the noise of his shouting. Valeria felt the tips of her fingers grow cold inside her gloves and her head was numb as if all the strength of her blood had been used in the climb from the river. She had thought, while she waited with General Hendrick in the cabin, that all the arrangements had been made. That the casket would be unloaded and sent ahead of them for the body to be washed again and the clothes changed and the traces of salt cleaned from the pale silk lining. That is how she had hoped it would be, remembering the procession that had moved down off the bluff at Natchez. He had been an officer in the Fencibles and the company had gone through town with the body on a caisson, the drums muffled, the uniform sleeves banded in crepe. To Valeria all this had seemed proper, or at least no more than the dead might have a right to demand. But for her, the widow, once was enough; and she shrank from the eyes of the river-front loafers who watched now to see them drive away.

She discovered, however, that this was not the reason Aaron stayed. "Naw, sir," he said, "I done got all that 'complished." He looked toward the boat as if he expected to see another passenger get off, somebody else who would want to ride in the surrey. "It's jist that Young Mistress' girl ain't come up yet."

"Girl?" General Hendrick said. He paused, staring down at Aaron. The sun was warm and he was sweating a little, the wrinkles in his face were damp with perspiration. Then he seemed to understand what the old Negro was talking about and he turned to Valeria. "He means your maid," the general said, leaning forward, not quite certain, his lips parted under the white mustache. "I should have attended to that."

"No, sir," Valeria replied. "I didn't bring one." She spoke, forming the words in her slow mind, comprehending at first only that she had been spared the ride with the casket—the display before the pitying and the curious. But slowly it came to her what old Aaron had meant, what he had known all along from the time he had seen the general take her arm and support her on the stairs.

Aaron stood, gazing toward the river, his eyes distant and focused on nothing as if he were having some sort of vision. Seeing his red-rimmed eyes, too big for the face that had grown small around them, tinged blue where they should have been white, Valeria felt her lip tremble and she set her teeth and pulled the flesh tight on her cheeks.

"Can't you hear?" General Hendrick said. "There's not any girl."

Valeria did not expect him to get in at once, to accept what the general had said immediately and let her off with no more than he had done already. She knew he would tarry for a moment longer, staring at the landing, his hat off, the hair thick and as white as cotton above the black forehead. But when he turned toward them and spoke, his face placid, his gums showing above the stained teeth, she felt the heavy beat of her pulse and the blood rushing to her face.

"Plumb from Mississippi," Aaron said. "You say yo'self she travel plumb from Mississippi."

"Never mind," General Hendrick said sternly. "You just drive on."

Aaron got in and they drove on, across the river and through a settlement called Edgefield and north along the pike toward Gallatin. They went through the rolling country on a day that was warm enough to have been July, past fields that were just a little brown from drought and woods where the leaves had not yet begun to turn. But the tobacco was in and the corn was picked and they passed a man with a hound on a leash. I have done wrong, Valeria thought. She sat beside the general, her feet braced against the jolts of the road, thinking, I have done wrong to come alone. Her aunt had foreseen this, her last surviving relative who had sat before the fireplace in the parlor at Natchez and said, "Do you intend to take any of your people besides Louella?"

"No, no," Valeria had said. "Not her either. I can get along without a maid."

"Ah!" the old lady had said, quickly, scornfully, as if she could demolish the idea with the one sudden expulsion of breath. Then after a moment her brow wrinkled, the white, powdered skin forming in ridges above her nose. "But don't you see?" she said. "You can't. What will people think? What will *they* think?"

And Valeria had said only, "I must." Believing then that for a while at least she could not stand up under the sight of another living person—eyes that would see her when the veil was removed, a voice that would require an answer. That was the reason she had given herself, the excuse she had offered her aunt, seeing then no further into the future than the end of her journey; denying what was to come as she had denied the past in order to soften the stern fact of the present.

There was time for her to think of this as they moved on through the late afternoon, past a farmhouse with its lonely, smoking chimney, through the last broken sunlight that slanted against the horses' dusty rumps. Time to spare from what she thought would be a lifetime of mourning, for she was certain of the immortality of her grief. She had put her mementos safely away, and she believed in the authority of a lock of hair, a portrait, a letter written in haste to help her memory stand firm against all the years. Valeria looked at the general riding beside her with his head tilted forward, his chin stuck out; but she could not tell whether he felt in his mind that she had disgraced his name by coming alone, unattended, on a boat where gamblers walked the deck and the bar was never closed.

I have done wrong, Valeria thought, holding the words of Aaron's reprimand in her brain. But it did not matter. In a week she would be gone, in two weeks she would be back in Natchez with all that she remembered, all that she cared to remember of the Hendricks of Tennessee. She would walk through the house, among the familiar chairs, beneath the chandelier and the velvet draperies, for whatever was left to her would be there, above the ground, far from the carved stone. The sun was down and they rode in the first clear twilight, across a shallow stream, beside a rutted, washing pasture.

"Now, then," Aaron said to the horses, speaking to them softly, almost with respect. "You come on git up there now, Gen'l Jackson. You, Mr. Lafayette. You all got to git on home to git you' feedin'."

The horses quickened their gait and Valeria closed her eyes and leaned back against the seat. She felt the movement, the pace of the surrey that carried them on toward Gallatin and Cedarcrest, and she thought, It will be over soon and I can leave. She could go back, away from the grave and the man who shared her loss and the impudent, scolding Negro. Then all this too would be a part of the past, an aspect of her tractable memory.

She lived through the day of the funeral, the preaching, the songs, the procession through the garden to the stone wall that enclosed the little cemetery. She stood with the general, firm in her resolution to be brave until the end, while around her the slaves wept, and the priest read in a sad voice from his prayer book. She did not give way to the feeling that even then had not defined itself—the sadness that is pure and almost abstract until the shock is passed and the days resume their pattern. The sun glinted on a silver hinge, the wind soughed in the leaves of a maple tree and she felt tears on her cheek, wetting her veil, rolling past her lips to her chin.

"There is a boat to Natchez on Friday," she said to the general after the funeral had been over for several days and they walked on a path in the garden beside the lake. She watched the swans that drifted tall and white across the dark water, under the cloudy sky. The weather had turned cold and the grass in the field was brown.

"Perhaps," General Hendrick said, "perhaps there is. But now we must go into the house." He spoke quickly, as if somehow he had known what she was going to say, as if he had been waiting like an actor for his cue that he might deliver the line he had memorized. He walked beside her into the house, tapping the gravel walkway with his cane, wearing a faded blue military cape that made him look stout.

They went directly into the parlor, the room that had appeared to Valeria quaint and old-fashioned and almost bare when she had first come from Natchez. The paint in the floral design of the wall was faded and dim against the plaster, and the mantel was plain and just slightly carved, but she discovered later that the window sills were marble. Now General Hendrick helped with her coat and then went to the table and mixed himself a toddy.

He stood for a moment, the steaming cup in his hand, his back to the fire, and after a while he said, "Valeria, I intend to repair the carriage." She knew what he was talking about; she had seen it in the carriage house, old and unpainted, the upholstery moth-eaten, one of the wheels broken and sagging toward the ground. It had belonged to his wife and it had not moved since her death fifteen years before. "Repair it," he went on, "or get a new one." He spoke quickly, his voice louder than usual. "A surrey is no kind of conveyance for a lady."

"No, sir," she said. "You don't understand. I have already stayed longer than I meant to."

But he went on, sipping from the cup and talking as if he had not heard the sound of her voice. "I will fix the carriage and give you a driver and then we will go to Nashville and buy you a maid."

"Wait," Valeria said, "wait, General Hendrick."

He waved his hand, his palm toward her as if to cut her off. "No," he went on, "the girl who's been helping you won't do. By rights she belongs in the kitchen."

He paused, his head turned to one side, his shadow cast long by the firelight and dancing on the carpet, and once more she was struck by the similarity, the family resemblance that she had discovered on the boat. She saw the profile, the hair that would not comb flat, the eyebrows a bit too heavy and not quite as gray as his beard. For an instant she felt that she stood now as close to John Hendrick as she would ever stand on earth again, but she had made up her mind. "No, sir," she said. "I cannot stay."

He looked at her in surprise, his mouth half open, and his teeth were small and uncommonly white. Then his features relaxed and he smiled sadly, the lines deepening in his shaded face. "Ah, Valeria, I am an old man," he said. "I am an old man and I have an honest name."

There was a pause. For she did not know at first what it was that he meant, what he was trying to make her understand. She sat a little bewildered in the quiet, firelit room, breathing the warm whisky-scented air, turning away finally toward the darkness outside the window where rain had begun to fall. At last it came to her that he was promising to respect her virtue and she was embarrassed and did not know how to answer.

Valeria remained silent, staring down at her lap, at her hands that were limp and cold against her dress. But the general seemed to know that she still held out against him, seemed to feel the strength of her resistance as if it lay between them, palpable above the figured carpet. "Damn it, missy," he said, his voice soft and hoarse and almost hopeless. "It will be easier here. It will be better than going back."

She thought of her home in Natchez, remembered it fondly and with a kind of faith in its power, not to heal the wound, but to hold forever what little would be left. She saw the house in her mind's eye as she had seen it that day when she rode in the surrey, next to the brooding general, behind the presumptuous Negro and the horses with their ridiculous names. She recalled the bed they had slept in, the upstairs sitting room, the balcony that looked out over the river—over all the steamboats and the fishermen and the boys who swam splashing in the water on the other side near the woods. He is wrong, she thought, he will have to be wrong. But she remained silent. The log broke in the fireplace and sparks scattered on the hearth.

"Valeria," General Hendrick said finally, "I am alone in the world and I want you to stay."

"Then you have abandoned Major Hendrick?" she asked. On the night before her wedding her husband had told her about Marcus— how he had married a Negro girl from New Orleans. ("I do not know why Marcus has done this thing," he had spoken slowly, wonderingly. "I only know what Marcus says. But he is too visionary and the world will not allow it.") She looked past the general at the pitcher of water that had grown cold on the sideboard, the decanter of spirits dark as mahogany, taller than the silver cups. "Don't you still have him?"

"No," General Hendrick said. "Marcus has abandoned me."

They both waited, with only the sound of the rain outside and footsteps from the back hallway near the dining room and the tinkle of glassware and china, as clear and faint as a distant bell. She stood up, and, holding to the back of her chair she said, "I cannot tell now." For she still believed that she wanted to go back, but the look in his eyes, the sad, lined face with its thin nose and the beard that grew soft as a woman's hair had told her something. She saw the fine detail of his sorrow, clear before her as lines drawn on a slate, and around him the furniture, the walls he had built, the accumulation of his life stood cold in the shadows.

"Oh," she said, "I cannot tell you now."

She went out, into the dark hall, up the stairs toward her bedroom, toward the trunk that was almost packed, the little picture, the lock of hair. She went up and lighted her candle and stood near the window that looked over the garden, searching, straining her eyes against the darkness. But she could make out nothing beyond the misted, dripping glass.

◇ 3 ◇

AND SO AT LAST she gave in, not to the force of the general's arguments or the elegant sound of his voice, but to the image that his wasted face had made in the yellow firelight. *It will be better here,* he had said; and now as she remembered the twitch of his slender nose, his quivering lip below the white mustaches, the sentence sounded again in her ears and her mind multiplied its meaning. Better to stay than to test the dream. Better to remain forever away than to return and find that the past was gone and the memories withered and brittle. Not yet, she thought. I cannot go yet. And she turned away from the window, back toward the strange room, toward the rocking chair and the pilastered chest and the bed with its high tester. If the old man was right, and all was lost, she could not bear to know it now.

She went down the twisting stairway, her hand on the railing, her skirt slightly lifted and rustling as she moved. She crossed the hall and opened the door, and, standing just inside the parlor, she drew her breath to speak. She hesitated a moment, facing the general, looking beyond him to the chimney piece and the paneling that reached up to the ceiling. It was all the same. The velvet drapes still hung at the windows; the rug still lay upon the floor. The old man stood as if he had not moved, but the cup was no longer in his hand and he had thrown a shawl across his back.

"General Hendrick," she said. "I am going to stay, General Hendrick."

Her voice was low, almost a whisper. But the words were loud enough, and the general crossed the room to take her hand.

Valeria remained at Cedarcrest. General Hendrick moved permanently into one of the downstairs sitting rooms. He took his clothes and his hatboxes, his escritoire, and his porcelain bathing set; and one chilly afternoon he came upstairs for the last time to show her the master chamber and to insist that she take it for her own. It was a big room, as large as the parlor, with doors that opened on a veranda and maple wainscoting and delicately blocked paper on the walls. The floors had been polished, the furniture was dusted; fresh candles had been placed in the sockets and wood was stacked beside the hearth. But it seemed that day to Valeria too grand; it was too long, too bright, and the late sun fell too gaily across a brocade couch.

"No, sir," she said. "I'd rather keep the place I have."

He was disappointed. He turned his head away and fumbled at his watch chain with his hand. "Stay where you will," he said. "You are free to choose." And then a little later, when they were moving toward the stairs, he went on, "The one you have is a good room too. It is the one that Marcus used when he was with me."

In the room that had once belonged to Major Marcus Hendrick she took up her life, and through the quiet days she watched the world, framed in the narrow window where she had stood and peered into the night. She saw the season change, the land turn brown. The leaves curled up on the hickory tree and the cedars grew rusty along the drive, and beside the creek, weeds were twisted and withered, dead from the heavy frost. Late in October she began to hear hunters, the sound of a gun far away and muffled, like the pop of a cork drawn from an empty bottle. And occasionally she saw the sudden flush of the covey, quick, turning specks against the sky as the lead cock drove for cover.

Winter came on, damp and cold, with a little snow that melted as soon as it touched the ground. Aaron moved between the quarters and the kitchen door, his head wrapped in a piece of blanket, the green coat pinned tight around his neck. Fires burned all day in the cabins, and Valeria would gaze out toward all the smoking chimneys, toward the swans on the lake and the bare willow branches and the children who played in the lot behind the smokehouse. She could see the grave too, the stone bright and just beginning to weather, the mound boxed with heavy slabs of marble.

Once a week she wrote her aunt in Natchez.

In October, when the sky was still blue, the weather mild enough for her to go about in comfort, the letter ran like this:

> *I went abroad today for the first time in the carriage with General Hendrick. We stopped with a family named Rutledge in a house all full of horsehair and extra harness. The corners were swept full of dirt. The slaves, needless to say, were worthless and impudent, almost as sassy as the insufferable Aaron. Mr. Rutledge fought in the war with General Hendrick and while the gentlemen stayed in the parlor calling each other "general" and "captain," I walked about the grounds with daughter Katherine. She is young and some, I don't doubt, would say pretty, but her nose turns up altogether too much and her way of talking grates against my eardrums. Her voice is a degree too hoarse, like she had the croup. She was home on a holiday from the Nashville academy.*

Later, just before Christmas, she wrote on a board laid across her lap with the ink on a table beside her:

> *Tired, tired, tired. There is so much sickness among the children we have turned the ballroom into a regular hospital. As General Hendrick will allow no other nigger man to pass the night under his roof, Aaron must stay up to stoke the fire. Only this gives me strength. I rejoice to see his villainous eyes droop for want of sleep. Dr. Anse Weaver comes twice a day, always in full costume. Fawn-colored breeches, flowered waistcoat, coat tails brushed, and oiled hair gleaming. There is, I think, some scandal in his past. But I have not yet made it out, more's the pity. The Rutledges say they are distantly connected with Mrs. William Chester of Vicksburg. Who knows? It may be, dirty house and croaking daughter notwithstanding.*

Valeria's mail was answered. The letters came, as regularly as she posted her own—one-page messages closely written on lavender stationery.

> *I have taken to my bed with a headache and a camphorated rag around my neck but will try to set down a few lines to you just the same because I don't see any promise of getting any better as long as you insist on behaving like a sinful, wretched woman. However old he is just makes it worse, and no nigger woman and a slave at that sleeping outside your door is going to hinder him if he takes the notion of meanness in his head. Why don't you come on home and live here at home where you married your husband and where you belong by rights and decency? No woman in her right mind ever craved to live in the country which is a place fit only for men to live in and hogs and horses that God made to work and not have any gumption. The Rutledges cannot be related to Bessie Chester who always kept a spotless house if they let you come under their roof for anyone would think you are a fallen woman the way you act. I know you don't give any thought to my poor headaches, but I am about ready to rub arnica on my brain to ease the hurting.*

And when this did no good, when the question of Valeria's return to Natchez remained unanswered, the old lady resorted to subtlety and began to send packages of books. Volumes of poetry by Shelley and Byron and Robert Burns; novels by Trollope and Thackeray, Mrs. Oliphant and Walter Scott; and devotional books, *The Sermons of Reverend Charles Tomes* and a bound set of the *Millennial Harbinger* for the year 1843. Toward the end of February, as a crowning insult, she sent a copy of the *Orthographical Spelling Book.*

"I don't see why you want to keep writing for those things," General Hendrick said. They were at the breakfast table, and he leaned toward her over the cloth, his fork still in his hand. There was an edge of testiness to his voice. "I've got books enough in the office to put your eyes out, and what ain't there can be had in Nashville."

"No, sir," Valeria replied. "It's just Aunt Mary. She pretends to believe that Tennessee is as far away as Texas."

"Thunderation!" General Hendrick said. "Don't she know we're right here at the other end of the Trace?"

"She's just pretending," Valeria repeated. "She only wants me to come home. She thinks that sooner or later I'll want to talk about a book that nobody around here has read."

"The reading don't signify," General Hendrick snorted. "And as for the talk, I calculate it's better here. The words ain't swallowed up by the swamp."

Valeria smiled, thinking how, during the six months she had been at Cedarcrest, the pattern of the old man's speech had changed. Or rather, how he had come to lose his formality when he was around her, and to allow himself to fall back into the idiom that he must have used when he came out to the West from Maryland over fifty years before.

"Don't worry, General Hendrick," she said. "I'm not going yet."

"No," he replied, "and if I have my way, you won't go ever."

But, as Valeria came to see, he recognized the threat. He sensed the presence of the enemy forever on his flank, forever operating just out of his vision, just beyond the range of his guns. He scowled at the lavender envelopes with their thin, curling inscriptions. He took up the novels, when she had left them in the parlor, and peered at the fine print through his narrow spectacles. His brows would wrinkle, his lips form a hard line across his teeth; and he would hold his gaze on one page for an incredible length of time, as if the text were spelled out in Chinese characters, or as if the words themselves were darkly obscene. But at length he hit on his own plan of operation: he asked her to tell him the stories of the books she read.

"What is in that one?" he said one afternoon in January. "What adventure does the hero have in there?"

They were sitting in the parlor. Outside, beyond the window, the day was bright and a few wispy clouds hung at the edge of the horizon, almost brushing the tops of the hills. The novel she had been reading was *Henry Esmond* and the general sat with his hands folded across his stomach, his eyes half closed, while she told how the boy relinquished his title to his cousin and married his stepmother in the end.

"So you see," she said, "it finally comes out very happily. And they settled in Virginia, General Hendrick, and they raised a daughter there."

"Happy?" he said. "That's a curious kind of happiness for a man to spend half his life fighting wars and the other half mooning over a worthless woman." His voice sounded gruff, but a little smile played at the corners of his mouth and twitched the ends of his mustache. "Not to mention the time he spent in jail," the general went on, "with a sword wound in his gizzard."

"In his hand, General Hendrick," Valeria replied. "People don't have gizzards."

"It don't matter," the old man said. "It ain't much to talk about. In real life it never would have happened." He grinned once more and his eyes glittered above the rosy cheeks.

So they laughed together at the quaint stories that she read in the books which came from Natchez, but at other times they were both sad, and Valeria thought often of her husband. She would remember a moment they had spent together, an evening at the theater, a night alone by the fire, and the old pain, the ache of her heart would come back. It did not last so long now, and the sense of loss was somewhat softened, but she mourned nonetheless, and she felt at home in her somber widow's habit.

She noticed, when she had been for a while at Cedarcrest, that the general too had fits of melancholy. He would sit sometimes staring off into space, his cigar dead between his fingers, his lips set tight across his little teeth. There were nights when he went early to his room and afternoons when he drank too much and occasions when he would not eat at all, but merely fumble with his silver at the table. He feels it too, Valeria would say to herself, he thinks of John too. And she was comforted to have him share her grief.

Now and then she spoke of her husband to the general.

"Oh, he would have loved this," she said one morning when they were looking at a foal; a chestnut colt that nuzzled close to its mother, and snorted gently, and moved its lips up and down over the toothless gums. "He loved any kind of animal uncommonly well."

And later, on a gray morning when they sat at the breakfast table, "He would have been twenty-nine today, General Hendrick. He was born exactly a week before Washington's birthday."

"Yes," he replied. "I had not remembered that."

Then after a pause he put down his fork and went on. "It is hard for you, my dear. There are not many things that appear more bitter than death."

But this was only a hint, and she was taken up with her own thoughts and she did not stop to analyze his words. Twenty-nine, she repeated to herself, dwelling on the ages, the numbered years, and I will be eighteen in April.

At last, however, on a day in March, he spoke to her of what was on his mind. They had been to the Rutledge plantation, and throughout the tedious afternoon she had sat in the parlor with the two old men, for Kate had gone back to the academy in Nashville. She had listened to Captain Rutledge talk, as always, of that ancient war, and after a while her mind began to wander. Valeria heard the start of the old familiar story. How General Hendrick had taken command of the troops at Fort Wayne, Indiana, and how they had marched down the bank of the Maumee River and avoided an Indian ambuscade. Then she let the voices drone on while she examined a picture that hung above the mantel. It was a new canvas, the portrait of a boy in uniform, Captain Rutledge's son. In one hand he held his hat, the other clutched the hilt of his sword, and Valeria noticed with faint distaste that his features were pretty and his nose turned up at the end.

She studied the buttons on his coat, the highlights painted on his boots, and still the talk went on, the movement of the army, the fight through the heavy woods. They had reached Michigan now; the attack in the snow had already begun. And she knew from the tone of Captain Rutledge's voice, sad, halting, almost breaking with age and emotion, that he would stop soon, for he could never quite force himself to describe their defeat. Then suddenly it happened. He spoke the words, without introduction, with no remark to let them know what was coming, no time to prepare for the name he meant to speak.

"I thought Marcus was going to cry when we had to surrender. He was only a boy, but he had a veteran's pride." His voice broke off, died in the abrupt silence like a match or a candle in the wind. He was an old man, older than General Hendrick; he was touched with palsy and his head rocked perpetually above his slender shoulders. It jerked forward once or twice violently now, but he steadied himself and pursed his lips and spat into the fire.

"No, no," Captain Rutledge went on, moving his hand, brushing the air as if he were trying to erase the words, scrape them away with the tips of his wrinkled fingers. "There's no call for a man to recollect the past. We impose on Miss Valeria . . ." And he stopped again, the tone hopeless, the sound trailing off.

They left then, and for a long time they rode in silence, side by side in the carriage, over the muddy road. Valeria looked out of her window. The day was cold, overcast, and windy, but already forsythia was in blossom, and the branches of the elm trees were green.

"Ah, Valeria," General Hendrick said finally, his voice a little wistful. "That boy, that William Esmond."

"No, sir," she replied. "His name was Henry. Henry Esmond, General Hendrick."

"Yes," he said, "Henry." He paused, took out a handkerchief, and wiped his lips. "I was mistaken about him. What he did was nothing. Compared to Marcus he behaved as sane as Greece."

They went on, the horses trotting, the wheels slipping in the shallow ruts. They passed a fence, a closed gate, a stand of short-leaf pine. Then the road turned and they moved by a pasture again, the brown grass sprinkled green with wild onions.

"But he did not cry," General Hendrick said. "Rutledge is wrong about that. He would not cry."

She weighed the general's words for a while, startled by the firm tone he had used, surprised by the sudden turn his thoughts had taken. And then she knew. She understood why they went to visit the Rutledges week after week, even when the roads were bad and the weather bitter. Sitting there in the quaintly furnished room, listening to Captain Rutledge talk and watching the play of the firelight, there was always the possibility of capturing that other moment, that hour in his life when the worst thing that had ever happened to him was the defeat he had suffered in the war. He preferred to remember his own disgrace, to recollect his own ignominy and his old broken ambitions, than to reflect further on his own son who had married a Negro.

The carriage jolted, swayed at the turn, and then they were riding on the Cedarcrest drive over the scattering gravel. In the time before they reached the walk, Valeria tried to visualize the face of Marcus Hendrick. She searched her brain for some hidden clue, some hint that she might have forgotten. The color of his hair, the quality of his teeth, the length and shape of his beard and his mustaches. But there was nothing. No point of beginning, no single fact to go on. When she had heard of him at all—from her husband, from the general, and now from Captain Rutledge—it was to hear that he was visionary or handsome or brave in the field when the defeated army had surrendered.

Often, when she was a child, Valeria had tried to see in her mind the figure of Sampson straining at the pillars or the baby Moses crying in his basket or the face of David as he mounted to the tower, weeping against the loss of his rebel son. But she was never able to capture the image. She could never get beyond the impalpable word, the simple concept of strength or wisdom or distraction. So it was now with her thoughts of Marcus Hendrick. He remained a step beyond her grasp, a shadow that played at the edge of her imagination.

The carriage stopped, the general helped her down, and they moved up the brick walk between the cedars. Halfway to the house he paused and touched her arm.

"How do you reckon . . . ," he began, "how do you suppose . . . ," and he broke off and for a while he studied his boots in silence.

Then he continued. "I mean, what do you think we could tell from his looks if we were allowed to see him?"

She was startled. It was, she thought, as if he had read her mind. "He would not be much different," she said. "He would not have changed much. He would look almost the same as he did when he left you."

"When he left me?" the general asked, his tone puzzled.

"Twenty years ago," Valeria said. "Perhaps he is gray now and wrinkled. But the shape of his face would be the same."

"No," General Hendrick replied, poking the ground with his stick, "not Marcus. It was the child I was dwelling on. I was thinking of the boy who is my grandson."

◈ 4 ◈

FROM HER CHAIR near the doorway Valeria watched them, the general and the three boys in the shade of the hickory tree, sheltered from the fierce rays of the July sun. General Hendrick stood with his back to the house, dressed in linen with a straw hat on his head, and the boys slouched in a row in front of him, all barefooted in denim and calico, and almost the same size, except for one who was a little taller and thinner than the other two. The boys were grinning, their eyes shifted slightly away, staring beyond the general, past his head or toward the ground beneath his feet.

"Now, then," the old man said, pointing his cane at one of the Negroes, "let's hear you."

"Here they come," the boy said. It was meant to be a shout, but it passed his lips not much louder than the general, himself, had spoken, and it ended in a high, embarrassed giggle.

"Hell-fire!" General Hendrick said. "Can't you yell any louder than that? What do you do to make your mammy quit whipping you?"

"I don't know, sir," the boy replied. "I reckon I cain't do it when nobody watching."

"Watching, the devil!" the general said. "You couldn't call for help if you fell in the privy. You." He pointed to the next one.

It came out loud this time, the words distinct and clear, with the *come* drawn out like the final note in a song.

General Hendrick paused a moment after the sound had stopped, rubbed his nose thoughtfully with his finger, then nodded to the tall boy with the slender arms.

"Yo-ho," the boy screamed. "Ole Massa General. Here they come a-trotting down the big road."

The noise reached a climax and rolled across the countryside; it flooded the house; it echoed in the hall where Valeria was sitting. The boy remained standing in an attitude of speech, his head raised, his lips slightly parted. The general took a step backward and turned his gaze toward the driveway and the hill that rose on the other side of the creek. He looked off into the distance as if he expected to see the words themselves, solid against the horizon, following each other over the crest of the hill.

"By God," he said at last. "You're the one I've been searching for all morning. You come on with me and I'll take you to the belfry."

So they came into the house, the old man first, and his lookout, his sentinel, behind him. Valeria watched in amazement as they crossed the hall, the general dignified, serious in his purpose, and the boy smiling, capering slightly, rubbing his toes against the carpet on the floor.

"Were you listening?" the general said as he moved toward the stairs. "Did you hear the way this boy can yell?"

"They heard him in Gallatin," Valeria replied. "They heard him in Nashville if the wind was right."

"Never mind about that," the general said. "Just so I hear him when the time comes."

For it was his plan to have the boy watch the highway until Marcus and Allen Hendrick came in sight. Then, when the cry was raised, Valeria and the general would move out of the house and stand at the head of the drive to meet them.

"This is foolishness, General Hendrick," Valeria said after the old man had returned to the hall.

It was not much after eight o'clock in the morning, but already the day was hot. The sun had heated the steps that led to the doorway, and wave after wave of scorching air swept through the room, past the ancient, dusty furniture, the lazy, circling flies. Valeria was seated in a hickory rocking chair, an edge of lace she was tatting spread out on her lap, her dress wet in the back from perspiration. Across from her, the general fidgeted on a leather davenport, drumming his fingers on the arm of the couch, pulling, from time to time, at the edge of his whiskers.

"General," she said, for he had not answered her, "there is no sense in staying here. We could see them soon enough from the parlor window."

"No," he said, his voice serious now that his guard was posted and the long wait had finally begun. "I want to be there. I want to see them when they come up on the hill."

She took her shuttle and began to work once more on her piece of tatting. "You could do that from the window," she replied. "You could see them just as plain from there."

"Damn it!" the general said, "I want to be as close as I can. I want to see the color of his face."

She remembered, then, how at breakfast General Hendrick had questioned Aaron, not only about Marcus, but about the boy as well —Allen, who had in his veins his mother's Negro blood. They had eaten early in preparation for Marcus Hendrick's visit, and the old slave was tired after his night in Gallatin, a little cross that he had been sent to wait at the house with the keys; to welcome home the prodigal son and the colored wife whom he had refused to abandon. This morning Aaron moved between the sideboard and the table, the dishes held a little precariously in his soft, wrinkled hands, his lips pouting, his cheeks sunken where some of his teeth were gone.

"Did you think him?" the general said, his voice a little formal to match his diction. "Did he seem to you to be much altered?"

"Considerable," Aaron said, and resumed his silence.

The general waited, his chair pushed back from the table, his hands folded in his lap. Then he said, "How was he changed, Aaron? How was he different?"

"He gray," Aaron replied. "Hair as gray as mine and his limbs is thin. He smell like he passed the last week in the jungle."

"Jungle?" General Hendrick said. "What jungle?"

"The jungle in Nashville," Aaron said. "Drinking in one of them Water Street saloons."

"Wait a minute," the general said sternly. "Who do you think you're talking about? What do you mean, saying such a thing as that?"

The old Negro was standing with his back against the wall, his arms hanging at his sides, his stomach pushing out against his waistcoat. He was looking at General Hendrick, but his eyes were blank, expressionless and round and slightly bloodshot.

"Use yo' own nose," he said. "Sniff him for yo'self when he get here."

"That'll do," General Hendrick replied testily. He took a sip of water, wiped his mouth on his napkin, and then in a voice that was softer, he said, "And the boy? Did you get a look at him before you left there?"

"I seen him," Aaron said. "He look like any other boy, I reckon."

"I know that," General Hendrick replied. "I know he would look like a boy." He paused. "Does he resemble Master Marcus?"

"No," Aaron said, "but I only seen him by the lamplight."

To Valeria, who was watching, the general's face seemed to lose its color. He grew pale, and the ruptured vessels in his nose, the veins in his forehead stood out blue against the shrunken, faded skin. Then, with a sudden anger he rose from his chair and said, "Damn you! You show some respect for Master Marcus or I'll have you whipped!"

Now, while they waited in the hot hall, listening for the shout from the top of the house that would tell them that their visitors were coming, the general was pale once again and he got up occasionally to walk toward the door, or to pace back and forth with his watch in his hand, the old repeater chiming out the hour.

"General," Valeria said, "sit down. They would have had to start last night to be here now."

He made no reply. He continued his steps along the rug and closed his watch and replaced it with a flourish. His suit, which he had put on fresh, was wrinkled now, the seat of the trousers creased, the sleeves a little baggy at the elbows. His hair was ruffled in back, the edge of his collar was stained with perspiration; but his boots were polished, his tie still fresh, and he wore a masonic badge upon his coat.

"They ought to be here," General Hendrick said. "It's almost nine o'clock and they ought to be here."

He took another turn down the hall. He walked in the shaft of sunlight that fell through the open door past a small walnut table, a slender, Empire chair, a brass candle stand that wanted polish. He moved toward the foot of the steps, cocked his ear toward the stairwell, then stepped once more to the place where Valeria was sitting.

"He's gone to sleep," the general said accusingly, looking down at her with narrow, glittering eyes.

She was only half listening. "Sir?" she asked.

"That boy," he said. "That damn nigger boy has gone to sleep."

"General," Valeria said wearily, "you're going to wear yourself out. If you don't sit down you'll have to go to bed yourself before they get here."

But he did not sit down, and he did not tire himself either, for when the signal came, the shout loud as a clap of thunder, the sound rattling through the old house like hail upon the roof, the general was standing with his watch in his hand, peering up the staircase. He jumped, shied back like a horse, then turned and went quickly to the doorway. Then he came back, for he had forgotten Valeria, waited impatiently for her to get up, found his hat and his stick, and they went together, across the lawn to the shade at the edge of the driveway.

There was no one in sight, and as the minutes passed, Valeria, too, began at last to be impatient. Now that they were somewhere near at hand, close along the big road, or perhaps already on the drive, she felt something of the old man's anticipation, his fearful curiosity to see the boy. Her hands were damp, her breath was sharp in her throat, and her eyes burned from staring at the brilliant sky that lay beyond the hilltop.

The general, standing at her side, seemed to have become completely calm. He held his head high; the blood had returned to the flesh of his cheeks. There was only a slight trembling, a jerk or two at the corner of his eyelid.

"Now," he said softly, as if he had been counting the time. "We ought to see them any moment now."

And all at once they were there, the two horsemen, both looking small at a distance, and silhouetted by the morning sun.

They seemed to hesitate, pause for a fraction of a second, then they were coming down toward the creek, the figures growing larger, the separate faces coming into view.

"He is older, Valeria," General Hendrick said. "He is past fifty and he shows his age."

But he was not, she noticed, quite so gray as Aaron.

He left his horse at the mounting block, and followed by the boy, he came toward them, his hat off, his body erect, his movements graceful. His hair, which had been blond to begin with, was turning slowly white, changing at the temples, fading in irregular streaks across his head. He was a small man, like the general, and fair, his face recently sunburned, and wrinkled at the corners of his mouth and eyes. His suit was brown linen; he wore a white waistcoat, and there was about him an air of elegance that she had not expected, a certain graciousness in the way he inclined his head and let his crop dangle from his fingers.

But all of this she saw in a single glance, in the fraction of an instant before she looked past the man to catch her first glimpse of Allen Hendrick. He moved behind his father, a little awkward in a nankeen roundabout and a string tie knotted tightly at his neck. He was thin and tall, taller than his father, larger than the general, and in no way resembling the picture she had drawn of him in her mind. For almost unconsciously she had patterned him after the Negroes she had seen on the plantation—coarse of feature, with thick lips, a wide nose, eyes large and brown and somewhat wistful.

A fit playmate for the boy who had called from the belfry, the son of a black mother with the mark, she thought, of Ham upon his brow.

But he was none of these things and his face was handsome. His nose was slender, his lips no more than full; his eyes were blue and his skin was white. He seemed bashful, and he hung back, away from her and the general.

For a moment it appeared to Valeria that General Hendrick had lost his voice. He stood with his cheeks drawn in, his old lips slightly pursed, looking at Marcus Hendrick, then at the boy, then back again to his own son in the manner of a man confused by alien surroundings. But he was merely biding his time, gathering his strength for the proper word, the note on which to found a reconciliation.

"I would have known you," he said at last. "I could have picked you out of a crowd. Or recognized you on the street in Nashville."

"And I would have known you, Father," Marcus Hendrick said. "But you never changed. You never showed your age."

So after twenty years he began his conversation with a compliment. His voice was gentle, husky, but with a mellow quality like a horn heard from far away, trembling on the hot air of the morning. He bowed to Valeria, an easy, practiced bow, made in a sort of rhythm, as if it were a movement in a dance, and then he turned to introduce them to his son.

"Allen," he said, for the boy hung back still. "Father, this is my son, Allen." And then, "Miss Valeria, may I present your nephew, Allen Hendrick."

But she did not notice what he had said, the impudent turn of his phrase which had stressed her relation to a Negro. She was looking at the boy's face, and she saw that he was unhappy and afraid. He was breathing heavily, the slender nostrils dilating slightly; his chest heaved and the blood ran to his face. With his chin trembling, his eyes cast down, he seemed on the verge of tears, and he twisted the cloth of his cap between his fingers.

"Oh," she said quickly to break the silence that had fallen, for the general did not speak, "oh, we are glad to see you, Allen. We are glad to see him, aren't we, General Hendrick?"

"Yes," he said, poking the ground with his cane. "But we must not stand here. It will be cooler in the house."

They went back through the hall, into the parlor where the blinds were kept closed in the summer and the air was musty and the light poor. General Hendrick and Valeria sat down together on a love seat; across from them Marcus took a chair. And finally Allen found a stool, close to the feet of his father.

They spoke of the trip first, empty speeches concerning the condition of roads, the price of ferries, accommodations to be had along the highway. And then of the people Marcus Hendrick remembered, neighbors and friends he had had in Gallatin.

"Is Captain Rutledge dead?" he asked.

"No, no," the general replied. "He is living." Then as an afterthought, he went on, "but he married after you left and he has children."

"He has a wife?" Marcus asked.

"No," the general said. "He married a girl from Hartsville, but she is dead."

And in spite of the sadness of it all, their poor effort at conversation, their abortive attempt to bridge the years that stood between them, Valeria looked at the floor and bit her lip to keep from smiling.

"And the Weavers?" Marcus said.

"The boy is a doctor now. He comes out here sometimes to treat the slaves."

"Does he treat you too?"

"I'm never sick," the old man replied. "I've got no need for pills."

Then as the men paused, the boy spoke from his stool near the corner.

"Sir," he said, "Father says you knew General Jackson."

It was not a question. He made the statement and leaned forward waiting for General Hendrick to speak. He was eager, blushing again, his eyes sparkling and reassured, but showing still a faint trace of fear. It was, Valeria thought, as if he were not talking of General Jackson at all, but rather of something nearer home, some person or time or event in the past that held the key to all his future.

"I knew him," General Hendrick said. "He came to Cedarcrest often. He was in this room less than a month before he died."

The old man relaxed in his seat, crossed his legs, and stared off toward the wall, toward a slit of light that came in through the blinds. He was frowning, his brow wrinkled, as if he were trying to recollect the details of some half-forgotten story. But when he spoke his voice was gruff and his manner distant.

"I knew him," he repeated. "But that was a long time ago and the country was different. He is dead now and Tennessee is changed."

The boy sat back, his face expressionless. Marcus Hendrick was silent. The general, sitting with his head still turned away, seemed to sulk at the end of the love seat and view the world around him with despair. He was confused, uncertain, with no words to speak, and he delayed and let the moments slip away.

Then, from the doorway, Valeria heard a loud, familiar voice.

"Marse General."

It was the Negro boy, his face gleaming, wet with perspiration, his thin arms hanging halfway to his knees. He had thrust his body forward so that he stood with his feet in the hall, his head beyond the doorjamb in the parlor. His eyes were open wide, his neck stretched long, so that he looked like a timid, gentle bird, and he waved his hands like wings to keep his balance.

"Marse General," he said, "is you 'specting no more gent'men this morning?"

"What?" General Hendrick said, startled. "What did you say?"

And that was a mistake, for the boy thought he had not spoken clearly.

"Is they nobody else?" he said, and the sound roared, caught in the closed room vibrating back and forth between the shutters. "Is they somebody else to look for on the big road?"

For a moment, while the echo died away, the general stared in astonishment at the boy. Then he said, "Get out of here! You get your black hide on back to the quarters!"

Marcus Hendrick waited, a puzzled smile on his face, his lips half parted, showing his worn teeth. Allen sat perfectly still, and the general regarded the floor and rubbed his ear.

"I had him watching for you," the old man said at last. "I had him waiting up above to give a signal."

There was silence again. Marcus Hendrick took out his glasses, rubbed them with a handkerchief, and clipped them to his nose.

"Father," he said and stopped, blinking through the spectacles at the general. "Father, you need not have done that. You did not have to meet us at the driveway."

"But I wanted to," the old man replied. "I longed to see you when you came in sight upon the hill."

And because this was spoken to Marcus Hendrick and not to the boy at his side, it seemed to Valeria to be no better than a lie. For it was Allen he had watched for, and perhaps the general was thinking of this too. He spoke again and this time to his grandson.

"And I was watching for Allen," he said. "I was anxious to see him, too, from the very outset."

Valeria looked at the boy, at the slender, delicate nose, the blond hair, the bluest eyes she had ever seen, the color clear and deep, as bright as the painted eyes on a porcelain doll.

"Grandfather," Allen said.

And when they all turned to hear him, he stopped in confusion. He let his head bend forward. He shifted his feet noiselessly on the carpet.

"Grandfather," he said at last. "We are glad to see you."

He said only this, but it was enough, and in the years that followed, Valeria liked to think that it was here that the boy made his fortune. For the old man was touched, moved by Allen's sincerity or the innocence in his heart, or shamed by his own deception, the little lie that he had told about his lookout. He got to his feet, supporting himself on the arm of the couch, moving slowly as if his joints were stiff.

"I will show you the land," he said. "I will show you the fields and the stables and the quarters."

But they did not go with him that day to walk his fences and admire his crops and see his pasture.

"No, Father," Marcus Hendrick said. "Not today."

"There is time," the general replied. "Time enough before dinner, and the boy will like it."

"No," Marcus said softly. "This time we cannot stay for dinner."

The general was silent for a while, chewing at the corner of his lip, biting at the hairs along his mustache.

"You can go to John's grave then. You can go that far before you leave us."

They went out into the blinding sunlight, along the hot gravel path, through the gate, to the little cemetery. There, beside the cool stone, under the shade of the maples, they stood and studied the inscription and looked at the flowers in their vase.

Then Marcus Hendrick said, "Miss Valeria, John was a fine man. I loved him deeply."

But this, Valeria knew, was only politeness. For he turned back to the general, and with his eyes full of tears he said, "Father, I would not have had this happen. I would have given the world to save you John."

The three of them were standing close together, and there was in the still air a scent of brandy overlaid by a faint smell of cloves. This, Valeria thought, was what Aaron had meant when he spoke of the jungle, and she noticed it, now that he had made his pretty speech.

"General," she said, "let us go back to the house."

They moved again on the walk, the two men in front, Valeria and the boy behind them.

"Was he . . . ," Allen began. "Miss Valeria, what did he do?"

"He was a lawyer," Valeria replied, "and we lived in Natchez."

After a moment Allen Hendrick asked, "Did he go to court? Did he try cases?"

"Ah, yes," she said. "He went almost every day during the session. They trusted John in Natchez, Allen."

"Father is a lawyer too," the boy replied. "But he does not try cases."

They were at the mounting block. A pair of grooms waited with the horses. The general and his son stood together, reluctant to part, uncertain as to how to say good-by.

"You must come again, Marcus," the general said. "You must come again prepared to stay for dinner."

These were the conventional speeches, spoken almost as he would speak them to Captain Rutledge, but not quite. The voice was a little hesitant; the tone was flat and rigidly controlled.

"I will, sir."

"And Allen. I will see you often, Allen."

"Sir," the boy said, "we have enjoyed our visit."

He was doing what he had been taught, performing according to his breeding, but the words had a wistful sound, a slow cadence that fell a little at the end. He seemed to have, Valeria thought, a gift for sadness, an unconscious talent for a sorrowful turn of phrase.

"Come back," General Hendrick repeated helplessly. "Come back again."

He nodded to Valeria and they went once more toward the house, toward the hall where they had waited, toward the parlor, shuttered and gloomy, where they had sat.

"Valeria," he said.

"Sir?"

"What did you think, Valeria?"

He did not fool her this time. This time she knew.

"Oh," she replied. "He is a lovely boy."

"Yes," the general said. "I liked him too."

◊ 5 ◊

So ALLEN HENDRICK made the transformation, changed from a nigger to a white man in the course of a morning in July. For at the instant that he rode away from the house at Cedarcrest, away from the old man and the girl three years his senior who was his aunt, he rode away not as the son of a Negro woman but as the grandson of a planter and a gentleman. The taint in his blood was almost balanced out by the glory of the old general's name, made tolerable to the people in the town by all the general's land and slaves and money.

General Hendrick called for him the next day, and they rode through town in the surrey, twice around the courthouse square, where a few loafers were lounging in the shade of a maple tree, whittling and spitting at the brown, dry lawn, and where on the other side of the street a few women were shopping from their buggies and a few more moved beneath their parasols. To each man and woman the general bowed and touched his hat, and Allen, in his turn, lifted his nankeen cap, and the boy's debut was over.

For that is what it was—his introduction to the town, his presentation to society, and when the surrey had stopped, the general leaned slightly toward Allen, faced him on the warm leather cushion, and said, "You are a Hendrick. Whatever you do, you must always remember that."

He did remember it. And often in the days that followed, he remembered too something his father had told him on that afternoon in Memphis when the old trapper from Arkansas had come to the store and told him that his mother was a nigger.

"Is she?" Allen had said. "Is she what he called her?"

And Marcus Hendrick had replied softly, "She is your mother." Then after a moment he said, "Come here," and they went to the front of the building and watched the people passing in the street: a bearded man in an old buggy pulled by a lean horse, a pair of Irish boys in denim pants and frayed homespun jackets, and then two women from Pinch-Gut, one with dirty fingernails and a dirty, painted face, and the other with dyed hair and heavy eyebrows.

"Are they white?" Marcus Hendrick said.

And when Allen did not answer he went on, his voice a little stern, "Is that what you mean? Is that what you want to be?"

Then, his tone a little softer, he stooped and put his arm around Allen and said, "They are people, Allen. They may even be good people, but being white does not make them good. And whatever your mother is, whatever her grandmother may have looked like, or wherever her people may have come from, she is a lady, and that is why we love her. And that is why you must be proud to be her son."

To an eight-year-old boy these were words, phrases not empty but unfathomable, and on Marcus Hendrick's breath there was the strong scent of brandy.

But Allen Hendrick remembered what his father had said. And now years later he had moved to Gallatin, and he had enrolled in the academy there and gone to parties and danced with girls, and he called the judge's son his friend. And sometimes at night, or at an odd hour in the morning, he would recollect how his grandfather had told him to remember he was a Hendrick, and it would occur to him that all his life he had been his mother's son or the general's grandson, and never himself, never simply a boy named Allen Hendrick. . . .

But not at first. He did not think of this at first, for his new world lay before him like a dream.

He took up his life in his new world of Middle Tennessee, and a part of his world was Anse Weaver, a doctor and a bachelor thirty years old, or perhaps a year or two older. Allen Hendrick saw him for the first time on a morning in October when the frost still glittered on the Cedarcrest fields and the sedge flashed red and gold in the early sunlight. Anse Weaver had come out to hunt and he rode up the drive in a black coat and a white stock so that he looked like something out of an English hunting print with his gun case tied to his saddlebags and an Irish setter following his horse. He was handsome, clean-shaven, with oiled hair and long, delicate hands, and he appeared at first glance to be a little effeminate, for he moved slowly and his voice was soft when he spoke. But as Allen came to find out, he could shoot a gun.

They hunted the ground together, Anse Weaver with his double-barreled Belgian fowling piece, and Allen with a lighter gun that the general had given him.

"Lead them," Anse Weaver would say. "Keep leading them after you shoot."

And he did, and more of his birds began to drop.

Allen spent most of his week ends at Cedarcrest that fall, and one night when the hunt was over and Anse Weaver had gone home, the general sat for a long time staring into the fireplace, his lips puckered up and his forehead wrinkled, and from time to time he would sniff a pinch of snuff.

Then at last he got up and, standing with his back to the mantel, said, "He's after Valeria. I'm damned if he comes out here in search of birds."

"Sir," Allen Hendrick said. "Who, Grandfather?"

"Nothing," the general said. "I was just musing. The truth is I didn't aim to speak."

But he had spoken, and if what his words implied were true, then Allen for Dr. Weaver was simply a means to an end, and the days they had spent together signified nothing. If the general were right, Anse had come only to see Valeria, and his friendship for Allen was merely a device, a means by which to circumvent her mourning.

So on the next morning—it was a Sunday with the air clear and the sky blue and a heavy frost that lingered in the valleys—he asked Anse if he loved Valeria. He put it simply, baldly in a single question, with no introduction, no innuendo to lead up to the subject, and with no facility either, but in one quick, sudden burst, as they walked between two rows of ruined corn. "Dr. Anse," he said, "do you like Aunt Valeria?" For he would not say love; he was still too young for that. And he was too innocent, even now at the age of fifteen, to realize the extent of his own impertinence.

For a moment Anse Weaver said nothing. Then, as they reached the end of the row, he stopped and smiled at Allen, his teeth white, his eyes narrowing slightly and the flesh wrinkling at the corners of his nose.

"Yes," he replied, "I love her, young Hendrick."

Allen turned his head away, looked out over a pasture, out over the dry, brown grass toward a sumac thicket and a clump of tall, bare locust trees. The dog ahead of them had come to a point, his front leg pulled up, his head forward, the feathers on his flank and tail fluttering in the autumn breeze. And the wind was cold on Allen's cheek, cold against his hands and through his coat.

"But what about me?" Allen Hendrick said at last, and he heard in his own voice a tone of anguish.

"Well," Anse Weaver replied, "what about you, young Hendrick?"

"When you come out here," Allen said softly, "you don't really come to hunt, do you? You don't come to see me."

"Yes, I do," Anse Weaver replied. "You're right in thinking I want to see Valeria. I do love her, and I hope she will marry me someday. But I come to see you too. I am your friend, Allen. I will always be your friend. You remember that."

So with his mind almost at rest he returned to the everyday business of his life, to the house in Gallatin, to his mother and father, to the schoolroom where the tall professor paced back and forth in front of the class to the rhythm of Latin verse and pounded the table to give emphasis to Euclid. He returned to town and the days passed, and in the afternoons he walked home from the academy with a boy named Houston Knott, a short, barrel-chested boy who was the son of a judge and the godson of the general. They would walk through the early winter twilight, and sometimes Houston would discuss the law that he had already begun to read at odd hours in his father's study. But most of the time he would talk of his dream, his ambition that some day he might run for public office. There were moments when he spoke of starting as a judge, of filling the bench of the circuit court, and of moving from there directly to the Capitol. But more often he was faithful to a saner plan, that of making a slow but orderly progress through the legislature to the governor's chair and then to a seat in the nation's Senate.

"You've got to be sure of yourself," he said one day to Allen Hendrick. "You've got to know what you're about when it comes to speaking and stumping around the country."

As they moved on up the brick walk, past a fence that was wet from the light December rain, Houston went on to tell how he rehearsed in secret for the hour of his glory.

"I pick out somebody to run against," he said, "and then I calculate a means to skunk 'em." He looked down at his boots for a moment and then he went on, "For an instance, take Joe Henry Witherspoon."

"Joe Henry Witherspoon?" Allen said.

"Yes," Houston replied. "Pretend he was running against me for the place of judge."

"But he wouldn't," Allen said. "He's bound to work in his father's livery stable."

"That don't matter," Houston said. "You've got to practice on somebody. Pretend it was him."

So Allen did his best to pretend while Houston told how he would start by making fun of Joe Henry's buck teeth and reach a climax when he told in detail of the way Joe Henry once ran from a crippled bull.

"You've got to go easy on the teeth," Houston said. "You've got to bring them into a speech like it just slipped out. If you do it wrong you'll get people to feeling sorry for him."

"Yes," Allen said. "And a judge's work don't require a whole lot of biting."

"Hell!" Houston replied in disgust. "That's not the point. You've got no understanding of elections."

They went on a few steps in silence and then Houston began to talk once more with his old enthusiasm. A serious expression came over his face; his eyebrows arched and his brown eyes opened wide as if in surprise. And in an intimate, somewhat histrionic voice, he heaped praise on the poor decrepid bull and shame on the coward it had intimidated.

"Did it happen?" Allen asked when he was through. "Did Joe Henry really run from a bull like that?"

[55]

For a second Houston looked hurt. His lips pursed slightly into a pout and he sniffed once or twice in the damp, cold air.

"No," he replied finally. "Not exactly that way, it didn't. That thorn the bull had in his hoof didn't slow him down much."

For Houston was honest, and he had no grudge against Joe Henry Witherspoon. He was merely practicing, sharpening his wit against the time to come when he meant to use it.

"And what would you say about me?" Allen asked him one day. "What if I decided to make the race for judge?"

"Not you, Allen," Houston replied. "You wouldn't want it. You wouldn't even like to make a speech."

"Why wouldn't I?" Allen Hendrick said sharply.

"No, no, Allen," Houston repeated. "Not you."

Allen stopped and reached out and caught Houston's arm and made Houston stop, too. Allen was panting, and he kept his grip on Houston's sleeve, and his hand, his whole body began to tremble.

"Why wouldn't I?" he said again. "Why in the hell wouldn't I stand against you for office?"

Houston jerked his own arm free.

"Because you——"

Houston Knott's voice stopped, broke off abruptly, leaving a vast and complete silence, a void in the dim, gray afternoon, as if the whole world had suddenly paused to listen.

"Because what?" Allen Hendrick finally shouted. "Because what?"

Then he set himself and waited for the word to come. He leaned forward and doubled up his fists; he drew his right hand slightly back and kept his eyes on Houston's face—but his gaze did not meet Houston's. He and Houston did not quite look at each other, they made no attempt to stare each other down. Allen felt all the heat and pain of his anger tingle in the warm surge and fall of his blood. He stood very still, holding rigidly to his position, and after a moment the muscles in his legs began to ache.

He will say it now, Allen Hendrick thought. He believed he saw Houston's lips move, part slightly to make the sound, and Allen knew that when the words came, the simple reason given in barely more than half a dozen syllables, his friendship with Houston would be irrevocably over. For when Houston said, *Because you are a nigger,* Allen Hendrick would ram his fist into Houston Knott's face.

But Houston did not speak these words. He allowed the silence to lengthen, to wear itself out, and Allen Hendrick opened his fists and slowly stepped back.

Then Houston said, "Because you are my friend."

They began walking once more, and after a while Houston asked, "What are you going to be when you grow up, Allen?"

Allen Hendrick felt a great fear clutch his heart.

"I haven't decided," he replied stiffly.

And he thought, What *will* I do? What about me?

While Allen Hendrick worried over this question, followed it around and around the circuits of his brain, the world speculated that a great change was coming, that the nation would be split into two governments instead of one. Of the men who discussed the matter with Allen—his father, the general, Anse Weaver—none was in favor of a Confederacy in the South.

"Allen," Marcus Hendrick said one night when his newspapers were finished and his brandy glass sat empty on the table. "Allen, I love the Negro and I think he should be free."

This was his way of talking, Allen realized, his way of using words as if he were always in public, always in front of a crowd making a speech. But suddenly, on this night, his tone changed, became reminiscent and a little intimate, and he looked past Allen Hendrick toward the wall.

"When I was younger," he said, "in the years back in Memphis just after I was married to your mother, I believed that all the problems of our nation might be solved simply by letting the people know the truth."

He took out a cigar, lighted it with a lucifer match, and then went on.

"The truth," he repeated. "And every evening I would go to my study and write pieces for the papers, for Brownlow's Knoxville *Whig* and for the *Freeman's Advocate.* For they stood for abolition then, just as they do now. And I spoke, all over West Tennessee, for emancipation."

He leaned back and blew smoke toward the ceiling, the slender, prim man now turning gray; his face was wrinkled, the creases showing deep in the glow of the lamplight, but his mustache was trimmed neatly, and his teeth were firm.

"The truth," he said once more, speaking the word in the way he spoke the name of Cedarcrest as if it were gold, as if the sound itself could be spent like money.

"I made a speech once at Jackson, and when I was finished a man came up to me, came up to the platform, and took my arm and introduced himself as Mr. Drake. Doubtless he is dead now, for he was old even then and his breath was short and his eyesight was failing badly."

Then while Allen sat with his back to the fire and his straight chair turned to face his father, Marcus Hendrick told how the old, birdlike man had leaned forward a little on his cane as if his thin legs were no longer able to hold up his belly. And he had said, "Son, I am too old to give a damn. I am too old now to be concerned with it any more. But there is always something. When first I come to the West it was the Indians, and I helped to kill 'em. And now it is the niggers, and I own some of them too, and they fetch me my toddy of a morning and my pot at night. In the world there is always meanness, and there is always a bottom rail to any fence."

"And I did not know it then," Marcus Hendrick said, "but *that* was the truth."

He paused and took the decanter from the sideboard and filled his glass with brandy.

"Listen," he went on. "They can tear the country apart. They can fight a war. They can kill all the white people or all the Negroes, and they can even make old Aaron emperor and Vernon chief factotum of the court. And nothing will be altered, nothing changed. For there is evil in the world and it is strong."

And the boy, who was fifteen now, and deep in the mysteries of calculus and on his way to a mastery of the Latin verb, did not understand this. For he was looking that night only at the words themselves, only at the statements his father made, and not at the lifetime of bitter frustration that lay behind them. So he remained silent and a little confused, and the log burned in the fireplace, and the scent of brandy drifted like perfume in the air.

He listened to the gloomy utterances of Marcus Hendrick; and a short time later, on a day in December when the sky was gray and the ground hard and there was a film of ice forming at the edges of the creek, he heard Anse Weaver talk of the war that was to come in a tone of voice less dour than his father's. It was afternoon and for most of the day they had been riding with the hounds. But the fox had eluded them and the dogs had been called in, and Allen and Anse rode together, over a smooth hill, up through the tall, dead grass toward the bare trees that stood out above the skyline.

"They will fight, young Hendrick," Anse Weaver said, smiling slightly in the dark afternoon. "There will be a war, you can count on that."

He glanced at Allen Hendrick and smiled, his teeth flashing in the poor light and his eyes narrow beneath his black eyebrows.

"Up in Washington," he said, "they talk of compromise. They lecture each other on Kansas and Nebraska and stay up nights drawing lines across a map. But they will fight because man is naturally bound to be a fool, and you do not have to be a doctor to notice that."

He rode on for a moment, watching the trees at the top of the hill, and all the time he was fondling his mare, patting her neck and running his fingers through her mane. Then he laughed softly and said, "It is a curious thing. When I was in medical school, my cadaver was the body of a nigger man who had drowned himself trying to swim the Cumberland River. You see," Anse Weaver went on, "he could not swim very well and the water was cold.

"And he knew all that, young Hendrick. He was sober and sane and getting along all right, with a few potatoes in his cellar and a girl he visited twice a week. But there was something in his mind that told him to try it, something that painted a picture of what a figure he would cut if he happened to make it, of how the news would travel and the story grow, and of how the girls would turn to look at him on Sunday."

They had crested the hill now and were going down, through the cold, still afternoon, through the grass that swished beneath the horses.

"So I searched for it," Anse Weaver said. "As soon as we started dissecting, down at the feet, I began to count the days until we got to his brain and I could see it. For I thought the answer would be there, in some little fold or line or crevice; I thought I could touch the reason he had acted a fool.

"But it wasn't there, young Hendrick," Anse Weaver said. "His brain was just like yours or mine, like those of the men laid out on the other tables. I noticed in the dissecting room that they were all alike, all the brains and all the hearts, with now and then a bone that had once been broken."

They rode on a few feet, the horses warm and smoking in the twilight.

And Anse Weaver said, "A war is another way to swim a river. And that is what they ought to do: go out in January and line up and each man take his turn jumping in the water. Slavery and states' rights would take care of themselves. And everybody would get the notion of being a hero out of his system."

There was another silence and they rode a few feet more.

Then Anse spoke again, lightly, with a touch of laughter in his voice. "Ah," he said, "there will be a war. And you will go to it. And all the girls will smile to see a soldier."

"And what about you, Dr. Anse?" Allen Hendrick asked, laughing himself now, remembering the days when he had played with the brassbound rifle. "And what about you?" he repeated. "Will you go too?"

"No," Anse replied. "Not I, young Hendrick, but what a lot of brains a man might see after a battle."

And it was later still, on a day in spring, when the general spoke his piece about secession. He had been reading, in a newspaper, a speech that Mr. Stephens of Georgia had made before the House in Washington, and when he had finished, he sat for a long time staring over the rims of his spectacles toward the distance. Staring across the garden where the hyacinths were in bloom, across the lake that was motionless in the warm sunlight toward a field of tobacco newly set and a new growth of pasture on the hillside. Then he turned to face Allen Hendrick, to gaze down at the boy who was sitting on the floor with his back against a column.

"It is talking," the general said. "They listen to the wag of their own tongues, and they'll speak the nation to death before they are finished."

There was, in the old man's voice, a note of anger, a certain harshness that Allen had never heard before, and his words came rapidly, crowding out of his mouth. He remained silent for a moment, drumming his fingers on the arm of his chair, and then he said, "You would not remember it. You were too young, and at the time you were in Memphis. But they were all here once, Rhett and Barnwell, Butler and Cheeves, convening in Nashville to break the Federal Union.

"Listen," he said, leaning forward a little, stretching his neck, and blinking his wrinkled eyelids. "I went down to watch them. I saw what they were. It was a convention of fowls, a gathering together of peacocks; and they squawked like parrots and milled about like chickens in the aisles."

He paused. "I thought at the end of the Nashville Convention they had talked themselves out. But they keep on inflaming the people with their speeches."

At that moment, to Allen Hendrick, his face seemed infinitely sad, the flesh wrinkled and shrunken on his cheekbones, the veins swelling blue beneath the skin. "It is wrong," he said. "It is wrong to break the country; it is wrong to fight a war. I know it is wrong for I have seen it.

"In the old days," he went on, "we chased the Indians and fought them sometimes, and it always struck me that a dead man, red or white, was a monstrous waste. For when a man is dead, it is all over then, and all the land that he would have plowed will have to be plowed by somebody else, and all the meat that his children use will have to be cured by another hand, and all the game that he would have shot will have to wait for another hunter's rifle. Of all the sins that man can commit, prodigality is the most grievous."

He sat back then, huddled in his chair with an old shawl thrown around his shoulders and his hat pulled down close above his eyes. He took out his snuff box, took his pinch of snuff, sneezed, and blew his nose on a cotton handkerchief. Then he remained silent for an instant longer, his eyes bright and his nostrils trembling as he breathed.

"Look," the general said at last.

And Allen looked where he was pointing. Out toward the land, toward the tobacco field soft and green in the sunlight, and the dark clumps of cedar on the hillside, and the channel of the creek between the sycamore trees that marked the direction of the river. He looked at the cows in the pasture and the swans that swam in the lake, and as far as he could see the land rolled away toward the blue sky and the misty clouds in the distance.

"It is beautiful, Grandfather," Allen Hendrick said.

"No," the general replied.

Allen leaned forward. "Sir?" he said, a little startled.

"No," the general repeated. "It is not beautiful. It is money."

He waited a minute and licked his lips, and then he said, "They can free the niggers and make slaves of the white men. They can do away with states' rights or outlaw whisky-drinking or make it against the rules to cuss on Sunday. But the land is still there. They can't abolish that. And whoever's got the land has got the money."

Then he said, "You bear that in mind when the bugles start to toot."

So the world raged and men talked of war, or of truth or of the land or of human motivation, and in Allen Hendrick's heart there was something like peace. But at odd times—at the quiet hour of a fading afternoon, or on Sunday morning when he was alone in his room, or in bed at night when the candle had been extinguished—at these moments the old question would disturb his mind. *What about me? What of Allen Hendrick?* What of a boy who would never be white? What could you be on this earth, if you could not be a white man? Sometimes he would lie in his bed and feel the pillow soft beneath his cheek and think of himself and wonder, more or less placidly, about the future. But at other times his heart beat furiously; and he would stop suddenly in his passage across the sunlit garden; or he would turn away from the window where he had been watching the day fail into the first twilight. And he would strike the palm of his hand with his fist and say, "God damn! God damn them all!"

A year passed and he was sixteen, another year, and he was in his last term at the academy run by Professor Stuart. He owned his own horse, and he was General Hendrick's grandson; and his mother seemed almost contented, almost happy. In the afternoons, when he returned from school, she would be waiting for him in the parlor, a book open on her lap or a tatting shuttle in her hand; but when he entered the room she would put aside what she was doing and question him about what he had done or learned that day. He did not know why she should be so much interested in the dull subjects he was forced to pursue, but often, when he told her of a recitation, or of his walk through the Gallatin streets with Houston Knott, she would clasp her hands at her breast in a gesture of happiness; she would smile and say, "My dear, you are very bright."

One day, when the weather was bad—a cold rain was falling out of a cold gray sky and the wind blew and twisted in the treetops— Allen invited Houston to come into the house with him, and they entered through the front door into the hallway, and stopped there to take off their coats and wipe their boots. While they were standing near the hatrack, Allen saw his mother come out of the parlor, heard the rustle of her skirt as she turned toward the stairway, and her figure disappeared in the upper dark. Later, when Houston had gone, she returned to the parlor.

"Mother," Allen said, "that was Houston Knott."

"I know," she replied gaily. She was moving about the room, touching, fondling the furniture. She lifted a vase, then replaced it on the table; she let her hand glide over the backs of chairs. "I know," she said, "I heard you call him Houston."

She moved close to Allen, raised her hands, and put them on his shoulders. "Oh," she said, "I am glad Houston came. I am glad you have a friend to come and see you."

He considered a moment. He was glad too, he supposed. But he had never thought of it quite so bluntly.

He moved over to the window and stood by the drapes and looked out at the rain and the fence and the muddy street. Then he said, "Mother, why did you go upstairs? Why didn't you wait down here to speak to Houston?"

"Ah," she replied, still smiling, her eyes wide and sparkling, her teeth very white. "He is your friend. He came to be with you, my dear, not with me."

But Allen knew that this was not the real reason she had avoided meeting Houston. Or rather, the excuse she made was no reason at all. At Houston's house, Judge Knott did not run out of the room when Allen entered it, simply because Allen was not his but Houston's friend. Among all the people that Allen knew, no other parents retreated before the acquaintances of their children. The truth was that Lucy had run away because she did not want to embarrass Allen; she did not want to offend Houston with her Negro blood.

Allen turned back toward the room to face his mother. When he spoke, his voice was harsh and loud. "You don't have to run away. Not from him. Not from Houston."

"Oh, yes, my dear," Lucy replied gently. "He would not know what to say to an old woman like me."

Allen Hendrick hardly heard her; his thoughts and his anger were racing ahead.

"You do not!" he shouted. "You do not have to leave your own parlor for Houston! If he doesn't want to talk to you he can go to hell!"

She did not reply immediately. In silence she drew up her shoulders and raised her chin. Then she smiled slightly, indulgently, and said, "My dear, you must not allow yourself to get so angry. You only make things worse when you lose your temper. Anger is a sin."

"But—" Allen began.

"No," she interrupted, "anger solves nothing. And as for me, I have nothing to say to your Houston Knott."

After that day, when Allen came home from school, he found her waiting in the upstairs sitting room rather than in the parlor. And though Houston visited Allen many times after this, she never came downstairs until Houston's visit was over.

So his life went, and the months passed, and only once did the old fear return to Allen. One afternoon, late in April, he was stopped on the street by a farmer, a lean, wrinkled, middle-aged man in homespun trousers and homemade shoes who had a large wart above his left eyebrow.

"Son," the man said, "ain't you Major Hendrick's boy?"

Allen stopped short, seized by a sudden panic, caught by the cold memory of that other voice in another city, long ago.

"Yes," he said a little shortly—although he knew that even to a man in homespun his grandfather or his father would have said *sir*. "Yes," he said. "I am Allen Hendrick."

The farmer rubbed the wart on his forehead slowly and shifted his eyes. Then he said, "Son, would you consider tellin' me whether Genul's set his 'bacco plants out yet?"

And that was it, what he had meant to ask all the time. For the season was uncertain, and the general was reckoned to understand the weather.

So time continued on into another summer, and it was then that he made his first mistake. It was the night after his graduation from the academy and he went to a dance at the home of Houston Knott. He went alone, dressed in a new linen suit, a dark blue cravat, a watch and chain his grandfather had given him as a present; and when he left his hat with the butler and was moving up the stairway, up toward the sound of voices and the fiddles playing a reel, it seemed to him that the world lay before him and that the music would drift forever through the hall.

"Ah," Houston Knott said, "you are here at last. My enfair will be successful now that you've come."

He was still the politician, consolidating his strength, laying votes away against the future. And Allen knew this. But the words were pretty and in the ballroom the candles burned brightly and the marquisette skirts draped gracefully over their hoops.

Allen smiled. "I am here," he said. "But I came to see the ladies."

He saw the ladies. And he danced with them, figure after figure, set after set. And when the fiddlers paused, he drank punch with Amy Douglas. She was a small girl, fifteen perhaps, or a month or two older, with dark chestnut hair and dark eyes and lips that were red enough almost to have been painted. He had seen her before. She was the sister of one of his classmates, and he remembered her during his first year in Gallatin as the little, frail, graceless girl, flat-chested and narrow-hipped, who had tried to follow him and Houston and Henry Douglas when they went hunting. He remembered her crossing a field behind them, her dress held up to show her skinny legs, her movements awkward as if her joints were improperly hinged.

"Go back," Henry had said. "You can't come with us. Go back." And she had turned away pouting, her lips puckered and her face round, like the face of an unhappy elf, and she had wept a little, moving away from them through the grass. But that was years ago, and now she sat in the warm parlor, a lady dressed in yellow silk with a green sash tied around her waist.

He went to see her the next day. He cut a bunch of roses from his mother's garden and carried them on horseback through the quiet Sunday afternoon, past the square and out Main Street to the red brick house with its wide veranda and the short, ugly columns that supported the roof of the porch. He rode slowly, dressed once more in his linen finery, and as he made the turn into the driveway, he saw them sitting there, the four of them immobile, frozen in their seats, composed in a group like the subjects of a family painting. Mr. and Mrs. Douglas and Henry and Amy, seated in a row before the windows, the ladies with their skirts in decorous folds, the men with their hair combed and their boots polished. Then Mrs. Douglas turned and spoke, and Amy rose and went into the house.

He did not see her that day. At the last minute he lost his courage and gave the flowers to Mrs. Douglas and sat silent and a little morose, only half listening to the summer talk, only half seeing the buggies that passed on the street. But the truth repeated itself in his mind: they had seen him coming and they had put her out of his way.

When Allen rose to go, Mr. Douglas walked with him, down the walk to the hitching post, a prematurely old man with bowed shoulders and bad teeth and a wide streak of gray in his chestnut beard.

"You were kind to come," he said. "It was good of you to bring that bouquet to Mrs. Douglas."

Allen mumbled something, tried to reply and found no words and looked off toward the driveway.

Then, when they had reached the mare, Mr. Douglas stopped and put his hand on Allen's arm. "Son," he said, "how is your grandfather?"

"Very well, sir," Allen Hendrick replied. "He asks about you."

"Allen," Mr. Douglas said, "I admire the general. I have always counted him one of my closest friends."

Then, almost without pausing, without changing his position or moving his hand from Allen's arm, he said, "And what about you, son? You're out of school now, what do you aim to do?"

"Mr. Douglas," he replied, "I just don't know." He was holding the reins of his mare, slapping the ends of them gently across his palm. "I don't know," he repeated, "but I guess I'll think of something."

6

FOR THE REST of the long summer the question that Mr. Douglas had raised remained unanswered in the mind of Allen Hendrick. Every morning he went with his father down to the office that Marcus Hendrick had rented on Front Street, the single room above a dry-goods store that contained a desk, an old iron safe, a few chairs, and a table strewn with newspapers. And there, when Marcus had studied all the news and had posted his notes for exchange at a Nashville bank, they would speak of what Allen Hendrick should do in September. They would sit, Allen facing the window that looked out over the street, out over the dusty walk toward the livery stable and the blacksmith shop, and Marcus Hendrick with his back to the door that opened into the dim and dingy hallway.

"You could be a physician," Marcus Hendrick would say, letting the ribbon of his glasses slide between his fingers. "You could study medicine in Nashville. But you would have to practice somewhere else."

And he tried to think of it, how it would be, sitting in an office, staring down throats, or riding through the country on a lean horse, lancing boils and drawing teeth at fifty cents a visit. He tried to imagine himself as another Anse Weaver, to see himself cutting the same figure in another part of the country, with all the citizens addressing him as doctor, and he in a white stock and a broadcloth coat. But he was not Anse Weaver and to him the sight of a bleeding knife was repugnant, and he found no joy in the thought of examining brains.

"Or the bar," his father would say. "You might study law."

"But not that here either," Allen would say, smiling with a faintly bitter gentleness.

And he would think then of Houston Knott and of politics. Of how Joe Henry Witherspoon had been born with large, protruding teeth and had run once from a mildly crippled, but still capable, bull, and of how difficult it was for a lawyer to remain neutral when any kind of election was at hand.

"No," he would say. "Not that either. But I ought to leave. I ought to go to college somewhere, and I ought to learn to do something I can do somewhere else."

They debated the matter, argued with their own consciences, round and round in a closed and continuous circle. And day after day Marcus Hendrick read his newspapers, the New York *Tribune* and the Philadelphia *Inquirer,* the New Orleans *Picayune,* and the Charlotte *Observer,* storing up in his mind information on crops and the market, studying the weather reports and the statements of banks, and consulting occasionally the government handbook on money. For he was a broker; or, at any rate, that is what the legend on his door made him out to be:

MARCUS HENDRICK
ATTORNEY AT LAW

*Broker in Private Notes and State Paper
Business of Itinerants and Travelers Respectfully Solicited*

Once in a while, once a month perhaps, a man who was making a journey would seek him out. A drummer on his way home to Kentucky, who would buy at a discount notes on a Louisville bank and pay for them with currency issued in Nashville. Or a man pushing West who wanted gold. Or a planter home from New Orleans, who had forgotten to change his money before he boarded the steamboat. For paper came from a hundred different sources and its value was never certain, and it bought the most when it was spent next door to the place where it was issued.

But he did not make his living trading with strangers and men who meant to travel far from home. Values fluctuated, wherever the money was found, and Marcus Hendrick kept up a running gamble with the banks in Nashville, trying always to buy currency from them when it was low and to sell out when the price rose, and most of his business was conducted through the mail.

Sometimes, when Allen went to the post office, carrying a bundle of notes to be mailed for his father, or an order to buy from one of the firms in the city, the thought would come to him that he, too, might spend his life this way, prying a living out of the world with a sharpened wit. But he did not entertain this idea very often; and his father would not hear of it at all.

"No," Marcus Hendrick would say. "It is too uncertain. It is too hard to live with when you get along in years."

"Yes, sir," Allen replied. "I reckon that's so."

In the end he decided to enroll in Transylvania College. He wrote the letter asking for admittance; he forwarded his matriculation fee. And then he packed up his clothes and went to Cedarcrest for a visit. He rode out to the plantation on a golden day in August when the air was still along the highway and a few clouds hung motionless in the sky, and only the birds moved—the tanagers and the waxwings and the robins feeding in droves near the pasture fence. He rode out on the horse that the general had given him, carrying his portmanteau, and it seemed to him that the country around had never been so bright, nor the hills so gentle, nor the trees so green beneath the summer sun. It is beautiful, he thought. And the answer echoed in his mind. No. It is not beautiful. It is money.

That night his grandfather offered it all to him.

They were alone after supper, not in the parlor, for Valeria was there with Anse Weaver, but in the general's office among the dusty furniture and the old ledger books and the portrait that hung above the mantel. Throughout the meal the general had been in good spirits; he had eaten well, and he had pressed dish after dish upon Anse Weaver.

"You've got to eat," he had said, his eyes sparkling in the last faint light that fell through the open window. "You've got to have food, my boy, to keep up your strength."

"Sir?" Anse Weaver replied, looking up at the general with his fork still in his hand and his mouth slightly opened. "My strength's all right, General Hendrick. I ride all over the country every day."

"No," the old man said. "You're right there. I didn't mean your strength exactly. I meant your heart."

He sniffed once and hid his face behind his napkin so that only his glittering eyes showed above the cloth.

"Your heart," he said. He put down his silver and sat back from the table, his thumbs hooked in his waistcoat pockets. "You know," he went on, "you won't remember this. You are too young. Even Valeria is too young——"

"General!" Valeria said. "Shame on you. Where is your glass? What have you been up to all this evening?"

"You won't remember it," the general said, his face almost serious, his lips half pursed, but trembling at the corners. "But thirty or forty years ago there were two very famous men in this part of the country by the name of Harpe."

"Harpe?" Anse Weaver said. "The highwaymen?"

"Doctor," General Hendrick said, "they were called worse than that. Wiley and Micajah Harpe, and they were famous."

"Did you ever see them, Grandfather?" Allen Hendrick asked.

"No," the general replied. "That is to say, not all of them. They were called Big Harpe and Little Harpe and I only saw Big Harpe's head after it was nailed to a tree."

"Well, sir," Allen replied, catching the spirit of the old man's performance, recognizing in the general's voice a tone he had heard his father use when his mirth ran high. "I reckon that would have been of more interest to Anse than it was to you."

"Hush," Valeria said. "Both of you, hush. What kind of talk is this for the supper table?"

"My dear," the general said, "you are perfectly right. It was hearts I meant to talk about from the introduction."

He nodded to Valeria, half bowed from his sitting position. "Hearts," he said. "Hearts and Harpes." He turned toward Anse Weaver. "They came, these two gentlemen, to an unhappy end at the hands of some outraged citizens. And I have always contended it was the women who brought them to grief."

"What women, General Hendrick?" Anse Weaver asked.

"Those three women," the general replied. "Those three wives they brought over the mountains from North Carolina."

"General," Anse Weaver said, carefully putting down his cup and wiping the tips of his fingers with his napkin. "You said there were two of them, Wiley and Micajah."

"Yes, sir," the old man replied evenly. "Big and Little we called them."

"But you said three women," Anse Weaver persisted. "Who in the name of goodness did the third woman belong to?"

"Both of them," General Hendrick said. "All three of the women belonged to both of them. It was the idea they had concerning matrimony."

[70]

"General," Valeria said, "this is not much better to talk about than heads."

"No," the general replied. "This is the point. It was those women that drove those boys to take to the road. You've no conception," he said, turning his gaze once more on Anse Weaver, "you can't imagine what the cost would be to keep up those females. With buying cloth here and paying the dressmaker there and laying out for new slippers in the bargain. My boy, it affected their hearts and they took to the highway."

"Hearts, General?" Anse Weaver said.

"Yes, sir," the general replied. "There is where it begins. It starts with the heart when a man falls in love and it ends with the heart when he weakens and turns to stealing."

"Sir," Anse said, "you've got a curious notion of physiology."

But the general seemed not to hear this. "Listen," he said, pointing his slender old finger at the doctor, "you've got to be set when the bills start coming due. I want you to eat to keep up the strength of your heart."

He laughed, chuckled rather, but with no effort to hide his glee. Then he left the table and Allen followed him to his study.

"Grandfather," Allen said when the old man had seated himself and sat nodding and smiling at the thought of his own wit, "what did you mean by all those things you told to Anse?"

"Nothing," the old man replied. "It was a kind of shivaree. I was only deviling them because they mean to marry."

"Marry," Allen said, not questioning and not exactly in surprise, but simply repeating the statement of the general. "Valeria and Anse are going to marry."

For a moment he remembered that morning long ago when he had asked Anse if he were in love with Valeria Hendrick. He remembered the wind and the coldness of the day and the bewilderment of the dog when they failed to flush the covey. He recollected this and then recalled the day when he had first come to Cedarcrest and stood by John Hendrick's grave with his Aunt Valeria.

"Ah," the general said, "don't you worry. You will still have your hunting companion. You will still have your crony to help you catch pneumonia in the fall."

"Yes, sir," Allen replied. "It is not that. I settled that myself three years ago."

"Allen," General Hendrick said, leaning forward slightly, his old face showing in profile by the dim glow of the lamp. "She is young, Allen. Not as young as you are, but young nonetheless. John would not want her to be alone, Allen. I do not want her to remain a widow."

"Yes, sir," Allen said again. "I understand that. Dr. Anse can help you on the farm."

"Hah," the old man said, "be the court physician. Be the midwife to the sows in farrowing time."

He moved to the desk and unlocked it and took out a book, a brown ledger, covered in leather that was beginning to crack at the spine. He laid it on the table and opened it beneath the lamplight, opened it near the front and turned the pages slowly, one by one, until he found his place.

"Look," he said. "It is all here. Look at it, Allen."

And written in purple ink in a meticulously legible hand it was all there: all the expenditure for calico and shoes, all the outlay for iron and rope and sugar. And in another column a list of the slaves with their ages and values; and further over still the figures the crops had brought in dollars. *Money*. The memory of what the old man had said returned to him for the second time that day. *It is money*. And here was the evidence, the proof of the general's view.

"Since your father lived here," General Hendrick said, "no one else has ever seen it. But I have kept it anyway, Allen, month by month to the final penny."

He left the table, moved toward the open window, and stood for a moment gazing out at the night, at the fireflies that still moved in the early darkness.

"In the old days, when I was by myself, after Marcus and John had left and before Valeria came, I used sometimes to study it at night. To add up the figures and calculate what I was worth and determine how much I had been able to make in my lifetime."

He turned back to the room, an old man with a gray beard, pink cheeks, and a slender, feeble-looking nose.

"It is a comfort to be rich, Allen. A comfort and an advantage. A toe hold above the common run of men."

"Grandfather," Allen began, but the general cut him off with a wave of his hand.

"Wait," he said. "I know what you heard in church and what you read in Marcus Aurelius and what your Latin poets say about the simple life. And part of it is true, for money is a responsibility, and there are many things it will not buy. But the poor man is plagued with trouble, the same as the man who is rich, and in addition he has the worry of being poor."

Allen said nothing. He remained standing above the open ledger, looking down at the column of figures, the list of names.

> *Amanda Wilcox, 38, cook, $600*
> *Young Jeremiah, 43, coachman, $900*

And down further:

> *Jim White, about 50, hand, $75*

He stopped reading, and his grandfather moved to his side.
"Allen," General Hendrick said. "Do you want it, Allen?"
"Sir? Want what, Grandfather?"
"All of it," the general replied. "The last acre of it will be yours when I am gone."

So his luck, that had begun when he left Memphis and held good through his visit to the general and his drive with the old man around the courthouse square—his fortune held good still. He knew that it was better to be a white man than a Negro, and the general had almost made him white. And he believed that it was better to be a rich man than a poor one, and now the general meant to make him rich. And if he could never simply be Allen Hendrick and be accepted for good or bad as what he was, he preferred being a planter in Middle Tennessee to being a nigger woman's son in Memphis.

"I am going to accept it," he told his father. "It beats practicing medicine in another city or being a lawyer somewhere else."

They were in Gallatin in the cluttered, dusty office, talking to each other once again across the table strewn with papers, and Marcus Hendrick said, "Yes, you must go."

He took his spectacles off his nose and tapped the edge of them lightly on his finger.

"It is your duty to go. Not to your grandfather but to your mother."

He paused for a moment, the glasses still in his hand, his head tilted upward and his eyes half closed.

"It was her dream. It was your mother's great hope. It was what made her force me to bring you here at the outset."

Marcus Hendrick smiled. "Listen," he said, "this is an accident, a happy accident. And I am glad for her and for you and even for Father. But she did not know it would happen."

He got up and moved toward the doorway, then back again toward the ancient, battered desk.

"You will hear all your life about female clairvoyance, about how a woman can know that a thing will happen beforehand and how she tells the future by a feeling in her bones. But it is not so. It is misplaced sentiment. It is foolish romanticism. It is too much Byron and Shelley and not enough Spinoza and Descartes."

"Oh," he went on, smiling, the lines in his face less distinct, the expression gentle, "oh, she plagued me, Allen. From the time almost that you were born she would not leave me alone. 'Take him,' she would say. 'Take him to see General Hendrick.' For she believed—oh, yes, she told me—she believed he could not resist the look in your eye, the innocent sweetness of your countenance. She was like the daughter of Levi, the mother of Moses, and she would put you out for Pharaoh himself to find. 'I know it,' she would say, 'I know General Hendrick will love him.' And when I asked her how she knew, she could only reply, because you were beautiful and her heart told her so."

Pacing still, smiling still, and with a tenderness in his voice that softened his bombast, he went on, "She will tell you that she knew this would happen. She will tell you that she felt it in her heart. And she will cry when the time comes for you to leave.

"But remember this. It is chance, the blind concatenation of events. And to know the future is given to no man—or woman either."

They left then. They locked the door and went down the steps to the street where a boy was leading a pair of mules up to the blacksmith shop, and a buggy passed them and a man on horseback.

"Allen," he said as they moved off down the sidewalk, "I wanted this too. I wished for it as strongly as your mother did. But I could not believe it would happen. Not to you. Not to us, after all these years."

They continued walking, on to the corner of Water Street and past the apothecary shop. "But I would remind you of one thing," Marcus Hendrick said. "I would call to your memory a story Herodotus tells in the *Persian Wars*."

"I have not read Herodotus, Father," Allen Hendrick replied.

"Ah, it does not matter," Marcus said. "I will tell you the story."

"It is of how King Croesus, who was wealthy and powerful and blessed with promising children, called all the sages of Greece to him and among them was Solon, the author of legal reforms. And he asked Solon who was the happiest man in the world, expecting to hear his own name from the lawgiver's lips. Solon replied that Tellus was happiest, because after a life spent in comfort he died triumphant.

"Croesus was enraged, but he asked his question once more, saying that if Tellus was happiest, surely he, Croesus, was next to the happiest man beneath the sun. And once more Solon risked his wrath. He replied that such was not so. That next to Tellus, Cleobis and Bito were happiest, for they, too, had lived well and died at their moment of glory.

"In a word, Solon told Croesus that in every matter we must mark well the end, and that often the gods give a man a gleam of happiness and then plunge him into ruin. And so it was with Croesus, for soon after this his son was killed and his grief made him the most miserable of humans."

Along the walk the sun was warm and dust lay heavy in the street, and in the distance the clock on the courthouse tower began to strike. And Allen Hendrick thought, why was the son of Croesus killed? And how, indeed, could a man be happy after he was dead? But that was not it. He understood enough to know that that was not what his father had been saying. It was simply that when a man had completed his life, those who were left might look back and say that man was happy. Yet what of the man himself when he was gone?

"My boy," Marcus Hendrick said, "the word Solon used was fortunate. A man was fortunate if he was virtuous and wealthy, sound of limb and comely to look at and blessed with good children, but concerning happiness . . . no man could judge while he still lived."

He was silent for a long time. Then he said, "You must go to your grandfather. And I wish you all the good that is in the world."

He moved to Cedarcrest in September. He went out to live with his grandfather when the days were still warm but the nights chilly, and in the evenings they sat in the parlor, or, when Anse Weaver had come to see Valeria, in the general's office, where already there was usually a fire. For the old man's blood was running thin and habitually now he wore a shawl and the damp night air brought on rheumatism in his back. He would sit huddled down in a Queen Anne chair, his feet propped on the fender, his snuff box open at his hand. And he would lecture to Allen like a teacher in a schoolroom, but his voice was tired and he seldom turned his head.

"We have never had orchards here," he would say. "For tobacco and beef are generally money and fruit is cheap and perishable and the market is flooded in season. But times change and the day may come when you might plant apples or peaches to advantage. So remember this: If you plant, plant on the northern slope and you stand less chance to lose your crop to the weather."

Or, pulling the shawl tighter around his shoulders, he would say, "Tend to the tobacco. Tend to it first and see it through to the end. For if you cannot get to the corn it will stay there. Get a good scarecrow and the corn will hang for a year on the stalk, and it seldom gets too old for cows and horses."

So it went, evening after evening, and during the day he rode all over the land, following the Negroes and the overseer, Mr. Finch, from pasture to tobacco barn, to the chicken house and to the blacksmith shop and the stable. He came to know the farm; and he came to know the people, the names that were listed in the general's book with the values set down in ink beside them. Amanda Wilcox, who was fat and stern and who wore pewter earrings that had been given her by old Mrs. Hendrick. And Jeremiah, who was tall and black and gentle with the horses. And Jim White, who was often sick and who worked in the fields and was worth only seventy-five dollars. He learned these by name and many more, and when he rode into the quarters the old women smiled at him from their rocking chairs and the men bowed and called him "Young Master," and the little boys begged him for pennies as he passed.

"They love you," General Hendrick said one night when they sat in the office by the fire. "And the land has got to have niggers. If they hate you they are bound to run away."

"Not all of them love me, Grandfather," Allen said. "Not Uncle Aaron."

"He is as old as I am," the general replied. "When you are old it is hard enough to love the Lord."

Sometimes, in the evening, when he had left General Hendrick, he would read in his room at the top of the house—history from his grandfather's library or the novels that had been sent from Natchez years ago. But most of the time he went to bed and lay between the cold sheets, alone in the quiet and peaceful darkness. On rare occasions he was still awake to hear the barking of the dogs and the sound of Anse Weaver's horse as he rode out the driveway. Then he would smile and sniff the night and be happy that again the time for hunting was upon them.

He went to the fields again that year, not as the city boy on a visit to the farm, but as the scion of the ancient house, the acknowledged heir to all the general's treasure. He went out again, whenever he could, with Anse Weaver, and it was a good season, good for quail and better for dove, and in the afternoons they returned with their game bags full and their feet wet and the barrels of their pieces fouled and dirty. They shot a good deal and ran out of powder by the first of November and replenished that and then ran out of land. Or rather, they grew tired of the same fields, the same hills to climb, the same trees in silhouette against the skyline. So they moved off the general's place, south to a farm that belonged to a man named Wilson, and then, a little later, across the road and north to hunt the fields on Captain Rutledge's plantation.

It was called Roseneath, named out of Scott by the captain, and it was a beautiful establishment, neat and well kept, in spite of the dirty house and the old man's infirmity. The fences were in good repair and the quarters tight, and rye was already coming up in the winter pasture. There was cover for the birds; there were springs to drink from. And the land was mostly flat and the walking easy.

When they arrived in the mornings they would leave their horses in Captain Rutledge's stable, and then move across his lawn and along his drive to a path that led near the barn toward the open country. And it was there on the driveway, when they were returning early one afternoon, that Allen Hendrick first saw Katherine

Rutledge. Or rather, he got a glimpse of her features, a quick look at her handsome face framed in the window of the passing carriage. In the moment that he touched his cap and returned the greeting of the Negro driver, he thought only, she is the captain's daughter. She is the sister of the boy whose picture hangs upon the captain's wall. He noticed only the family resemblance: the nose that turned up at the end, the large eyes, the chin that was firm and slightly rounded.

"It is Kate," Anse Weaver said, and they both stood for a moment with their heads turned watching the slowly disappearing carriage. "I reckon she is home from Nashville to visit the captain."

And when Allen Hendrick did not reply, he said, "It is his daughter, Kate."

"Yes," Allen said at last. "I know it."

"Ah," Anse Weaver said. "You have met her, Allen?"

"No," he said. "I knew her from the favor."

They were at the stable now, and the Rutledge groom was saddling their horses.

"The favor's not that strong," Anse said. "You recognized the carriage and you guessed it."

Allen went over the face again in his mind, the mouth wide, the cheekbones a little high, the skin white in the shadow of her bonnet.

"Maybe so," he replied. "But I knew it was Katherine Rutledge."

Later as they were riding home in the cold November wind, south and then west toward the gray, November twilight, Anse Weaver reached out and touched Allen on the arm.

"She is pretty, young Hendrick," he said. "And they tell me she cuts a figure down in the city."

Allen made no reply.

"She is pretty," Anse Weaver repeated. "But she will likely come back home to find a husband."

"Anse," Allen said, "listen. I am never going to marry. Not even if I live a hundred years."

"You're too young to know," Anse replied, smiling. "Some woman will get you sooner or later. Even an old fool like me can fall in love."

And so can I, Allen Hendrick thought. For once he had gone with flowers in his hand, up through the shade of the maple trees, up the walk to the shaded porch, only to find an empty chair and the family waiting in silence for him to speak. It was not for him, not ever again, not even now with the general's wealth to back him.

And as if he had been reading Allen's thoughts, Anse Weaver leaned over in the saddle and said, "My boy, when the time comes you cannot help it."

⋄ 7 ⋄

SO ON THAT BLEAK November afternoon Anse Weaver said, "My boy, when the time comes you cannot help it," and they rode on over the muddy pike, on into the pale and hasty twilight. But the time of which he spoke did not come for a while, and in the interval Allen was able almost to forget the face he had seen that day in the carriage window. Christmas came, and Kate was at home with her father, and the general and Valeria went to Roseneath to call on the Rutledges. But Allen did not go with them. He went instead back to Gallatin, back to his parents and the rented house with its gloomy hall and its long stairs and its parlor with the massive cherry woodwork. He returned to the old familiar landmarks: the bed he had slept in, the chairs where he had sat; the French novels that his mother kept on her sewing table, the rosewood piano, the slender, gilded chairs. And when he had walked through all the rooms, out to the stable, and through the kitchen, and back once more to the house and the parlor fire, it seemed to him that nothing had altered, nothing changed.

And not only the house but his father's office was the same, the table still cluttered, the desk still covered with dust, his father's voice still mellow and scented with brandy. He was full of politics, full of Bleeding Kansas and the Dred Scott decision, full of hate for President Buchanan and shaken by the financial panic they were in. But he was neither bitter nor hopeful. He was simply resigned and a little ironic, a little annoyed by all the evil in the world.

"And what does the general think of Old Buck now?" he said,

smiling at Allen across the folded papers. "What does he think of the Democrats and the price of crops?"

"The same as he always did, I guess," Allen said. "He's a Whig, Father. He voted for Mr. Fillmore."

"I know it," Marcus replied, "but I thought he'd be fussing."

He got up and moved to the corner of the room, to stand for a moment with his hand resting on the safe.

"I know," he said. "I know what the general is saying. 'The land. Stick to the land. They can turn the White House into a privy and the land will stay.' He told me that once, Allen. On the day I left for Memphis he lectured to me on the land. And he was right; the earth is surer than paper."

"Father," Allen said.

"No, no," Marcus Hendrick interrupted. "I am solvent. I have weathered the panic. I will even make money out of it. But it is too fast now and I am old."

He moved back to his chair and sat down once more.

"I am old, and it is hard to keep moving. Hard to get my paper to Nashville, hard to beat the news when you know that a bank is due to fail."

"Do you still use Ben Hill, Father?" Allen Hendrick asked.

Marcus Hendrick nodded.

Then he said, "Yes, I still use Ben. But he is heading for trouble, Allen. Ben doesn't trust me any more."

And that was the reason for all that followed, the circumstance that lay behind Allen's visit to Nashville, the first link in a chain of events that was to make Ben Hill hate Allen for the rest of his life. . . .

Allen Hendrick never knew where Ben Hill had been born, or how he had made his first dollar, or even whether he had come into the world free or had been manumitted at the death of a kindly master. For when Allen Hendrick saw him for the first time, Ben Hill was a middle-aged man, fifty or just under that, with a pot belly and a heavy gold watch chain and cunning eyes that stared from a handsome face. Round, bright eyes set closer together than was common in the Negroes that Allen had seen, and short, sparse whiskers barely flecked with gray, and skin as smooth on his cheeks and forehead as the skin of a baby.

Allen Hendrick saw him for the first time on a day three years before, looked up from a book he was reading to see Ben Hill standing inside Marcus Hendrick's office, holding his beaver hat in his hand, smiling to show his slightly yellow teeth. And beyond the clothes that he wore on his back and the diamond ring that glittered on his finger, there was nothing unusual about him: no humility and no pride, no arrogance and no timidity either. He was simply a man who happened to be black.

And that was it, of course, the thing that made him unusual beyond the most fantastic dream, beyond the most visionary expectation. There was something in the way he stood, the tilt of his head, the posture of his body which seemed to indicate that it had never occurred to him to consider the fact that he was colored and that other men were white. Or, if he had considered it, thought of it at all, the possibility that he might be deemed inferior had never once crossed the circuits of his mind. He looked around the room, his gaze sure but not impudent, as if he half expected to see another Negro on the other side of the table, or as if he meant to invite Allen out for a drink or down to the Gallatin Inn to get his supper. It was as if he had never heard the minstrel song about Jim Crow, or never passed a field at setting time, or never seen a slave exposed on the block for auction. But this was not true, for Ben Hill made his living buying and selling other Negroes.

On the day that Allen first saw him, he was planning a trip to Mississippi, and he came to Marcus Hendrick simply as a traveler, to buy notes issued by a Vicksburg bank. But because of his business, Ben Hill traveled a good deal, frequently to Nashville and sometimes to Memphis; south to Montgomery and even to Natchez and on rare occasions as far as New Orleans. So they formed a partnership; and Ben Hill furnished his mobility and Marcus Hendrick, his wisdom and his wit. Each time, before Ben left on a trip, he would come to the office and Marcus Hendrick would give him money: paper issued by a bank at his destination, gold that was good wherever he happened to be. When he arrived at the end of his journey, he would wire Marcus Hendrick. And Marcus Hendrick would telegraph back for him to buy or to sell. So they both prospered, Marcus Hendrick because he had a new way to exploit distant markets. and Ben Hill because he was always in on the secret, free to take advantage of Marcus Hendrick's advice. But Ben continued his old trade too; he hauled his people chained in wagons over the muddy roads into Alabama or down the river fastened on the lower decks of boats.

"Ben," Allen asked him once, "why do you do that? They might even be your cousins you put on the block."

They had met on the street in the shade of a tree near the courthouse. It was a year later and spring and the air was warm and a few pigeons pecked back and forth in the manure near the walk.

"No," Ben said, "I'm a lone-born child. I've got no mama or daddy. No uncle or aunt."

"But they might be," Allen Hendrick insisted. "Some half-brother or sister you never heard about. And you truss them up and sell them for what you can get."

"You hit it right," Ben said, frowning a little and looking away across the courthouse lawn. "What you can get and the market the way it is, you can't get much.

"Allen," he said, for that is the way he always spoke to Allen Hendrick, called him by his first name as any other man would do. "It ain't because they are darkies. It ain't that. It is because they are slaves. Because they was born slaves and sold to me as slaves and will have to die slaves unless somebody is willing to stand a loss and free them."

He paused and picked at his teeth with his fingernail. Then he smiled slyly. "To me," he said, "it ain't a matter of principle. I would sell a white man too or buy him either. But I never yet come across one up for auction."

"You ought not to sell anybody," Allen said. For nobody else Allen knew would ever sell a slave. Not his grandfather, not Anse Weaver, not Captain Rutledge who owned more than he could use. He went on, "With Father to help you, you could make your living on paper."

"No," Ben replied. "The major is cunning. But even with him, I'm not smart enough for that."

So he went on, selling flesh and changing money while the blue diamond sparkled on his finger and the gold chain glittered on his vest.

Not only was Allen distressed by the trade that Ben Hill followed, but he was disappointed too, a little hurt, that his father would continue a partnership with a man who refused to abandon his speculations in slaves. For although Marcus Hendrick claimed to believe that all the world was evil and the cause of freedom hopeless, Allen knew that he did not condone slavery—did not hold with it now any more than he had twenty years ago when he had written essays praising abolition and stumped the country setting forth his aims.

On a summer night Allen raised the question with his father. It was in June, three months before he went to live at Cedarcrest, a week after his rebuff by Mr. Douglas. His mother had gone up to bed; they were alone on the porch. And the moon was full and a mockingbird was singing.

"Father," Allen said, "it is not right. It is not right to help him, if he will not give up his trade in slaves."

"Ah," Marcus Hendrick said. "But he helps me too."

In the silence that followed, Allen turned to look at his father, shifted his weight in the chair and moved his whole body, not quite certain that he had heard correctly, not quite believing what his ears had heard. But before he found his tongue, Marcus Hendrick spoke.

"Wait," he said. "I offer you that only as a possibility. For no man can ever be sure of his motives, and he is a fool who dares to think he can. But I do not believe that I deal with him to feather my own nest, Allen. Or, at least, I think there are other reasons stronger than that."

He paused; then he said, "Let me tell you something. I know that slavery is a stain on the earth and that right is right and wrong is wrong and that man is free to choose between good and evil. That is acknowledged generally to be true. And if it were given to man to see the world clearly and to separate the good from the bad like a grocer separates apples in a barrel, then the land would be full of heroes and life would be sweet as honey and villainy a thing to read about in books. But it is not that way. It is not so simple. For the moral choice is never pure, and nothing is completely good or bad, and in the end there is always the circumstance to be considered."

He stopped, puffed his cigar until it glowed in the darkness, then stared for a while at the shadows on the road.

"No," he went on, "never simple. For the better sometimes appears to be the worst and iniquity wears the mask of virtue and walks in the sun.

"But grant your own wisdom," he said, moving his hand, waving the burning cigar in a narrow arc. "Grant that you can know the truth and separate the wheat from the chaff, where are you then? You have only brought yourself to another question.

"Yes, it is wrong to own slaves, and worse to trade them. But what of Ben? Where did he come from? And what has he had to live with all his life? Allen, Ben is not free. He has got his manumission papers and they are recorded in the capitol—maybe not in Tennessee, but somewhere, signed by a governor and approved by a legislature and stamped with the great seal of the state. But he is not free, he will not live long enough to be free, and the only thing to save him from the white man is his money. He has got to have it. And perhaps if we work together long enough and our luck holds good he will get enough to give up trading people."

He took a last pull on the cigar and threw it away. "But if he never stops his dealings, remember this. The slaves will keep on being sold, whoever sells them. And it is better to have one Negro rich and secure in a white man's world than to make a saint out of Ben Hill and perhaps to impoverish him.

"Perhaps," Marcus Hendrick said, "they will have to do it this way. Rise by spending their own blood, by mutilating their own flesh in the process."

This was what he said. And Allen Hendrick, sitting in the shadow of the wide and silent porch, knew that part of it was right and part of it wrong: part of it the last vestige of his old abolitionist spirit, part of it the dregs of all the frustration a bitter age had made him bear. But what, indeed, of Ben Hill? And what of Marcus Hendrick? And who was to tell Allen now how a man should live?

"Allen," Marcus Hendrick said, "a gentleman named Augustine, one of the saints of your mother's church"—for she was a Roman Catholic, or had been once, long ago, before she ever moved to Tennessee—"Augustine wrote some words to the effect that we do not cast off our sins; we outgrow them. He was wrong there. Man does not improve. He grows no better as he nears the end. But Augustine had the seed of an idea. For life, itself, is given to irony, and time destroys the evil as well as the good."

There was a pause.

"He is greedy, Allen," Marcus Hendrick said. "Ben is avaricious and he wants to move too fast."

Then he said good night and went into the house.

So Allen Hendrick had his explanations, for what they were

worth, one from Ben Hill and one from Marcus Hendrick; and the partnership continued into the panic of 1857 and on into the uneasy period of recovery and speculation. Some railroad stocks had weathered the storm; some banks had come out stronger than before; and in 1859 Ben Hill took up residence in Nashville and stayed by the telegraph wire and reaped the harvest. It was here that Ben's duplicity began.

Or rather, it was not duplicity but foolishness, a kind of folly born of innocence—ignorance of the ways of the world and of the man with whom, for four years now, he had been working.

"It is," Marcus Hendrick said to Allen, "that he has been persecuted every day for fifty years. He has been cheated and duped by the white man ever since he saw the light of morn. He had no reason to expect the next one to be honest.

"No," Marcus Hendrick went on after a moment. "Ben was acting from experience. By rights he should have taken my gold too, and sold his traps and run for Texas."

"Does he believe you cheated him, Father?" Allen asked. "Does he still think that?"

"Yes," Marcus Hendrick replied. "With all his heart."

What had happened was this—as far as Allen was able to tell, for his father was reluctant to speak of it and said very little. What had happened was that somehow Ben Hill had made himself believe that Marcus Hendrick was holding out on him. He had convinced himself that the profits he made were the smaller profits and the tips he got were the minor tips, and that Marcus Hendrick by some other means—with some other messenger or method of communication—was making money on deals that he was not sharing.

But how? Allen thought. How could he believe this? Or believing it, how could he possibly conceive of another *modus operandi* for Marcus Hendrick? For there was no way to achieve quick profits beyond that of keeping a cohort in a financial center, and where secrecy was important, why trust two men instead of one? And that was the answer: Ben Hill was a Negro. And he had never been given any reason to think that any white man would ever trust him. And now, at last, Allen understood that his father had foreseen this moment all along.

Allen understood. He saw it all in his mind's eye, how at night when the business of the day was over Ben Hill would have gone home to total up the profit and the loss. Home to a shack built on poles down near the river, or to an outhouse some white man no longer needed for wood, a room no bigger than a cell for a monk, with cracks in the walls and dirt on the floor and a cornshuck mattress on a shaky bed. And there, in the light of a smoking lamp, he would count the fruits of another white man's wisdom. Or rather, he would simply sit and gaze at the white man's magic. For that is what he would consider it, this manipulation of paper, this eternal trading that somehow made a fool of time and brought one to riches in the end.

In his imagination, Allen could see him, how he must have leaned forward toward the yellow light to examine a note more closely in one more effort to divine the secret, to learn the hidden trick of this abstruse trade. And for the old slave dealer, nothing there: no teeth to examine, no muscles to feel, no fingers to pull or limbs to test for strength. Only the thin and whirling lines; the mystic numbers and the faces of men, the engraved pictures of trains and wagons and horses. And here and there a signed name, the signature of a person he would never meet. So at last he must have lost his powers of distinction; he must have believed that once one had the knack there was no limit to the amount of money that could be made, no logical restriction to be placed on an act of magic. It was a trick, like hiding the ace of diamonds in your sleeve, and it could be performed as often and as quickly as the cards could be dealt.

And then Old Ben must have brooded some more, stared some more at the pink and green and purple paper certificates. And ultimately, it may have occurred to him that it was not a trick after all, but a touch, a power in the flesh like that of Midas—but he would not have found the simile, he would not have known the name—and at last he began his attempt to outfigure Marcus Hendrick.

Ben left Nashville and came to Gallatin on the day after Christmas when the general and Valeria were visiting the Rutledges at Roseneath and Allen was staying with his father and mother in the rented house. He arrived on the cars and came directly to Marcus Hendrick's office, still the portly, handsome man, still in broadcloth and a golden watch chain, but not rich any more, no longer a gentleman of means. He had brought Marcus Hendrick's money back with him in a carpetbag, and without speaking a word spread the notes out on the table, dumped them on top of the old newspapers, and then took a talley sheet, an account of all his transactions from his pocket.

"It's all there," he said. "I will wait here while you count it." His voice was expressionless, completely neutral, denying somehow with its inflection all possible difference between black and white, all prejudice and all distinction.

"No," Marcus Hendrick replied. "There is no need of that. Sit down, Ben."

He hesitated for a moment and then slowly let himself down into a chair and sat leaning over the table, his shoulders bowed, his hands in his lap, his tired eyes slightly averted. He seemed to droop over the pile of money like an old and weather-beaten pigeon, his strength gone and all his handsomeness ruffled. And Allen Hendrick thought: he is a nigger, after all. After all his careful progress through the world; after all his impeccable years of restraint and decorum. For the first time that Allen remembered, Ben looked like a nigger.

"What is it, Ben?" Marcus Hendrick said.

"Nothing," Ben Hill replied. "It is nothing, Major Hendrick."

Marcus Hendrick looked at him for almost a minute, watched him through the shaft of golden sunlight that fell through the misted windowpane.

"What is it, Ben?" he asked.

"It is what I said," Ben replied. "It is nothing. It is all gone now. Down to the last hand I had on the market, the last greenback dollar I had in my sock."

There was another long pause, with dust motes floating in the sunlight, and no sound, not even voices from the street.

"How, Ben?" Marcus Hendrick said at last.

"No," Ben replied. "Not how. Why, Major Hendrick? All this time I done your work and paid you honest. But you never gave me the secret or the truth."

"I did, Ben," Marcus Hendrick replied. "There is no secret. It is a matter of reading the papers and having a little experience and a lot of luck. There is no secret, Ben," he repeated. "And I did tell you everything I knew."

"Honest," Ben said, his head lowered, his eyes round and white and looking up. "And all your money back and all your winnings.

Major, if you can make a hundred dollars, you can make a thousand. And if you can make a thousand, there is no heading, there ain't no place where a man is got to stop. It is that way with people, and, the market strong or off, you can hold your own."

"Ben," Marcus Hendrick said, "people are people. They are only one thing, one commodity to deal with, and you can look at them and tell if the wind is good and the sinews strong and the heart likely to continue with its beating. But paper: paper is not like people. It is not like blackberries or trees in the woods, and you can never be sure. You can never bet all you own on a single venture."

He was holding his pince-nez in his hand, tapping them against his slender finger.

"What did you do, Ben?"

And still looking up, the eyes still white and round, Ben replied, "I put my money in Georgia Railroad Bonds."

"All of it?" Marcus Hendrick asked.

"All of it," Ben replied. "And you said it was good."

So at last it was out, and Allen Hendrick, listening from his corner of the room, knew now what had happened to Ben Hill. He had drawn on his old experience with slaves; he had invested all his money in one issue, in the same way he would have bought a new stock of people from a single dealer in Memphis or Paducah. He had lost because Marcus Hendrick had been wrong, but Allen knew that his father had told Ben to go lightly. He had lost, and the pity of it was that with a little luck he might have made a fortune.

"Ben," Marcus Hendrick said, "you didn't do what I told you."

"You never told me enough," Ben replied. "You never told me the secret, and I never seen it clear."

He started to leave then. He cast one, last, pain-filled glance at the pile of money that still lay spread on the table, and he got up and put on his beaver hat and moved slowly toward the doorway. He walked with deliberate, almost faltering steps, his head tilted forward, his eyes on the ground, and at his sides his arms swung loosely. Allen Hendrick knew that Ben Hill was back where he had started twenty or thirty years ago: a nigger with manumission papers, but not free and no longer rich; defenseless now against the poorest white. He thought this, and he was sorry for Ben; he was touched by the sight of Ben's grief and his great weariness.

Without thinking, without considering what Ben might feel or say or do, Allen snatched a few banknotes from the pile of currency on the table and rose quickly and said, "Wait, Ben."

The Negro man stopped and turned around slowly; he raised his eyes slowly and looked at Allen Hendrick.

"Take this," Allen said. "Until you can get on your feet again. To tide you over."

And once more without haste, as if slowness had become with Ben a disease or a habit, he extended his hand and took the money and for a moment held it limply in his hand. Then he seemed to think of something: an idea seemed to strike him. His eyes opened a bit wider, his jaw pushed out, and in the light from the doorway the line of his face grew hard. He licked his thumb and carefully counted the bills.

"Seventy dollars," Ben said. His voice was cold, flat: it had no timbre, it caused no reverberation.

"Seventy dollars," Ben Hill repeated, "and that given me by a boy, handed out like you would give candy to a child, like you would give a penny to a field nigger."

"No," Allen said. "Ben. It was not like that. I didn't mean it that way."

"How did you mean it then?" Ben Hill asked evenly.

Allen hesitated. "Like I said. To help you out. To tide you over."

"Yes, by God," Ben Hill replied, "like I said too. Like giving whisky or a string of beads to a damned Indian."

There was a moment of silence while Allen stood and looked into Ben's eyes and felt nothing. He had reached an equilibrium, a stasis of passion, with the pity he had felt for Ben obliterated now, and the anger not yet quite started.

Then there was a sound of ripping paper and a quick motion of Ben's hand, and Allen saw the scraps of colored banknotes come up to hit his face and drift and flutter in the air around his head and fall in little arcs to the floor of the office.

"Keep 'em," Ben Hill said. "The day may come you need 'em more than I do. Worse come to worse and you can use 'em to wipe your ass."

Allen started forward. He doubled up his fist and half drew back his arm before he felt his father's hand on his shoulder and heard Marcus Hendrick's voice sharp in his ear.

"Wait!" Marcus Hendrick shouted. "Wait, Allen!"

So he did not strike Ben Hill. He said, "You black bastard! You get out of here, you slave-trading, nigger son-of-a-bitch!"

Ben Hill said, "Who are you to be talking about a nigger? Who was your mammy that made you so Goddamned white?"

Once more Marcus Hendrick said, "Wait!" shouted at Allen and held tightly to his shoulder, and Ben Hill turned and went out through the door and the room was quiet.

The room was completely silent, and Marcus Hendrick poured himself a drink of brandy and his hand shook when he held the bottle and when he lifted the glass. Allen was aware that he himself was trembling and he thought for a moment that he was going to cry. But he moved to the window and looked out at the street, stared out at the sunlight and the pigeons around the courthouse, and got control of himself at last.

"Father," he said, "I didn't mean to make Ben mad."

"I know you didn't," Marcus Hendrick said. "But try to understand Ben. He is proud and he has been hurt, Allen. We would act the same way, you and I, if we had suffered Ben's misfortune."

"I reckon so," Allen said, "but damn his soul——"

He broke off and did not try to speak again for a moment.

Then he said, "I mean, he thinks we cheated him somehow. He thinks what happened to him is all our fault."

"Yes," Marcus Hendrick replied. "I'm afraid he does."

❖ 8 ❖

So THE TORN BANKNOTES, the green and purple and yellow scraps of paper, had fluttered about Allen's face and had fallen to the office floor, and the partnership between Ben and Marcus had ended. And if this had happened ten years or even five years earlier, in the old, easy days before the financial panic, Marcus Hendrick might have gone back to doing business through the mails. But now times were hard and gold was scarce, and Marcus Hendrick was holding too much paper. He explained to Allen how, through a seemingly endless series of transactions, he had been inflating the value of his money by trading in banknotes; it was now time to start changing the currency back into silver and gold. "I will have to ask you to go down there and act as my agent," he said to Allen. "Time is of the essence, and, as you know, I cannot go myself and leave your mother. There is no one left for me to ask but you."

Allen Hendrick did know this, and a week later he traveled to the city. He made his trip to Nashville on the coldest day of the year when the sun hung for an hour small and yellow and far away among the thin, white clouds and then went down in a cold and rosy twilight. He rode on the train, and throughout the frozen afternoon he was jolted along over the iron rails, his breath misting on the car window and his feet chilled by the draft that swept along the floor. Mile after mile he went past brown country and distant, lonely houses and an occasional horse or man shivering in the cold; and at last he reached the city and found a hotel and took a room.

He settled himself in the St. Cloud in a large chamber that was never quite completely warmed by the wood fireplace, and in between his sorties out to do business for his father, he spent his time huddled close to the hearth in his overcoat reading or pacing back and forth between the poster bed and the mahogany chest and the tarnished mirror, absently counting his steps on the figured carpet. "It is a good room," he wrote his grandfather, "but bigger than Texas, and I have no conveyance to fetch me from the chiffarobe to the chair."

He had carried with him to Nashville a copy of Gibbon, *The Decline and Fall of the Roman Empire,* and during the first few nights, when the banks were closed and his day's work of changing money was over, he attempted to read the small print on the old and foxing paper. But after the exertions of the afternoon he found his mind unreceptive, and in the dull hotel chamber his brain seemed to cool like his backsides as he leaned across his book toward the pale, inadequate fire.

So at last he gave up his reading and tried for a night or two to entertain himself at the public amusements offered by the city. He went once to see a play, full of aphorisms and romantic love and a father's advice to his daughter on the subject of matrimony. He went to a minstrel show at the Odd Fellow's Hall, and finally in desperation he tried an evening at the St. Cloud bar, staring at himself in the looking glass while the talk of politics and horses went on around him. In the end he followed his father's lead and attempted to interest himself in the available papers.

He began to buy issues of the *Daily Gazette*, the *Republican Banner* and sometimes the Nashville *Patriot*, and while the old copy of Gibbon rested on the chimney piece, he read how Mr. Toombs of Georgia had grown choleric on the Senate floor and how all hell kept breaking loose in Kansas. Sometimes, when the hour was late and the hotel quiet and there was no longer the sound of carriages from the street, he fancied he heard the general's voice cursing secession and the Democrats, swearing allegiance to the faded colors of the Whigs. Saying, "Damn the hotheads and the niggers too. Hang John Brown and Langdon Cheeves and leave the land in peace." His voice, through a trick of the cold night, saying this, as he had in fact said it before, and Langdon Cheeves long dead now, and the statement itself a simple affirmation of agrarian idealism, a declaration of faith in the grand and profitable mystery of the fertile earth.

Then, thinking of home, Allen would smile.

He was lonely in Nashville. Lonely in the morning when he had breakfast at the soiled hotel table, eating in silence amidst the noisy talk of the drummers and horse traders and farmers' sons, heavy-eyed from a night of pleasure in the jungle. Lonely then, and lonely too in the telegraph office where he waited for the message from his father, his feet extended toward the belly of the stove, his senses lulled by the clacking of the key. For Allen there was no pleasure in the city streets, the fine stone house fronts, the neat, fenced yards. No joy in the capitol building or the courthouse on the square. He took no interest in the parades of the militia or in the gilded steamboats at the landing; and the ladies of fashion in their equestrian costumes, the gentlemen in their polished boots and flowered waistcoats passed and made no impression on his mind.

He found himself, after a week in Nashville, looking forward to the simple transaction of business with the clerks in the banking houses, anticipating with a kind of doleful eagerness the opportunity to count money and to speak of the weather with the man behind the grille. He sent letters home to his mother and father and to his grandfather. In one of his letters to Lucy Hendrick he wrote:

You will remember it was summer when we came through here, you and Father and Vernon and I on our way from Memphis. It was afternoon and hot, and I recollect that there were few people on the streets and these mostly men and niggers. But now, since it is winter, much society may be seen abroad, and the carriages are fine, the horses well caparisoned, the ladies decked out in such finery that it startles the eye. It is curious to me to note the customs of the city. In Gallatin, when a train of cars arrives at the station, a great crowd of people gather to see who will disembark. But here, the cars may come and go, even the packet boats may arrive and depart, and only those who happen to be nearby raise their heads to look. It is true that the landing attracts a group of idlers: but these are generally regarded as vagrants and do not count for much. It is a sight to see the street lamps lighted at night, and the fine houses on Vine Street lighted too, and at a place called the Vauxhall Gardens there is a miniature train which is run nightly over its own course and which carries passengers in its small cars for their jollification. Amusement runs rampant here, though many poor are to be seen too, and many of Irish and German blood live here as they did in Memphis.

She answered his letters in her curious copybook English, interlaced here and there with a word or two of French. She compared the city, as he had described it to her, to the other cities where she herself had lived—to New Orleans with its tall and secret houses, to Memphis with its gravel streets that turned to mud. She told him of the health of his father and Vernon; she sometimes mentioned a book that she had read. But most of all, she urged him to seek pleasure in the city; in her letters his happiness was an ever-recurring theme:

We are well here, and well contented. I sit and sew and your father attends his office; we make our lives and the days move quietly by. Sometimes, as you know, from my sitting room I watch the traffic, and the other afternoon I saw Houston Knott march by on his horse. Ah, mon cher, *your friend goes handsomely, but he does not go so handsomely as you. You must fret not at all about us here, but make your own diversion and allow your father not to set you too great a task. We miss you, but stay till your heart is filled with amusement. Go yourself to ride on that cunning train of cars.*

He kept an account book in which he figured his transactions for his father, and he marked each day on a calendar that hung in his room. But there was no way of knowing how long he would be in Nashville. He could not predict the market, and he knew little of Marcus Hendrick's plans. So he sat in his chamber, an exile under an indeterminate sentence, and in his loneliness read the papers and stared at the fire.

One evening, when he was looking at the *Daily Gazette,* he came across an account of a ball given by the legal society of Nashville, and in the list of guests he saw Katherine Rutledge's name. At first he was reminded simply of Sumner County, of Cedarcrest that he missed so much, and of the palsied old captain whom he had visited with the general. But after a moment he remembered too the day he had seen Kate's face in the carriage window: how he had stood with Anse Weaver in the late November twilight and watched the Rutledge rockaway come up the drive, and how she had looked at him from behind the glass, her face framed like a picture, her nose short, her lips full, her head tilted back to show the whiteness of her throat.

He remembered this, and yet for all the power of his recollection that brought to his mind the bright detail of the moment, he could not say whether she was beautiful or ugly, haughty or merely bored by the autumn day. To Allen, there in his hotel room, she was another traveler away from home, a part of the land that he longed to see again. It was perhaps because of this that he made her a visit.

He thought of her that night as someone to talk to, someone more interesting than the bank clerk, more coherent than the men in the St. Cloud bar; and it occurred to him that he might simply go to call at the Female Academy, arrive there at teatime or a little after, and send his card in by the porter at the gate. But on consideration, the idea of approaching the school seemed almost appalling and he figured his accounts and snuffed his light and went to bed.

He went to bed on the night that he read her name, halfway convinced that he would never go to see her, and through the day that followed he occupied himself with the dull routine of his father's business. But the night came again, as empty as those which had gone before, and the thought of Kate returned afresh to plague him. I might go, he thought, and stay for an instant and ask after her father. He saw in his mind's eye his own figure moving through the dim halls of the Female Academy—he saw them that way in his imagination, dim and wide and a little musty, dim and quiet like the aisles in an empty church—he saw himself standing in a parlor, standing before her and hearing some news of home. I might go, he thought, and crossed to the window of his hotel room and looked down at the poorly lighted street: at a chaise that passed and behind that an open wagon, and beneath a lamp post a man with his coat buttoned close up under his chin. He might go. And he made his decision and turned away from the window.

For what, in all the world, did he have to lose?

So he went to see Katherine Rutledge because he was young and away from home and infinitely lonely when the day was through and he sat in his room with his newspapers and his Gibbon. He wrote her a letter, asking permission to call, and she answered it a little formally, but politely nonetheless, setting a time that he might wait on her at the academy. He made some preparations for the visit: he bought a new waistcoat and a pair of boots and a mahogany stick with a polished silver head. He went to the barber shop and bathed and had his hair trimmed. Then he went to the livery stable and hired a rig and drove the few blocks down the hill to the Female Academy.

He hitched his horse and passed through the iron gates, and on down a covered portico to the door, where he was admitted by one of the teachers. She was a large woman who introduced herself as Miss Clayton, and on first glance she seemed far from beautiful, for she wore glasses and her nose was big and there were a few freckles showing beneath her powder. But she was well shaped in spite of her height and the fullness of her limbs, and she held herself erect and moved with considerable grace.

"Mr. Hendrick," she said. "Katherine is expecting you, Mr. Hendrick."

Her voice was soft, her diction almost precise, and her words came faster than was usual for Tennessee. It seemed to Allen that, in her large and graceful ugliness, Miss Clayton was uncommonly well suited to the academy itself, to the wide, carpeted hall through which they were moving, to the faded, ugly wallpaper and the standing candelabra and dim oil portraits in gilded frames. She led him to an immense double parlor with a fireplace at each end and red velvet draperies drawn across the windows and red and blue velvet upholstering on the couches and chairs. There was in the room no paneling, no brocade, but there were pictures, pastels and water colors that were bright enough and which must have been done, Allen thought, by the students at the school. It seemed to him a pleasant room, safe and decorous and little given to frivolity, and it did much to still the beating of his heart.

Miss Clayton left him and came back with Katherine, who was a little taller than Allen had expected, and a little paler than the face in the carriage window, but familiar to him nonetheless, reviving his memory of the turned-up nose, the soft chin, the wide eyes and the hair done in ringlets. They sat down near the hearth, Allen on a love seat, Kate in a rosewood chair with her hands lightly folded and her dress draping over her legs down to the floor. She was slender, her waist narrow, her arms thin beneath the fitted sleeves. But her eyes seemed to catch the yellow glow of the firelight and her teeth were white and even when she smiled.

She asked him about his family, about the general and Valeria and his father, and in the intervals when she waited for him to answer, she leaned forward a little, as if she feared he would speak too softly for her to hear. She inquired after the Cedarcrest servants, Uncle Aaron and Amanda, the cook, and Jeremiah, the general's coachman, and her voice was animated and pitched low as if it trembled always on the edge of a breathless whisper.

"And you, Mr. Hendrick," she said at last. "How have you fared since you have been in Nashville?"

"Thank you," he replied. "I have been well."

Then, seizing on his chance, he looked a little past her toward the heavy curtains, toward the valence and the molding at the top of the wall. "I have been lonely, Miss Kate," he said. "I have been homesick for Gallatin and Sumner County."

He said this not so much for the sake of truth, not simply to answer the question she had asked, but rather because he did not feel quite secure, quite safe even now that he had passed the gates and sat before her, facing her across the corner of the hearth. He believed that he ought to offer some excuse for having written her at all, some circumstance that might soften his presumption.

"I am not accustomed," he said, "to living in the city."

"Ah," she said a little sadly, "I understand."

She smiled and shifted in her chair and the silk of her skirts rustled softly.

"I remember when I first came here," she said. "It was a long time ago, before the railroad was built, and I made the trip in the coach with Papa and Percy."

Allen knew who Percy was though he had never seen him: her brother, in the army now, stationed somewhere in the West.

"I was twelve years old then, Mr. Hendrick," Kate Rutledge said. "And when they left me alone here at the academy I cried."

"Cried?" he said, half startled. For he could not picture Katherine as a child, and sitting there now with her chin raised, her hands completely still and folded, she seemed to him a study, the epitome of fortitude and composure.

"Yes," she said, "I cried. At first because I missed Percy and Papa, but later I cried sometimes at night because I missed the house and the garden pavilion and the chickens and the horses in the stable."

"Yes, ma'am," Allen said. "It is pretty much like that with me. But I never thought much either way about the chickens."

They laughed. Her lips parted and her eyes seemed to catch the light, and she lifted her fingers to touch the brooch at her neck.

"Even the chickens," she said. "They were my pets, and I was allowed to feed them."

For a moment they were silent, and then Kate said, "Did you ever go to the bluff above the river? It is on your land, on Cedarcrest."

"I know," he said. It was high ground, higher even than the hill the Cedarcrest house was built on, and in the summer it was shaded by a group of oak trees, and cool when the wind blew off the water. "Yes," Allen said. "I have been there."

"I used to go there every spring with Percy," Kate said. "We had heard Papa and General Hendrick talk about the big flood, and we used to go there when the river was rising. Or Percy did, and I always followed."

"To escape the river?" Allen asked, smiling, for not even a deluge could have threatened them at Roseneath.

"No," she said, smiling too. "But it was just as silly. Papa had told us how once when the river was very high a lot of things were caught in it. Houses, squatters' cabins, I reckon, from upstream and dead stock and boats adrift and big trees pulled up by the force of the water. Percy always thought that if it had happened once it might happen again, and he wanted to be on hand to see it."

She paused a minute, her head tilted to one side as if she were thinking. Then she grinned and went on, "The houses especially. He wanted to see a house floating in the water, and the cows too, as if they were swimming."

"Did you see it?" Allen asked.

"Oh, no," she replied, "we never did. Nothing but trash. Nothing but old sticks and pieces of lumber."

She leaned forward, looking into his eyes. "Oh," she said, "we were foolish children, Mr. Hendrick."

"No, ma'am," Allen said. "It would be a sight at that. If we have a flood, I'll watch the river for you."

They sat for a while longer before the fire, talking of Roseneath and Cedarcrest, of the land Allen had hunted with Anse Weaver, of the neighborhood house and the people in Gallatin. And all the time the teacher, Miss Clayton, sat on a couch near the wall and peered at them occasionally over her tatting.

At last, just before Allen rose to leave, Kate's face became serious and she let her eyes drop and she twisted her handkerchief between her fingers.

"Tell me, Mr. Hendrick," she said, "are we going to have a war?"

"A war?" Allen replied.

"The Yankees," she said. "Are they going to make us fight?"

"I don't know," he answered. "Grandfather doesn't think so. He believes it's just all talk and politics."

Kate pulled once more at the handkerchief. "Percy thinks so too," she said. "His letters all share General Hendrick's view."

Allen was ready to go now, but he stayed a moment longer.

"Where is Mr. Rutledge?" he asked.

"In the army," she said. "He's a lieutenant with Colonel Pemberton in Minnesota."

Allen thought of this. He thought of the portrait that hung at Roseneath, and he considered soldiers that he had seen, and the militia that paraded often on the streets. But to Allen, Minnesota was a space on a map, a name and boundaries printed on a piece of paper, and the picture at Roseneath remained for him a picture, unrelated somehow to all flesh and blood.

Allen said, "He is most likely right then, being in the army."

"I hope so," she said. "I truly hope he is."

Then both Katherine and Miss Clayton walked with him to the door, past the candles in the standing candelabra, noiselessly across the heavy, padded carpet. At the end of the hall Miss Clayton stood off a way, back of them and a little to one side.

"Miss Kate," Allen said, "I thank you for letting me come."

"No, Mr. Hendrick," she said, "you were kind to visit me. You must come again before you go back home."

There in the poor light of the doorway he searched her face. He looked at her eyes, dark now in the shadows, at her short nose, at her lips and her chin. But he could read nothing, and there had been nothing in the sound of her voice: nothing to tell him exactly what she meant, whether her words expressed her desire or merely her breeding.

And perhaps she felt some of this, sensed his uncertainty and his indecision. For she said, "Wednesday is a good day. You must come back here on Wednesday and have tea."

❖ 9 ❖

KATHERINE RUTLEDGE was seventeen years old during the winter that Allen spent in Nashville, younger than the scandal of Marcus Hendrick's marriage, younger by two years than Allen himself; and because her father had married late and her mother had died young of typhoid fever, she had lived a good deal of her life in the Nashville academy. She had come to the academy for the first time, as she later told Allen Hendrick, when she was twelve, traveling the dry September roads in the Rutledge rockaway, with her father nodding sleepily on the seat beside her and her brother Percy riding with the driver on the box. Or at least, riding outside until they reached Edgefield, and then removing his duster and getting in the coach that they might arrive at the school with some appearance of gentility and breeding. Percy, taller than she and blond, but with the same turned-up nose; and her father, wrinkled and drowsy in the heat of the day, but not yet showing any sign of palsy.

And when they left her—when Percy had kissed her on both her cheeks and her father had touched his lips, affectionately but a little absently, on her forehead—she did cry, just as she told Allen five years later, but not quite for the reasons that she gave him. She stood in the hall on the same flowered carpet, surrounded by the same candelabra, the same dour portraits that peered gloomily from the wall, and wept not because she was parted from the two human beings she loved most in all the world but because she had misunderstood the terms of her education; she had believed that she was to be a day student in the academy and that she would live with her aunt, her mother's sister, who kept a red brick house on Vine Street. She had not been misled; she had simply made a wrong assumption, miscalculated the conditions on which her father at last gave in to her Aunt Lucille's continual harassment.

Kate was seven when her mother died, and for five years before she came to Nashville she lived in the house at Roseneath with only her father and her brother and the kitchen maids, and for a little while, a few months immediately after Margaret Rutledge's death, a governess to keep her on the premises. Or that is the way Captain Rutledge had put it in his instructions to the old Negro woman. "Keep her," he said, "out of the hayloft and off the big road, and bring her to me if you think she needs a switching." And that is all old Sarah endeavored to do, and Katherine was left, for the most part, to her own devices. Left to roam free on the Roseneath land, up the hill to the high bluff and down again to the lower fence rows, to the pastures and the cornfields with Sarah following on her heels. And by August, Sarah, who was never trained to be a governess in the first place, who was a retired seamstress whose fingers had grown stiff—by August, Sarah petitioned the captain for relief.

"Well, damn it," Captain Rutledge said. They were in the parlor, already cluttered with harness in the short time that Margaret Rutledge had been dead. "Damn it," Captain Rutledge said to Sarah, "I told you to bring her to me if she needed switching."

"No, sir," Sarah replied, an old Negro with wisps of gray hair peeping out from under her headcloth and a million lines in her dark and shining face. "It ain't that," she said. "It just that I too old to dog her footsteps."

"Well, slow her down," Captain Rutledge said. "Put a halter on her and slow her down to a walk."

"Massa," the old lady replied, "I old and she young. She just a slip of a baby girl and I'm old as you are."

He turned away, silent, pursing his lips, working the muscles in his cheeks. He looked at the wall and the dusty mantel and at a piece of plow line coiled beside the hearth. Then he shifted his gaze toward the chair where Kate was sitting.

"Come here, Mistress," he said.

She crossed the room to stand before him, a tall girl, her head almost level with his above the chair back.

"Missy," he said, "are you trying to wear this nigger woman out?"

And without blinking her eyes, without looking away or hesitating even for an instant she said, "Yes, sir. I aim to keep her moving."

He pursed his lips again, shifted his teeth which did not fit very well, and then finally let his mouth relax and his lips drop open.

"Father," Kate went on, "I don't need a nurse. Aunt Sarah is slow and she gets sleepy after dinner."

"Well, damn it," he said, finding his voice at last, "what do you want? A hound dog? Or a mammy mare from the stable?"

"No, sir," she replied. "I want to go with Percy."

"Kate," Captain Rutledge said softly, "he don't want you. He's a boy, Kate, and older than you are. Percy does things a girl can't be allowed to accomplish."

"I want him," she replied, still looking in her father's eyes, but feeling in her own the first sting of tears, feeling in her throat the first contraction. "I want Percy."

"Missy," Captain Rutledge said. "He hunts. He shoots guns and rides horses, and sometimes he even swims down in the river."

"I can do that," she replied stubbornly. "I can ride and I can learn to shoot and I can come home when Percy goes in swimming."

"But, Kate," her father began, and the old Negro, Sarah, interrupted him.

"Massa," Sarah said, "she a good girl. You give her her head and she'll promise to stay off the big road."

"I reckon so," Captain Rutledge said after a pause. "But she'd better keep her ground from the cistern too."

So they gave her her head and Percy accepted her company, not without complaint, but with no great show of irritation either, and he undertook to instruct her in the ways of his strange and fascinating life. He was five years older than Kate, twelve when she was seven, and he was short for his size and well built with wide shoulders and large arms and short, thick hands, browned by the sun, but generally kept clean. He was, for a boy, uncommonly neat, and in his way almost handsome, with a nose like Kate's but with smaller eyes, a harder jaw, a broader forehead. He took her with him to the woods, allowed her to follow him along the paths that led between the beech trees, toward the river. He would let her walk behind him or ride on one of the captain's older mares, and he taught her a little of what he knew about nature. She learned first to identify birds, not the easy ones that she had always known—the robin, the mockingbird, the sparrow—but the others that were harder and more seldom seen—the titmouse and the phoebe, the female tanager and the yellow-breasted chat. They went from birds to snakes—the moccasin, the rattler—and then to fish and animals and back to birds when the time for hunting came. Back to the partridge and the mourning dove and the rosy-breasted, blue-winged passenger pigeon, and he taught her how to shoot, a fowlingpiece at first and later a double-barreled shotgun.

"Like this," he said, "up tight against your shoulder."

And she squeezed, as he had told her to do, she heard the noise and felt the blow, harder than any man could hit, and he laughed because the gun had kicked her over.

"Kate," he said, smiling, his small eyes bright, "you should have been a man. If you were a man you would make one hell of a soldier."

He spoke that way sometimes, cursed before her, out of forgetfulness, out of the habit of not remembering that she was a lady.

And they came in time to live in a way like soldiers, to spend their days when they were not in school cleaning guns and firing pistols and charging on horseback toward a canebrake or a fence. In the house there were maps from General Hendrick's campaign against the Indians and the British, the positions of the armies marked, a red line for the route the troops had taken. They would sit with it sometimes on rainy afternoons reconstructing the battle, seeing in their mind's eye the snow and the ice and the frosty breath, the Indians wrapped in furs against the Michigan winter. And Captain Rutledge talked of the old war, and occasionally General Hendrick spoke of it too, but not as often or as enthusiastically as their father.

They lived in a house where the war was never forgotten, and they seldom visited anywhere but Cedarcrest. They would go once a week in the rockaway the three miles to see General Hendrick, the other old widower who was completely alone, with one son disgraced and the other in Mississippi. Kate remembered for the rest of her days the contrast between the general's house and Roseneath, the spotlessness of the Cedarcrest parlor, the dusted mantel, the brushed rug, the way the silver shone in the light from the window. And yet, at that time, at eight or nine or ten, it did not occur to her that one manner of keeping house might be looked on with more favor than another. She thought simply that General Hendrick's life was different from the life she led with Percy and her father—that the general liked books instead of guns and horses. She admired the general, but she admired her father too, and there, for her at least, was an end of it. She was happy in the clutter of old maps or iron bits and bullet molds and bridles.

She was happy, for a while content with the man's life she lived with the captain and her brother, but not for long and not completely, for there was a vague uneasiness in her female brain. Sometimes in school, in the one-room frame building with its hard benches and unfinished walls, she would look around her at the other girls who had come from other plantations: girls who had never shot a gun or ridden on a horse without a saddle, girls in starched pinafores with white hands and braided hair and voices soft and sweet as the springtime wind, and a loneliness, an undefined longing, would clutch her heart. Then, too, there were times in Gallatin, the occasional trips that she made to town with her father when he went to see his factor or to buy a horse. She would wait then in the rockaway, her face pressed close to the window, watching the ladies that passed along the street. The ladies in their silks and feathered bonnets, in their velvet capes and cloth shoes, each with a parasol to keep her from the weather. And each in her finery was beautiful to Kate. Often she could see in her girlish fancy, her own figure dressed in taffeta, herself grown up and suddenly transformed like the girl who went to the dance in the pumpkin carriage.

But in the end her father always returned and they drove back to the fields and to the Roseneath parlor.

It went that way for three years, the golden days stitched through here and there with a single hour of yearning. With the simple desires of a girl's mind, with a wish for a valance on her bed, a pair of gloves, a painted vase for flowers. She would ask for a dress or a petticoat, and her father would buy the best of cloth and then have it cut by the seamstresses in the quarters. He allowed her the vase and curtains for her room and he ordered them himself and they arrived, expensive and ugly. He agreed that the mealtime service was poor, then failed to notice the defections of his butler. He was kind and good, and he meant exceedingly well, but he was old now and he lacked a woman's perception.

So when the letter came on her tenth birthday—it was from her aunt, who had kept track of the time, who knew Kate's age, and who must have suspected more although since Kate's mother's death she had not been to Roseneath—when the invitation came, Kate accepted it and went to Nashville. She went down in the rockaway, the first of the many trips she would make, the first of the long journeys in the carriage, and she carried with her the letter from her aunt, the pale blue stationery, sealed with darker blue wax. And she read it over and over as if it were a document, a visa to a part of the world she had never seen. She did not remember her Aunt Lucille. Or rather, she remembered only a tall woman who smelled of lilac and talked in a low voice and who had been present at the burial of Margaret Rutledge. But there were some facts for her to go on: her aunt was her mother's sister, childless and forty—Captain Rutledge had told the age—and married to an engineer who had an interest in the railroad. She tried at first to work from there, to visualize the man and to move from him to the woman. For she had seen surveyors, bearded gentlemen in boots and denim coats, sighting along their transits toward the horizon. But this was a bad start, in fact as well as in fancy, for her uncle, Mr. Richardson, did his surveying from the back of a horse or the seat of a buggy, and he studied his plats on a table in his private car. But not knowing this, thinking only of the boots, Kate thought of her aunt and attempted to create an image. She searched her mind for the handsomest lady she knew, the most beautiful woman she had ever seen on the trips she had made to Gallatin with her father. And she hit at last on a kind of composite of them all, on a faceless figure dressed in the latest fashion. In this respect, at least, Aunt Lucille lived up to Katherine's expectation.

She was not a handsome woman. Her eyes were too small, her forehead too broad, her upper lip short and her large teeth almost prominent. But she was, beyond any cavil, the most beautifully turned out lady Kate had ever seen. She was wearing, on the afternoon that Kate arrived, a dress of lightweight summer brocade, a pale yellow, almost cream-colored background, stitched with a pattern in dull red and blue and gold. It was plainly designed, with a simple red sash at the waistline and a cameo brooch pinned at the neck; but it was cut fuller than any garment Kate had ever seen, it draped over the hoops in delicate ripples, it swung in a perfect balance, in a kind of rhythm, when her aunt moved down the steps.

Kate never forgot the moment of her arrival, that first sight of the elegant lady who was her aunt. She stood for an instant alone with a servant in the hallway, alone in the varnished rococo house, beneath the crimson glass of the chandelier. Then at the top of the stairway, above the carved banister, the beaded running board, she caught a view of the bright brocade and, looking up, the toe of a satin slipper.

"It is Katherine," Lucille Richardson said. "You have grown, my dear, but I would know you anywhere."

And Kate said simply, "You are the prettiest lady I have ever seen."

So perhaps intuitively, because they were women, they knew already what they were going to do, how they were going to trick Captain Rutledge, understood each other with no necessity for speaking. For the next morning, as soon as breakfast was finished, they started at the shops on Deaderick Street and worked their way toward the public square, buying cloth and laces and buttons, shoes and bonnets and white cotton stockings, ruffles for pantaloons and embroidery and binding; and, at the jeweler's, a seed-pearl brooch and a small gold ring set with a garnet. That was the first morning, and part of the afternoon; and the rest of the day they spent in the sewing room of Lucille Richardson's seamstress. Sat while the dressmaker showed them patterns, and waited a while longer to see the material cut, and returned, three days later, to try on the finished outfit.

Kate could not believe it at first, this grand transformation. When they had left the seamstress and were riding home in the carriage, she fingered the cloth of the dress she wore, and touched her hand to her head to feel her bonnet; she caressed the brooch and the gold ring; she wriggled her toes in the confinement of her slippers. Then, content that they were real, she fell asleep.

She saw in the month that she remained in Nashville a world that she had never dreamed existed, a way of life that she could never have pictured in her mind. In the mornings when her uncle was out of town, the house remained quiet until late in the day and Aunt Lucille had breakfast at nine in her dressing room. But after noon, in the hours before dinner, and later in the time before supper at seven o'clock, there were often carriages at the curb, and a maid moved softly in the hall, fetching a calling card on a silver salver. There was tea for the ladies served in the drawing room and sometimes rum for the men in a cut-glass decanter. And when callers came, Kate met them all, a banker's wife and the widow of a general, an Episcopal bishop and a retired judge, and the younger ones, the doctors and lawyers, the politicians and speculators and a storekeeper here and there, looking a little uncomfortable, a little too intent on his tea, but extremely well mannered and very conservatively dressed. All these and many more, and to each she curtsied and spoke a few words and then retired to her room at the top of the stairs.

But her aunt was not always in the house, and on the afternoons when Lucille was visiting or attending a bazaar, Kate would spend her time with Lucille Richardson's maid, watching the traffic that passed on the street below. They would be in Lucille's dressing room, Kate at the window, seated on a stool and the maid moving from chiffarobe to chest, brushing clothes and changing ribbons, cleaning shoes and sweeping up powder off the floor. And whenever a carriage passed, Kate would call her to see it.

"Here's one, Louella," she would say. "Here comes one now."

The maid would look and tell her whom it belonged to—the banker's wife, perhaps, or one of the lawyers—and if she knew them, remembered the name and the face, she would clap her hands for the joy she felt in her heart.

"Louella," she said one afternoon, speaking in the final hour of daylight, in the moments before the gas was lit in the hall. "Louella, I am going to be a lady."

Speaking as if they were in another country and perhaps another century too: as if "lady" began with a capital letter and stood at the beginning of a name, like Senator or President or Queen.

But Louella did not notice this. "Maybe," she said. She was a short Negro with a round face, firm teeth, and hair that was almost straight. "Maybe Mistress mean for you to be."

Louella paused and pressed her mouth together. Then she said, "Is you rich?"

"Yes," Kate replied thoughtfully. "I don't know. I think so."

"You got to be rich," Louella said. "In the city it don't amount to much being well-to-do."

So the next day—it was almost September, a bright, hot, dusty day, when the blinds were drawn against the heat and inside the house was dim and all in shadows—the morning following her talk with Louella, she went to her aunt and asked the point-blank question.

"My dear," Lucille Richardson said. She hesitated and bit her lip with her large front teeth. "My dear, a lady shouldn't speak that way of money."

And Kate said softly, "Am I a lady?"

"You're going to be, darling," Lucille replied. "I'll see to that."

And she did see to it, but it could not be accomplished all at once. For the first visit, the initial phase was over, and Kate returned to Roseneath, to the dirty parlor and the wide fields, to the hard benches of the one-room school and the girls with braided hair and her brother Percy. Her departure was noted in the Nashville *Daily Gazette*, and the paper printed a description of her clothes: a dimity dress figured with sprigs of roses, a matching bonnet and leather button shoes. But it said nothing of the bills packed away in her trunk. They had been paid, of course, discharged in full by Lucille Richardson, so there could be no question of returning the shoes, sending back the ring or the brooch or the uncut ribbon. And Katherine's father, the poor, helpless captain, grown old now and only a man to begin with, could only blink and purse his lips and shift his ill-fitted teeth in astonishment, before he made out his draft for the full amount.

The next year there was not any need to trick him. Captain Rutledge knew when the invitation came, the blue envelope, the darker blue seal, that the journey to town was going to cost him money. A week before Kate's departure he assumed a gloomy mood, his face wore a frown, and he began to sulk at the table. He sat beyond his bedtime poring over his accounts, figuring with a scratching quill pen, making entries and corrections in his ledger. He was petulant with his overseer and cross with his slaves; he brought more harness to the parlor to be mended. He complained of high prices and the poor yield of his land, and he was almost blasphemous in his comments on the weather. Then at last, when his testiness had played itself out, he threw himself on the mercy of the ladies.

"Kate," he said on the night before she left, "damn it, Kate, I'm an old man. Don't buy out the stores when you get down to the city."

It was, she thought, a disjointed remark, and she studied a while over what he had said before she answered.

Then she replied, "Father, you are not old. I would not have you younger. I would not like you any other way."

So he was vanquished, defeated, his week of pouting brought to naught, and he paid once more when she was home again from Nashville.

And perhaps because it had been so easy, because, in the first two skirmishes, he had been so readily driven from the field, she believed that he could not stand up against them, that he could never refuse what she and Lucille asked. And therefore when the business of her schooling had been settled—Lucille herself had come up for this, bringing her own maid, her own laundress, her own coachman on the box of her Rogers coach—Kate simply assumed that she was to live in the house with her aunt. She visualized the succession of afternoons, the visitors, and the tea at the house on Vine Street, through the fall and the winter and on into the spring, with shopping trips to be made on Saturday mornings, and, when she grew older, the concerts and the balls. But the captain, in spite of being a man, in spite of being old and a little sleepy, had enough imagination left to foresee this too. He would not allow it, and he required her to be a boarding student at the school.

So Captain Rutledge carried his point, and she wept when they left her at the academy, just as she told Allen Hendrick, but she did not tell Allen Hendrick the reason why. And in the years that followed, she saw her aunt only on week ends or occasionally in the afternoon when Lucille visited her at the school. But one night when Kate was sixteen years old, they met, the girl, almost indeed a lady now, and the aunt looking rather youthful still and groomed as always to perfection; they came upon each other at a dance in the City Hall. They chatted briefly over a cup of punch, and a little longer in the ladies' dressing room, but it was not until Saturday that she saw her aunt alone.

They were alone in Lucille Richardson's house, together in the parlor when the guests had gone and the silver service had been taken away and only a hint of cigar smoke was left in the air.

Lucille was on a love seat, half reclining, her feet lifted a few inches off the floor, and Kate sat on a low stool near the hearth.

"And was he the one?" Lucille said, smiling, her large teeth astonishingly white. "The dark-haired boy you were with at the City Hall?"

"The one?" Kate said, her tone innocent. "Which one, Aunt Lucille?"

"Ah, my dear," Lucille replied. "You know what I mean. I want to know who has captured my lady's heart."

Kate laughed at the reference, the old joke between them, but she did not answer, not at once; she looked down at her hands, at the bracelet on her wrist, the wide gold band that caught the glint of the fire. Then she said, half seriously, "No. No one. I think I have been spoiled for the common run of men."

"Oh?" Lucille said.

"Yes," Kate replied. "I lived too long at Roseneath. I compare every man I meet to Percy and Father."

Lucille smoothed her eyebrow with the tip of her finger. "And they don't measure up?" Her voice was gay. "Just wait, my dear. One will."

"I hope so," Kate replied brightly. "I would hate to wind up like Miss Clayton. I would hate to be an old maid and spend my days teaching school."

10

So ALLEN WENT TO VISIT Katherine Rutledge, to sit with her an hour before the fire, to watch the play of shadows on her handsome face, to hear the sound of her whispering, breathless voice. And when he had left her, he did not return directly to the hotel but went instead up Vine Street, up the hill to the capitol grounds, and then on foot to the building itself and sat down alone on the wide, cold steps. It was a dark night, gray with a fog that had risen off the river, and the city beneath him was completely silent and the street lights were dim and far away and twinkling through the heavy mist like stars. Here and there a carriage lamp moved, slow, and weak as a firefly, in the distance. Allen looked up, and above him the columns swept away, out of sight into the darkness, and on the lawn before him was a statue of Andrew Jackson, mounted on horseback, the bronze wet and gleaming slightly, blurred like a ghost of his boyhood dream. He rose and walked down the portico, and his footsteps echoed in the darkness; he stopped and looked once more down at the town. He counted off the intervening days on his fingers, the time that remained between now and Wednesday afternoon; he breathed deeply in the cold, damp night and clasped his hands together at his waist. Then he hurried back to the gate and his rented rig. It occurred to him, as he drove back toward his room, how they would not believe it, his mother and father and General Hendrick. They would find it hard to believe that he had visited Kate.

And he himself found it a little hard to believe in the yellow winter light of the day that followed. Or rather, he found it difficult to account for his luck, for the concatenation of events that had brought him to see her name and to write to her and to go on through with the visit. But the evening itself was engraved in his mind, complete to the last detail of her dress, the flash of pearls in the brooch at her throat, the embroidered corner of the handkerchief she carried. And the spell of the night before remained as he followed the dull routine of his father's business. There was a charm in the telegraph office that he had never caught before, a beauty in the red, glowing belly of the big iron stove, a music in the clicking of the key. The streets were bright beneath the sun and cleaner than he had ever seen them, and the dray carts rattled pleasantly. The walks were full of people elegantly dressed, women in capes and polished walking shoes, men in broadcloth coats with velvet collars. On the strength of his happiness he ordered a suit, stopped at a tailor's shop and prowled among the bolts of cloth, and then stood to be measured by the proprietor himself, a fat man with a gold tooth and sleeve garters and a tight black waistcoat. He took a drink before his noontime dinner and joined in a conversation at the bar. He carried his cane and wore his beaver hat and took a stroll by the steamboat landing before he went to change his money at the banks. And at last, when the day was over and he had gone back to his room, he studied his calendar for a long time and then circled the date that Katherine had set for him to come to tea.

He found on Wednesday, and on other Wednesdays that followed, that she was as beautiful in the afternoon as she was at night, or perhaps, seated by the window, her hands busy above the silver tray, more beautiful, with her white skin showing to perfection and the color rich in her cheeks and eyes and hair. There were more people at the academy in the afternoons, and Kate and Allen were not always alone with their Meissen cups and the cakes on a polished salver and the little sandwiches of thin white bread. There were others, other gentlemen, other girls, and often several couples would sit together grouped in a circle around the table where Kate poured. Allen met them, the young men of the city, most of them enrolled in the university, studying to enter the professions, and the girls whom they came to visit, the classmates of Kate. There was a boy with red side whiskers who liked to pun in Latin, and the fat son of a banker, who would not have understood a pun, even in English, and a man named Gibbs, who was out of school and already a partner in a land company, and one named Wilderson, whose hair dripped with oil, and who had just returned from a trip to Eastern Texas. There was a girl from Louisville, and one named Ford from Franklin, and a tall, blonde girl from near Knoxville who played for them sometimes on the Aeolian harp.

One day, a rainy afternoon, when the lamps were lighted at **four** o'clock and the curtains already drawn over the misted windows, the Latin scholar with the red whiskers turned to Allen and asked where he was from.

"Mr. Hendrick," he said, "were you born in Tennessee?"

He was seated across from Allen, and his voice was high and piercing and his accent strange as if he had spent too much time reciting his Virgil.

"Yes, sir," Allen said, and he knew he would have to look, turn his eyes toward the narrow face, the sharp, hooked nose, the high forehead, pale and smooth as a woman's. He looked toward Watkins, for that was the scholar's name, and repeated, "Yes, sir. I live near Gallatin."

There was no sudden silence. He was conscious of that. Voices continued to talk around him, and nearby a teaspoon rattled on a saucer. But he knew that Kate was listening, straining her ears, as he was, watching Watkins who pursed his lips in thought.

Then at last Watkins said, "There was a General Hendrick, I believe, from Sumner County."

"He is my grandfather," Allen replied. "He is still alive."

"Living yet," Watkins said sententiously. "A ripe old age, indeed. I remember reading of him in a history of the war with England."

And that was all. Watkins tugged once at his red whiskers, sniffed through his long, hooked nose, and quoted a line from one of the *Georgics* that Allen Hendrick failed to understand. But Allen was shaken nonetheless, amazed to find that General Hendrick was known so far beyond the bounds of Sumner County. In the days when he had heard the general talk of war, when he had sat with his grandfather and Captain Rutledge and listened while they spoke of the old campaign, it had never occurred to him that the general's name would be in a book, or that the battle would be written up, or that anyone would remember a minor skirmish in a war that took place fifty years ago. He was strangely conscious, in the moment of relief that followed his sudden fear, of a glow of pride in the family record, a sense of joy at the breadth of the general's fame. But he was aware too, for the first time, of the danger that lay before him— even here so far away from home. For if Watkins knew of his grandfather, there was always the chance that someone else would know of his mother—some traveler who had been to Memphis, some old lady interested in family history, some girl who had relatives in

Sumner County. There would now be the constant threat of the fortuitous remark, the natural inquiry of *Where were you born?* or *Where do you live now?* or *Young man, what branch of the Hendricks do you come from?* The question waiting to be asked, and what then would Miss Clayton have to say to Kate?

He left that day, earlier than was his habit, and went directly to his room and thought for a while of what he should do, and of the responsibility Watkins had placed upon his shoulders. The duty that he had was to shield Kate, to protect her from the scandal that was his, alone, to bear, from the pain and the hard words and the recriminations. On the day that Mr. Douglas had turned him away from his door, he had returned home and stood by the looking glass, examining each detail of his own features; and he did that now, there in his hotel chamber. He held a lamp up close to his face and peered into the mirror, at the blue eyes, the thin lips, the blond hair brushed thick above his ears. And the image returned his wistful stare, and in the end it told him nothing. It made no suggestion; it gazed back and kept its own secret.

I will not return, he thought. I will not go back on Friday.

Then he walked to the window and then to a chair, his eyes averted deliberately from the mirror. And after a while he thought, I will go back once more. I will see her one more time to say good-by.

So he went back to the academy two days later to say good-by to Kate, dressed in the suit he had bought from the Nashville tailor, carrying his walking stick with the silver head. He left the hotel and moved up Church Street, and he noticed that the night itself was one to remember, the sky clear and full of stars, the February air warmed by the hint of spring. There was a breeze blowing soft and damp off the river, and shutters were opened on some of the houses, and a smell of earth rose from the city lawns. He felt it, sniffed it in the air, the first break in the winter; and he thought, as he moved along the walk, that at home the willows would soon be in bud and the creek would run high from the heavy rains and the jonquils would bloom along the paths in the garden. He thought of the house as it looked in spring, gray and old in its plot of new green grass, rough behind the cedar trees and a little streaked by the weather; and from the balcony you could look out over the hills at the maples and elms and hickory trees, at the fields and pastures and clumps of sedge, at the beach grove and the canebrake near the river. He thought of this, and then he thought of Kate, considered for the first time how it would be to move with her through the garden in the spring, to sit with her at night on the Cedarcrest veranda.

But in spite of his vision his resolution held, remained firm as he moved through the iron gates, was unshaken as he took his seat in the academy parlor. Miss Clayton went to fetch Kate, and when they returned, Kate smiled at him from the doorway and crossed the room in a gray dress trimmed with lace at the neckline, and gold earbobs hung with a golden fringe.

"Ah," she said, "you left me early Wednesday."

He made no reply and they took their seats near the wall.

They sat down in the shadow of a bracket lamp, beneath one of the water colors done by one of the students, and for a moment he believed that he could not do it, that he could never bring himself to speak the words, never force his lips to open and say good-by. He turned away from her, looked past Kate toward a corner of the room, but her image lingered in his mind's eye, the short nose, the white neck, the dark hairline. He looked at her again, and she leaned toward him and smiled—she was saying something, he did not know what—and the scent of her perfume filled his nose, not lilac this time but something more pungent, something sharp and sweet like lemon verbena. He saw her hands move and the ring on her finger sparkle. He saw the curls that hung down at her back; he examined the wide gray bow at the V of her neckline.

"Kate," he said.

She waited.

"Kate," and he paused again. He felt warm and slightly light-headed as if he had fever. But he went on this time. "You know about me, Kate?"

"What?" she said. "Know what, Allen?"

"About me," he repeated. "About Memphis and Father and Mother."

"Hush," she said. "Hush, Allen."

But he had started now, and all that he had planned to say, the speech he had so carefully formulated and rehearsed came back to him and he went on. "No," he said. "Somebody will find it out. Some teacher here at the academy or some fool like Watkins."

"Hush," she said again. "Not here. Nobody here will ever know."

"Except you," he replied, and he heard in his voice a note of bitterness that he had not meant to be there. "No one except you."

"Ah," she said. "But I've known it all along."

He was silent for a moment and the clock on the mantel struck, the gears whirring softly, the chimes tinkling thin and frail before the hour.

"Kate," he said. "Somebody will make it known. Some drummer who has passed through Gallatin. Some man who knew Grandfather long ago."

She did not answer. She simply leaned back in the lady's chair, back further into the shadow of the bracket lamp, with her chin raised a little, her eyebrows arched, her head tilted slightly to one side. It occurred to Allen how once long ago she had looked at him this way, examined his face through the glass of a carriage window. The day came back to him in all its bright detail, the white clouds in the blue November sky, the last sunlight that struck across the gravel. The rockaway had come around the bend, the horses blowing from the pull, the coachman straight on his box and chilled by the weather. Then Allen Hendrick had touched his cap to the pale and inscrutable face of the captain's daughter. He recollected this, and the rest of it came back to him too, the afternoons he had come to tea, the evenings he had spent with Kate here in the parlor. Suddenly, under this spell of the past, he said what he had schooled himself not to say, he spoke of the secret he had not meant to tell her.

"I love you, Kate." And then, without pausing, he said it again. "I love you, Kate. And I have come to say good-by."

This time she did not say hush. She covered his mouth with the palm of her hand and then got up quickly and walked toward the center of the room. He rose and followed her, conscious that Miss Clayton must have seen them, must have been watching all the time just out of earshot, and was watching still as they moved into the hall.

"I'm sorry," he said. "I did not mean to tell you that."

"No," she said. "None of it. You did not call tonight to say good-by."

Before he could answer she had opened the door and handed him his stick. "You will come again," she said, framing the words so they did not ask a question. "You will come back and we will talk some more of home."

Then she moved away and left him alone in the hall.

She left him, and he returned to the street, passed out through the gates to the warm night and the star-filled sky and the soft breeze that blew from off the river. He walked to the corner and paused for a while, to breathe the air and to think and to get his bearings. And when the wagon passed him and stopped in front of the school, he could not quite believe what his eyes had seen. It was a simple, open, four-wheeled wagon, pulled by a pair of brown Percheron horses, but at one end, near the driver's seat, there was a piano with a stool beside it and a boy sitting on the stool, and there was another boy with a violin, and another with a flute, and two or three others who had no instruments at all. They stopped and lighted candles in hurricane lamps and put two of the candles on top of the piano and placed the others around the wagon bed. Then the musicians began to play a song. Allen was able to see then that Watkins was there; he was the man with the flute, and holding the violin was the boy who had been to Texas. They played "Camptown Races" first, but in a sad, slow, mournful way that seemed to fit the character of the Percherons that drew the wagon. They played one chorus, then stopped a moment, and struck up another tune and the boys without instruments began to sing. It was "Believe Me If All Those Endearing Young Charms," and it was pretty, Allen thought, the voices blending with the violin and the flute and all of it subdued and muted by the night.

In a moment lights began to appear in the windows of the academy; the sashes were thrown open and girls peered down from up above. They had come, some of them, from out of bed, with cloaks and robes put on over their nightgowns, but others like Kate had still been dressed when the music began. For she was there, her face lighted by a lamp that she had placed upon the sill. She was there, listening to the singers, and down below, in the shadow of the academy wall, Allen wondered if she stood in her own room, and if the music were perhaps being played for her, and if one of the boys in the cart was in love with her too. He wondered whether, when the serenade was finished, she would remain for a while staring out at the night, counting the stars and breathing the springlike air. Or whether she might turn back to her room and pace the floor or toss in her bed or sleep, perhaps, untroubled until the day.

He did not know. And he felt, of a sudden, the grand extent of his own provincial ignorance. For never before had he seen a cart rigged out to furnish a serenade for the ladies, or a flute player playing in a wagon bed, or hurricane lamps set up to light the music. He felt that the song itself had some grave significance, some meaning beyond the words and the tune, and the candles lent a ceremonial air to the whole performance.

A small crowd had gathered now; a few passers-by had paused to listen. One of them, a tall man in tight worsted trousers, stopped near the wall and spoke to Allen.

"It is pretty, now, ain't it?" he said. "I never before knowed 'em to bring along a piano."

"Do they do it often?" Allen asked. "I mean just the singing and the fiddles?"

"You never heard 'em before?" the man asked, apparently startled. "They commence as soon as the weather breaks and keep it up all summer. All the boys. If it ain't one group outside the academy it's another." He hesitated an instant, then added, "It's a pretty thing to listen to of an evening."

"Yes, sir," Allen said. "But what does it signify? I mean what do they come to do it for in the first place?"

"Son," the man said, "you're new here. You're from somewhere else, and you just got in to the city. That's a school for girls, and they're up there in the windows. Them in the wagon is boys, as you can see."

"Yes, sir," Allen replied. "They come and sing to compliment the ladies."

"Yes," the tall man said. "It's a way to court."

Allen left them and returned to his hotel.

But after his visit to the academy and the talk he had had with Kate and the serenade he had heard by the boys on the wagon, there was still one more surprise left in the night. When he got back to his room, he found Anse Weaver.

Anse was sitting in the tapestry-covered rocking chair, his feet on a stool, the copy of Gibbon open before him, and he smiled broadly at Allen and crossed the room and took his hand.

"Young Hendrick," he said. "I have come to see about you. I have come to see if you are behaving yourself in the city."

"You've done the wrong thing then," Allen said, smiling too. "You should have written. I could have made a better case for myself through the mail."

They sat down and had a drink together, and Anse told him of all that was happening at home, of a cold that the general had in his chest, of a new mare Lady Susan had foaled, and of Marcus Hendrick, who continued well, and to Aaron, who continued in his sour disposition. He got everything else out of his system first and then he settled down to talk of Valeria. "You will not believe it," he said, "but she is prettier than when you left. Though you must have thought then that she could not be improved upon."

"No," Allen said in mock seriousness. "I thought nothing of the sort. I always considered Valeria a trifle homely."

"You will go to hell for lying, young Hendrick," Anse Weaver said. "You have put yourself beyond the hope of Christian salvation."

"All right," Allen said, laughing at Anse. "She is a handsome woman. You came all the way from home to tell me that."

"Yes," Anse said. "To tell you that and to attend a medical meeting."

He got up and poured some whisky in his glass and added some water from the pitcher. Then he sat down again and took a few sips before he spoke.

"No, damn it," he said, grinning a little shyly. "The meeting is only an excuse. I came to buy a wedding ring, young Hendrick."

Allen remained silent for a moment, moved by what he had heard, and in the few seconds that passed before he rose to congratulate Anse he thought of Valeria in a wedding gown moving down the Cedarcrest steps with the general beside her. He thought of the flowers and the yards of lace, the music from the harpsichord and the people who would come and Anse and the priest waiting in front of the mantel. Somehow to Allen it seemed a little sad; beautiful but touched somehow with melancholy.

"I am glad, Anse," he said. "I am very glad for you."

"I know that," Anse Weaver replied. "And I thank you, young Hendrick."

Then he gazed at Allen and he noticed something: the new suit perhaps or the pin in his cravat, the line of his mouth or the wrinkles in his forehead.

"Allen," he said, and then stopped.

"Allen, do you remember what I said to you one day? How the moment would come and when it did you could not help it?"

"Yes," Allen Hendrick replied. "I remember."

"Is she the one?" Anse Weaver said. "Is it Kate, young Hendrick?"

"Yes," he said again. "I have been to see her."

Anse picked up his glass, saw that it was empty, but continued to hold it in his hand.

Then he asked, "Did she send you away, young Hendrick? Did she turn you out?"

"No," Allen replied. "I turned myself away. I said good-by."

Anse waited, sat for a long time while footsteps passed in the corridor outside and a train whistle blew somewhere down near the station. He waited and at last Allen Hendrick broke the silence.

"You know me," he said. "You know who I am. The moment can come now or next year. I can fall in love a thousand times, and nothing on earth can change me from a nigger."

"No, by God!" Anse said. "Look at yourself. Walk over there and look at yourself in the mirror."

"I have done that too," Allen said. "With me it is not color. With me it is not anything but being a nigger."

"Then show it to me," Anse said. "Tell me where it is. In the cells of the blood? In the muscles? In the nerves or the bone?"

"It is being a nigger," Allen said. "I can't tell you why."

"I will tell you then," Anse replied. "It is not there."

Allen said nothing to this. He moved to the window away from the light to stand and look down at the dark and silent street.

"Young Hendrick," Anse said at last. "What about Kate?"

"Yes," Allen replied. "I am thinking of her. I would not hurt her, Anse. That is why I said good-by."

"Ah," Anse said. "But what if she loves you too, Allen?"

He did not know. He had not thought of it this way. He had concerned himself only with the embarrassment she would feel if the old scandal, the facts of his birth, were told.

"Allen," Anse said. "Are you really thinking of Kate? Or are you frightened for yourself, Allen? Are you afraid to take the chance you would have to take?"

"Afraid?" Allen said, turning back toward the room. "Afraid of what? I am used to it now. It has happened to me before."

"No," Anse replied. "It hasn't, young Hendrick. You were never really in love with Amy Douglas."

Anse rose then and got his hat and moved toward the doorway. "Go back to her," he said. "Call on her tomorrow night. And remember this. It is easier to see her here than it will be at Roseneath. It is an opportunity, Allen. It may never come again."

◊ 11 ◊

THAT WINTER, when Allen was in Nashville, there was much crime in the city and much talk of war, and many slaves ran away and were advertised for in the local papers, and there were grave robbers at work in the city cemetery and a lawyer named Robinson was shot and killed near the courthouse square. Often at night, regardless of the weather, slaves would be loitering at the corners of the streets, and sometimes they had enough money for whisky and they would drink and shout insults at the white people passing by. One evening, when there was more whisky than usual, two slaves were killed by the night watch, and their owner, a man named Wilkerson, brought suit against the city to recover the value of the Negroes he had lost. Then the feeling ran higher than ever, and the watch was increased, and at last there were few slaves at all to be seen after dusk in the business district. But later, a young Senegalese was caught with his face in a lady's dressing-room window and he was tried and whipped and sent to prison. It was a winter of violence, a season of anger, and the social life of the city seemed to Allen to have a military cast. Most of the balls were given by or in honor of the militia companies—the Rock City Guards, the Governor's Guards, the Nashville Blues, the University Grays. The companies were frequently parading, most of them infantry, but some with field guns too, some light artillery complete with limbers and ammunition chests and caissons. Once, while Allen watched, the Grays halted on Vine Street, stacked arms, and entered a residence for tea. And while the boys marched, the men in the hotels and the banks and the taverns peered at each other with narrowed eyes, and talked of war. For it was 1860, and the hope of compromise was almost gone, and the dream of an independent South raged like a fever.

On the morning after Allen's talk with Anse Weaver, the day after he had tried to say good-by to Katherine, he went as usual to the telegraph office to get his instructions, and from there to the banks to make his trades. In the State Bank he was waited on by a clerk named Harding, a tall, middle-aged man with a sharp nose and small blue eyes and white hair. When the exchanges were over and the bills had been counted and Allen Hendrick was closing his valise, Mr. Harding leaned forward across the counter and said, "You know, a curious thing happened yesterday."

"Oh?" Allen said. "What was that, Mr. Harding?"

"Well," Mr. Harding said, speaking softly, "as soon as you had left yesterday morning, a nigger man came in, came directly over here to the window. He wanted me to tell him what paper you had traded and what you had got."

"Who was he?" Allen asked.

"I don't know," Harding replied. "A nigger, like I told you. You don't need to worry, Mr. Hendrick. I sent him on his way."

"But what did he look like?" Allen asked quickly. "How old was he? How was he dressed?"

"I didn't really notice," Harding said. "I was—" and suddenly, for no apparent reason, his voice stopped. He was gazing past Allen's head, peering with his small blue eyes over Allen's shoulder.

"Why, there he is now," Mr. Harding said, "over yonder in the doorway."

Allen Hendrick turned and looked where Mr. Harding was pointing and saw Ben Hill. From where Allen was standing, Ben appeared in silhouette, framed by the door against the strong light of the morning. But there was no mistaking who he was, for he stood with his head slightly tilted to one side, his shoulders set back, his stomach protruding.

At first Allen felt only mild surprise. Then the memory came rushing back, the recollection of the torn banknotes that had fluttered in Allen's face, and the sound of the words that Ben had spoken about Lucy Hendrick. And with the memory came the old anger, sharply felt like a constriction in the chest.

Allen moved to the door quickly, but Ben did not run away. Ben stepped out onto the street and waited there, and when Allen came out, he was standing with his back to the wall and with the round, dark face showing nothing, the eyes blank, the forehead smooth, the mouth tightly shut.

"What are you doing?" Allen Hendrick said. "What did you mean going in that bank and asking about my business?"

There was no answer.

"Right now," Allen Hendrick said angrily. "What are you doing here now?"

"I'm standing on the street," Ben Hill said slowly. "I'm a nigger like you are, but I reckon I've got a right to stand on the damn street."

This time there was no hand to fall on Allen's shoulder, no voice to speak sharply in his ear. He jumped forward and grabbed the lapels of Ben's coat, held him with both hands, and gave the first preliminary jerk that allowed him to feel the solid weight of Ben Hill's body. But that was all. As if the touch itself somehow had power to communicate, the cloth of Ben's coat against his own taut flesh brought him back to his senses. In the midst of his anger he was suddenly conscious of the extent of Ben's poverty, which was attested by every garment that Ben wore. The broadcloth of the coat had grown thin and rusty; Ben's trousers were patched and his shoes were broken and the brim of his beaver hat was badly creased. For Allen Hendrick there was a reversal of what he had felt on that other day, that other meeting with Ben in the office in Gallatin. Then his pity had turned suddenly to hate and rage. Now he released Ben, and his anger temporarily subsided, and Allen looked down at the ground in embarrassment, almost in shame.

Then he said softly, "All right. I'll put it another way this time. Do you want to say anything to me? Do you have a message you would like to send to Father?"

Ben hesitated. He frowned and pursed his lips, and his eyes did not meet Allen's: he gazed blankly off in apparent indecision. After a moment he let his face relax; though he did not smile, he did not look friendly. He reached into his pocket and withdrew the hand empty. Then he reached in again, slowly this time, and took the hand out more slowly still, as if the effort were costing him great pain, and held out a package of bills toward Allen Hendrick. They were notes issued by the Planter's Bank in New Orleans.

"What would your daddy advise a man to do with this?" Ben asked.

"It's good," Allen replied. "It's worth as much as any paper. But if you can get seventy-five cents on the dollar, change it into gold."

Ben seemed to think for a moment; then he reached in his pocket again and brought out some small yellow bills which were unfamiliar to Allen. They were certificates of deposit issued by the Augusta Savings Bank, Augusta, Georgia, and Allen Hendrick had no idea of their value.

"What about these?" Ben Hill said.

"I don't know," Allen replied. "We never traded with them."

Ben Hill licked his lips and his eyes grew narrow. "You don't know," he said scornfully.

"No," Allen replied testily, "we don't."

"You don't know," Ben repeated. "You trade money here day in, day out, and I ask you about one kind of paper and you say you don't know."

Ben's mouth tightened, his upper lip stretched long, his breath came unevenly, and his chin quivered. He was leaning against the wall of the bank, and he slapped his open hand once or twice against the brick.

"Look at me," he said, and in his anger his diction changed; he slipped into the patois that he had spoken in his childhood. "Look at my coat and the hat on my head. Look at my shoes and the pants I got on, with a hole in the seat to show my butt to the elements. I git up of a morning and put on these clothes, I think about you. Every morning I git put in mind of your daddy. I say, 'These here Hendrick breeches. This here Hendrick shirt. These here the clothes them Goddamned Hendricks git me.' I poor because of you and because of your daddy. I rich man once and now I poor, and you won't even tell me the worth of a dab of money."

"I don't know," Allen said, feeling not only anger but a terrible frustration. "By God, I tell you I don't know!"

"All right," Ben said, "we let that pass. I don't know about them banknotes either. But there's one thing I do know. You young and rich now and eating high off the hog, but there's one thing I can tell you. Times change. Folks change. Years go by and everything changes, and the fleas don't bite on the same dog's ass all the time. You think about that. You study it hard while you ridin' so fancy."

He paused. Then he went on, "We meet again, you and me. I see you another time and things might be different."

Ben said this and turned and walked away, but the threatening tone that had been in his voice seemed to linger after he was gone; his anger seemed to vibrate still in the bright air of the morning.

And that night at the Female Academy—Allen took Anse Weaver's advice; he returned to the school as Anse had told him to do and passed through the iron gates and entered the hallway—that night, for a few dreadful minutes, Allen believed that Ben had made good on his threat. For Miss Clayton did not offer to take him to the parlor. "Mr. Hendrick," she said when she had closed the door, "Dr. Cox has asked if you will spend a few minutes with him."

Allen did not know who Dr. Cox was. He assumed he was an official of the school, and as he moved with Miss Clayton down the academy corridor, he glanced at the portraits that hung along the walls—stern-faced men in high neckcloths, women with pinched mouths and black dresses—thinking that one of these might be the face of Dr. Cox. And then when he saw that the pictures bore no names, he tried to fashion a composite face, a conglomeration of features from a number of the portraits. For during the long walk to the doctor's office he felt a sense of foreboding, a premonition that something had gone wrong; and he believed that he ought to prepare himself by fixing in his mind an image of the man he was to meet.

But he failed in this, for Dr. Cox did not look much like a scholar. Or rather, he looked too much like a scholar and not enough like a schoolmaster, for he was a slight blond man with teeth worn away from chewing tobacco and brown tobacco stains on his light mustache, and blue eyes that seemed rather rigid, restricted in their motion by the narrow frames of the glasses that he wore. He was myoptic and probably, Allen thought, a little absent-minded. His clothes were wrinkled, and there were grease spots on his coat.

Dr. Cox was standing before the fire in his office, and he advanced to meet Allen and shook his hand and offered him a chair.

"Mr. Hendrick," he said, smiling with his stubby, worn teeth. "Are you related to the Hendricks in Paducah?"

"No, sir," Allen said. "I am from Gallatin."

"Miles Hendrick," Dr. Cox said. "That was his name. I knew him long ago up in Paducah. I taught school there once, Mr. Hendrick. When I was young, I taught school in Paducah."

He looked around the room vaguely, turning his head to keep the glasses straight before his eyes and blinking as if to clear his vision. He looked at the bookcases, the desk, the leather davenport, and then finally he looked back at Allen Hendrick.

"Paducah," Dr. Cox repeated. "But you are not from there. Your family lives in Gallatin, Mr. Hendrick." It was not a question. He was getting the fact straight. He was repeating the salient point of the day's assignment.

"Do you know where the springs are?" Dr. Cox asked. "The Castalian Springs?"

"Yes, sir," Allen replied. "Our place is nearer the springs than it is to Gallatin."

"Yes," Dr. Cox said. "The Castalian Springs. Our girls like to go there to imbibe the water."

Then he clasped his hands at his waist and chuckled gleefully, his eyes blinking and growing a little misty.

"That is what they maintain," he said as if he were repeating a joke. "They claim, sir, that they go to drink the water." He laughed some more, his thin shoulders shaking.

"Yes, sir," Allen replied lamely.

"No, sir," Dr. Cox said. "No, sir, Mr. Hendrick. You don't understand. You see, they don't go there to drink the water at all."

There was a long pause, while Dr. Cox raised his eyebrows and stared at Allen expectantly through his glasses.

"Mr. Hendrick," he said. Another pause. "Mr. Hendrick," his voice was triumphant now. "They go to Castalian Springs to see the boys."

Allen tried to grin. He forced his features into what he hoped was the proper attitude, and a specter of a laugh sounded in his throat.

"Now," Dr. Cox said. "Now, then, sir. You wonder why I called you to my office." There was a tone in his voice that suggested some transgression, some equation missed or sentence misconstructed.

Allen hesitated for a moment and then said, "I am glad for the chance to meet you, Dr. Cox."

"But you wonder, nonetheless," the doctor said sharply.

"I do, sir," Allen replied. "I wonder."

"Why, to see you, sir," and the hands went back across the stomach and the shoulders shook and the blue eyes blinked in mirth.

"Yes, sir," Allen replied. "I am glad to see you too."

"No, no," Dr. Cox said, serious again. "I wanted to see you, sir, I wanted to get you back here and have a look at your face."

And now, Allen thought, after all his foolishness it is coming. He knows, and he has sent for me to warn me from his door. And in the instant before Dr. Cox spoke again, Allen wondered who had told him. He thought first of Ben Hill, who knew the truth and might have imparted it out of malice, written a letter or appeared in person and spoken the scandal to one of the teachers or one of the maids. But it could have been Watkins, who might have stumbled on the truth. Or perhaps Dr. Cox had known the story all along and had only just now made the connection in his mind, thought of Allen as the son of Marcus Hendrick.

"I am a teacher," Dr. Cox said. "I educate girls and I am responsible to their parents."

"I understand that," Allen replied, and growing a little impatient, he went on, "but what was it that you wanted to say to me, sir?"

"You are hasty, young man," Dr. Cox said. "You must learn patience. I told you, sir, that I wanted to see your face."

He reached in his pocket and took out a plug of tobacco. Then he carefully cut a chew with a penknife, and speared the chew with the knife blade and took it to his mouth.

"I am a judge of men, sir, of people," Dr. Cox said. "I have to be. Your face, Mr. Hendrick," he pointed the knife, still open, at Allen's nose. "Your face to me is an open book. I can read it, sir. I can see through your eyes to the bottom of your heart."

Allen felt at first a little naked, exposed to the eyes of a stranger and to the world. Then he was angry, resentful at the old man's senseless sparring, at the time Dr. Cox was taking to reach the point.

"Yes, sir," Allen said, returning the doctor's stare.

"And what do I see?" Dr. Cox said. "Enough, Mr. Hendrick. In your eyes I see enough."

He leaned over and spat in a cuspidor that sat on an India-rubber mat at the side of his desk. Then suddenly he rose and extended his hand to Allen. "I am glad to make your acquaintance, Mr. Hendrick. You are welcome here. At the academy we welcome young gentlemen of your stamp."

Allen was standing too, gripping the cold, faintly damp hand of the doctor, and at that instant he could not believe his ears. For if Dr. Cox were not aware of the scandal of Allen's birth, why then had the doctor sent for him in the first place? And if he did know, if in some way he had been informed, why now this travesty of politeness? Allen remained silent, and Dr. Cox seemed to sense his confusion.

"My boy," he said, "much as I should like to, I cannot meet every gentleman who comes here. We have many girls, Mr. Hendrick, and my duties are heavy. I can only check up on those who call with regularity." And this, Allen saw, was another joke. The eyes blinked, the shoulders shook, and this time the hands patted the stomach gently.

"And you have checked up on me?" Allen asked, beginning now to relax, beginning now almost to appreciate the irony.

"I have seen your face, sir," Dr. Cox replied. "I have read your features."

Allen turned away, and when he had reached the door, Dr. Cox said, "You come back, young man. Katherine will be here again on Monday."

"Sir?" Allen said, halting now with one foot already in the hallway.

"She is at her aunt's, young man, at Mrs. Richardson's on Vine Street," Dr. Cox said. "Is that what you desired to know?"

"Yes, sir," Allen replied. "Thank you, sir."

"And Mr. Hendrick," Dr. Cox said. He paused and shifted his chew from one jaw to the other. "Procrastination, my boy, is an inveterate thief of time."

And he did not chuckle now. He laughed, threw back his head and roared like an old, emaciated moose, and Allen closed the door softly on his laughter.

So he left Dr. Cox and the Female Academy and passed once

more through the iron gates and moved down Church to High Street and there he stopped. He stood for a while on the corner, leaning on his stick beneath a lamp, and he thought at first that he would not go, that he would not risk appearing where Kate might not want him to appear. Or more than this, he would not take the greater chance that Mrs. Richardson—whoever she was, for he had never seen her—that she might know more from gossip or hearsay than Dr. Cox had been able to see in Allen's face. He half decided to spend the evening with Anse Weaver, drinking with him in a tavern, or visiting the Vauxhall Gardens or simply talking once more in the hotel chamber. But this was Friday and Kate would be gone from the academy till Monday, and Allen knew that time was running out. In another three weeks, another two if they were lucky and his father's guesses right, his business in Nashville would be over, and what Anse called his opportunity would be gone. He breathed deeply and straightened his cravat and then moved off toward Mrs. Richardson's.

When he reached the house, there were several carriages parked in front and two or three buggies, and a horse at the hitching rail, and because the night was reasonably warm, the coachmen were gathered under the street lamp, talking and jostling against one another, and one of them was throwing rocks at a cat across the street. Perhaps if Allen had known where he was, he would have been frightened off at the sight of so much company. But he did not know, he had never been there before; and he stopped and asked one of the Negroes to direct him to the place where the Richardsons lived.

The coachman turned at the sound of Allen's voice, a tall, handsome Negro in livery. He stood better than six feet, with broad shoulders and narrow hips, his skin coal black, his eyes clear and sparkling, his teeth good. He looked at Allen, a little contemptuously at first, perhaps because Allen had not arrived in a carriage, and then he answered with respect, perhaps because he had looked at Allen's clothes.

"You there, Young Marster," he said. "This is the Richardson residence, this one here where the company is gathered."

Then, for Allen, there was nothing to do but to go in, or else to walk away, to retreat amid the derision of the Negroes. He moved slowly up the steps and across the porch to the doorway and paused there before he pulled the bell. He could see through the fan-shaped window, the hall lighted by the red glass chandelier, the ornate stairway, the carpet, a few chairs and, on a table, some wax flowers in a vase. Then he saw, sitting in a corner, a maid wearing a starched uniform and a white cap.

When he had rung and the maid had let him in, he heard voices and the sound of music from the drawing rooms that were somewhere to his left. But he did not go in this direction. The maid took him instead to the other side of the house, offered him a chair in a small parlor that overlooked the street, and took his card on a silver tray and disappeared. Then, in a very short time, she was back, and they crossed the hall again, and she opened a door and stood back for Allen to enter. It was a parlor, almost as big as the one where he visited Kate at the Female Academy and he noticed in the split second, before he moved into the room, the white dental-work molding that ran around the ceiling, the carved white panels above the chimney piece. The furniture was in gold cloth and carved rosewood, the floor was bare and polished and the draperies were gold too, and adorned with tassels. There were many people in the room, and most of them were considerably older than he, and few of them were even looking in his direction. As he moved through the doorway, he searched the room for Kate, and he saw her, smiling, dressed in green, green embroidery on her slippers, a narrow green ribbon in her hair. She was coming toward him, and at her side was a tall lady in a black velvet evening gown, cut low at the neck and falling away at the shoulders. And on the other side of the lady—he could hardly believe his eyes—was Anse Weaver in a ruffled shirt and diamond studs.

Allen spoke to Kate, bowed to her, a little awkwardly, he feared, and Anse said, "Miss Lucille, may I present my young friend, Mr. Hendrick?" and he bowed to Mrs. Richardson and she offered him her hand.

"Yes," she said, smiling at Allen. Her teeth were good but slightly prominent. Her face was long, too thin to be handsome, but her expression was pleasant and there was a certain elegance in the way she held her head.

"Yes," she said. "I have heard a good deal about Mr. Hendrick already. It is a pleasure, indeed, to see him in the flesh."

And Allen could say only, "Thank you, ma'am. You are kind to receive me."

Mrs. Richardson introduced him to some of her guests, to a man who, to Allen's annoyance, reminded him of Dr. Cox; and to a short, fat woman named Pickett, who had a son Allen's age who was a student now at Yale; and to a young lawyer, who, Allen suspected, took a fancy to Kate. A Negro man was busy in the room, passing out cups of punch, and on a sideboard near the windows there were trays full of food and opposite the sideboard a small orchestra was playing, but the music was not dance music and the people seemed content to talk in groups, with occasionally a lady and gentleman walking together the length of the long parlor. Allen looked for Kate and saw that she was occupied, talking to a middle-aged couple and a younger man near the fireplace. Then he caught sight of Anse, alone beside one of the love seats, and he bowed to the lady whose son was in Yale, and moved across the floor to Anse's side.

"Young Hendrick," Anse said—he was puffing a cigar, and he blew a smoke ring toward the ceiling. He was in good spirits, and his eyes had a vague, dreamy look. He had already been to the punch bowl many times. "Young Hendrick," he said. "You came a little late."

"I can see that," Allen replied, smiling. "I can tell that by the tone of your behavior."

"Sir?" Anse said. "What was that, young Hendrick?"

"Anse," Allen said, "what in the hell are you doing here?"

"Ah," Anse replied lightly. "I never miss a chance to attend a Richardson levee."

"Levee?" Allen said.

"It's the only word that will fit," Anse replied. "Morning, afternoon, or night. When Lucille Richardson gives it, it's a levee."

Allen looked at Anse, his question still unanswered, and after a moment Anse said, "Never mind, young Hendrick. Never mind why I am here."

He dropped his cigar in a porcelain ashtray and then looked at Allen. His eyes became narrow and his face assumed a serious expression.

"Listen," Anse said. "Listen to me. Don't waste your time here tonight. Don't spend the evening following after Kate."

"What?" Allen said almost angrily. "What do you mean?"

"Hush," Anse said. "Don't talk so loud. I mean this. Tonight you have an opportunity."

For a while Allen looked at Anse in silence. Then he replied, "You have said that once before, if I'm not mistaken."

"I did," Anse said. "This is the second one you have had. This is the best thing that has happened to you since Ben Hill lost his money."

"What?" Allen asked again.

"Miss Lucille," Anse replied. "You'd better court her tonight instead of courting Katherine."

He did not understand, but there was no time to press Anse, for Lucille Richardson was moving toward them. She was alone, and her face seemed pensive and she tapped her fingers with the edge of a folded fan.

"Good night," Anse said softly, his lips close to Allen's ear. "Good luck, young Hendrick."

Then he smiled at Mrs. Richardson and moved away.

Allen did not think over what Anse had said; he did not weigh his words and mull over them in search of meanings. For Lucille was standing at his side, smiling with her prominent teeth and saying:

"I am glad to find you free. I want so much to get to know you better."

"Yes, ma'am," Allen said. "I would like that too."

She was silent, looking at him, not staring, for her eyes were very soft, and the expression on her face was one of polite concern, almost tenderness. There were small wrinkles at the corners of her mouth that made her appear a little sad.

"Come," she said at last. "I must talk to you, Mr. Hendrick."

He followed her through another door, not the one he had entered, and through a smaller hallway dimly lighted by a single gas jet, and finally into a small private sitting room, carpeted and finished in plain cherry woodwork. She sat down, her wide velvet skirt swinging on its hoops and bobbing up to show her slender ankle; then she motioned for Allen to be seated too, and said:

"Mr. Hendrick, I am Katherine's aunt."

It came out weak, a bit uncertain, as if she had changed her mind, as if she had started to say one thing and said another.

"Yes, ma'am," Allen said. "I know that, Mrs. Richardson."

"Mr. Hendrick," she began, and then she paused and leaned forward in her chair. "Allen," she said, "why did you come here?"

"I'm sorry," he replied, embarrassed by this. "They told me at the academy——"

"No, no," she interrupted. "I did not mean that. I meant to the city, to Nashville; but it does not matter."

"Ma'am?" he said. And when she did not reply, he said. "I came down here on business for my father."

"I know that," Lucille Richardson said. "It was a foolish question."

Suddenly she rose and walked to one end of the room, to the windows, and idly straightened a drape and then returned and rested her hand on the back of her chair.

"Oh," she said, "you can tell me nothing. I see it all." She regarded Allen for a moment without speaking. Then she said again, "I see it all. Your face and those wistful, beautiful eyes, and that sadness that runs in your voice as pretty as music. But damn you," she said, taking a step toward Allen, "why in all the world did you have to pick my Kate?"

After a silence, a long hiatus of time, Allen said, "Mrs. Richardson, you ought to see that too."

"I do," she replied. "Try to forgive me, Allen."

She was very quiet now, thoroughly composed, and she went to a small sideboard and returned with brandy for herself and Allen, and it occurred to Allen that never before had he seen a lady drink.

"Attend me," she said. "Understand this. I have nothing to say of it. It is up to you and Katherine. Or to you and Captain Rutledge. Or to you and Percy. Percy," she repeated thoughtfully, almost as if she were alone, "if he will dare kill you knowing that Kate will never forgive him. Oh, yes," she went on, rapidly now and with great animation. "She loves you. If knowing that, if being sure will dim your fire, I will tell it to you a million times. I will follow you about the street just to repeat it."

Allen sat, stunned by what Lucille had said, and the voice now seemed to come to him as if from a great distance, but the words that she spoke, he understood quite clearly. He gave a start now and sat up in his chair.

"No," she said, smiling faintly. "You have that virtue too. You are constant."

Then she said, "Allen, I am getting old."

"No," he protested, "no, ma'am——"

"No," she echoed sharply. "You are right. Not old enough to want compliments from boys. Now be quiet and hear what I am saying."

He did not speak.

"I am getting old," she repeated. "And I have no children, and Kate has no mother, and I have raised her, Allen. I have made her what she is. And I will not lose that," she said emphatically, setting her glass on a marble table top. "I will not lose her. I do not flatter myself that I could keep her from marrying you. But if I could, she would hate me, Allen. She would never forget it."

Then very quietly, very softly, she said, "If you must, you must. We will have to make the best of it. With your money and my money and the Rutledge money, we will perhaps be able to cram it down their throats."

And strangely, surprisingly to Allen, she gave him what amounted to a warning. "But remember," she said, "there is still her father. There is still Percy."

"You will not try to stop us?" Allen asked finally.

"No," she replied. "I thought I made that clear."

Then, with that touch of inspired innocence that had won him General Hendrick's heart so long ago, he said simply, "Will you help us?"

"I will do," she replied, "whatever Katherine asks."

And she turned away from him and left the room.

⋄ 12 ⋄

IN THE HAPPY DAYS that followed, Allen went to see Kate as often as visitors were allowed to come to the school. And on a Monday evening, three nights after his meeting with Lucille Richardson, he sat in the parlor at the Female Academy and asked Katherine Rutledge to marry him. They were seated on a couch near the windows, not very close together, for Miss Clayton was watching them from near the door, and beyond the room a March rain was falling, and a March wind rattled the drops against the glass. He made no preliminary speeches. He had just entered through the wide, dim hall, past the portraits he had examined so carefully on the day that he had had his interview with Dr. Cox. And when Katherine had joined him and they were settled on the couch, he took a deep breath and looked past her toward the fire—toward the hearth and the mantel and the ticking clock, toward a table where a vase of daffodils stood and the Aeolian harp that stood behind the table.

Then in a voice that was flat and did not show much feeling he said, "I love you, Kate. And I want you to be my wife."

He felt vaguely that he had done it wrong. In the books he had read, the plays he had seen, proposals were always introduced by pretty speeches. There should have been, he knew, some talk of her virtue, some compliments on her beauty and her maidenly charm, some hint of the respect he had for her and her family. But he could not do this. He lacked the courage and the conscious gift for words. And time seemed to him short and the moment fleeting.

"I love you," he said. "And I have no right to ask you. But I do ask you to marry me just the same."

"Allen," she said and stopped. When she had come into the room, she had taken one of the yellow flowers from the vase near the hearth; she turned the green stem now between her fingers and she looked down and watched the petals catch the light.

"Will you, Kate?" Allen asked.

She raised her head and smiled, weakly so that her lips barely parted. Her face was half in shadow and in the shadow the plane of her cheek was flat.

"How?" she replied softly. "Yes, I will marry you. But, oh, my dear, please tell me how?"

"I don't know," he said, speaking rapidly. "Some way, Kate. We will think of something."

And it occurred to him then, though he did not express it, that they might simply go out of Tennessee and marry. That he might meet her late at the academy gates, and carry her in a rented rig north into Kentucky or south down over the Alabama line, and there in some little country town wake the clerk and find the preacher and have it done. But then? he thought. What after that? Could they then come back to Middle Tennessee?

"Allen," she said, "we will have to talk to Father. I don't know about Percy yet. I cannot think that far ahead."

She was tearing up the flower now. The stem had broken and she was picking off the petals and dropping them one by one upon the rug.

"Listen," she said. "I love you too, Allen. You know that. Aunt Lucille told you that. But, my darling, Papa is old. And he is a good man. A fine, brave man like General Hendrick. He lost Mother. And Percy is in Minnesota. And I love Papa too, Allen. And I cannot break his heart."

Allen was silent for a moment. In his mind's eye he saw the old captain, ancient and palsied, his skin wrinkled, his teeth forever shifting on his shrunken gums, his eyes pale and blinking through the endless drowsy hours of the day. How long can it be? he thought. He is not Methuselah. And then Allen was ashamed of this, ashamed of wishing that Katherine's father would die.

"I know," Allen said at last. "We will not break his heart. But we will think of something."

And in the days that came after, he tried to think, tried to consider the problem in all its facets, but his mind continually wandered and all his hours were filled with a dream of Kate. When he passed the shops around the square, the dressing box and the jewelers and the stores where ribbons and fabrics were sold, he would linger at the windows and pick out gifts for Kate. He could not give them to her, of course. Not until they were married. But he selected watches and bracelets and rings, lengths of brocade and pieces of lace, hats and shawls and a dolman with elegant fringe. He saw her in a million different costumes, bejeweled and handsome, her head held high. Her head covered in an azure silk bonnet with frills and roses sewed inside the poke.

At other times, when he was in the bar before supper, or in the barber shop in the middle of the afternoon, or waiting in the telegraph office early in the morning, he would think of her and try to decide what she was doing at that moment and how she looked, and what book she might be holding in her hand. He was not very good at this. For he had no idea of the routine of the Female Academy; he did not know when the classes met or when they had dinner or when the girls went up to their rooms for their afternoon naps. He could not imagine how the bed chambers were furnished; he could not visualize the curtains or the chairs. But the face of Kate was always there before him, smiling at him from the corners of his mind.

So he thought of her and not of how they would marry; he dreamed of the moment and did not consider how it might be brought about. And even when he was with Katherine, they did not speak of marriage very much. In the afternoons, when tea was served, they would sit as close as possible to the window, and there, with the sunlight on the carpet at their feet, they would look out at all the world that passed below. They were, in a way, prisoners of the academy. Or at least so it seemed to Allen when at last the spring had come and the pods were forming on the maple trees and leaves had begun to fall from the magnolias. He would see other lovers strolling through the town, gentlemen with ladies on their arms, and sometimes a couple in a buggy or a chaise, always with a chaperone to watch them. Then he would wish for his freedom and wish most of all that the blood in his veins were pure.

But even then he did not speak. And at night he did not talk much of their marriage either, though the sight of Kate's beauty often made him sad. To Allen her face and her figure now had a quality of delicacy that he had never seen before. Her eyes gained depth and her skin was whiter, her cheeks more rosy now and her lips more red. Sometimes when he looked at her beneath the bracket lamp, the nerves in his breast seemed to quiver, and he felt himself in the grasp of a great despair. We can never do it, he would think. She will never marry me. And at those times tears would almost fill his eyes. Occasionally the girl from Knoxville would be in the parlor, and she would sing and accompany herself upon the harp. She was in love too, Kate told Allen, and most of her songs were very sad and one of them, Allen thought, was the prettiest song he had ever heard. It was about love that had never come to fruition; or perhaps the love had been consummated and then cut short by death. He was never sure, but he liked to hear her sing it, and he thought the last verses the most beautiful of all.

> *'Tis down in yonder garden green,*
> *Love where we used to walk,*
> *The finest flower that ere was seen*
> *Is withered to a stalk.*

> *The stalk is withered dry, my love,*
> *So will our hearts decay;*
> *So make yourself content, my love,*
> *Till God calls you away.*

It did not apply very well to his own situation, but the mood of it suited the climate of his heart.

So he listened to music and looked at Kate's face, and days passed and they came to no decision. Then, during the second week of March, their time ran out.

One morning, while Allen was eating breakfast, he received a telegram from Anse Weaver, telling him that General Hendrick was sick and advising him to return to Cedarcrest. He went to his room and packed his bags, then went to the square and closed his accounts at all the city banks. On the way to the railroad station he stopped to see Kate.

It was the middle of the morning, classes were in session, and the porter at the Female Academy did not want to allow Allen through the gates. He was an old Negro man, white-headed with most of his front teeth missing, and the ones that remained were yellow and worn with age. He looked at Allen through the iron bars, squinting his eyes and tilting his old, rust-colored face.

"It ain't time," he said to Allen. "Young gent'men cain't come to see the ladies 'fore this evening."

"I know that, Uncle," Allen said. "But I've got to go home. I've got to go a long way, and I want to ask Dr. Cox to let me see her."

"You might, you might not," the old man said. "I open these here gates, and you free to ramble."

"Look at me," Allen said, peering into the old man's face. "Look at me, Uncle. You know I wouldn't lie to you. Get out your key and I'll give you fifty cents."

So the old man opened the gates and let Allen through, and when he rang the bell at the main building, the maid was very much surprised to see him. But she took him to Dr. Cox and Dr. Cox allowed him to spend five minutes with Kate.

They were together, not in the parlor, but out in the hall, which now, in the daytime when no lights burned, seemed dimmer, gloomier than ever. They were not alone. Dr. Cox watched them from his office door, and a few girls passed, carrying books, and they showed how startled they were to see Allen there by not even looking at him, by not daring to turn their heads for fear they would stare. Kate herself was disconcerted—perhaps because she disliked to infringe on the rules, or maybe because of the way she was dressed, in plain gingham and plain black shoes, with a bow of ribbon in her hair. She was holding a piece of paper in her hand and she folded and unfolded it while they talked.

"Kate," he said, "I'm sorry to come in on you like this, but I have to leave."

"Leave?" she asked. "Now?"

"Yes," he replied. "Grandfather is sick and I'm on my way to catch the cars."

"Oh," she said. "I'm sorry, Allen."

He waited a moment, glanced past her toward Dr. Cox, and Dr. Cox in turn looked at his watch.

"I don't know when I can come back," he said.

"No," she replied. "Of course not."

They were silent again. It seemed to Allen, standing there in the hall with Dr. Cox and all the portraits watching, that somehow they had reached a dead end, arrived at a blank, a hiatus in time, and there was no way to see beyond it to the future.

"Darling," she said, and the word sounded very beautiful to Allen, spoken in her soft, mysterious voice. "Darling, I will come home. I will be there by summer if I cannot come before."

"Yes," Allen said. "But till summer is a long time to wait."

"Maybe I will see you before then," she said. "And, Allen, don't do anything. Don't try to talk to Father until I get there."

"I won't," he replied. "I will wait for you."

He left then. He told her good-by and turned away and moved back down the hall and out through the gates, and along the street to the depot and the train. And that afternoon as he rode through the March day, past the tobacco beds still covered against the frost, and across the streams that were high from the rains, and between the same fields and fences he had seen in the winter, he thought of all that Kate had said when they had stood together in the darkened Female Academy hall. And he knew, suddenly, why it was that they had never discussed their plans, why through the afternoons and evenings they had never decided what they would do, or when they would marry, or what Allen would say when he went to the captain and asked him for her hand. She had told him not to see her father, because she must have believed that he would fail. That the old man would say no and order him from the house, and then, until the captain's death, at least, there could be no wedding.

One night at the academy she had given Allen an account of her life at Roseneath. Of how, with the help of her Aunt Lucille, she had come to Nashville and bought new clothes, and how the next year she had come back again, and how always the captain had pouted and fussed and always, at last, had granted her her wishes. Even down to allowing her to live at Lucille's house, but later she had changed her mind and remained at the academy. She did not want Allen to speak to her father, because she believed that he would be refused the favor that she herself might be granted. And thinking of her face, the beauty of her eyes—loving her, Allen believed this too.

So the train went on, and another hour passed and he was home. He had expected to see his father and perhaps old Aaron too, for he thought the general might have sent a coach to fetch him. But they were not there, and Anse Weaver met the cars. He shook Allen's hand and helped him with the luggage, and he appeared the same as ever, except that he looked tired. His eyes were bloodshot and his face was pale.

"Anse," Allen said, "what is wrong with Grandfather?" The wire had told him nothing. Only that the general was sick and that he should come home.

"Wait," Anse said. "We are going there now. Wait and I will tell you in the buggy."

They loaded Allen's trunk and climbed up into the seat. Then they moved off down the old familiar roads, past the courthouse, past the maple trees and the village loafers and the pigeons that strutted near the walk. At the house fronts forsythia was blooming; and hawthorne was red and green down near the fences; in the gardens the tulips had come out. It was too late for the jonquil and crocus, too early for the blue flag and the rose. But the bright, almost yellow leaves hung on the limbs of the poplar and the days had grown longer and the air was very damp. It had not changed much, Allen saw, except for the weather. Except that winter had given way to spring. The horse pulled over a rise and they were on the highway, in the country now, on the road to Cedarcrest.

"Anse," Allen said, "is Grandfather going to die?"

And after a long time Anse said, "Yes, young Hendrick. By next week the general will be gone."

There was another silence, for Allen found he could not speak at once. He had not believed it. He had feared, yes. He had been frightened by the message. He had known that someday the general would have to die, and he had known, too, that the general was old and the day would come soon. But now that it was here, and death was a fact and the fact had been put into words and spoken, he was very sad and tears came to his eyes.

"Young Hendrick," Anse said, "he has pneumonia. And it would kill him whether he wanted to go or not. But he has been here a long time, young Hendrick. He is very tired and he doesn't seem to want to stay around here any longer."

Then Anse told Allen how on the night before, when they were certain that the general had pneumonia and not just a cold, Anse had prepared a mustard plaster and taken it to the room and got ready to put it on General Hendrick's back. He had taken the lamp up close to the bed and unfastened the old man's nightshirt, and he told Allen how at first the general did not appear to know what Anse was doing.

"He just lay there," Anse said, "relaxed in the bed, and let me work on him as if he were weak and simple as a baby."

But suddenly he had tried to stop Anse. He had raised his old, white, fleshless arm and turned to the doctor and said, "Get the boy."

"Sir?" Anse had replied.

"Get the boy," the general had repeated. "Send for Allen and then let me die in peace."

Looking at Allen now, there on the road, Anse Weaver said, "And that is what I did, young Hendrick. And it does not matter. For whatever I were to do, I could not save him."

"Yes," Allen replied softly, "you were right."

He clamped his lips together and put his face into the wind.

But when they got to Cedarcrest, General Hendrick's mind had begun to wander, and he did not know who Allen was. The bedroom was dark, the light was shaded, and there was a smell a little musty, a little sour, that was strange to Allen, and the air was still, for the windows were all closed. The general lay in bed, thinner and older than Allen had ever seen him. He was propped up on pillows, and his breathing was heavy; his chest lifted the cloth of his nightshirt when he took a breath. His eyes were half closed, and one hand lay outside the cover, a skeleton hand with the flesh and blood dried up beneath the skin.

"Grandfather," Allen said. "I am home, Grandfather."

"Who?" the general said, his voice weak. "John?"

"No, sir," he replied. "It is me, Grandfather. Allen."

The old man did not look at him. He did not look at anything, but his eyes remained slightly open.

Then after a while the general said, "Where is Marcus?"

Marcus Hendrick moved up to stand beside the bed.

"He doesn't know me either," Valeria said to Allen. Her voice was tired and she spoke in a slow whisper. "Not always. He is worn out at night. He will be better in the morning."

Then she looked at General Hendrick and said, "He will not wear his nightcap. He ought to wear it, but I can't make him keep it on."

It was no different the next day or any of the days that followed. He never came to himself sufficiently to recognize Allen, and when he spoke it was of Marcus or John or, toward the end, of his wife, who had been dead now for almost thirty years. For two days and a good part of one night Allen sat in the room and watched the general die. His breath grew shorter as the lungs became more involved. He spoke less frequently and became unable to eat or drink, and with his fingertips he plucked gently at the cover.

When he was dead and the body had been washed and bathed, he was brought by some of the slaves into the parlor. At first they did not put him in a casket. They put him rather on a high, narrow bed and covered him with a satin quilt and lighted the candles in the standing candelabra. Now, with his hair combed, his beard trimmed, his face in something like repose, he looked much younger than he had looked when he was sick; but he was old still and his nose and lips were thin. He had come out to Tennessee from Maryland over sixty years before, when there was no village at Gallatin and no hotel at Castalian Springs, and his slaves had quarried the stone and he built his house. He had fought the Indians and his brother had been killed by them; he had fought the British and many of his soldiers had died. He had buried his wife and one son and he had lived to see the other son marry a Negro. And through it all there had been the land; through all of it he had watched while the green tobacco grew. Maybe, as Anse Weaver said, he had finally got tired. Maybe, in the end, he was willing to give it up.

Standing there beside his grandfather's corpse, looking down past the candles at the worn, old face, at the skin drawn taut across the head, the sunken cheeks, the fine and silky beard, Allen thought that perhaps he ought to say good-by. He formed his mouth to speak the word, but he did not speak it. Instead, he turned away and left the room.

◆ 13 ◆

ON THE DAY that General Hendrick was buried, some rain fell in the morning and the sky was overcast till noon. But by two o'clock the sun had broken through and the services were held out on the lawn. Many people came to the funeral. There were almost a hundred of the general's slaves, and fifty or more other Negroes from neighboring plantations; and there were more white people than there were black and these had come from everywhere, from the city and from the farm, from off the river, and from out of the hills, and they had arrived at Cedarcrest in every imaginable kind of conveyance. Parked along the driveway, there were carriages and buggies, chaises and gigs and unsprung wagons, and plantation horses were tethered next to mules. One old lady had come on a jenny, with her barefooted children walking at her side. Some of the people did not speak to Allen; some of them doubtless did not know who he was. But all of them remembered Marcus Hendrick, and they filed by one after another and shook his hand. They agreed that man was mortal and that ultimately God took back what He had given, and among themselves they told many anecdotes concerning General Hendrick. There were two clergymen: the Episcopal priest from Gallatin, to whose church Allen's grandfather had belonged. And a tall, skinny Methodist parson named Brother Gardenhire. He was a circuit rider, and he had often stayed at the general's house. Both of them prayed and read the Scripture. The Freemasons were in charge of the ceremonies at the grave.

When the funeral was over and the congregation of mourners had gone home, Allen packed his bag and got his horse from the stable and rode with his father back to Gallatin. Mrs. Finch, the mother of the Cedarcrest overseer, had moved into the house to chaperone Valeria. But she was very old and known to be hard of hearing and her eyesight was beginning to grow dim. In actual fact she knew little that went on around her, and to avoid gossip Allen decided not to sleep at Cedarcrest. At least, not until Valeria was married or until a more suitable lady or a couple could be found.

"I ought to go home," Valeria said to Allen when he had sent for his horse, and they were standing on the porch. "I ought to go back to Natchez and not put you to the worry of this move."

"No," Allen said. "It is no trouble. But even if it were, you would have to stay here anyway. Grandfather never meant for you to leave Tennessee."

"I know," she said, and tears came to her eyes. Her eyes grew wet and she turned them away, looked out toward the garden and the swans on the lake, toward the sunlight that struck across the hills. She was three years older than Allen. She was twenty-three. And she had buried her mother and father and her husband, John Hendrick. And now she had nursed the general and buried him too. She had seen enough death, Allen thought, to last her a lifetime. She had spent her life losing the people that she loved.

"I know that," she repeated, looking once more to Allen. "And when I marry now, you will have to give me away."

"Yes," Allen replied. And he thought, for who else is there? Who else, now that the house and the land were his?

So he said good-by to Valeria and returned to Gallatin with his father; and every morning after that, he rose early and rode out to the farm, tended his business there, and came back to town at night for a late supper. All things considered, it was not a bad time, though he missed the general very much and was sorry to have lost him. Often when he was riding over the place, or giving orders to Mr. Finch, or visiting in the quarters with the people, he would remember a remark the general had made, or the sight of the old man on his horse, or the expression his face had assumed at moments of pleasure. He would recollect the glitter in the fine blue eyes, the curve of the lips behind the beard, and the memory would fill his heart with sadness. But there was no bitterness; at Cedarcrest there was no desolation. For the trees still lined the gravel drive, and the water ran yet in the creek, and the general's house stood firm upon its hilltop. The things he had built and loved, he had left intact.

But things were different in the town where Allen spent his nights, for Marcus Hendrick took the death of his father very hard; a great deal of his time he spent alone, and when he was by himself he was usually drinking. Often, when Allen had finished supper and was sitting in the parlor with his mother, they would hear Marcus Hendrick moving, pacing the floor of the library up above. And if it were late enough and he had been there long enough, they would hear a chair fall sometimes, or a glass would drop and shatter on the hearth. But he was not always in his library, and he was not always drunk, for often at night he took long walks—or they assumed he did. He was gone for hours from the house, and he would return very tired and go to his bedroom. But drunk or sober, morning or night, his manners remained impeccable; and though he had always been gentle, it seemed to Allen that he was kinder now than he had ever been before, and he treated Lucy with increased tenderness and consideration.

One evening, when Allen came home from the farm, he found Marcus Hendrick sitting in the dining room. There was a decanter of brandy on the table in front of him, and he had removed his coat and loosened his tie and he had put a shawl around his shoulders. Dressed as he was, he looked out of place, a little forlorn in the formal room with the chairs pushed back against the wall and the candles lighted in the silver sockets and the chafing dish cold and polished on the buffet. He was not reading; there was no book or newspaper near his hand. But his face wore a look of concentration: there were wrinkles on his forehead and his eyes were squinting and occasionally he wet his lips with the tip of his tongue.

"It is late," he said, looking up at Allen. "When it got late I wasn't sleepy, so I came down here."

"Yes, sir," Allen replied.

"It is late," Marcus Hendrick said again. "Your mother went to bed and I did not want to disturb her."

"Father—" Allen began and then stopped. He did not know how

to put the question. It seemed to him that he ought to offer something; some comfort to ease his father's grief, some word of encouragement or understanding. But, in truth, he did not know why his father was so sad or why the death of General Hendrick had touched him so deeply.

"You have a letter," Marcus Hendrick said. "It was given to me by mistake, and I brought it home to you."

He handed Allen the pale pink envelope, sealed at the flap with Katherine Rutledge's initials. Allen took it, studied the address for a moment, put it in his pocket, and started to leave the room. He turned away from the table and made a step or two toward the door, then paused and turned once again and looked back at his father.

"Father," he said, "do you know Katherine Rutledge?"

"I know who she is," Marcus Hendrick replied. "I have never met her."

"This letter is from her," Allen said. "I'm in love with her, Father."

He did not know why he said it. Why he chose this moment to tell Marcus Hendrick of his fancy. It was perhaps simply an impulse, a sudden compulsion. Or perhaps looking at his father now, at the lonely man in the cold room, he saw how deeply Marcus Hendrick had loved and how much he had suffered.

"What does she look like?" Marcus Hendrick asked. "Is she pretty?"

"Yes, sir," Allen replied. "She is beautiful, Father."

"I am glad," Marcus Hendrick said. "Sit down, if you are not too tired, and tell me about her."

So he sat down at the table and poured himself a drink and told his father how he had fallen in love with Kate. Told him how on that night in Nashville he had seen her name in the newspaper and how he had written her a letter and how she had looked when at last he met her at the Female Academy.

"And that was the first time you had ever seen her?" Marcus Hendrick asked.

"No, sir," Allen replied. "I saw her once before that. I was out hunting with Anse, and I saw her pass in a carriage."

"And you remembered her all that time," his father said, but this was not a question.

Before Allen could answer, he spoke again. "I know about that. It is a quality of beauty. It stays, it lingers in the mind."

"Yes, sir," Allen said, and he went on with his story, told Marcus Hendrick of the night he had gone to the academy to say good-by and of the boys who had sung in the street when he had left there. He related how he had seen Mrs. Richardson's house and some of the things that Mrs. Richardson had told him. But a good deal of what she had said and most of what Anse had said, Allen left out for fear of embarrassing his father.

When Allen had finished, Marcus Hendrick did not speak at once. He filled his glass and took a sip, then set it down and drummed his fingers on the table. His face had changed very little. If anything, the look of sadness had become more pronounced. The lines in his forehead had deepened. His eyes fell away from Allen's and searched the shadows in the corner near the door.

"Will she marry you?" Marcus Hendrick said at last.

"Yes, sir," Allen replied. Then after a long pause he said again, "Yes, sir. She will marry me sometime. We will work it out somehow, but I don't know when."

"I see," Marcus Hendrick said. "I understand."

He rose suddenly and pushed back his chair. He moved to the buffet where the chafing dish stood, then across to the mantel where a clock was ticking, and once more to the table where he stopped and resumed his seat.

"Allen," Marcus Hendrick said, and his voice was very soft, "Father forgave me, Allen. And he forgave Lucy too, I think, though he never saw her. But he never understood it. Never knew why I had cost him so much pain and brought so much disgrace to his name and his reputation. And I could not tell him, Allen, for I could only have said, 'I love her, Father.' And that would have meant nothing, because many have turned away from love for the sake of honor. Or I could have told him that I did what I thought was right, and that too would have been meaningless, for he would have said that God made the black man black, and the Negro was the son of Ham and marked for slavery. So he forgave me, and there was nothing I could give him in return, no hint of excuse, no word of explanation. He died believing that a whim of mine broke his heart."

"No, sir," Allen replied. "He was happy at the end, Father. You made him content when you came back here to live."

But even as he spoke, at the very instant that the words were on his lips, he knew that they were not so. And Marcus Hendrick did not even bother to deny them.

Marcus leaned forward and looked at Allen, watched him across the decanter and the half-filled glass, and then turned away from the dripping candles. His face was half in shadow, his head tilted to one side, as if he were listening for the sound of a voice, or the noise of a footstep in the kitchen. Then finally he said to Allen, "But it is different with you. You will not only have to forgive me now. You will have to go on forgiving me over and over again, every day, every hour that you live. Or, rather, you will have to forgive us. Your mother and me. Go on forgiving both of us until your life is over. And I do not know how to explain it to you either. But I will try. At least I will tell you how it happened.

"Or I will try to tell you," he said. "For it is hard to see the juxtapositions of life. It is hard to know where the tale begins, or to discover, looking back, just when the die was cast, and few men can say when the seed was sowed to make the harvest. But to start at the beginning, or what must be the beginning, for I can remember nothing else that went before, I must make you understand that the country was different in my day from what it is now. The year that Father built his house, my uncle, whom I never saw, was scalped by the Indians near the creek that runs through Cedarcrest, and even in my own recollection there were Cherokees who raided the stock pens at night, and day or night the doors to the house were always bolted.

"But that is not what I meant to tell, because by that time the Indians were no longer of importance. They were doomed and they knew it, and the movement to the West had already started, and what we saw was the rear guard, the last bitter holdouts against the course of history, the reactionary element that is found in any society. What I do want you to see is that there were fewer white people, and there was much land, surveyed, yes, but not yet cleared, not tenanted; and the courts were quite imperfect then and the laws of the state as we know them now had not been codified. There were great things to be done, Allen. There was land to be got and money to be made, and the country lay before us to be settled. And that is the way we thought of it. Father too. We did not work for freedom or for the nation's glory. Pioneering was a business like any other.

"But that is not all of it. It was not simply the time. Father was already rich. He had been rich before he ever left his place near Baltimore, and there were others too, all men of power and all moved by the same desires, the same ambitions. Jackson, Oliver, Winchester, looking toward the West, searching for more square miles of land, searching for a place on the river to found a city. In a way, they brought me up to be one of them. When they would come to Cedarcrest with their plats and their deeds, the reports from their surveyors in the Chickasaw country and letters from men they had bought in the legislature, Father would allow me to stay up and greet them, and sometimes to sit in the room while they discussed their plans. They were an impressive group in their square coats and ruffled neckcloths; Oliver with eyes set too close together in a face wide at the forehead and narrow at the chin, his whole head shaped like a large, inverted drop of water. And Jackson with a long face too, but with bigger eyes and a squarer jaw, and gray hair that was thick and as long as the mane on a pony. And General Winchester, small, with a brick-red beard and a sallow, almost yellowish complexion, but in spite of this, the handsomest one of the three. They were already at work on Memphis, already buying some of the land, from people who had no claim to it and no right to sell it. For the ground itself, the bluff still belonged to the Chickasaws then, and the incorporation of the city was twenty years away.

"But they were planning, scheming, and one night when they had finished their meeting, Judge Oliver came over and spoke to me. We were in Father's office, and I was sitting in the alcove between the fireplace and the windows, listening to the talk of acres and dollars and of rights to the river that the proprietors meant to reserve. Oliver was the oldest of the speculators, though he was not as old then as I am now, and he had more patience and more experience than the others, and he could see that the founding of Memphis was still far off.

"He got up from the table, and standing with his back to the chimney piece, his coat lifted up to warm his buttocks by the fire, he looked at me out of the corner of his eye and said, 'Boy, what do you aim to do when you leave the schoolroom? What do you mean to make of yourself when you are grown?'

"He had never spoken to me before, except to grunt and frown when he saw me in the room with Father, so I did not know at once what to answer. But in all likelihood he did not intend for me to speak, for he turned immediately to Father and repeated his question.

" 'What are you going to do with him, General?' Judge Oliver said. 'He is almost grown now, sir. He must think of making his fortune.'

"That is the phrase he used. 'Making his fortune.' Said those words with no trace of self-consciousness, and he was being neither facetious nor bombastic. He was Oliver and the time was ripe, and he was not accustomed to thinking in niggardly figures.

"Father was standing near the table, tracing a route across a map with the tip of a penstaff. His hand stopped, and he looked up very slowly and spoke very slowly and said, 'I will make nothing of him, sir—' he emphasized the word *make*. 'He himself has a preference for the law.'

" 'Then encourage that preference, sir,' Judge Oliver replied quickly. 'A man who knows the law is a step ahead of the run of people. I know that from experience, and Jackson will bear me out.'

"Father did not reply, and General Jackson, who was across the room talking to Winchester, started when his name was called, but he did not break off his own conversation.

" 'Come here,' Judge Oliver said. 'Let me show you something, Marcus.'

"He let his coattails drop with a flap against his trousers, and I followed him to the table and looked down beside him at the map. It was a chart of the United States and the western territory, and I remember how each state was individually tinted, and Tennessee was colored a muddy red. Beyond the Mississippi much of the land was white, the color of the paper the map was printed on, but a few rivers were marked there, a few mountains.

" 'Look at it, my boy,' Judge Oliver said, sweeping his hand west across the blankness. 'How many miles do you see there, sir? How many plantations, how many cities will it hold?'

"Once more I did not know what to tell him. It was not ours; nothing that his hand touched was the property of our nation. So far as I knew it would never be, and if it were, it was still full of Indians, not to mention the rattlesnake and the panther. But he had come to the world ahead of me; he remembered when Louisiana belonged to France, and he remembered what Robertson had done to the Cherokees at Nicajack and Running Water.

" 'Look at it,' he repeated when I did not answer. 'It will be ours someday. Not in my time, but in yours. And in all that wilderness one lawyer will be worth a hundred muskets. A good lawyer can settle half a state and never raise his backsides from his chair.

" 'But not only all of that,' he went on. 'It is nearer home, boy.' He did not seem to care now whether I replied to him or not. I do not think he ever listened to anybody else's talk except that of General Jackson. 'Look here,' he said and traced his thumbnail down the Mississippi. At the southwest corner of Tennessee a circle had been drawn in black ink, and under the circle, written in Father's hand, was the word, *Memphis*.

"He pressed his thumb hard against the paper, as if the convolutions of the earth might be changed by the strength of his flesh. 'We will need a lawyer to represent us in Memphis; when the streets are laid out and the houses are built, voting time will come around and our man will have to be there.' He turned away from the table and moved toward the hall where Aaron was waiting with his hat and greatcoat. From the door he said, 'Be a lawyer, boy. Read the books and watch the trials at court, and come to me when you know enough to have some gumption.'

"But after that I did not think much of what Judge Oliver had told me. I took my leisure to get an education; or rather, I pursued the long, the circuitous way to reach the bar. I went to Princeton and the years passed and I was still no lawyer; but neither was Memphis a city, and when I returned and began to read the law in an office in Nashville, the speculation was yet in progress, the last move in the gambit had not been made. Judge Oliver pointed out my opportunity again.

"He invited me to dine with him at the Nashville Inn, and when we were finished, we walked along the street in the darkness by the river, and he talked of Memphis and of how their plans got on; although I expected him to chide me for wasting precious years at Princeton, he did the opposite and congratulated me, and spoke at length of the pleasure he took in classic literature, in Virgil and Homer, in Catullus and Horace.

"It was a night in late April, the evening cool after a warm day, and above us in the clear sky there were many stars. Judge Oliver pointed out the constellation Hercules, and speaking half to himself, almost as if he were musing, he told the story of how Hercules had built his own funeral pyre and then had been snatched from the flames and placed in the heavens. He seemed to be very much moved by the story, though he was obviously familiar with it and had told it over to himself many times. He grabbed up a rock from the ground and threw it in a high arc into the river. After a while the splash came back, faint and far away, and he said in the same detached voice, 'Too stout, too stout and powerful to die; he was greater even than the earth he trod on.'

"Then suddenly he seemed to recollect himself, and he turned to me and said, 'Not yet. We do not need you yet. But we will have our city soon, and you can serve us.'

"I did not see Judge Oliver for a long time after that. And the next year, when Father sold his land in West Tennessee, I put the idea of ever going to Memphis out of my mind. I was admitted to the bar and I began to practice.

"I had done my reading in the office of a lawyer named Seymore Wilson, a fat man with a red face and strong teeth and a jolly manner. He was then around fifty years old, and I knew that he had not been born in Nashville and that he had not been born rich, although he had made a great deal of money in the days before I met him. But I did not know exactly where he had come from except that it was somewhere in the Cumberland hills, and beyond that I can tell you only that he had been an orphan from his earliest recollection, and until he came to the city he worked on a mountain farm that belonged to his cousin.

"Seymore Wilson conducted himself with a kind of obverse pretentiousness that you will discover occasionally in men who are inordinately proud. I call it obverse, for it consisted of a score of peculiarities, idiosyncrasies that he cherished, nourished in the way a mother nourishes her brood. His office, even after I had joined him in practice—for he made me his partner when I was admitted to the bar—was a single room, south of the square on Union Street, and it was seldom dusted and seldom swept and the cuspidor beside his desk was seldom emptied. There was no place for his clientele —which was numerous—to wait, and on any given morning you might have found two or even three of Seymore Wilson's clients standing on the walk outside the office door while he talked to another at his desk inside.

"His clothes had the appearance always of being old, and it was rumored in Nashville that he would bring a coat new from the tailor's and hang it on a tree behind his house and leave it there exposed to the weather before he put it on. His neckcloth was plain and often frayed, and though he was very punctual, he owned no watch.

"I tell you all this, for I know of no other means by which to explain him; his habits were a key to his character, and an asset to him in the pursuit of his profession. He was a great trial lawyer, specializing in criminal cases, and his looks and his homespun demeanor set the jury at ease. But it was not for the sake of winning suits that Seymore Wilson conducted himself in this curious fashion. He could have made a name in the law no matter how he dressed. Rather, I concluded, he wanted nothing in his surroundings to enhance his own personal luster. He was determined that the public should see him and his genius without benefit of luxury or the trappings of success.

"It was 1828 and I was thirty-three years old, when we were retained by a man named Richard Tyree. This was the same year that Memphis was incorporated as a city, but as I told you earlier I had not seen Judge Oliver for a long time, and for equally long I had not thought of West Tennessee. I had become a full partner of Seymore Wilson; I was already well on the way to what the judge had referred to that night as 'making my fortune.' And on the morning in January, when I saw Tyree come through the office door, I had no sense of premonition, no thought, that this case would be any different from all the rest. Tyree was a man of medium stature, clean-shaven, with a round, almost moon-shaped face that from a distance would look forever like a boy's. But on closer inspection you could see that his flesh bore many wrinkles, and his eyes seemed tired and somehow weakened, as if he had been staring too long at a clear blue sky. He stood for a moment just inside the room, gazing first at me and then at Mr. Wilson. Then he took off his coat and hat and hung them on a peg and crossed the room to shake our hands. He wished, he said, to hire us to defend him. He was charged with having killed one of his slaves.

"I will not burden you with an account of all that followed, though even now the trial is etched in my mind down to the last detail. It is enough to say simply that Tyree was guilty. He was not an evil man, but he was quick to anger; he had an ungovernable temper, and he knew this, of course, though to my knowledge he made no effort to control it, even so. In the courtroom he was unable to sit still while the lawyer for the prosecution spoke to the jury, and before the trial ended he was fined for contempt of court. He was, I say, guilty. His groom, whom I never saw, but who was described to me as a mulatto boy, barely twenty, failed one night to rub down one of Tyree's horses, and subsequently the horse took a cold and died. Tyree found the animal when he went to inspect his stables one Sunday morning. From appearance the horse had been dead since the night before, for its flesh was hard, its limbs were stiffened, and a froth of mucus that had formed around its mouth had dried. The groom, who had been whipped already for neglect of duty, had left the premises and hidden in some woods.

"Tyree went into a rage when he saw the horse; he returned to the house and got his gun—a large fowlingpiece loaded with duckshot; he sent to the quarters for some of his Negroes, then he cast a pair of his hounds on the trail of the groom. They found the boy in less than an hour. He was huddled on the ground in the midst of a scrub oak thicket, and Tyree said—oh, yes, he told us the story, all of it, even before Wilson had accepted his case. Tyree said that he could see only the face, round and yellow and set with two round white eyes, peeping out through the maze of black branches at the dogs that were scampering and snapping at his nose. 'Then,' Tyree said, 'he saw me. And he let his eyelids drop and I shot his head off.'

"That is the way he told us that it happened. And there was no reason to doubt him, for who would make up such a lie to tell on himself? It was not strange either that he told us the story, because we could not, of course, testify against him, and it was commonly understood in Nashville that Seymore Wilson knew the secrets of half the free murderers in Middle Tennessee.

"When Tyree had finished, Seymore Wilson leaned back in his chair and fumbled at the buttons on his waistcoat. For a long time he said nothing; he stared at the ceiling as if he were lost in thought.

Then at last he said, 'And you want to be done with your nigger and go scot-free?'

" 'That is the gist of it, sir,' Tyree replied. 'But I am already done with the nigger. I managed that alone. I only need you to keep me out of the pen.'

"Mr. Wilson was disconcerted by this speech. He was himself addicted to the use of irony; but he saved his own performance for the court. His face flushed, slightly but perceptibly; there was a perceptible reddening of his cheeks.

" 'Then to get to it,' Mr. Wilson said. 'Who saw you kill the nigger?'

" 'My people,' Tyree replied. 'The slaves I had brought along to help me track.'

"Mr. Wilson checked them off on the tip of his finger. 'And they can't testify. That's good so far.'

"He leaned toward the cuspidor and spat into it. 'Now,' he went on, 'who beside your niggers knew about the horse?'

" 'My wife,' Tyree said.

" 'That's good again,' Mr. Wilson replied. 'For the same reason. They can't make her testify against you in a court of law.'

"He went on that way, asking questions and listening to the answers, and when he was certain that all the evidence against Tyree was circumstantial, he expressed the conviction that he could win and he took the case. He did win. He had very little to say while the prosecution built its case against his client; he called only character witnesses on behalf of the defense. But on the final day of the trial he plead for three hours and his eloquence won an acquittal for Richard Tyree.

"When all was finished, we left the courthouse together, the three of us—for Tyree came with us—walking along the street toward the Nashville Inn. For the first time in my life I felt shamed before the public, embarrassed to be discovered in the company of Tyree and Wilson, and it seemed to me that the life I had built, all I had worked and striven for, had fallen down in ruins and rubble about my head. I refused to drink with them in the bar of the inn; I declined to break bread with them in the hotel dining room. I insisted, instead, that Mr. Wilson meet me at the office when he had had his meal, and he agreed to do so, though it was against his custom ever to go to his place of work at night. He knew, I believe, what it was I meant to tell him.

" 'Mr. Wilson,' I said when he had finally joined me, 'I do not like to see murderers walking free upon the town.'

"Oh, yes, I began that way, with no preliminaries or courteous preparation. I was young, you see, and though I was familiar with criminal practice, I had never before seen a case which circumstances so little extenuated or where guilt was so black.

"He had dined well and he had used the bottle freely. That was apparent from the set of his eyes and the scent of his breath. But he was not drunk; his behavior was merely deliberate. He stared at me for a moment or so before he spoke.

" 'None does, sir,' he said at last. 'I know of no murderer who goes unmolested on our streets.'

" 'Mr. Tyree is at liberty,' I replied sharply.

" 'And so are you,' he said, 'and so am I, but that signifies nothing. You yourself this afternoon heard the jury. The charges against Mr. Tyree were found to be untrue.'

" 'But I know better!' I shouted, pounding my fist on the top of the office table. 'I heard what he said to you. I know what he did.'

" 'You know,' Mr. Wilson repeated scornfully. 'You know better. You would set your judgment over the legal procedures of the state of Tennessee. That is your privilege for the comfort it will bring you. But the court says he is innocent. I am satisfied to be guided by a court of law.'

" 'Law, the devil!' I replied. 'You have circumvented the law. You have duped the jury with your cajoling, silver tongue.'

" 'This is enough,' he said evenly. 'We are alone here, Major Hendrick—' it had been his custom before to call me Marcus—'and there is no public to obligate either of us to take offense. But alone or not we find our tempers rising. You want to dissolve our partnership, I take it. Well and good then. Let us do so, but no more of this.'

" 'Yes,' I said. 'You are right. I am going to leave, Mr. Wilson. I will move my books and papers in the morning.'

"I rose then and fetched my stick and hat, but just as I reached the door, Mr. Wilson stopped me. He had remained seated behind the desk, his body in the same attitude, his face still bearing the marks of his dissipation. But somehow his features had softened;

he regarded me with the expression a father employs when looking at a child.

" 'Marcus,' he said, 'you are a lawyer. You have spent a decade learning the law, and there are worse things in life than cheating the hangman.'

" 'Undoubtedly there are,' I replied. 'But there are better things too and I must find them.'

" 'You will have to search a long time then,' he said in resignation. 'And in the end you will have to abandon your profession and set out and change the notions of the world. Reconsider, Marcus,' he went on. 'Stay with me, and in the years to come you will see this all with a different eye.'

" 'That is most likely true,' I replied, 'and therefore all the more reason that I should go.'

"I turned away and left without shaking his hand. And that night as I walked back toward my room, I resolved to call on Judge Oliver at his earliest convenience."

⋄ 14 ⋄

So FROM THE BEGINNING he was an idealist, a visionary, as his brother later called him, and he abandoned his law practice in Middle Tennessee and went to Memphis. As he explained to Allen Hendrick that night in the dining room, he did this because he believed that Seymore Wilson had set himself not to live by the law but to circumvent it. "At that time," he told Allen, "the fact that Tyree had taken life, spilled human blood to assuage his own anger did not weigh with me so heavily as the almost abstract consideration that he had broken the law and we had supported and comforted him in the breaking. For I had set myself to live by the law, you see. I had put my faith in what we sometimes call its majesty. And I did not then concern myself with the rightness or the wrongness of the statutes that were written on the books. The law was the law, and to my eyes nothing reprehensible could be done within its bounds. Conversely, all things done outside the law were deserving of censure. It was my final arbiter; the code of Tennessee was my moral strength."

This was what he thought, and he settled down in that wild country where rivermen wore feathers in their hair and tramped the wharf and made their boasts and had their gouge fights; where in a swamp called Pinch Gut the banjos strummed all night in the houses of the painted ladies; and where Indians wrapped in cheap blankets walked the muddy streets. For ten years he represented Oliver, and in between times—when no election was brewing, or when no land was to be bought, or when there were no settlers suing for rights to the wharf or complaining about the price of the ferry —in the off seasons he ran a general store. He sold hardware and dry goods, sugar and cheap jewelry and whisky, and for a long time, as he told Allen later, he did not look beyond the legality of the orders that he received from Oliver. He did not question the ethics of the things he was asked to do.

When candidates announced for mayor of Memphis, Marcus Hendrick made no effort to judge the men involved or what they stood for. He simply waited for the letter that would come from Nashville, and later for the load of whisky that would come by boat, and a week before election he would start giving the whisky away. Or he would settle a lawsuit against the land company out of court —to avoid a public hearing, a taking of testimony; or he would remit payment on a plot of ground if a promising settler threatened to go north or cross into Arkansas.

So time passed, and Marcus Hendrick prospered. But one day in the fall of 1838 a note came from Oliver—economical, succinct, written in a small hand and sealed securely—telling Marcus Hendrick that a railroad was to be built from Memphis to St. Francis, Arkansas, and directing him to buy up land on the right of way. Oliver was as usual beforehand with his information. He had sources close to the government in Washington, and he urged Marcus Hendrick to secrecy and speed, lest the news of the railroad become public and land values increase. "I particularly desire," he wrote, "that you purchase the holdings of a Mrs. O'Connor, whose boundaries are marked on the enclosed plat." He named a figure that Marcus Hendrick should pay: a high figure for a backwoods farm, but a low price for land along a railway.

"I went," Marcus Hendrick told Allen, "to do his bidding. With no sense of compunction, no pangs of guilt, I took the ferry and crossed the river and rode for a day along a small trail through the woods. The weather was miserable. It was November and a hard rain was falling, and the wind blew strong and the water dripped cold from the trees. Late in the afternoon, just as the dusk was gathering, I came upon a clearing and saw the O'Connor house."

He moved through a grove of pin oak and came suddenly to the edge of a large lot, and he saw through the half-darkness a common log house with a dog run in the middle, and the dog there too, a hound that raised its head and sniffed and barked.

"Inside there were two of them," he said to Allen. "One a lady of fifty, perhaps, but very gray and wrinkled and looking considerably older. And the other a boy of fifteen with blond hair and pale blue eyes who came out and helped me with my saddlebags and took my horse. And there was nothing remarkable about either of them. They were simply two people like other people that I had dealt with. You must understand that there was nothing unusual in this situation. The house was poor, but I had been in much poorer houses. The woman was a widow, but I had purchased land from widows before. They fed me, they gave me a place to sleep, but this was what one expected in the wilderness; it was the common, the accepted, thing to do. What happened to me that night was no fault of theirs. It was something that came over me like a spell. It struck me as a disease will take a man; and who, when he is sick, can say exactly where he first contracted the fever, or when the contagion had its first introduction in the flesh?"

What happened to him was that he saw his error, and in the morning he refused to buy Mrs. O'Connor's land. He lay that night on a pallet, thinking of his journey, watching the lap of the shadows on the wall. And suddenly his mind turned back to the past, to the days in Nashville and Seymore Wilson and to the murderer, Tyree, who had paid nothing for his crime.

"I pondered the past," he told Allen Hendrick, "I considered it in all its facets, and it came to me then that even the law with all its ramifications was not enough to sustain a man through life. For if Tyree were guilty of murder, though the jury had set him free, was not Oliver guilty, too, of a kind of theft, even though the purchases of land that he made were made inside the law? And hadn't

I, through all the ten years that I had been in Memphis, been an accomplice to his crime?"

The next morning he did not even make Mrs. O'Connor an offer. He left the deed and the bill of sale in his saddlebag and when he got back to Memphis, he wrote a letter to Oliver and resigned. He quit as representative of the land speculators without anger and without apology, feeling only, as he later told Allen, a sense of loss. A sharp regret for all the years he had wasted, the time he had spent pursuing the ends of the law.

"And yet," he said, "now that I had gained my freedom, now that I was at liberty to search for justice, I did not know at first where to set my sights. It occurred to me that I might go once more into the wilderness and search out Mrs. O'Connor and give her warning not to sell her land. But the chances were that she knew already of the railroad, and the judge had lost his opportunity for profit, and even if this were not so, even if she were still unaware that her land was her fortune, what would I do when I had seen her and returned to my home? I had no long-range project, you see, no goal on which to set my sights. And in all my education, in all the Greek and Latin I had read, whose word was to guide me, what philosophy could show the way? I attempted, after all the time that I had been away from Princeton, to discover a formula by which to live. But I could think only on the one hand of men like Epictetus and Epicurus, who addressed themselves to the individual behavior and, on the other, men like Plato, whose design for a republic seemed to me dictatorial and more evil than the law. So I turned at last to Mr. Jefferson, who was a better classicist than I, and embraced his idea of freedom and equality for all."

He had an idea, an end, a dream to follow. And he began by setting Vernon free. A week after he had come out of the Arkansas wilderness, he called the Negro to his office at the back of the store. It was a small room, poorly lighted even in the daytime, and it was poorly furnished too, with only a table, a lockbox where the accounts were kept, two chairs, and a lantern hung from a beam. Marcus Hendrick remembered this, for he told Allen that in the pride of his increasing wealth he had become ashamed of the office and had meant to refurnish it. He wished on this day, for Vernon's sake, that he had.

"It seemed to me," he said, "that Vernon was to start on a new life, that he was to be born again as the preachers like to say, and I would have chosen more elegant surroundings for his birth. At any rate, I told him to be seated at the table, and I asked him then if he wanted to be free.

"He did not answer at once. He looked at me for a long time, not past me, or through me, as slaves will sometimes do, but right into my eyes. Then he said, 'Free for what? Free to be caught by the paterollers on the big road?'

"He did not understand what I was offering him. He felt that he was being rejected, discharged from his job, deprived of his food and shelter, stripped of the little protection that he now enjoyed. I know you have heard stories of slaves who refused to be freed. Who would not take the manumission paper when it was tendered to them, and who became famous thereby, examples to be used on the stump against abolitionist speakers, and written about to show that bondage is a happy state. Do not believe it; do not think for an instant that they cherished servitude. They simply preferred their slavery to starvation. They needed an owner to keep them from the world.

" 'Not to be caught,' I said to Vernon. 'I would like to have you continue to work for me.'

" 'That suits me,' he replied. 'Make me free and I will find a girl to marry.'

Marcus Hendrick made out the papers and sent them to the legislature. Manumission was granted and Vernon ceased to be a slave. But this, in its way, was like warning Mrs. O'Connor would have been; once it was done, there was no project left to work on, for Vernon was the only Negro Marcus Hendrick had ever owned. "I could see," he told Allen, "that there were many things upon this earth which wanted doing. But I could not be sure what I was suited best to do. I thought of it for a long time. For a week or more I spent my evenings in my parlor, casting about for some scheme that might serve the human race."

Then one night it came to him in a flash, the answer so obvious that he had been unable to see it, the solution so close to him that heretofore it had escaped his view. The next morning he went to the auction block and bid in two single Negro men. One of them was a small, wizened little man named Prentice, about forty years old but looking sixty, who in his youth had been apprenticed to the blacksmith on a large plantation. The other, named Victor, was a hand, younger than Prentice, and tall and very strong. It had been Marcus Hendrick's design originally to buy a piece of land outside of Memphis. His Negroes would clear it, and he would sell the timber. They would plant it and he would sell the crop. And regarding the land as a permanent investment, an expenditure never to be amortized, he would free the Negroes as soon as they had made enough cotton to repay the price he had paid for them at the sale.

This was his plan in the beginning, but when he discovered that Prentice had the mind of a blacksmith and Victor the muscles of one, he set them up in a shop next to his store, and bought a bellows and some iron and put them to work shoeing horses and banding wheels. Then he bought three more Negroes—one a woman this time, for the free Vernon refused any longer to cook—and got his land. Horses shod by his own smithies, pulled loads of timber cut by his own slaves; and he thought, with a touch of irony, that he resembled not so much a New England utopian as he did his father or Judge Oliver, or any other Southern planter who made his plantation pay. But in truth, it was not paying. For in the shop two men were doing the work of one. And on the land where he had no overseer, where he left everything to honor and the slaves' desires and inclination, the work faltered and sometimes was not done at all. After two seasons not a bale of cotton had been made.

So he hit upon another scheme. From the profit he had accumulated running his store, he set aside a thousand dollars. Then he began to study the government money book in earnest, he subscribed to all the Eastern papers, and he became a broker in currency and notes. With the original thousand dollars as the capital, he made the five slaves his partners, shareholders in a corporation. They continued at their own tasks; they did not even know what he was doing. But as his venture in paper succeeded, he set aside the profits to accumulate until he had saved the price of his slaves. Then he intended to set them free and buy some more.

So he became known up and down the river as a visionary fool, a simple-minded philanthropist who had respect for neither land nor social tradition, and occasionally, to visitors in Memphis, he was pointed out on the street. But he gained a reputation too, as a financial wizard, a man who could foresee the failure of a bank, one who, in spite of his indifference to the land, could predict a harvest. He was often consulted by his friends on matters of investment.

That is why, on a day in February, Thompson Jervis came to see him.

Thompson Jervis owned a plantation in Western Kentucky, in Hickman County at the very tip of the state. He was a young man, not over twenty-one or two years old in 1840, but his fame was as great as Marcus Hendrick's, though for a different cause. He had been raised the only child of a Presbyterian elder, a stern man who refused to talk of secular subjects on the Sabbath, who neither drank nor chewed nor swore even mildly and who gave a tithe of all his earnings to his church. He was so crusty and his attitudes so full of brimstone that very few people ever came to see him, and his abhorrence of the world's evil was so great that he refused to let Thompson leave his farm to go to school. He hired, instead, a tutor, a bachelor from Massachusetts, who was, if anything, even more strict than the elder Jervis. Every morning and through the long afternoons they sat in the library: Mr. Primrose, the tutor, tall and thin, beak-nosed and emaciated but adept with a birch switch; and Thompson, the boy, thin too, but short and rather wiry, with black hair and black eyes that glowed with hate. There was no mother. She had died when Thompson Jervis was born.

Marcus Hendrick had heard all this, and he knew too that when Thompson Jervis was eighteen, his father had decided at last to send him to college. Whether he reached this decision from a precocious infirmity, a weariness from having fought the Lord's battle so long against such overwhelming odds; or from a kind of overweening pride which made him think that his mark was on the boy, ineradicable now and Thompson was safe from all temptation: from what motive he sent Thompson to college, Marcus Hendrick never knew. Nor did the old man ever know the results of his moment of weakness. Thompson left early in September for Lexington with only a horse, and a poor one at that, a change of socks in his saddlebags and an extra shirt, but not one cent of money. Payment for his fees and his board had been sent ahead.

He protested mildly to the old elder.

"I will need some money, Father," he said. "I will need to pay for my food along the way." He said nothing about lodging. He was willing to sleep in the woods. The weather was fine and his blood was warm and he enjoyed an outing.

Old Jervis was reading the Bible on his veranda. It was late afternoon, and his eyesight was none too good; but because he was frugal and he believed that God was hard, he had not lighted a candle. He glanced up, blinking his eyes at Thompson, licked his lips, and said loudly, "Look to the Lord!"

"Sir?" Thompson said.

"I have cast my bread upon the waters," his father replied. "I have fed many a traveler who has asked for food at my door. The good I have done will come back to succor you."

And he would say no more, even when Thompson insisted that he ought to be able to pay, able to offer something for a kindness received.

"If you are asked for payment," the old man said, "you must require credit. When you return, bring me an account and I will settle your bills."

The next morning Thompson left to beg his way across the country. And that evening old Jervis was thrown from a horse and killed. Or rather, he was found in the evening, when he did not answer the dinner bell, but he had been dead for a long time. The tissues of his body had already begun to stiffen. His neck had been broken and his head lay over to one side.

They sent for Thompson. The white overseer went himself, tracing him from one plantation house to another, arriving in the morning where Thompson had had supper the night before, pulling up at night where Thompson had eaten dinner. He did not catch up until Thompson had stopped at Lexington. Already the corpse had been out of the ground for a week.

The overseer, a man named Hamilton, a fat, round-faced man who did not ride very well, found Thompson Jervis in a tavern. Thompson had borrowed some money from a fellow student he had met that day.

"We'd better send them word, Mr. Hamilton," Thompson Jervis said. "We'd better send a message telling them to bury Father."

"Send it by who?" Mr. Hamilton replied. "Cain't nobody git there no sooner than you and me."

"I reckon they can, Mr. Hamilton," Thompson Jervis said. "Considerably sooner than I can, for I don't aim to go."

Hamilton thought he was drunk. He looked at Jervis' face for some sign that he was intoxicated. He examined the features, the eyes; he sniffed at the breath. Then he saw that Thompson was not drunk, not even close to drunk, and he saw too that Thompson was not joking.

"It's yo' own daddy," Mr. Hamilton said. "Yo' own pa that give you life and breath and you've got to come back, Thompson, to the burying."

"I appreciate your interest, Mr. Hamilton," Thompson Jervis said courteously, "but this time I don't believe I'll go."

"This time?" Mr. Hamilton replied. "I ain't never heard of it happening to 'ere human man but once."

"No, sir," Thompson Jervis said. "Neither have I." Then before Mr. Hamilton could answer, he said, "Do you have any money?"

"A leetle," Hamilton said. "Two dollars and fifty or sixty cents."

"Never mind then," Thompson replied. "Make a good harvest, Mr. Hamilton. Make a dandy crop. And have Lawyer Frank send me a thousand dollars."

Mr. Hamilton had never had a thousand dollars. Not at one time. He was a middle-aged man, and he had worked hard all his life, but he had ceased expecting to accumulate that kind of money.

"A thousand dollars," he said in disbelief.

"Yes," Thompson Jervis replied. "That much to start on. Tell Frank he will hear from me when I get to New Orleans."

Hamilton left. He took a stiff drink of whisky and returned to his tired horse, resolved that he would not pass the night in Lexington, Kentucky. He felt suddenly that the world, for no reason good or bad that he could think of, had been turned upside down, thrown off its proper moral course by some strange power. All the rules by which he had been taught to live seemed to have been abrogated by Thompson Jervis when he refused to go home and see his father to the grave. But Hamilton was faithful, and two weeks later Jervis had his cash.

He journeyed overland to Louisville, riding the same horse, though he could have afforded better, wearing the same clothes too, and stopping at houses along the way to get his dinner. He traveled frugally, just as his dead father had taught him to do. But when he got to Louisville and found accommodations at an inn, he gave his horse and saddle away to the Negro porter. Then he ordered new clothes and when they were ready, he gave his old suit to the tailor's boy. Before he boarded the packet boat for New Orleans, he had spent a little over four hundred dollars.

He had already begun to be talked about. Already his fame had begun to spread. But by the time the steamer reached the Gulf, he had become a legend, like Mike Fink, or perhaps, more properly, like Jimmy Fitzgerald or Napoleon White. For long before they passed Owenboro, Thompson Jervis sought out the gamblers who had set up in the barber shop—not the gentlemen looking for a friendly game, but the real gentry, the men in black broadcloth and French boots with their golden watch chains draped around their collars. Never before in all his life had Jervis gambled. He didn't even know the rules of the various games. He passed up the poker table and chuck-a-luck cage, and chose that easiest of all ways to commit financial suicide: he played faro, he tried to buck the tiger. Or rather, he did buck it, for three days and two nights without leaving his chair except to go and relieve himself in his cabin. The shop began to fill up with men who were watching; the poker players and the monte dealer stopped to look on. Toward the end an awed hush, a silence as in a church, fell over the crowd. The stewards bringing food and rum punch moved on tiptoe; the barbers folded their cloths and put away their shears. Thompson Jervis leaned over the board, his hair very dark against the green baize, his black eyes watching the dealer pull the card from the box. He had begun to grow a beard, to hide his youth probably, for at that time beards were not in fashion, and he looked a little like old Pharaoh himself, the king of spades pasted on the cloth. And maybe Pharaoh had blessed him, or maybe the queen had. Or maybe after all his years of enforced godliness, the devil at last had marked Jervis for his own. The gambler abandoned his board and left the boat at Memphis. Jervis had won eight thousand dollars. He had broken the bank.

His luck continued to hold good. He gave up gambling; there was no one else on board the packet who wanted to play with him. But when he reached New Orleans, he started a different kind of game. Almost as soon as he stepped onto the levee, before he had even gone to his hotel, he met a young Creole boy named Pierre Clovet. The meeting was accidental, the result of pure chance, just as it had been chance that he chose the faro board and not the monte. Clovet had come to put his sister on a boat for Natchez, and Thompson Jervis asked him directions to St. Charles Street.

Clovet told him and walked a part of the way to St. Charles with him. And if Clovet had been a month older, or if Jervis had taken time to bury his father before he caught the boat, it would have ended there, and in all probability they would never have seen each other any more. But Clovet had just reached his maturity, had just that week come into some money, and he was intoxicated with the idea of the pleasures he was about to enjoy. On their way through the city, they passed the Orleans Ballroom, and Clovet told Thompson Jervis about the Quadroon Balls.

He would have heard of them anyway, of course. He had probably heard of them already coming down on the packet, the *Bals du Cordon Bleu,* and doubtless he would have gone to one, simply to see what it looked like, and to find out if the ladies were really as beautiful as rumor claimed. But most likely it would never have occurred to him that he himself might participate, might dance to the fiddles and choose a woman and show her mother the color of his gold. He would not have thought of this if it had not been for Clovet. But Clovet was almost his own age, dressed very much as he was dressed. Indeed, because both of them were dark and small, Pierre Clovet bore a physical resemblance to Thompson Jervis.

For money, Jervis thought. A man can go in there with money, and talk to the girl's mother and then talk to the girl. He did not know what a house on the Ramparts cost. "That is what you do," Clovet told him. "You buy them a house and furnish it, and keep them in money enough to live well on." He did not know the price of silk or net or beads or even wine or roast beef. But he had eighty-five hundred dollars in his pocket and at home he had three thousand acres and seventy slaves.

"Mr. Clovet," he said, "I told Mr. Hamilton to make me a dandy harvest. I think I'll get me a house on the riverbank too."

So that night he put on his evening clothes and went to the ballroom. He paid his two dollars and passed through the doors, moved between the statuary and up the stairs, to the ballroom proper with its oak floors and its crystal chandeliers. Then he stopped, for he could not believe his eyes. The men, and there were many of them, were all white. There was no doubt of this. They were dressed, if anything, a little better than the people he had met on the boat, and since the music had not yet started, they were moving about, talking and bowing courteously to the ladies. But he only glanced at the men. He stared at the women.

At that moment he would have sworn that some of these too were white. Not all of them, for many were obviously dark, not as dark as mulattoes, not yellow, but golden, with black hair and a very slight broadness of nose and coarseness of feature. But the others, the lighter ones had fairer skin than Pierre Clovet, paler faces than some of the Creole ladies on Royal Street. One in particular attracted his attention. She was an inch or two taller than Thompson Jervis and very graceful, with full lips and a wide forehead and black hair that reflected the candles' glow. He saw her walk across the floor; he saw her stop and turn in his direction. She was wearing a deep green satin dress, short-sleeved and cut low at the neck, and he noticed when she faced him that her waist was rather high. Her limbs were long. And seeing the shape of her arms, the slender wrists, the smooth elbows, and above these, the flesh fuller but not fat, he tried to fancy what the rest of her would look like when the gown and the petticoats had been removed.

"Mr. Jervis," Pierre Clovet said at his side, "would you like to meet her mother, Mr. Jervis? The girl's name is Lucy Martineau."

"Yes, sir," Thompson Jervis replied. "I think I would."

He got his house on the Ramparts. He went the next day to see the old lady—who did not look old. Who looked less than forty, and youthful for that age, but who looked old enough still to be Thompson Jervis' mother. He went to her house at the end of Esplanade; he pulled the bell and waited at the door until a Negro servant came and escorted him down a long passage and across a garden—green and lush and to him exotic, even now in October—and up a flight of stairs to a living room, small by Kentucky standards but large enough. The parlor, the house itself, seemed to Jervis somehow fragile, too lacy, too ornate, trimmed with too many curlicues, loaded down with too much porcelain and damask. A faint perfume seemed to hang in the close, still air.

He was required first to talk about his family. To tell how his father had come out from Virginia in 1815, and then he described his land and the house on it, and at last gave an accurate and complete statement of his total wealth. When he had finished, Mrs. Martineau sat for a long time looking at him as if he were a slave on a block, or as if their situations were reversed and it was she who was, in a sense, making the purchase.

Then she rose, tall and stately, darker than her daughter, but handsome, the same high waist, the same delicate features.

"Go back, monsieur," she said. "You do not belong here. Even now your heart remains in that other land."

"No, ma'am," he replied. "Miss Lucy has my heart."

She put her hand to her throat, to the lace collar that she wore at the neck of her dress. "I will leave it up to her," she said. "To Lucy. But you will have to pay. This is all she will ever have and I fear you will leave her."

He did not see Lucy that day or the day that followed. Mrs. Martineau believed perhaps that the notion would leave him, that he would convince himself of his own folly or blunt his desire on Royal Street and they would never hear from him again. But in the end she was forced to admit him to Lucy's presence.

It was in the afternoon, around four o'clock on a still, wet, foggy day, when drops of water gathered on the green fronds of the garden and dripped noiselessly on the sodden ground. He moved across the flagstones and up the stairway, and along an open passage to another sitting room, smaller and less comfortable than the first. Or rather more completely decorated, the furniture more intricately carved, the hues in the engravings more vivid, the nap of the velvet upholstery more recently brushed.

Lucy was seated near a window. Her hands were folded in her lap, her shoulders were covered in a thin cashmere shawl. The face, the limbs were the same, yet to Jervis, blurred somehow, softened by the fading daylight and the room's shadows. He stood inside the door, and the room seemed filled with the girl's physical presence, with the heat and flavor of her flesh, with the very fragrance of her breath and being. He looked at her, at her lips and the smooth flesh of her neck, at the hands in her lap and the cloth of her dress that draped fully and gave no suggestion of her thighs. He looked at her slippers, embroidered with silver thread.

"Miss Lucy," he said. "I do not know how to begin. I do not know what to say to you, except that you are beautiful beyond anything I have ever seen. If you will have me, I will do what you require."

She made no reply. She turned her head and looked out at the fog, her face placid and almost blank, as if he were not there, or as if the day were bright and she could see out into the garden.

He crossed the room and stood beside her chair. He felt a weakness in his joints, a trembling in his fingers. Beyond this he felt a sharp and urgent longing to put his hand on her shoulder and let it travel down her arm.

"Will you?" he said.

"Not yet, monsieur," she replied. "Don't be too hasty. Sit down, now and let us talk."

But at last she did say yes, and he was free to touch her.

A month later she had her own house on the Ramparts, her own boudoir and her own slaves bought with Jervis' money, and night after night he left the St. Charles Hotel and walked through the damp darkness into the candlelit dining room where she waited. She had a good cook, a woman trained at one of the New Orleans restaurants, who had cost Jervis almost two thousand dollars. The wine was old and the service good, the porcelain was thin and the silverware was polished. But he did not know this. He did not taste or see it. He saw only the hair that caught the light, the play of the silk around her hips, the shoes and stockings, the pearls around her neck. He knew every measurement, every dimension of her figure. Sometimes he would buy her a complete outfit of clothing and become excited in the shopping with the mere thought that the cloth would touch her flesh. He would have the garments wrapped and take them with him, and through dinner he would fidget in his chair with the package on the floor beside him. When they were finished, they would have their coffee served in her dressing room, and there she would change clothes for him, strip off what she was wearing piece by piece, and replace it slowly with the new things he had brought. Then she would drink her coffee and thank him for her clothes and they would both undress and go into the bedroom.

So it went, through the winter, and on into the spring, and through the sultry heat of a New Orleans summer. He called on her sometimes in the afternoons, and on the fine days in March and April they would stroll in the garden where the cool moss covered the stones of the walkway. When they climbed the stairs to return to the parlor, or to sit on the balcony with its wrought-iron rail, he took great delight in letting her go before him, that he might see her ankles as she took the steps. The body, the flesh, which he had seen a hundred times remained for him somehow secret, mysterious beyond any final knowledge, and he longed always to see that which was hidden, to examine once more the parts beneath the cloth.

It was this way even when they did not make love. When his body, his organs, were wearied by the performance, and the tired blood would no longer flow to the sensitive tissue. Even then they would sit with their chairs pushed close together, and his knee would press hers through the material of her dress. Or he would pull up her dress to see her thigh and to stroke it gently with the fingers of his hand. When she went to her bath, he often went with her, to sit in the small, hot room, watching her through the steam that rose from the water, feeling her breasts that were warm and slick with soap. For him the act was never finished; it prolonged itself day after day, month after month. Consummation served only to feed his desire, and when he lay back on the sheets, exhausted after his passion, a part of him still remained beyond satiety, and he trembled when her hips brushed against him in the night.

His grand passion was never diminished, the heat of his ardor never cooled. But all around him the life of the world went on. In the city, business flourished and the banks were open every day. There was cotton in the warehouses, and there were ships to be unloaded in the port. From time to time he got letters from Kentucky, from the lawyer, Frank, at first, discussing the estate, but later from Mr. Hamilton asking directions. Should a certain field be planted in pasture or corn? Should some of the stock be sold? Should he clear one of the fields and sell the timber? Jervis answered all of his letters with the same reply: do what you think will be best for the land and make the most money.

But they began to annoy him, these messages from home. He found himself less and less able to forget all the years that had gone before, the mornings and the afternoons in the library with his tutor, the evening meals when his father had quoted the Scripture and questioned him on the lessons of the day. He did not love old Jervis' memory any more than he had loved old Jervis when he was alive. But he could not control his own recollections; not even his love for Lucy could crowd the past with all its images out of his brain. He thought of the land and the trees and the house. He remembered the old man and the way he sat his horse, the way he held the Bible when he read on the shadowy porch.

Then, in the fall, after Jervis had been in New Orleans for a year, an itinerant artist came through Hickman County, Kentucky. He was a portrait painter by profession, and he called at the Jervis house looking for subjects, expecting to do the lady, or the master, or perhaps a canvas of two children, but there was no one home. No one living in the big house, but as he turned to leave, Mr. Hamilton came up the driveway. Mr. Hamilton, who himself would never be painted, who would die and leave no memento, not even a daguerreotype for his children to cherish, conceived a notion. He commissioned the painter to make a picture of old Jervis' grave. When it was completed, he posted it to Thompson.

It arrived in New Orleans, no miniature, but a two-by-three-foot landscape, the canvas held taut in a wide mahogany frame. It was not a very good painting; it lacked perspective and the colors were rather drab. The grave, however, was visible for what it was, and the name on the stone could be read: Lucius McClintock Jervis and the dates and the inscription from St. Luke. It was poorly done and highly sentimental. The artist had put in a willow tree where none existed, and a few brown maple leaves were scattered on the sod. But it served Mr. Hamilton's purpose. It was a reminder to Thompson Jervis. Kentucky was still up the river and his father lay buried there.

When Thompson had unwrapped the picture and set it up against the wall of his hotel room, he looked at it for a long time and thought of old Jervis and of himself and of the deprivations of his youth. He considered all that he had endured during the first seventeen years of his existence, and now, as he had never done before, he turned his thoughts to the future, to the long decades that lay ahead. To the time when he would be forty and then fifty, and, if he were lucky, sixty, and with each changed digit, an added sluggishness in the blood, a slow mortification of the sentient flesh. Maybe, after all, there had been something to the rules his father had lived by—some value or virtue or even pleasure that he had not seen. He was not afraid of hell. He was too young for that, or at least too young to be scared of damnation for very long. And he had no active thirst for Christian glory either. But he felt a little tired, a little wary. Already his good fortune, his luck, had held too long.

He left the picture propped against the wall of his hotel room, and one afternoon when he was not with Lucy, he met a man he had known since he was a boy. Or rather, the man, whose name was John Murdock, sought out Jervis and they had a drink together in the St. Charles bar. They did not talk about anything very important, and Jervis did not speak very much at all. He simply listened while Murdock rambled on about Kentucky, about deaths and births and marriages and the state of the land.

"Are you married?" Jervis asked.

"For two years," Murdock replied. "I have a boy, and we're going to have another baby."

"Children," Jervis said dreamily, wonderingly. "A boy."

He took a drink and squinted at the bottles on the back bar.

"Does it still snow in Kentucky?" Jervis asked. "I mean did it snow last winter?"

"Yes," Murdock replied. "It snowed."

"Yes," Jervis echoed.

He remembered the whiteness of the snow in the sun, and the glittering branches of the leafless trees and the smoke that rose in the clear, sharp air from the quarters. The smoke dark against the pale and distant sky, and beyond the smoke the last flight of geese above the marshes.

I will have to see it one more time, he thought. At least I will have to go back there for a visit.

⬦ 15 ⬦

WHY DID HE LEAVE HER? He could not have said, not then or ever, though he knew that it was not simply because of the picture, or because of his conversation with John Murdock, or even because of the memory of home that came to him so sharply there in the St. Charles bar. There was something beyond all this, some mark, some cast of his disposition that had been made by the old man, buried now, and the tutor who had gone home to New England. He was not strong, not stalwart in the face of temptation as Lucius McClintock Jervis had always been, but as things turned out, he was not quite a sensualist or a Creole either.

He left New Orleans and returned to Hickman County, and three months later, in February, he rode down to Memphis to call on Marcus Hendrick. He made the journey alone through West Tennessee with ten thousand dollars in gold in his saddlebags, and when he entered the store, his face looked somehow familiar to Marcus Hendrick. Marcus Hendrick felt that if he searched his memory, he would be able to call his visitor's name and say where he had come from, and ask about the members of his family. He himself, Marcus, was standing at the back of the room, feeling the end of a new bolt of denim, and he examined Jervis, who had paused inside the door. The dark eyes and the black beard, the heavy brows and the little hands and feet. Then it came to Marcus Hendrick that he did not know this man but that his visitor resembled a picture he had often seen: the face that was printed on the king of spades.

Thompson Jervis told Marcus Hendrick his story. Not all of it, of course, not even, in a way, the most significant part, the passion that had kept him down the river for a year. But he told some of it. There in the plain office where Vernon had been given his freedom, under the lantern that hung from the beam, surrounded by the lockbox and the ledgers, he told Marcus Hendrick how he had talked to Lucy's mother, and how he had bought Lucy a house, and how he had abandoned her to come home to Kentucky.

It was very difficult for Marcus Hendrick to understand what Thompson Jervis told him. He had never, to his knowledge, seen an octoroon. He had never been to New Orleans or to a quadroon ball, and he had never even known a woman who was another man's mistress. In a city like Memphis, or even one the size of Nashville, there were respectable women and there were the others, the girls in the jungle or in Pinch Gut down beneath the bluff. Nobody he had ever heard of would give a bag of gold to a whore. He did not understand, but he was sorry for the woman, perhaps because she was legally a Negro and he had enrolled himself in the Negro's cause, or perhaps he felt pity because he had a tender heart.

"Mr. Jervis," he said, "why did you come to me?"

"You have a reputation, sir," replied Thompson Jervis.

And so have you, Marcus Hendrick thought, but he did not say this. "Oh?" he uttered, making no commitment.

"You are said to be able to make money, Major Hendrick," Thompson Jervis went on.

And the same thing is said about you, Marcus Hendrick thought, remembering how successful Jervis had been at faro. But Marcus did not say this either.

Jervis rose and walked across the small room to the window. He stood there in silence for a moment looking out at the blacksmith shop where Victor and Prentice worked.

"This is all I will ever be able to give her, Major Hendrick," he said. "But if you will take the job, I will pay you to invest her money."

"I will do it, Mr. Jervis," Marcus Hendrick replied. "But I will require no pay."

So it was settled. Marcus Hendrick went to the courthouse and made a bond; he gave Jervis a receipt for the money. Then he set to work, figuring and trading, as he had been doing now for a year with his own funds. As the spring came on, his business prospered. There was much travel up and down the river, and when each boat called at Memphis, there were always a few passengers anxious to have their money changed. He had a good location, and in Memphis he had no competition. The New Orleans notes he bought from a man returning to Cincinnati he often sold the next day to a traveler going South. Near the first of April, without touching the original capital, he was able to send five hundred dollars to Lucy Martineau.

Then came the shock, the great surprise, the letter he had never dreamed of getting. Even when he saw the envelope, sealed with a pale amber wax and addressed in light blue, almost violet, ink, he did not guess that it came from her. It had not occurred to him that, being a Negro, she would be able to write. Sign her name, perhaps, and read a little, but certainly not spell, nor would the penmanship be much beyond the scribbling of a child. Yet it was from her, and this is what it said:

Yesterday I received your letter with its generous enclosure. May I take this opportunity not only to thank you for the present favor but to express the boundless gratitude I have felt toward you since Mr. Jervis told me what you were doing in my behalf? In our world kindness is more rare than any jewel, and therefore more welcome when it is found. Your own kindness has exceeded Mr. Jervis' description of you, to say nothing of my own hopeful expectations and sanguine desires.

I pray daily to my patron, St. Agnes, for your comfort in this world and your salvation in the next. This, I believe, is a liberty your generosity will allow me, regardless of your own creed and beliefs.

I remain, sir, your most grateful beneficiary,

Lucy Martineau

For a long time he thought his eyes deceived him, and then for a long time after that he could not believe that she herself had written it. It had been composed and written for her, by a friend perhaps, or even by a priest. And yet, who else, beside one who had lived as she had, would put her thanks precisely in that way? It seemed to Marcus Hendrick that the letter was at the same time resigned and hopeful, experienced in the uses of the world and yet naïve. He tried to recollect what Jervis had said about her, what description he had given of her background and her education; and he discovered that Jervis had told him very little, except to discuss his relationship with Lucy and to give an account of his meeting with her at the Quadroon Ball. For the first time he tried to see her in his mind's eye, to decide what such a creature as this might look like, but no image would come. There was no way of knowing, no way for him to tell, beyond going there and seeing for himself.

And he did go there. But not immediately, not at once. He waited, rather, with an unbridled, galling curiosity, until he had enough money to send her another check and to receive another note of thanks, as literate and as tenderly grateful as the first. Then he compared the two letters—they were written by the same hand— and waited again and sent another check, and got another answer. Sometimes at night when he fingered the heavy paper, looked at the seals and the violet ink and the little flourishes with which her name was written, he felt that he was very close to her, that, unseen, she lingered with him in the room. For he was romantic. He was an idealist and he was past forty and he had never been in love. But in his saner moments he knew that the presence was only the scent of perfume on the paper and the working of his imagination which would not be still.

He made inquiries. When he dealt with passengers from the boats, he asked questions about the city at the end of the river, and slowly, subtly, he thought, he would bring the talk around to the Quadroon Balls. Many of his customers had been there, and most of them were willing to talk about it; but what they said did not tell him what he longed to know. For it was all simple, physical description, accounts of the ballroom with its terrace and its statues, recollections of the golden beauty of the girls.

"But where do they come from?" Marcus Hendrick asked one of the travelers: a man from near Louisville who had red hair and a thin, red face.

"Bastards," the redheaded man replied. "Bastard girls. You take one of them to be your mistress, and when the time comes, she takes her daughters to the Quadroon Balls."

"Are you sure?" Marcus Hendrick said. "Could you really do that?"

"Why not?" the man said. "They're niggers, you know."

Niggers. The word seemed to hang in the circuits of his brain, to vibrate there like a voice in an empty room. Once, in the old, dead days of his youth, he had known the difference in the races. The sons of Ham had faces that were black. And later, when he had practiced law with Seymore Wilson and then represented Oliver here on the Chickasaw Bluff, he had known that a slave could not testify in court, could not own real estate, could not even be freed without permission of the legislature. And until that day when Thompson Jervis had come into his store, he could look out his window at Victor and Prentice or go out to his land where his other slaves worked and say to himself: *here, this is the answer. Freedom leads to justice and justice is the alpha and the omega. Justice is all.* But now he knew of freedom where there was no justice; he knew of Negroes whose faces were not black. He knew he would have to go and see it, look at it with his own two eyes, if he never did anything else under God's bright sun.

He went to see it, not the Orleans Ballroom, or the *Bals du Cordon Bleu,* but the woman whom Jervis had left in the house on the Ramparts. Went in all innocence, believing that he might find her simply by inquiring on the street or knocking on a door or two in her general neighborhood. He began at his hotel by inquiring at the desk.

"I am looking," he said, "for a lady named Lucy Martineau."

"Ah, yes, Major Hendrick," the clerk replied. He was a medium-sized young man with brown hair, brown eyes, and a short mustache. "Is she a Miss Martineau, sir?" he went on. "Does she live with her father?"

"She lives alone," Marcus Hendrick replied. "She lives on the Ramparts."

The clerk stared at him in consternation. The brown eyes grew wide to show a full circle of white around the iris, then narrowed again and finally turned away.

"Perhaps you are mistaken, sir," the clerk said.

"No," Marcus Hendrick replied. "The Ramparts. I am sure of that."

"Major Hendrick," the clerk said. "Don't go there. You will have a duel on your hands if you are discovered. No woman is worth a bullet in the heart."

"Tell me where it is," Marcus Hendrick said. "I will risk it."

And the clerk told him and he set out on his way.

He moved toward the river to the Ramparts, walked through the quiet, warm afternoon to the row of houses that lay silent and shuttered in the sun. He stopped at a corner and looked around, walked a few feet and stopped again, and at last saw an old colored man standing in a doorway.

"Uncle," Marcus Hendrick said, "can you tell me where to find Miss Martineau?"

The old man stared at him blankly.

"Miss Martineau," Marcus Hendrick repeated, speaking louder.

The Negro nodded. *"Oui,"* he said, *"je connais Mademoiselle Martineau."*

Not quite this, for it was a patois that he spoke, not the pure language. But this is what Marcus Hendrick understood him to say, and he caught the meaning.

"Où est chez Mademoiselle Martineau?" Marcus Hendrick asked.

"C'est là," he replied and pointed up the street to another doorway.

Marcus Hendrick went where the man had directed him, and knocked lightly on the panel with the head of his cane. He rapped against the damp, painted wood, and the sound came back to him hollow, like the tapping on an empty box, and after a long time there were footsteps along the passageway inside. It was a Negro woman this time, a girl really, with a dark, wide, shining face, and her hair wrapped in a clean white headcloth. She left the door on its chain and peeped around it.

"*Chez Mademoiselle Martineau?*" Marcus Hendrick asked.

Her eyes grew wide as those of the hotel clerk had done. Her mouth fell slightly open.

"Yes, sir," she said at last.

"Is she at home?" Marcus Hendrick asked.

"Yes, sir," the girl said again. For she was not that kind of servant. She had been trained for the Ramparts, where chance visitors never called.

She did not offer to let him in. She continued to stare at him around the edge of the door, her face still puzzled, the edges of her teeth very white behind her lips.

"Here," Marcus Hendrick said, taking out a card. "Give her this and ask her will she see me?"

The door closed, the footsteps retreated back down the passageway, and after a while she returned and let him in. She came back and held the door open for him to enter, and led him without a word into the garden and through it and up the stairs to the balcony and then along this to another door and stopped. He waited but she did not open it.

"Here?" he said.

"Yes, sir," she replied and walked rapidly away.

So undaunted, or at least willing to try once more, though he felt like a man not in another country but on another planet, he knocked here, gently with the knuckles of his hand.

"Come in," a voice said, and he entered.

He was in the presence of Lucy Martineau.

It was a long, rather narrow room, with tall, shuttered windows that reached the floor and green drapes and wide velvet valances which were also green. The fireplace was carved marble, and above this was a mirror, heavily carved and gilded, and before the fireplace a high-backed love seat and a green chair. In one corner there was a small rosewood piano, and across from it a marble-topped table. On the table was a vase that held a rose.

He saw all this, but not before he saw the lady—Lucy Martineau in an afternoon dress the color of the amber wax she used to seal her letters. Because the shutters were drawn against the heat, there were candles burning in the chandelier, and her hair caught the light, shone almost purple as she turned her head and smiled at Marcus Hendrick. Her lips were full, her nose was thin, and her wrists looked very slender beneath the undersleeves of the pale ivory lace.

"Major Hendrick," she said. "Please sit down, Major Hendrick."

"Thank you," he replied. And after she was seated, he lowered himself carefully into a chair.

He remained with her that first afternoon for thirty minutes, a half-hour in that parlor where the candle glittered on the golden picture frames and threw shadows on the deep pile of the rug. He sat and talked to Lucy about his journey downstream, about the weather in New Orleans and the narrow New Orleans streets, and about the architecture of the house she lived in. He was aware of her beauty, acutely conscious of her smooth forehead, the line of her neck, the delicate articulation of her fingers. But he was fascinated too by her turn of phrase and the quality of her voice that was slightly foreign. Toward the end of his visit he noticed a book on the table at his side, a paperbound copy of a tale by Stendhal.

"Do you read French?" he asked.

"Ah," she replied. "As well as I read anything. I am not very learned, monsieur, I read only novels."

It seemed very sad the way she said it. There was a wistfulness in her tone that touched his heart.

How many novels must she have read, he thought, for what else could she do? On Sunday mornings she went to Mass. Once a month she left the house to see her mother. She had told him this. But through all the long days in between, only Stendhal and a little Balzac, only the books and the ticking of the clock.

"Do you read English?" he asked. "If you read English I will bring you some more novels. I would not trust myself to select one in the French."

They were his first gifts to her, leatherbound copies of the old English stand-bys, *Tom Jones* and *Pamela, Ivanhoe* and *Pride and Prejudice.* He gave her the books he had read as a boy, and many more which he had never gotten round to. He wrapped them in paper and tied them in ribbon and presented them to her with his card inside. And then along with the books, a bunch of roses, a box of candy, a bottle of perfume.

But he was not in love with her. Not yet. Or at least he did not recognize it as love, this great pity that he felt for her predicament, the pleasure that he took in being at her side. When they were together in the afternoons, for he did not see her in the evenings, she would sometimes play the piano for him—Mozart and Bach mostly, but occasionally a French folk song, which she would sing. There was one in particular that Marcus Hendrick liked very much, a slight thing about a girl and a shepherd boy and a piece of cheese and a bottle of white wine. He would often ask her to perform it for him and it became a kind of joke between them, his preference for this over a fugue or a minuet.

"Ah," she said one day when she sat at the piano, "when I was in school, we were not allowed to sing songs like that. I learned it from a girl from Tours and we got scolded for singing it. The sisters were kind, but they were very stern."

"Tours," Marcus Hendrick said. "The girl was from France?"

"Of course," Lucy replied. "It was in France, Major Hendrick. A convent near Poitiers."

To him, somehow, this was the greatest shock of all. It moved him more deeply than the letters she had written, or the sound of her voice, or the sight of her beauty when the candlelight struck her hair. For what had it brought her, this journey across the waters, this preparation for maturity, made in another land? Where were her classmates now? Where was the girl from Tours? The girl whose voice had joined Lucy's near the convent wall? It had not been long ago. She was not yet twenty. But her life, her happiness, was passed.

Turning to her, looking down at her face, at the dark eyes and the sensitive nose, the nostrils that quivered with her breathing, he said, "Why, Lucy? Why did you come back here?"

"It is home, Major Hendrick," she said simply. "I did not belong in Poitiers once I had finished school."

"All right," he said, "but why the rest of it? Why the *Bal*, why Jervis, why this house?"

"What else?" she replied. "If not this house, my mother's, which is like it."

She rose and moved away from the piano, over to the mantelpiece where a pair of Sèvres vases flanked the gilded mirror, and she picked up one of these and held it in her hand.

"Major Hendrick," she said, "they know who I am. All of them, all the men in the city, all the world. My name is in the record, the black book at the courthouse, so even if they did not know and could not tell by looking at my features, I am still known to be a free woman of color. There is still the 'F.W.C.' written after my name."

"Then go somewhere else," he said. "There is no black book in Philadelphia, none in New York."

"And what do I do?" she asked. "How do I live when I have gone there?"

He could not answer this. What, indeed, could she do, this single girl who had no friend to look to? He saw it now, as clearly as he would ever see it. He remembered stories he had heard, true stories of Negroes who had been freed and who had gone to the North and starved to death with their freedom. Perished because they had not been prepared, because nobody had taught them what to do to find work in the city.

"My dear," he said softly, "is it such a terrible thing to be a Negro?"

She said nothing.

"I mean," he went on, "there must be people you could marry. These unions," he said, pointing at the street outside, "these arrangements, like you yourself have made, produce boys too as well as girls. There are free men of color."

She set the vase on the mantel and let her hands fall to her sides. She was wearing a blue silk dress and there was a slight rustling of the cloth as she moved once more, walked to the center of the room, and stood there for a moment, gazing round at the furniture and the walls. At the velvet drapes and the green chair, at the love seat and the carpet and the marble of the hearth. Her eyes lingered for a moment on the silver tray where their coffee cups were sitting, then moved to the piano where she had sat to sing her song, then back to a Dresden figurine on a rosewood table.

"You ask too much, Major Hendrick," she replied softly. "Oh, monsieur," she said, "you are harder than the priest."

He took her hand and held it for a moment; he said good-by to her as gently as he could. Then he moved quickly down the passage and across the garden and through the door into the street. As he walked through the red, sultry twilight, along the street that was busy now, crowded with servants who had been out to shop, and gentlemen on their way to their nightly pleasure, he thought over the words she had said to him there in the house. Too much. He had always asked too much. Too much honesty from the lawyer, Seymore Wilson, too much charity from Oliver, who dealt in land. And too much from all the Negroes too, from Victor and Prentice, and the ones who were clearing his timber, too much from Vernon, even now that he was freed.

Twenty years later, in Gallatin, he sat at his dining room table with a glass of brandy in his hand. And he said to Allen Hendrick, "I saw then, for the first time, how long was the road that led a man to justice, and how difficult and devious was the way. There in the first starlight of a summer evening, there in that city where evil seemed to breed upon itself, I thought of them all, and I forgave them, each one in his turn. I forgave Seymore Wilson for his devotion to the law, because even an imperfect law is better than none to live by. And I forgave Judge Oliver for wanting to buy Mrs. O'Connor's land, because he had built a city which would survive when both of them were gone. I forgave Jervis, because I had seen Lucy. And I prayed that in the end I might find forgiveness for myself. For all my blindness and all my folly. And for all the uncertainty that attended what I meant to do.

"I turned around and walked back to the Ramparts, knocked again on Lucy's door, and was admitted to see her. She was sitting in almost complete darkness. There was only a single candle burning near the door. But I could tell that she had been crying. I could see the stains her tears had left on her face.

" 'I have come back,' I said. 'I have something to tell you.' I began to pace the floor and my shadow moved with me, cast long across the rug by the feeble light.

" 'I am past forty,' I said. 'I am old enough to be your father. When you were a girl singing songs at Poitiers, I was past my prime. But I have learned to love you and respect you more than any living creature, and I am here now to ask you to be my wife.'

"She said nothing. For a moment she remained immobile, rigid as a stone statue or a figure in the window of a church. Then she raised both hands to her face and hid her eyes from me.

"'Will you marry me?' I said.

"'No,' she said and her voice was muffled. 'No, Major Hendrick, I will not.'

"'Why not?' I asked. 'Can you not learn to love me? Can you find no regard for me in your heart?'

"She replied only, 'I cannot marry you.'

"I sat down next to her and put my arm about her waist.

"'Lucy,' I said. 'Is it because they say you are a Negro?'

"'I am a Negro, Major Hendrick,' she said. 'My name is on the record, it is in the book, and I cannot marry you.'

"'Is that the only reason?' I asked.

"'No,' she replied.

"And I knew what she was thinking. She was remembering Jervis, who had bought the house we sat in now, and she was refusing my proposal because she could not come to me in her maiden purity.

"'Lucy,' I said, 'we cannot change the world. I have tried to change it, and I will continue to try. But all the old evil has been with us so long now, it will take a hundred years to set things right. It will take two hundred, or three hundred or maybe a thousand years, and we will be gone then and our bones decayed. But we will do what is in our power. We will salvage what we can. If you marry me, then you will be one Negro who no longer has to live like a Negro. You will be one quadroon or octoroon who can forsake this life and place.'

"She rose and pulled away from my grasp and walked quickly to stand near the door where the candle flickered.

"'Oh,' she said, 'you ask too much again. Not of me this time, but of yourself.'

"'No,' I replied. 'Whatever I ask is not too much. Whatever I shall require of myself is nominal. It will be nothing compared to being deprived of you.'

"I moved to her side once more.

"'I love you, Lucy,' I said. 'I love you and I cannot leave you now.'

There in the dining room at Gallatin, he paused, delayed in the telling of his story to blow out the candles and to fill his glass one final time. It was daylight, though the sun had not yet risen, and outside a rooster had begun to crow.

"Oh," Marcus said, "I looked into the future. I knew of some of the happiness to come and some of the pain. I knew of the rightness of my intention and of your mother's virtue. But I could not know everything. I could not foresee it all. I could not know then about you or about Katherine Rutledge. And I never expected to see Cedarcrest for the rest of my life."

He hesitated for a moment.

"Allen," he went on, "it is like that always. Life is a labyrinth and a man's direction is doubtful, and every pleasure has its dregs of pain. I married your mother because I loved her. But I would have married her anyway, whether or not I had loved her, because she deserved an existence nobler than the one she led. But I am not sure that I gave it to her, for who recognizes her nobility now? And where is her happiness? And where was Father's for the last twenty years?

"And now you," he said. "You and Lucy. She made me bring you here, Allen. She cast herself into the lion's mouth that you might prosper. And her hope was realized when Cedarcrest passed to you. All her dreams, her wishes, seemed once to have come to fruition. But they will turn to ashes if you must have a broken heart."

"It is not broken yet, Father," Allen Hendrick said softly.

"And God grant it may never be," Marcus replied. "Not only for your sake but for hers."

◈ 16 ◈

DURING THE SPRING that followed General Hendrick's death, Allen did not see Katherine, although he thought of her most of the time and wrote to her often. He did not feel that he should go far from Cedarcrest as long as Valeria continued to live there, and Katherine was unable to get leave from the Female Academy. Or at least these are the reasons they gave themselves in the letters that traveled between Gallatin and Nashville. Late in April, two days after Marcus Hendrick told his story, Allen wrote to tell Kate that the tobacco at Cedarcrest had been set—a little early because of the weather's moderation—and that the river ran high beneath the bluff and that the chickens at Roseneath were well cared for. He reverted to their old, original joke, which was no longer funny, but somehow precious to them, and then in the final paragraph, he said:

> *More than anything else on earth I should like to see you. But I cannot come now for a variety of reasons. As you know, Valeria is alone at Cedarcrest, except for the company of Mrs. Finch, and though I have no apprehensions as to her safety, I feel it my duty, if only as a host, to be near her each day and to offer her my poor society. Beyond this, Father is much disturbed by the talk of war. He fears secession on the part of the Southern states, but at the same time he hopes for the nomination and election of a strong emancipation man. At this juncture his strength seems none too great; he is deeply moved by Grandfather's death, and the state of his health is a source of concern to my mother.*

He wrote this, put a period at the end of the line, and looked off at the wall and scratched his chin with the penstaff. He had never before mentioned his mother to Kate, and for a moment he was mildly surprised that he had done so now. It was as if the word had formulated itself in some secret part of his brain, as if his hand had written it, not by an act of will but through some curious instinct. He was not conscious of feeling differently about his mother, now that his father had told him of her past. Indeed, in a way, he did not feel differently, for he had always loved her and admired her beauty and respected her talents. Even in the early days in Memphis, the hard weeks that had followed the disclosure by the man from Arkansas, he was content to kiss her when he came in from the store, he was secure in her presence when supper was finished and the hour came for the light in his bedroom to be put out. He had always loved her, but with a kind of innocence, and though it pained him to admit it now, with reservation. He had loved her privately when the door was closed, when the blinds were drawn against the world outside; he had loved her secretly in the fair light of day, but with a love to be cherished darkly and always hidden. He had been ashamed not only of her but to a lesser extent of his father too, and it shamed him now that he made the discovery.

On that night when he had tried to say good-by to Kate, when he had returned to the St. Cloud Hotel with the sound of the boys' serenade ringing like a condemnation in his ears, Anse Weaver had said, *Look at yourself in the mirror.* And he had replied, *I have done that. It is being a nigger. I cannot tell you why.* And Anse Weaver had said, *No. Believe the looking glass, young Hendrick.* If he had not believed the looking glass, he had nonetheless wanted to believe it, and the fact that he did not say good-by to Kate, that he returned to her, proved that he must have believed it in his heart. And if he were not a nigger, then why was his mother a nigger, though her hair was dark and her skin not so light as his? And if she were not a nigger, then what was a nigger, and what difference existed beyond the shadings of the flesh? Two nights before, Allen Hendrick's father had said, *When I was young, I knew the difference in the races. The sons of Ham had faces that were black.* He had said this, and Allen understood that Marcus Hendrick now rejected this distinction. Yet, the difference was there, existed for the eye of man to see. There were those like Anse Weaver and the general, now dead, who were white and read Latin and walked with their heads held high. And there were those like Ben Hill and Aaron and Vernon who were not white and whose pride ran subtly beneath the surface.

There were many questions that he could not answer, but his train of thought brought him back to a paradox. He returned to the dilemma that was forced upon him by his mother's attitude: she had chosen for him not the way of his father, the rebellious emancipator who longed to change the world, but that of the old general, the man of power and of human property, the symbol of the persecution which had marred her life. Why had she done this? He could not truly say. But he guessed that she had little faith in the future, when she regarded mankind and the bright, round world as a whole. She had chosen for him a fulfillment of a dream which, in spite of her virtues, she herself could never encompass. Her ethics were personal and her sacrifice was great.

He looked back at the word he had written on the paper, the six letters that spelled a relationship and a name; and it occurred to him, for the first time, that he owed her something. He too had a debt that he ought to try to pay.

The next afternoon at Cedarcrest when dinner was over and he had finished his work on the plantation books, he left the house and went into the garden. He was searching for Valeria, who had begun to make her wedding clothes and who often went to sit by the lake and sew. She was there now, wearing a silver thimble, pushing her needle through a piece of white batiste. He sat down beside her on a wrought-iron bench, and looked out across the water and past the swans to the green slope of land that led up to the hilltop. It was the quietest part of the day, quiet and warm with only a little wind to shake the hawthorne, and down near the river a buzzard swinging wide against the sky.

He did not know exactly how to approach it, the question, the request he meant to make. And she seemed to sense his mood, for she merely smiled at him once and continued sewing.

Then he said, "Valeria, Father has been very sad since Grandfather died."

It seemed, even as he spoke, a curious way to begin a conversation. But he had come in the last few days to understand some of the complexity of human suffering. He saw that nothing was ever quite separate, ever pure, and he saw that his father's misery was to some extent his mother's too, and that hers, Lucy's, weighed heavily on Marcus Hendrick.

"Yes," Valeria replied. "I could see at the funeral that his grief was hard." She paused and looked down at her fingers. "I'm sorry," she said. "I am sorry for Major Hendrick."

"He thinks he hurt Grandfather," Allen went on. "He believes that when he married Mother he broke Grandfather's heart."

"Oh, no, Allen," Valeria said. "Don't let him think that. Your grandfather loved Major Hendrick. He held no malice toward him."

"Yes," Allen said. "Father knows that too. He says now that Grandfather forgave him and that he could give Grandfather nothing in return."

She made no reply to this, and for a while they were silent. She threaded a needle and Allen watched the landscape. He studied the drooping leaves of a green willow tree.

Then he said, "Valeria, Father loves Mother. He loves her very much, and he loved Grandfather too. And he did break Grandfather's heart, even though he loved him."

"Allen," Valeria said. "Don't, Allen. Oh, my dear, don't treat yourself this way." She put her hand on his, her woman's hand, soft except for the rigid end of the thimble. "You had nothing to do with it. It is no fault of yours. Don't you see that whatever happiness either of them had is what you brought them? It was because of you that they ever saw each other again."

"No," he said. "Not me, Valeria."

"Oh, yes," she said positively.

She turned her face toward him, the green eyes, the fair skin, the forehead high beneath hair that was almost red. She turned to him in surprise, and he saw her expression change. Her lips parted slightly, her eyebrows lifted, and she seemed suddenly to be looking past him, or rather not looking, seeing nothing, as if her vision had been drawn in toward her thoughts.

"Not you?" she said softly, questioning.

"No," he said. "It was Mother who made Father bring me here."

She put the batiste down on the bench and started as if she meant to rise, but she did not get up. She remained where she was sitting. She folded her hands in her lap, and her ruby birthstone glittered on her finger. Then she bit her lower lip and shook her head.

"What fools! What fools!" she said. "Oh, Allen, what fools we have been and how poorly we have used you!"

She did get up now and moved two steps away to a trellis where a rose bush was growing. She stood for a moment, holding a piece of budless stem between her fingers. Then she turned to face him once again.

"Yes," she said. "Your grandfather forgave Major Hendrick. But can you ever find heart enough to forgive us?"

"You?" Allen asked.

"Me," she said. "All of us. Even General Hendrick. Even Anse."

She moved back to the bench.

"Would she receive me now, Allen? After all these years, would your mother let me in if I came to see her?"

"Yes," he said. But he did not know really. He had not thought of it this way, and he had not asked Lucy. He hesitated a moment and went on, "I don't know, Valeria. I did not know whether you would go. I came out here this afternoon to ask you."

"I will go a thousand times," Valeria replied. "I will go twice for every time I should have gone. But only if she wants me. You must find that out."

"She will want you," Allen said. "She is lonely, Valeria, and she will want to see you."

"Ah, yes," Valeria said, "she is lonely. She is your mother and you know her ways. But she is a woman, too, and no man, not even you, can know her heart."

Allen let his hand fall on the bench, and he scraped his boot on the gravel of the walkway.

"What you say is true," he said at last. "You may be right. But I will ask her."

He stood up and looked at Valeria for a moment in silence. Then before he could speak again she turned and walked away.

He went back to Gallatin, and that night after supper he spoke of Valeria's visit to Lucy Hendrick. He found his mother in the parlor where a small fire had been kindled, for it was her nature, even in springtime, to be cold. She was wearing a blue dress and brown cloth slippers, and when he entered the room and saw her there alone by the fireplace with her eyes on a book, he was reminded of another evening long ago. For the furniture they had brought from Memphis was with them still, the rosewood piano, the gilded chairs; and the cherry woodwork still caught the lamplight's glow and the same shadows fell upon the carpet. They had been here six years now and much had altered. He was grown and General Hendrick was dead. He now owned Cedarcrest with all its land, and Valeria was going to be married to Anse Weaver. Ben Hill had come into their lives and gone. And he had fallen in love with Katherine Rutledge.

Yet it seemed to him that his mother did not change. Her hair was no grayer, her cheek no more lined. When she moved it was with the old girlish grace, and her dresses were still made to the old measure. It was almost as if, by stepping out of life, by cutting herself away from all society, from all the rewards and pleasures of the world, she had abrogated too the laws of time. Transcended the sequence of days and months and the endless circles of the turning globe. Thinking this, he felt a slight misgiving in his heart. But he went on, nonetheless, to state his case, as delicately as he was able.

He did not tell her that he had asked Valeria to come, for the letter of the truth was that he had not. Nor did he mention Valeria's apology, made there in the sunlight by the lake. He simply told his mother that Valeria would like to visit her and that he was the intermediary seeking Lucy's approval.

"She is very kind," Lucy Hendrick said. She had put her book aside and she sat now as gracefully erect as if she were posing for a picture. "She is good, and your father says she is very pretty."

"Yes," Allen said. "And I will tell her you expect her."

"No," Lucy replied. "I do not expect her. I will not see her, and you must not let her come."

"Mother," Allen said, "she would like to come." And he went further this time than he had planned in the beginning. "She thinks that she should have come earlier. She would have come if—" And here he broke off. If what? If she had known that Lucy wanted to see her? But she could have found that out. If she had thought of it at all? But that was worse. If she had known that it was Lucy, not Marcus, that brought Allen home?

"If you had asked her," Lucy Hendrick said softly, "for she loves you too."

"And I did not ask her," Allen said. He raised his finger to his mouth and bit it lightly and turned his face away from Lucy toward the door. "I did not ask her."

"So your father told you the story," she said with that faintest trace of an accent playing, whispering like a counterpoint to the words.

"Yes, ma'am," Allen replied. Then with vehemence he said, "But it does not matter."

"It does," she said, almost sharply. "It is all that matters. It matters beyond everything else in the whole world."

"Not to me," he said. "I love you, Mother. It does not count with me."

"But it does," she replied. "It matters to us all."

For a moment she looked down at her hands, at the long, tapered fingers, the smooth skin.

"Allen," she said, "did your father tell you why we spent our lives in Memphis? Why we didn't sell the store and go up North to live?"

"No, ma'am," Allen replied. "He did not mention that."

"No," she echoed him. "He would not. It is likely that he does not even remember, for I do not believe that he ever understood.

"But that was our plan," she went on, "to go to Boston, where he had friends, men with whom he corresponded about abolition. When we left New Orleans, we intended to remain in Memphis only a few months, a year at the most, time enough for your father to free his slaves and sell the stock that he then had in his store. But two things happened, one of them almost an accident, and I would not let him go, I would not leave. First, I discovered that you were coming. That is, not you; I could not be certain then, but some child, and I did not know whether to laugh or cry, whether to curse God or be thankful for His blessing. And the second thing was something your father said to me.

"You remember the room you used in Memphis, how it was on the back of the house, and you could see down to the river, and if there were no fog, you could see all the way across into Arkansas. Before you were born, I used that as a sitting room. I would go there to sew on your baby clothes and look down at the boats and barges as they passed. Look down and wonder and not know what to think. Look down, while inside of me you were taking shape, and I not able to understand any of the meaning or the glory of it.

"Then one afternoon in that room, one evening when your father had just come in from work and the blinds were drawn against the late, western sunlight, he happened to begin to talk of home. Of his home, which he had never spoken of before, because he is kind, Allen, and he believed such talk as that might shame me. Indeed, he then made only a passing reference to his father and the house in Sumner County, but I would not let him stop. I pressed him. I almost drew the words from his mouth, and in the end I learned about General Hendrick, who he was and how much he owned and what his name and the title he bore stood for. That was the accident, the casual word, the reference that your father made to home, which he would not have made if he had held his tongue for a moment to consider. But I understood then what God might help me do."

There in Memphis, with the cell dividing in her womb and the strips of sunlight filtering through the blind, the idea struck her, the ambition clutched her heart. She knew that it would have to be a boy. A girl would be worthless, a liability, and if when the moment came and the pain was over, if she were delivered of a female child, she would be content to leave the South and go to Boston. But if it were a boy, and her desire were fulfilled, then all the old hurt and the old guilt, the generations of suffering and tainted blood, might be paid off, receipted for all times by Allen Hendrick. For she had named him already, after her brother who had manned the fieldpiece at Chalmette.

"We cannot go," she told Marcus Hendrick. And when he sought her reason, she claimed the infirmity of her condition. She said that she could not travel until after the child was born; she temporized against the baby's coming. He complained that his business would be marking time; she suggested that he partially restock his store.

In the room where the idea had first come to her, she built an altar to the Blessed Virgin, and there through the mornings and the afternoons she would pray fervently that she might bear a son. Even during the late months, when her belly was large and the balance of her body shifted, she would kneel ponderously, holding her beads, and seek the Holy Mother's intercession. She prayed for a boy, and if her desires beyond this were to be met, she asked that he have his father's characteristics.

So the moment came and it was a boy and its name was Allen. Six weeks later, when she had apparently regained her strength, when her stomach had shrunk to almost its natural size and the color had returned to the flesh of her cheeks, Marcus Hendrick brought up the subject of their move again. He did not importune her; he was incapable of that. But one day in the same room, where she had sewn and where later the altar had stood and which now had been turned into a nursery, Marcus Hendrick looked up from the cradle where the baby slept, and suggested that the time had come for their trip to Boston.

For a while she made him no reply. She looked between the bars of the crib at the face that had just now lost its newborn redness, at the wisps of blond hair, at the tender lips, at the barely perceptible curl of the long eyelashes. She gazed at the child and Allen's father waited.

"No," she said at last. "We cannot go yet."

"Not yet?" he asked gently. "That is well, my dear. But can you tell me when?"

"Yes," she replied and stopped.

"Lucy?" Marcus Hendrick said, touching her arm.

"Not ever," she said. "We can never leave Tennessee."

Did he know then what she planned to do? He was a man of some foresight, he was called a visionary, and it was well known that his perception was acute. He dreamed of a world where slaves would be free, and in a way he cheated time with a pack of banknotes. But all his vision could not encompass this, could not penetrate her love or her desperate longing. He did not understand, and he did not give up; from month to month, from year to year, he urged the arguments that favored their migration. For a while he feared he had chosen the wrong place and he asked her if she preferred Philadelphia or Hartford. He tried to explain to her that in the North she need not even hide her past, for he shared the dreamer's glorious innocence. He spoke to her on Allen's birthdays, on their anniversaries; he chided her softly at the table or in bed. All this she endured with good grace and bided her time.

She fended off this manifestation of her husband's love and endured each painful moment as it came. She waited patiently as Allen's consciousness grew, as he began to sense his own and his mother's segregation. At last, when the final knowledge had come, when the man from Arkansas had had his say—though she did not know about this, did not know even yet who had told him—she marked the tear stains on his face and felt with her sadness a strange sense of relief. Then she launched her attack; she made her wishes known to Marcus Hendrick.

She harassed him, she argued, she cajoled. And he, who would deny her pleasure nothing, believed that this whim could only bring her grief. She pressed her suit and once more set up the altar and all the time hoped for the thing for which she dared not pray. She could have no more children; another child would spoil her dream. And in the end luck was with her, or her prayers were answered, or the planets were in the proper conjunction, or the ethical substance of the universe asserted itself to the proper alignment of the good.

For eventually, on a summer day in Middle Tennessee, she saw from her bedroom window a surrey pull up to the house. In the surrey was a gray-haired gentleman in a white linen suit and a white straw hat. She saw him wait until Allen came out and got in beside him, and then he drove with his grandson slowly around the square.

There in the parlor, six years later, she brushed her skirt smooth across her lap and said, "I have waited a long time, Allen. The time has been long, and I am not blessed with patience."

"Mother," Allen Hendrick replied, "it is over now."

"No," she said, "not over. It is only begun."

She turned toward the fireplace, toward the warm coals of the fire.

"She cannot come," Lucy said. "She cannot be seen to drive up here. For the world would talk, Allen, and we do not want that. What we want is that the world forget."

He did not know what to say. When he had finished talking that other night with his father, he had felt like one who has not kept the faith. He believed himself guilty of betraying his mother. And yet with all the corruptness of his heart, with all his selfishness and his shameful denial, he had done what she would have had him do. He did not need to explain, for she knew his motives; he could not apologize without accusing her. So he said, "I love you, Mother."

And she, falling back into that old idiom, if not the words she had spoken at Poitiers. "How many years have you now?"

He was aware that the question was rhetorical, that she knew his age as well as or better than he.

But he answered anyway. "I am twenty," he said.

"Yes," she replied. "You are twenty. And I suppose you are old enough now to see me weep."

⋄ 17 ⋄

IN MAY, on the date that had been set before the general got sick, Anse and Valeria were married. Whether or not it had been Valeria's plan to have a big wedding—a dinner the night before, champagne and dancing and supper afterward—Allen did not know; this was her second marriage, and she might in any event have thought such festivities unseemly. But now, since the ceremony came so soon after General Hendrick's death, there was not even music, not even a love song played on the harpsichord, and only a few people were invited to attend. Judge Knott and Houston, a Mr. and Mrs. Binkley, some people named Witherspoon and an old lady, a widow named Mrs. Dodson. All these were friends of Anse. Valeria's aunt from Natchez sent a present, but she did not come, and the bride invited only Allen, who gave her away; Marcus Hendrick; the Armstrongs, who lived on a plantation nearer town; and Captain Rutledge, who was too infirm to leave Roseneath. In keeping with the wedding, the journey that they made was short. They spent a night in Anse's house on the other side of Gallatin and then caught the cars to Nashville, where they stayed a week.

"I don't want to go anywhere else," Valeria said. "Trips are for those who suffer ennui, and marriage ought to be enough of a change to save one from boredom."

Whether she meant this or not, Allen could not say. He knew that John Hendrick had taken her to Saratoga.

When the guests and the priest and the newlyweds had gone, Allen walked out through the garden and sat down on the bench where a month ago he had asked Valeria to visit his mother. It was late afternoon and warm in the spring sunlight, and the sun lay warm and golden on the water of the lake. A few birds, the early ones, had already begun to feed: a few robins were in a field across the lake and a pair of waxwings were at the berry bushes. From somewhere in the distance a bobwhite called, and after a moment Allen whistled back to it. Then the bird called out again and Allen answered. It was not much to say, not much to do, but he sat there for a long time, whistling at a bird that he could not see, and then the bird gave it up and refused to whistle any longer. In his preoccupation with the things his mother and father had told him and with the thoughts of Kate that forever filled his mind, it had never occurred to him how quiet the day could be or how lonely the house when Valeria had left it.

Back in Nashville, it was the hour for tea, the hour at the academy when the curtains were drawn and Miss Clayton came in to sit near the wall, and Katherine—or someone else—poured and passed the teacakes. And in all likelihood it would be someone else, the girl named Ford from Knoxville, perhaps, who would later rise and go to the harp and sing sad songs in the first sad twilight. She or someone else to pass the cups, but in his mind's eye Allen could see only Katherine Rutledge. In his imagination he saw the room, the detail of the rug and the twin hearths, the drapes and the bracket lamps and the upholstered love seats. And by searching his recollection, he could say who would be there, call the names, not only of the girls, but of the boys too, Watkins, Jeremy, Simpson, but their faces remained for him indistinct and blurred, their figures had no substance in his memory. Only Kate, dressed in blue—he saw her that way—with golden ear bobs and a brooch at her throat, undersleeves of lace, embroidery on her slippers. Suddenly, foolishly, he envied

Anse, envied Valeria, who would stroll by the wall and get a glimpse of the academy yard through the gateway. And he envied, too, the boys who would be there now and who would sing at night beneath the open windows.

But he did not go to Nashville that spring, and May lengthened into June, and at last Katherine returned to Roseneath. She returned, as she always did, not on the cars, but in her father's carriage, driven by the tall coachman with the fine white teeth, accompanied by her maid, who slept through most of the journey. She arrived at night, weary from the trip, and on the night that followed, Allen met her in the Roseneath garden. Until the time for their meeting had almost come, he did not consider the difficulties that would attend their courtship. Lost in his dream of her pretty face, of the high cheekbones, the rounded chin, he had not thought, for example, of the fact that he would have to walk. He could not risk the sound of hoofbeats that might reach her father. Or more than this, he could not risk discovery by one of the slaves, or even be seen by a chance passer-by, for in the country it was easy to guess a man's destination.

He left Cedarcrest just after full dark, being careful at first of his own people, who were as dangerous to his plan as any others. There was first the problem of leaving a light, for it was his habit to remain up reading, long after the quarters were quiet; and a darkness in the house would perhaps be noticed. He filled a lamp, lighted it, and left it burning in his room, then went downstairs and searched the parlor and the office and the sitting room, went through the hall to the dining room and down the steps and through the passage into the kitchen. He went up again, the back way this time, the stairs that let into the ballroom. Then around the upper veranda and into the front wing where the bedrooms were, and down at last and out the door, the one on the side that was farthest from the quarters.

There was no moon. He was fortunate in this. And he was careful to make a slight noise, to let his foot fall just loud enough for the dogs to hear that they might recognize the sound and keep their silence. Then he went on, walking in the grass at the edge of the driveway until he reached the creek. Here, he tiptoed across the bridge and climbed the hill and passed down again to the big road.

Allen knew that in the darkness, in the springtime of the year, the woods, the countryside were never silent. There were always the insects to sing in the night; the owls called and the soft leaves rustled. And yet, when he walked, no matter how quietly, he walked not through the sound but surrounded by it. For it was always in the distance, the scurry, the snap of a twig, ahead of him or after he had passed it.

Allen came up from behind the Roseneath stable, downwind from the dogs and a hundred yards from the quarters. He moved in a wide circle through an elm and cedar windbreak, around some outbuildings, and then between the boxwood to the lawn. Ahead of him there were lights in the house. A lamp was burning in what he knew to be the parlor; the shutters were open, someone moved inside. His problem now was to get across the driveway. He had intended to follow it, swing with it in an arc up toward the veranda, but he saw that a square of light fell from the window and lay across his path. He took off his boots, crossed the gravel slowly in his stocking feet, then put the shoes back on and walked into the garden.

But when he got to the summerhouse she was not there. He sat down on a bench to wait, wishing he could smoke, and wishing even more that he could tell the time, strike a lucifer and see his watch. But he could not do this. He could not risk even pacing up and down, and of course he could not call out or give a signal. He waited and still she did not come. He folded his hands together and one of his knuckles cracked, his clothing brushed softly against itself when he crossed his legs and shifted his position. At last, when he had been there for what seemed a long time, he decided to go to the house and look in at the window.

He circled once more, once more crossed the drive, crept up to the wall, and then approached the yellow shaft of lamplight. But here he had to stop and think. If he stood in front of the open window, his shadow would be cast on the lawn, not to mention the fact that his face would be illuminated. If he stood back far enough to be out of the light, he could not see into the room at all, and standing where he was, against the house, he could see nothing but the other sill of the window. So he placed himself back and a little to one side and half the parlor came into his vision.

What he could see appeared to be exactly the same as it had been when he had first visited there with General Hendrick. The door to the hall was standing ajar; a shotgun and a crop were leaning in the corner. A piece of muslin was draped over the couch near the wall, and on the table next to a vase and on the top of a pile of books, there stood an empty cup and saucer. In the very center of Allen's gaze Captain Rutledge sat blinking sleepily at the fireplace.

He had aged. He had broken. He looked older now than General Hendrick had looked in his last illness. It seemed to Allen at first that the old man's palsy had strangely diminished, that the tremble and movement of his head were not so pronounced. But this was not so. The head still shook above the sharp line of the shoulders, as badly or worse than it ever had. It was simply that the rest of him had caught up with this symptom of age. His cheeks were sunken so that his teeth hardly fit at all any more; they pushed against his lips that were thin and bloodless. His thin gray hair stood up on his head, his eyes seemed tired and the lids around them were swollen. Though it was summer and the night was warm, he was wearing a wool roundabout with a muffler tied at his throat, and Allen could see by the play of shadows that a fire had been lighted.

"Long ago," Captain Rutledge said, his voice weak, worn thin by a million words and the years of a lifetime. "Long ago, and all this was not here."

It appeared to Allen that he tried to gesture with his hand. He raised it feebly off the arm of the chair, then lowered it again as if his strength had left him.

"Nobody here," he said, "nothing here except Cedarcrest. No neighbor except the general and Mrs. Hendrick. So long ago, Kate. And you would not believe it, how it looked to me, the valleys and the hills as fresh as when God made them, like it had been waiting for me to make it into a place and plow the ground."

"Papa," Kate's voice spoke from out of Allen's vision, the deep voice, the sound of it soft as rain, and so sweet to him that he almost flinched as he heard it. "Papa," she said, "it is past your bedtime. Let me call Uncle Henry to help you to your room."

But the captain did not understand a word she said. It was as if the vibrations were too low for his ear, the frequency of her voice beneath his range of hearing.

"Ah," he said, "I have seen it in my dreams. The way it was then, and the way it is now. We have done much for ourselves, and much, too, for the nation."

He paused, an old, old man, and there were tears in his senile old eyes, spilling over and running down through the cheeks' deep wrinkles.

"Much," he said. "We have done much. General Hendrick and I."

"Papa," Kate said, "please, Papa."

"Much," he said hollowly, like an echo of himself.

There was a pause and then Allen heard the sound of a footstep, and suddenly Katherine came into his view. She crossed the room and took a chair beside her father. It gave Allen a start to see the two of them sitting there, Kate so young beside the captain who was so old, she so beautiful and he so ugly. She was wearing a yellow dimity dress tied at the waist with a green sash, looped at the hem with a narrow green ribbon. Her hands were folded in her lap, long and slender and very white, and she was holding her chin up slightly so the skin of her neck was pulled tight and smooth, and the shadows from her father's summer fire made the flesh look a little thin beneath the high cheekbones. It struck Allen, when the first shock of delight had passed, the pleasure that he took in seeing her once more, it occurred to him that they looked a good deal like one of the tableaux that the girls of the Female Academy liked to perform. They sat, except for the captain's shaking head, erect and still as if they were posturing, as if they had been posed that way after long rehearsal. And in their great disparity of looks and age there was something almost allegorical.

Then he heard Kate say again, "It is late, Papa. You ought to be in bed."

His own mind echoed that sentiment, and he did not remain to watch any more. He returned to wait at the summerhouse in the garden.

He returned to sit and count the stars, to clasp his hands and cross his legs and drum his fingers on the bench beside him. It was a fine night, the air damp and a little cool, the world everywhere dark and very silent. Once he thought he heard a door close, and he got up and searched the path expectantly for her. But this was a false alarm and he sat down again, and when she did come, she was at his side before he heard her. It was hard for him to see her in the dark, or rather, hard to make out the fine detail; her features were vague, the face dimly seen, and the yellow dress reflected little light. But her voice was the same and the smell of her lilac perfume, and he remembered the sight of her he had had when he looked in the parlor.

"Allen," she said. "I am here, Allen."

And he made no reply. He moved close to her and put his arm about her waist and kissed her rather quickly on the lips. It was not much of a kiss. Her lips were dry and she kept them closed and he allowed his own to remain together. It was little more than a touch, a bare contact of the flesh, but it was closer than he had ever been to her before, and he felt considerably moved and a little embarrassed.

"Oh, Kate," he said. "It has been so long. You have been away so long, and I have missed you."

"I know," she said, half testily, half sadly.

Then she sat down on the bench and said, "Oh, Allen, why didn't you come to Nashville? It would have been better than this. I do not like seeing you only in the darkness."

"I couldn't," he replied. "You know that, Kate."

He sat down beside her, and he found when he took her hand that it was cold. She had been holding onto the bench and the iron had chilled it.

"Darling," he said, "I could not come. And we can be alone here. It is better."

"No," she said, "we do not need to be alone. Oh," she went on, "when you used to come, it did not make any difference who was there, Miss Clayton or any of the others. They were there, but they could not hear us talk and it did not matter whether they could see us."

"Kate," Allen said. "They are not even here now. It is at least the same. They did not help us."

"No," she said. "You don't understand. Listen to me. How long have you been here tonight, waiting?"

"I don't know," he replied. "A little while, I reckon."

"A long while," she said. "I am more than an hour late. Do you know why?"

He did know. Or at least he knew part of it. He had looked through the window and seen her sitting with her father, she herself, waiting while the old man procrastinated, delayed against the time when he should go to bed. But he did not say that he knew this. For he had no right to stand outside her window; he had no claim to see her when she did not know that he was there.

"You don't know," she said after his silence. "It was because of Papa. Because I could not come until Papa had gone up to his room."

She rose, freed the hand that he was holding, took a step toward the summerhouse, then moved back toward the bench.

"Oh, my dear," she said, speaking more gently now. "It is not the way to do things. To make you wait in the dark with no one to talk to."

These were her words, but they did not ring quite true. He could not say exactly what it was that troubled her, but he was wise enough to tell that it was more than this. She was considerate. He had recognized this from the beginning; she would think of him and his loneliness when she kept him waiting. But something beyond this weighed heavy on her mind. All her concern could not be for his comfort.

"Kate," he said softly, "I wanted to come. I would have come if it hadn't been for Valeria. But if I had, if I had spent the whole spring in Nashville and visited you at the academy every night, things would still be the same here at home. There would be no difference."

She still stood before him, very quiet, her face, her figure all but lost in the night's darkness.

"Kate?" he said. "There would be no difference, would there?"

"I don't know," she said, a very faint note of despair in her voice. "I don't know. I can tell you only that it was different when we were in town. And you let three months pass and you did not come to see me."

It was he who kept the silence now. He could not think of what to say to her, and it seemed to Allen that she was being a little unfair, not only to him but to Valeria.

"Perhaps," he said at last. "Perhaps it was different. But only because we were inside in the light and there were other people. Are you angry because I kissed you, then? Do you not like being alone with me in the nighttime?"

"No," she said sharply, "it is not that. Don't you see that what we did in Nashville, when you came and we were together there, it was honest and above board and according to the rules of Dr. Cox and the academy? Oh, Allen," she said, "don't you see that? And here I have to wait for Papa to go to bed and slip out then and meet you in the dark."

"Not exactly," he replied. "Not exactly honest at the academy either. If they had known who I was, you would have had to slip out there too."

"Oh," she said resignedly, "you don't see, you don't see, and I cannot tell you."

"Kate," he said, taking her hand once more. "It will have to be this way. I would give everything to change it, but it can't be changed. Until we are married, we will have to meet in secret when we are here."

There was a long pause, a full silence, then suddenly she came close to him and leaned against his arm.

"Forgive me," she said, her voice wonderful and mysterious and whispering in his ear, her breath warm on his cheek, her hand resting lightly on his shoulder. "My dear," she said, "I did not mean it. I said all those things and I did not mean to say them. I have hurt you and I did not want to do that."

"Hush," he replied, "hush, Kate."

His arm was around her now and he could feel her body, her leg beneath all the petticoats pressed close to his. She seemed to have finished. The mood that had brought her almost to tears seemed to be over. And yet he was aware that he was ignorant still, that he did not know the real source of her complaint or what it was about meeting him here that made her unhappy. When he had left Cedarcrest two hours before, his intention had been to speak to her of marriage. He had planned to urge her to seek her father's consent, and he himself was prepared to marry without the captain's permission. But now, after what had happened and the things that she had said, he felt that the time had not yet come to press her.

While he considered and held her in his arms, she seemed, unaccountably, to become lighthearted. She suggested that they leave the summerhouse and walk along the path to the other side of the garden. They did this, moving near the edge of the path where the grass encroached and they could walk in silence. They stopped at a boxwood gate that led to the stables. There was still no moon, but by the faint light of the stars Allen could see the trail that led across the field and the bare outline of the fence around the paddock.

"I have been here before," he said. "Did you know that, Kate? Did you know that I had been to Roseneath often?"

"Yes," she replied. "You came with General Hendrick to call on Papa."

"Sometimes," he said. "But most of the time I came with Anse Weaver."

"Yes," she said, "to hunt."

"I did not think you knew that," Allen said, smiling. "I thought that was a secret I had kept from you."

"Men have no secrets," she replied gaily. "Men are very foolish."

Then a little more seriously, though not sadly, her voice in no way tinged with sorrow, she said, "I saw you once. One day when I was coming home from school, you were standing by the driveway when I passed in the carriage."

He was touched by this, moved that she too was able to recollect that moment which for so long he had cherished in his heart.

"You remember that?" he asked. "You remember that too?"

"My dear," she said, "of course I do. And when I got in the house Papa told me who you were."

Somehow, when she mentioned her father's name, it came back to haunt them, the old ghost; they seemed both to think of the taint that was in his blood. He looked down at her face, but he could see nothing there. It was too dark and the flesh would tell him nothing.

"Do you love me?" he said.

"Yes," she replied.

"Will you marry me?"

And she said it again. "Yes," she replied. "I will marry you, Allen."

"You will have to," he said softly.

Then after a long pause he said, "Kate, you will have to marry me some time soon."

18

B UT WHEN WOULD SHE MARRY HIM? She would not say, though he urged her again and again to speak to her father. Sometimes on the nights when the moon was full and the ironwork of the summerhouse cast a fretted shadow in the garden, they would make an adventure of walking to the end of the path, slipping like hunters or Indians from the safety of one boxwood to another. It was a foolish risk, a chance to take, a challenge their love made to the world around them; but they were never discovered, and when they were safe once more, back in the full shade of the pavilion, they would laugh and rejoice in their triumphant passage and he would kiss her on the lips or on the cheek. He would press her hand in the darkness, let his arm go around her waist, and then he would say, "Kate, when are you going to marry me?"

Like that, lightly, the question asked almost with levity, in a tone of voice that was almost fraught with humor. And perhaps she understood that he spoke this way because in his heart he remained a little afraid. He was like a man cast under a spell, like a prince who walked in a golden dream, and he was apprehensive lest some harshness in his voice might tear the fragile tissue of his joy. "When, Kate?" he would ask. "When will the fiddlers play?"

Or at other times, when there were clouds in the sky, or when the moon was little or there was no moon at all, they would stroll at their leisure like masters of the domain, through the herb plot and between trellises, their practiced footsteps light on the gravel walk. Stealth, to them, had become a habit, the darkness a time to celebrate, and at a turn in the path or a corner of the hedges they would stop and he would look at her in the night. He would gaze for a long time at the figure so faintly seen, at the features that his eyes could not make out, at the ribbon in her hair which was a gray spot in the blackness. Then, softly, secretly, as suited the climate of darkness, he would say, "Kate, have you asked your father? Have you told him yet that you want to marry me?"

Or again when the ground and the benches and the leaves were wet, dripping from the late rain that had just now stopped, they would have to move single file among the flowers to keep Kate's skirt from striking the petals and getting wet. It was a fresh and cool and lovely time, the sort of evening they did not see very often. The cows would come out of the barn to graze in the night and their lowing could be heard from the pasture in the distance. The insects would start up again, and if it were early or Saturday the slaves would pick their banjos in the quarters.

And he would say, "When, Kate?"

And she would not tell him.

Or rather, she could not, for she did not know.

During the mornings and the afternoons, the long summer days filled with sunshine, he would try to discover what made her hold back, he would search for the reasons she might have for not asking her father. He would sit on the veranda and look out toward the lawn, out toward the grass where the hounds lay asleep, and he would say to himself, she loves me, but she loves the captain too. Or he would lie down after dinner in his room upstairs and stare at the fringe on his tester bed, and he would think, it is because she is afraid he will say no, and she wants to put off the time when she will disobey him. But would she disobey him when the moment came? This was the question that Allen could not answer.

One afternoon early in July, Allen went to call upon Anse Weaver. He had gone because he had nothing else to do, simply to visit and pass the time of day. But when he had got there and sat down to talk, he was seized with a sudden desire to speak of Katherine. The sight of Anse, the handsome face, the long hair that dripped oil, reminded him of that other time when Anse had been waiting for him in the hotel chamber. The night, six months past now, when Allen had first told Kate that he loved her. I should not speak of it, Allen said to himself. It is not Anse's concern. It will not be fair to Kate to talk of her to him, or fair to me, or even to Anse, who does not want to hear it. But the longer he sat in the room with Anse—it was his office, furnished with books and medical tools, decorated by a skeleton that hung on a stand in the corner—the greater the temptation grew, and at last he broke down and told Anse of his problem. How she would not ask her father and would not even set a date, plan the time when she would ask him, and so their love made no progress toward its goal.

"And if she loves me," Allen said, "why doesn't she speak to the captain? And if she does not, why does she meet me every night?"

"Ah," Anse replied, "I am only a doctor, young Hendrick. Only God can tell you about a woman's mind."

They were silent for a while, Allen on a wide, leather couch, and Anse across from him on a straight wooden chair, and the skeleton smiling down from his stand between them.

"I don't know," Anse said at last. "She may temporize. She may delay against her father's going."

"Going?" Allen asked, not understanding at once, though the thought had occurred to him one night in Nashville.

"He is old," Anse said, not unkindly, but not with great gentleness either. He was stating a fact. "He will have to die sometime."

"Anse," Allen said. "Kate would not wait for that. It is like hoping, like wishing for him to pass away."

Anse considered a moment, squinting at the floor. "Yes," he said. "I reckon so. I reckon you would be inclined to think of it that way."

"Then why?" Allen said.

"Young Hendrick," Anse replied, leaning forward a little. "Do not push her. How old are you? Almost twenty-one. And Katherine? Seventeen or maybe eighteen. And if you stick to good whisky and stay out of the rain and walk close to the rump when you go around your horse, you have got forty or fifty years more, and what is a month or twelve or twenty-four of them in a space of that magnitude?"

"A month is thirty days," Allen said. "Twelve months more will bring another summer."

"Ah, yes," Anse replied. "And a year may bring more than a season to one who is patient."

"Anse," Allen said a little wearily, with an edge almost of testiness in his voice, "we cannot wait for Captain Rutledge to die. We will not do it that way."

"No," Anse said. "But I did not mean that. Or, at least, not only that; life is not that simple. You do not know what is coming, or whether what comes will be good or bad. But you wait and watch like the preachers say. You keep your peace and look for the opportunity to come. And when the time is ripe, then you will know it."

Allen thought of this for a moment or two, sitting there with Anse and the skeleton and a pair of flies that turned and dipped near the sunlit window.

Then he said easily, half innocently, "Anse, why will she not ask Captain Rutledge?"

"Young Hendrick," Anse replied. "I am not sure, but I think the reason is that Katherine loves you."

Allen waited, feeling the heat of the afternoon, the perspiration that gathered on his back and on his forehead.

Then Anse asked, "What would you do, what would she do, if the captain said no and forbade her to see you again?"

Allen did not know, but perhaps this was it. Maybe she had looked ahead, had seen beyond the chance of the captain's denial.

"Honor," Anse said with irony. But his smile was kind, benevolent, like the smile of a father, or one seen in the picture of a saint. "Honor," he said again. "Beware of it, young Hendrick. It will scourge you sometimes. It is apt to act like a Campbellite preacher or an old-maid aunt."

"It has scourged me already," Allen replied. "It is worse than any parson I ever knew."

He left Anse then and rode back to Cedarcrest, and that night when the full darkness had come and the dishes had been washed and the slaves had gone back to their quarters, he made his inspection of the house and left the lamp to burn in his room and slipped out of the house and walked to the Roseneath garden. He made his circle around the quarters and crept between the boxwoods and on up the path to the summerhouse and the pavilion. She was not there. There was a lamp still burning downstairs in the parlor, and he stood for a moment looking at the square of yellow light, which was dim at a distance and feeble against the darkness. But he did not go to the house. He would not look again where he had not been invited to look, and the words Anse had spoken came back to him, and he thought, a little humorously, how honor did indeed make demands like those of a schoolteacher. Then the light went out and he waited some more and she was with him, beside him on the bench.

She was there to walk the paths once more, moderately tall and slender, with cheekbones that were high, with a ribbon in her hair and the scent of lilac all about her; and the long skirt swinging slightly on its hoops, and the hands slim and barely cold to his touch, and the ring her aunt had bought her on her finger. She spoke to him in a voice that was almost a whisper, even when she did not fear being overheard; and she seemed a little sad, as she always did, when she first came out from the house to meet him.

"Kate," he said when he had kissed her, when he had felt her girl's lips tight together against his. "Do you know what I did today?"

"No," she replied, "but I hope it was something honorable."

She meant nothing by this, of course. She could not know what he and Anse had talked about, nor the thoughts he had had before she joined him. But the chance remark halted him nonetheless, made him stop for a moment and be thankful for the darkness.

"I don't know whether it was or not," he said at last. "This morning I went without you up to your bluff and stood there and looked down at the river."

"Not dishonorable," she said, the tone of her speaking more cheerful now. "But not nice," she went on, "not really very kind."

"But I did it for you," he replied. "So I could tell you about it. Do you know what I did? I rode up there just to see it and call it yours. I looked down at the water and said, 'This is Kate's river.' And a tree limb came floating by and I said, 'That is Kate's wood.' And I looked at the trees and the grass and the rock ledges, and the birds and the crops in one of our fields, and I said, 'These are Kate's too.' Then a man came by floating on a raft, but I said, 'No. This is enough. One man is all she may have, and I will be that one.'"

"Darling," she said. "My dear. I did not want him."

He took her hand and kissed it, kissed the tip of each of her fingers. Then he said, "What did you do, Kate? Tell me about all of it. Everything from the time you first got up."

"Nothing," she replied half wistfully. "I have been here all day."

She rose and he followed her and they walked a few steps down the path that led to the driveway.

"No," he said. "Please tell me. I want to hear."

"Allen," she replied, "I don't do anything. I sit and sew or read or talk to Papa. That is all."

"But you think," he said. "What do ladies think about, Kate? Bonnets and cloaks? Teas and balls and fancy carriages? Or how many maids they will have when they are married? There," he went on, "that is good. How many maids will you have when you are married, Kate? Ten? Twenty? We will bed them all down in the ballroom and they can work in shifts, and do whatever maids are supposed to do. Or maybe thirty. Maybe ten different ones for each third of the day. I will sell all the hands to buy maids for you."

"Allen, Allen," she said, laughing. "One will do."

"No," he replied quickly. "Thirty at least. If they pass their time doing nothing else but admiring your beauty."

They moved on down to the end of the walk, then back again to the bench, and past it and on around the summerhouse and through a trellis into another part of the garden.

"Tell me," he said gently after a pause. "What do you think?"

"About maids," she replied. "About thirty maids and sixteen carriages."

Then another silence that took them near the herb plot and beyond this to pansy beds and then a turn that brought them round once more to the pavilion.

"Kate," Allen said. "I think of you. Always. All the time. Whatever I'm doing."

She moved closer to him and squeezed his arm with her slender fingers.

"I think of you too," she said. "You ought to know that."

Then suddenly, with no warning, or at least none that he had seen, she put herself directly in front of him and stood very close looking up at him with her face near his, her forehead near his lips.

"Oh, Allen," she said, "it is horrible in the daytime. I am frightened in the daytime without you."

He put his arms around her, feeling her dress beneath his hands and beneath the dress the thin waist and the firm flesh of her back and shoulders.

"Darling," he said, "afraid of what? What is it?"

"I don't know," she said, her voice trembling a little more than usual, whispering a little more softly, filled with more emotion. "It is nothing. There is not anything to fear, but I get frightened anyway. I cannot help it."

He rubbed his hand gently up and down her back. "Try to tell me," he said. "Is it me? Have I done something?"

She moved away from him and he followed her back to the bench. The night was very silent for July, quiet and hot with no wind, no voice to be heard, no sound of insects from the pasture. They sat down together. He took her hand, the right one which wore the ring, and he said, "Have I? Is it me who frightens you?"

"No," she replied. "I don't know what it is, but it is not you."

She paused and looked up the walk toward the house, which was dark now and as silent as the night and barely discernible against the sky.

"Oh," she said, speaking very rapidly, "it is the difference. It is the way things are now and the way they used to be. Allen. Listen to me. Try to understand it."

"My dear," he replied softly, "I am listening. I shall understand you."

"Do," she said, "do, and explain it to me. I cannot endure worrying much longer."

She stopped, broke off, and he could hear the sound of her breath, not panting, but a bit hasty, a little deep.

Then, after a moment, slowly, with almost complete composure, with her head erect and her voice almost normal, she said, "I keep remembering how it used to be. How it was back before I entered the academy. Percy was here then and Papa was strong, or at least stronger than he is now. And every day in the summer we would go somewhere, we would do something. Oh, Allen," she said, "it was a lovely time. On some mornings Percy and I would go to the woods and sit down and talk sometimes, and sometimes not talk. Sometimes just sit and watch the squirrels and hope that a deer would pass, or even a rabbit. Percy wanted to be a soldier even then, so he always took his gun when we went out walking. And occasionally he would shoot at something. A blackbird or a crow, or maybe just a leaf or a mark on the side of a tree, or maybe an acorn. The gun made such a terrible noise. There would be a boom close to our ears, and then it would echo, the sound traveling away, repeating itself over and over again through the forest. And we would argue about it, wonder how far it could be heard.

"I would say, 'Papa can hear it. Papa heard it back yonder at the house.'

"But he would never agree with me. He liked to tease me and he would laugh. It is funny. I remember so well how he looked when he laughed. He has blue eyes and when he laughs you can hardly see them. He would pretend to be stern and say, 'No, he can't, Kate. You are an idle, silly girl, and Papa did not hear it.'

"I would get angry then, and exaggerate and declare they had heard the shot all the way to town."

She paused, looked off at the night as though she were lost in thought. Then she looked back at Allen and went on. "But I was never really angry, and I knew that he did not think I was an idle girl."

"No," Allen replied. "The only thing he could possibly think was that you were pretty."

"My dear, forgive me," she said. "I am being silly and you ought to scold me for it."

"No," he replied. "What is it, Kate? Go on."

"That," she said. "The way it was then. And sometimes I would go to town with Papa, ride with him in the carriage all the way there and back, and whoever saw us would always speak and the men would alway raise their hats, and John Noble would grin and bow from up high on the coach box. It was not much," she said. "It was simply going with Papa and not being alone, or with just a maid to chaperone you. And there on the square in Gallatin there were so many people to pass along the streets, so many ladies and so many men, so many horses and wagons and buggies and people to drive them. Sometimes then I used to pretend that I lived in Gallatin. I would pick out a house that we passed in town, always a big house and one made of wood, for I liked so well the way they looked when they were painted. And I would think about how the parlor would be arranged and how I would hang the drapes and varnish the banisters. I could imagine it then. I could almost see myself, grown and dressed like a lady and receiving guests."

She stopped and moved closer to him on the bench. "You see," she said. "I told you it was foolish."

He did not reply this time and after a moment she went on.

"And even later, when I had been to Nashville, when I had seen Aunt Lucille and her house there, and the way people live in a city, it was still the same to come back home and to go into Gallatin in the rockaway with Papa."

"Darling," Allen said, "you shall have a house in town. You shall have one built anywhere your heart desires. And Percy may come and live with us if that will make you happy."

"No," she replied, turning her face toward him in the darkness. "Please listen. Please understand what I am talking about. I don't want those things any more. I only want to live with you at Cedarcrest or anywhere else. It does not matter. For it was not the house or the ride to town or the walks in the woods or even Percy. It was simply the way we felt then, the happiness that seemed to come day after day, and you could expect to be happy like you expect the sun to shine."

"And now?" Allen asked. "Aren't you happy now, Kate?"

"With you," she said quickly. "At night with you. But, Allen, you have not seen Papa lately. He is so old, and his palsy is worse; his eyesight is bad and he is cold all the time, even in the very hottest weather. He sits and thinks about dying, about all the people he knew who have already died, and about his own death, which he knows is coming. And he wants to die in a way, but he is still afraid. He is so tired, Allen, and he believes a dozen times a day that the end has come. He calls me and the servants to come stand around his couch and watch him die."

Allen thought of this, remembering the figure the old man had made on the night he watched from outside the parlor window. The flesh so thin, so wrinkled and traced with veins, the head shaking and quivering above the rounded shoulders. Like age itself, like the apotheosis, the allegorical representation of the end of man.

"Darling," he said. "I am sorry about your father."

"Yes," she replied. "I know you are. But I am doing it badly. This is not what I want to tell you. What I mean is this. That we are not happy any more. Five years ago I did not believe that anything in the world could ever change. The earth would go on and the years would pass, but the trees would still be standing in the woods and the bluff would be there with the river under it and Roseneath and Cedarcrest and the land would remain with the people happy always, winter and summer. But we are not happy. We are not the same. The woods are still there, but Percy is gone, and Papa would be better off dead than forever sorrowing."

She paused once more and looked down at her lap, and once more Allen lifted her hand to his lips and kissed it.

"It did not last," she went on slowly, softly in that wonderful, whispering voice that was full of infinite mystery and sadness. "It was a lovely time and now that time is gone, and I do not know any more what I should look for. Oh, Allen," she said. "Allen, in Nashville, in the winter, it was better than ever. On the nights when you came to the academy, I sang in my room while I dressed; I danced between the wardrobe and the dressing table; I took an hour to select my ear bobs. And in the parlor with you it was best of all, better than home or being in the woods, better than Aunt Lucille's or going to town with Papa. Oh, my dear, I love you. I have told you that a thousand times. But not ever enough. There is no word to use for the way I feel, no way to say it. But whether you were there or not, even when you had come back to Cedarcrest, the dancing and the singing and the loving you went on."

"With me. With me too, Kate," he said. "I love you too."

"But don't you see?" she said. "In the old days it was so good here, but it is not good any more and Papa is sad. Oh," she continued, "I told you it was silly. It is foolish, foolish, and Percy was right; I am an idle, foolish girl. But if Papa and I could have been so happy together then and so miserable, so discontented now, what then of everything else in the world, all the other happiness and love and expectation? I could not endure to lose you, Allen. I could not give you up, but more than that: I could not give us up, this time and the way we feel, the way it is when we sit here on this bench together. But, oh, if five years could destroy all my other peace, all the joy that I knew with Papa when I was a child, how can I look to the time to come without quaking? I cannot help it. I do not trust happiness. I can put no faith in joy or in the future."

He took her in his arms and held her very tightly, very close to him, and he spoke to her with his lips close to her ear.

"Kate," he said. "Listen to me. Believe me, Kate, it will never change. I love you. I have always loved you. From the moment I first saw you when you drove by in the carriage. It will never change. We will not let it. We will go on loving each other and no man can do us harm."

"Oh," she said. "It is not us. I am not afraid of us. It is something else in the way time moves. It is the world that is too big and we cannot control it."

"No," he said. "It is our world, Kate. And you shall have your happiness. I will stalk it to the end of the earth for you, Kate. I will capture it for you."

"I love you," she said softly. "I love you, Allen."

He kissed her, the lips that were damp and slightly parted, soft and full and not quite still against his, and he moved closer and pushed his thigh between hers, his knee bent, the hoops of her skirt pressing against his ankle.

"Kate," he said at last, "do you believe me?"

"Yes," she replied and he could feel her breath on his neck. "I have to. I could not bear it if I didn't."

⬥ 19 ⬥

THEY CONTINUED to see each other through the month of July and on through the first hot weeks of August. And in spite of the waiting and the uncertainty and the great distrust that Katherine had of the future, they were happy most of the time that they were together. Late in the summer when the stars began to fall, they would sit with their heads resting on the back of the bench, their hands clasped, their bodies close together. And when it came, the meteor, faster than sand through a glass, faster than time itself and twice as brilliant; when they saw the orange streak of it swinging down between the stars, they would catch their breaths and make their silent wishes. Then kiss, long and with some passion, and breathe again and look back at the sky.

Occasionally, if they were early enough, if the captain were tired and went to bed sooner than usual, they would be together in time to see the last firefly and be fooled by its tardy glow in the first full darkness. "Ah," Allen would say, "there is no good there. It is no use to wish on a lightning bug. There are too many of them."

And Kate would reply, "No. We will have to make it up. We will have to look close and find an extra star to wish on."

They would laugh and she would press his arm, and they would turn their eyes once more to the sky above them.

That was the way they passed their nights, sitting on the bench and wishing for luck and longing for the time to come when they might be married. But in the day it was a different world and then for Allen there was work to do, and frequently he went in to town to see his parents.

He would ride in to Gallatin on Sunday to have dinner with them in the white frame house, or he would spend an afternoon in the parlor with his mother, or he would call on his father sometimes at the office near the square. And if it was Sunday and they sat at the table, the shutters would be drawn against the heat and the candles lighted, so their shadows danced like ghosts on the papered walls. They would speak of mundane things, Allen of his farm and the way his tobacco was growing; and Lucy of the traffic she had seen when she watched the street from her chair beside the window; and Marcus of the trial he had heard in court. Now that Allen had returned from Nashville and most of Marcus Hendrick's money had been turned into gold, Marcus did not have much to do any more and he amused himself by sitting for hours in the courtroom and watching the tedious litigations unfold. He was at his best when he told about criminal cases, if they were not too serious and the punishment was not too severe. Sometimes, when they had finished eating, a silence would fall over the table and they would simply sit and look at each other, and Lucy would smile. Her teeth were as sound, as white as a girl's and she appeared very young in the dim light of the candles.

But when they were away from the house, Allen and his father alone in the office—still dusty and cluttered with old newspapers, the desk still there and the safe against the wall—they were likely to talk politics, for campaigning had begun for the election in the fall. There were four men running for President that year: Mr. Lincoln and Mr. Douglas of Illinois, Mr. Breckinridge of Kentucky, and Mr. Bell of Tennessee. Lincoln was a Republican and Douglas a Northern Democrat; Breckinridge was a Southern Democrat and Bell belonged to the Constitutional Union party. In the spring, as Allen had written Kate, Marcus Hendrick had hoped for the nomination of Lincoln. But now that the election was drawing near, his support of the Republicans was beginning to waver and he spoke more and more in favor of Mr. Bell. For until the Democrats' Baltimore convention he had not really believed that the South would ever secede.

"Allen," he said one afternoon. It was near the end of July and very hot. There was no breeze, no stir in the air, and the street outside reflected the glare of sunlight. "I do not believe in slavery. I do not believe in it any more than Mr. Lincoln does. Or less even. I believe in it less than he. I would do away with it with less compunction. But as much as I hate slavery, I love our nation and I cannot bear to see it torn in two."

He rose and went over to the desk, took out a bottle of brandy and two glasses, and poured a drink for himself and one for Allen.

"I am getting old," Marcus Hendrick said. "And things are not so simple any more. It is easy to believe in what is right, but there is so much that is right and so many things to believe in. I keep remembering back when I was young, and the war broke out and I went to it with Father. I was only fifteen then, and I served as one of Father's orderlies, as his pet really and general nuisance to the army. I did not belong there. Father merely indulged me. But I recollect how it was on the march north. It was bad weather, cold, the worst time of winter. And we went a long way with no road to follow, and the men freezing and the wagons sticking in the mud. But my clothes were good and I did not know much about suffering, and until the battle began I saw the whole thing as a lark. It was a game, a form of jollification, it was a journey made with a lot of company. This was the first time I had ever been out of Tennessee. I remember thinking all through Kentucky, through Indiana, and into Michigan, 'We have gone a hundred or two hundred or five hundred miles, and it is still the United States. We are still in it.' All of it good land and all of it fertile and settlements of people along the way."

He drank, refilled his glass, paced to the window where the heat of the street blazed up and the bright glow of sunshine lay across the sill.

Then he said, "I have believed in it, you see, all my life, in the integrity of the country, like I believe in justice for the Negro and freedom for all. I always thought that secession was talk, just as Father thought it was when the convention was held in Nashville, and I concluded that no citizens, no matter what their views, would take the final step and split away. For together we are strong and we will be good; apart, we are like sheep and we amount to nothing. But then, when the Democrats met in Charleston, some of the states bolted, and later, in Baltimore, the party broke in two, and they were intelligent men, and they knew that to break up was their doom. They were giving the Presidency to Mr. Lincoln. But they did it. They destroyed themselves as a party, as surely as the world is round. And I trust them no longer. I know not what they might do next."

"Are you going to vote for Mr. Bell then?" Allen asked.

"I don't know," Marcus Hendrick replied. "I cannot vote for Mr. Lincoln. He is not on the ballot in Tennessee. But whatever I do the situation is not changed. If Lincoln wins, we will have freed the slaves at the cost of the nation. And if Bell is elected, we will have temporized on slavery to save the United States."

He returned to the table, an old man, a gray-headed man of sixty-five with pince-nez glasses.

"I will vote," he said, "but it will not matter. Mr. Lincoln will be elected and we will have a war."

"Father," Allen said, "it may not be that way. Mr. Lincoln may not be elected. Or if he is, he may allow the South to go in peace."

"No," Marcus Hendrick replied. "It will be Lincoln. And in war or in peace, if we go it is all the same."

He paused and looked past Allen toward the office door, toward the doorway where once Ben Hill had stood, a rich man in a broadcloth suit and a gold watch chain.

Then he said, "Allen, you own slaves. I know that out of deference to Father, out of respect for the love he bore you, you have not thought yet of granting them their manumission. I do not judge you. I have for you only love, as I have for your mother, and I mention her because she approves of what you do. But think of it. For time passes, and before a man knows it, he is standing beside his grave."

And there was nothing he could say to this either: there were so many things to be considered, so many people involved. He knew that he wanted to remain rich, for if he did not, he would never be able to marry Katherine, and to marry Kate was what he wanted most and what Lucy wanted for him. But Marcus did not approve of slavery and would not approve of a civil war. And General Hendrick had advised against breaking the Union.

"Father," he said, "I don't know. I guess I will just have to wait and see."

"And what if a war does come?" Marcus Hendrick went on. "Will you fight in it? Will you help the South secede?"

"I don't know, Father," Allen repeated. "I have not thought about it."

Marcus Hendrick looked at him, his eyes a little large, a little magnified behind the glasses. Then suddenly the eyes narrowed slightly, and Allen saw that his father understood, knew he had been too busy thinking of Kate to consider the nation.

"Yes," Marcus Hendrick said softly. "You have your own worries. You bear your own burden and I bear it with you. And I should not disturb you with mine."

Allen did not reply to this; and after a moment he rose and shook his father's hand and went down to his horse and rode back to Cedarcrest.

But if Marcus Hendrick occasionally forgot about Kate under the stress of a troubled time and his thoughts of the election, Lucy did not. Lucy remembered, and when she saw Allen alone, the question of when he would marry hung between them. She did not ask it; for a long time she did not mention Katherine's name. But there was something in the way that she let a silence fall, sat with her lips slightly parted, her expression mildly expectant, her hands gently fondling the embroidery in her lap. She would look at him through the long pause, give him his chance to speak of his love, and when he disappointed her, go on with the conversation.

But one day, one morning that threatened rain, he brought himself to talk to her of Kate. They were in Lucy's upstairs sitting room, her high parlor that overlooked the street, a small room with three tall windows. There was a rug on the floor, some chairs and a table and a drawing of the convent at Poitiers framed on the wall. Lucy had been at her prayers when Allen entered, and she still held her rosary in her lap. For some reason that Allen did not at first understand she began to talk that day of New Orleans. Or rather, she began to talk of it in a different way, in a gentle, almost reverent tone that he had never detected in her voice before.

"It is different now," she said. "I am sure it is different. But some of the old places must be there, and the old people."

He made no reply. All he had ever heard of New Orleans was that Andrew Jackson had once paraded there and that later his mother had had a house on the Ramparts.

"Do you know," she said, "it is almost over now? I am proud of you, Allen. I watch for you to come down the street on your horse, the gray one with the black mane, and when I see you, you are so handsome I catch my breath. And when you come into the room dressed as you are, owning a plantation and a hundred slaves, I know it is all but finished now, all but done. Oh, my dear, it seems such a short time ago that I prayed for you and God gave you to me, and your father brought us to Middle Tennessee. It seems only a year, less then a year. In my memory it all happened yesterday."

"Mother," he said, understanding at last, seeing at last a little into her woman's heart. "Do you want to go back there?"

She smiled at him. "When we are ready," she said. "Your father will take me there when it is finished. But there is one thing more that I must stay here and see."

He gazed at her sitting so small in the chair, smaller and more delicate than Katherine, with the hair not even yet beginning to turn gray, the wrinkles in her face still shallow and vague, almost indiscernible in the light of the cloudy morning. And behind her the drawing of the convent on the wall, the beads in her lap, her embroidery on the table. In the moment before the summer rain began, the air was hot, lifeless, the room almost stifling.

"Mother," he said, "she is going to marry me, she has promised to marry me, but I cannot tell you when."

He paused and his conscience accused his tongue: she had, indeed, promised, but how could he be sure? In his memory he heard Anse Weaver say, *A year may bring more than a season to one who is patient.* And in answer he recalled the voice of Kate, *I can put no faith in joy or in the future.*

But he went on, rushed on to put his mother's mind at rest. And if he spoke a lie, he accepted the sin—freely, and he complimented himself upon the telling.

"We will be married," he said. "You need have no fear of that. If that is what you mean by completion, then your worries are over."

Did she believe him? He did not know. Her face was inscrutable, her eyes showed nothing.

"Ah," she said at last. "It is strange how quickly the time can pass."

Yes, he thought, quicker than a star, faster than a trail of light in the summer darkness. But he did not say this, for he did not believe that his mother would know what he meant.

"Mother," he said.

She had been looking out the window at the first fall of rain, the first drops that splashed against the tree leaves. Now she looked up and waited for him to speak.

"Do you believe me?" he asked. "Do you trust me when I tell you I will marry?"

"Ah, *mon cher*," she replied softly. "I love you. You are my pride. That is enough."

He left her then and rode back to Cedarcrest. He mounted the gray gelding and rode back past the square, back through the rain past the maple trees and the benches where, on good days, the village loafers congregated. But the benches were empty now and the pigeons had abandoned the gutters, and when he got on the highway, he saw that the fields and most of the pastures had been deserted. The Negroes had gone back out of the rain to their quarters. The cows were in their stables or huddled close in tight groups beneath the trees. It was very lonely with only the growing things, only the grass and the tobacco plants and the hickories and elms and blackjack oaks. Only the fence posts and the dull gray sky, the hills and the cedar trees dark on the horizon.

He left his horse at the stable and walked up to the house, poured himself a drink, and took the decanter with him to the office. He sat down there amid the trophies of the general's wars: on one wall some Cherokee arrows and a feathered clay pipe, on the other a British fife and a flintlock rifle. Above the mantel General Hendrick's portrait hung: a young man with a brick-red beard and golden epaulets upon his shoulders. Allen took another drink and lit a cigar and sat for a long time motionless, staring up through the smoke at his grandfather's picture. He looked at the eyes and the slender nose, the mouth that was thin and handsome but very determined. And he wondered what the general would tell him to do now, what advice he would give concerning Kate and Captain Rutledge. But he did not know, he could not even guess about this, and after a moment he left his chair and walked out the hall to the doorway and stood and watched the rain come down. Back in Gallatin, in his mother's sitting room, he had said, *We will get married. You need have no fear of that.* And the words had sounded very hollow;

he had detected a quiver, a note of uncertainty in his voice. Now, once more, his own mind had taken up the question: would they be married? And if so, when, in all the turning years to come, would it be?

Months ago, before the death of the general, the last time he had seen Kate in the Female Academy, they had stood in the hallway under the curious eye of Dr. Cox and she had made him promise that he would not speak to Captain Rutledge. Later that same day on the cars bound for home, he had stared out at the landscape just turning green with spring, and he had believed that he knew why she urged him to keep silent. She wanted to make the request herself, she had faith that in the end her father's love would be too great; when the objections had all been made he would submit to her pleasure.

But why now did she delay? He had asked her that one evening in July, a hot night that was very dry, with a dry wind blowing, soughing through the boxwoods. He had reminded her of the last time they were together in town, and he had asked her when she was going to speak to Captain Rutledge.

She had been carrying an ivory fan, and she had opened it and waved it once before her face and then closed it again and tapped it on her finger. "My dear," she had said, "I will when the time is right."

They had gone on a few steps, and then she had stopped and turned to face Allen and put her hands upon his shoulders.

"Darling," she said, "you must try to see. Things have changed since last spring and you must try to understand it."

Her voice trailed off and she took a deep breath that was almost audible, almost a sigh, and then she said, "Allen, I did not know it could happen this way. I did not know that God would let him go on living, year after year without alteration, without even seeming to grow old. For he did not change, Allen. Or only a little bit, only another line in his face or a hair or two less growing on his head. When I was at home last Christmas, his mind was clear. It was like old times, like when I was a child, and it was fair to argue with him then, to cajole with him, and to force him to furnish what I wanted. But it is not fair now." She paused. "Oh," she said, "you could not believe what has happened. Now there are times when his mind is not even clear, and he is sad and he thinks a good deal about dying. I cannot torment him. I cannot—" she hesitated, then said it vehemently, "I cannot devil him, Allen. I will simply have to try to catch him when the time is right."

He felt then a tightness in his throat, a constriction, not quite fear and not quite sorrow.

"Catch him?" Allen asked, "how, Kate? What is it that will make one time the right time?"

"He lives in the past," Katherine replied. "He spends his days remembering all the things he used to do and the people he used to know when he was younger. He talks about your grandfather, Allen. He loved General Hendrick, and he loves his memory now that he is gone. He cries when he thinks of General Hendrick's funeral. And one day when his mind is buried in the past, when he is thinking of Cedarcrest, where he used to visit every week and of the general whom he loved so dearly. . . . Then I will ask him if I may marry you."

Allen remembered how he had looked past her as she spoke, out toward the dark blue, star-filled sky; then he had turned his eyes to the ground and kicked at the gravel.

"Kate," he had said, "what if he answers no?"

"He cannot," she had replied. "That is why I must choose my time. Oh, my dear, I do not put it off to plague you."

"But if he does?" Allen had persisted.

"He cannot," she had said again. "He cannot, for if he did I could not bear it."

Nor could I, he had thought.

"Nor could I," he had said to Katherine.

This had been in the garden a month ago, for now it was the seventeenth of August. Two weeks more and it would be September, four months and it would be Christmastime again. If they were to know this summer, she would have to ask him soon. And even if he is going to refuse, Allen thought, I would like to know it.

He went to see Kate that night and the night that followed, slipped out of his house and made the distance on foot, then returned home to wait for the night to come again. They continued to walk the garden paths, to sit on the bench and look at the sky, to kiss and hold hands and talk of the time they would marry. And one night, three days after Allen's conversation with his mother, he found her already at the summerhouse when he arrived. She was standing in the middle of the pavilion in a brocade dress and a light shawl, for with August the evenings had turned cool. Her hands were folded in front of her. Her eyes were toward the ground. She did not see him till he was almost at her side.

When he thought of it later, he believed that he should have known. When he reconstructed it in his recollection, saw her again in his mind's eye, he recognized something of despondency in her posture, some sadness in the line of her shoulders and the tilt of her head. But at the moment of its happening he did not feel this. He was conscious only of his great delight in seeing her, and he moved to her quickly and kissed her on the cheek. Kissed her gently at first on the slightly cold flesh above her cheekbone, then kissed her again on the lips before she spoke.

"You are late," she said, not in anger but gently, as if in sorrow for the moments they had lost. "Don't be late. Not ever again."

"You are early," he replied. "But I apologize anyway. Next time I will be here as soon as the sun has set."

She said nothing. She had her arms around him, her own arms hooked beneath his, her hands resting on his shoulders. He felt her grip tighten, felt her fingers through the cloth of his coat, squeezing against the skin and flesh and muscle. The embrace so long and so possessive, the silence long too, and the sound of her breathing, not sharp, but deep and slow: and still he did not suspect it, though by now undoubtedly he should have known.

They walked between the boxwoods and past the chrysanthemums, not blooming yet but coming into bud. Past the dahlias and the late roses, to the end of the path and back to the summerhouse. Then he kissed her again and her face was wet with tears.

"Kate," he said, and at last he did know, understood what had happened, guessed what she would say.

She held to him again, one arm around his neck this time, pulling his head forward, his cheek and ear down close to her lips.

"Oh, darling," she said, "I thought it was right. I thought it was time to ask him, and I did ask him. I did the best I could."

"I know you did," Allen said softly.

He waited, feeling her body close to his, her breasts, her thighs, her chin close to his collar.

"I know you did," he repeated. "What did he say?"

"Oh, Allen," she said, "we came so near. He had been talking all day about General Hendrick. About how General Hendrick lent him slaves to help build his house, and let him apprentice one of his own men to the Cedarcrest blacksmith. He talked of all the old things, of the war, and how they lived so long here side by side, and of how General Hendrick stood up with him when he married Mother. He wept, Allen, and it almost made me cry too, just to watch him, to see him made sad by his recollection. But I did not cry. Not then. I made myself listen and I tried to gauge his mood, and just before supper when he was having his drink, when he was sitting in front of the fire drinking his toddy, I told him that I wanted to marry the general's grandson."

She broke off here, and after a moment Allen asked, "What did he say, Kate?"

She hesitated, pushed hard against Allen, tightened her grip around his neck.

"He will not allow it," she said in a whisper.

He had known this, known it from the moment that he had felt the tears, wet and cold upon her face. But now that it had been spoken, the phrase formulated, the fact put into words, he felt a kind of weakness, a slowness of the blood, and his head seemed very heavy on his shoulders. He waited, delayed to gather his strength.

Then he asked again, "What did he say?"

"I told you," she replied. "He said no."

"Kate," he said, "whatever it was, it cannot make it any worse."

"Oh, darling," she said, "forgive me. So near, so near. And perhaps if I had put it off another day—but it seemed the right time, Allen. It seemed to be the best opportunity we would have."

"Kate," he said. "Tell me, Kate."

She took a deep breath. "I asked him if I might marry you, and at first he said yes. He was sitting by the fire, as I told you, and when I mentioned it to him, I think he heard only the name Hendrick, and I do not believe he remembered who you were. He did not recollect that he had ever seen you, or whether or not General Hendrick had any grandchildren, boys or girls. And he said yes, I could marry any Hendrick, any man on all the earth who bore that name. But I knew it had not registered. I could tell by his face that he thought still of that other time, remembering only the general and no one else.

" 'Father,' I said, 'I want to marry Allen Hendrick.'

"And he looked at me for a long time, his eyes dull and sunk back in his head. He regarded me with no show of recognition, as if I, too, were a stranger, an intruder come to haunt his memory of the past. Then slowly it came to him, and his head began to shake more violently, and his lips trembled and he dropped his cup. Then he mentioned your mother, Allen, and said no."

Standing there with Katherine in his arms, he thought of his mother and what she would be doing now. How she would be in the parlor with her embroidery or a book, a slender, youthful woman with beautiful teeth, who spoke with an accent slightly foreign. And she had been to Poitiers and her brother had fought with Jackson at Chalmette, and once long ago in West Tennessee she had made an altar to the Holy Virgin. In the midst of his disappointment, sharply, cleanly felt through his desolation, was the first instant not of bitterness but anger. His mind's eye caught the vision of the captain's face, the very figure of age, the butt of time, the travesty of man's pride and his ambition. Who was he to deny Allen the fruition of his love? Who was he to thwart the heart's desire of Lucy? There in the garden Allen's hands grew cold, and he felt the strong pulse in his throat and the warm blood pounding through his temples.

So, being angry, he did not speak at once. He let his arms fall and stepped back from Kate, and breathed deeply and clamped his teeth together. When at last he did speak his voice was almost calm.

"I love you, Kate, and whether he likes it or not, I mean to marry you."

"Darling," she replied quickly, "don't talk like that. He is an old man, Allen. He is sick and feeble."

"Sick he may be," Allen Hendrick replied, "but what of me and what of you? If he could make the whole world miserable that would not improve his own condition."

"Allen," she said sharply, "I cannot help it. I did my best. You seem to forget that. I asked him. I tried."

Allen took a step toward her.

"I know that," he replied. "I do remember. And you failed through no fault of your own, and that's over and done with. He said no and he can stand and be damned on his own negation. But we do not have to stand on it. We can marry without his blessing. We can marry on our own."

"Hush," she said, the words broken by her quick breathing. "Please, Allen. Hush."

But he went on. "Listen. If it is a parent's blessing that you want you can have my father's. Or my mother's. But you had not thought of that, had you? It had not occurred to you that you might please or sadden them."

"Allen!" she said. She was weeping quite audibly now, sobbing, and she pounded his arm once or twice lightly with her fist. "Hush, Allen! Do not say those things to me. Do not speak to me that way. I cannot bear it!"

She paused. Then she said, "Oh, never talk to me that way again."

They were quiet for a moment, and Allen felt the August wind in his face. He clenched his teeth together and looked up at the stars, looked east where Hydra stretched its head toward Cancer.

"All right," he said, and he put his arm around her. "I'm sorry, darling."

"Oh," she said with feeling. "I know. I am sorry too."

Then after another pause with only the sound of her breath, with only the sound of her breathing, and in his own ears the sound of his heart and beyond the summerhouse the sough of the breeze through the Roseneath garden, she said:

"I am going to Nashville as soon as I can. Next week, if Aunt Lucille will have me."

"To Nashville?" he said, echoing her dumbly, his voice almost completely flat.

"Darling," she said, "think for a minute, listen to me for a minute, try to understand me. I have got to go. Father has forbidden me to see you again. He has asked me to promise that I will not see you, and I have used a subterfuge. I have circumvented him. I told him I would go to Nashville and get out of temptation's way. So I did not actually make a promise and you can come down there, don't you see? And we can be together. Whatever I do, I cannot meet you again out here."

She waited and he said nothing.

Then she said, "Oh, my dear, it will be better there. I will enjoy seeing you inside once more, having you in a light where I can see your face."

He kicked at the gravel walkway with the toe of his boot.

"No," he said. "I will not be there. I am not coming."

"Not coming!" she repeated incredulously. "I am leaving home and deceiving Papa. I have done the same thing as lie to him. And you say you will not even come thirty miles to visit me. Then don't. Then stay at Cedarcrest. It does not matter!"

"Wait," he said. He took a step toward her and grasped her by the arms. "It does matter. It matters more than anything else. I love you. As much as I ever did. More than I ever did. But where in the name of God are we headed when we go on this way? Katherine, I cannot keep it up. I cannot go on courting you forever."

"I did not ask you to," she replied. "I have promised to marry you."

"You will not say when," he said.

"I cannot say," she replied.

Again they were silent for a moment.

Then she said, "My darling, my darling, this is not my fault. I do not hate your mother. Though I have never seen her, I admire her because of you. And Papa does not hate her. Not really. He does not hate her or you. He does not fear her or you. It is everyone else, Allen. It is the world and what they will say that Papa fears. Oh, my dear, I know it is difficult for you. I know because I love you and I have felt it too, felt it for you in my heart. But Papa is only a part of the world. You must not despise him alone. You must not make him the butt of all your anger and bitterness."

He knew that there was much truth in what she said. He knew that at least partly the captain was thinking of a time to come, of the slights that Kate would receive as Allen's wife, and of Katherine's children. But this was not all of it. Captain Rutledge was thinking of Allen Hendrick, too, and of Lucy Hendrick, of Allen Hendrick's mother.

"Kate," Allen said with exaggerated patience, "I do not despise your father. But I cannot wait his pleasure forever. As much as I love you, I cannot wait yours. If you will name a day—I do not care when—just give me a time to look forward to, and I will follow you to Nashville or to the end of the world. I will come to the city, just to stand outside the academy wall and think of you."

He stopped.

Then he said, "Will you name a day?"

"Oh," she said with tears in her voice, with her voice filled with sadness and weeping. "Oh, you do not understand. I cannot name a time, and I cannot make you see why."

"I do see," he said with irony. "I understand perfectly."

"You don't," she replied quickly. "You don't! You have never seen it."

She turned and ran up the path toward the house, ran across the drive and up the veranda steps and was lost at last from his view in the heavy shadows. He waited to hear the latch on the door, strained his ears to catch the sound of her step. But there was no sound; in all the deep blue night there was only silence. He knew that by now she was in her room, alone in the quiet and dark of the house, except for her father, who doubtless would be sleeping. He stood with his hands in his pockets, motionless, gazing off into the darkness. Then he left the garden and took the road for home.

◈ 20 ◈

HE THOUGHT OF HER continuously in the days that followed; she was on his mind from morning till night through the long and lonely months of a bitter autumn. Wherever he went, on his farm or in the town, the memory of Katherine went with him. It was a subtle thing, this constant recollection. She came to him in a series of images, appeared like magic before his mind's eye: dressed in a gown that he recognized, striking a posture that he had seen her strike before. He remembered her as the girl at the academy seated on the love seat beneath the bracket lamp. He saw her in her aunt's drawing room or sitting on the bench at Roseneath or walking the path in the garden, her skirt lifted slightly to keep it out of the dew. She wore many costumes, her face assumed many expressions, and there were moments when he believed that he could hear her voice in the keen of the wind that shook the leaves on the trees. He thought of her with yearning and with considerable sorrow; in his heart he felt a desolate sense of loss.

But he did not write her, he could not bring himself to go to

Nashville, and after a while he stopped expecting a letter from her.

He spent a good deal of time that fall riding over his land, watching the hands at their harvest tasks—the cutting of tobacco, the baling of hay, the hilling of potatoes. In September the weather was very dry; the sky was blue, the air hot, and the wind came strong and dusty out of the west. Then October, and the sky bluer still, and a little rain to dampen the ground and a chill in the air at night and the dogs growing restless. And later, into November and the cold, damp days with the first coveys flushed by Anse Weaver's setter and the shock of the gun butt when the birds began to sail. And the first killing frost and the first days of December and the trees completely bare and the sky bright again. He lived through it all and learned to contain his sadness, learned to exist with the sorrow hidden carefully away. He could converse without losing the thread of conversation; he laughed at a jest and read books at night; and on Sunday afternoons he visited his parents. He even told his mother that Kate had returned to school, heard his voice speak the words in an almost tranquil tone, and no tear rose to betray his grief; his throat did not choke, his fingers did not tremble. He listened to Marcus Hendrick talk politics and law; he ate heartily, drank brandy, smoked cigars, and only once did he feel his passion stirring, rising to the surface, out of his control.

It was a day in October, a quiet afternoon when the leaves on the maples had begun to turn and to fall, singly, gently through the breathless air. They were in the parlor in Gallatin, Allen and his father, in the room that seemed to Allen to hold all that was left of that other time, the old days before he had come to Sumner County. The piano, the slender, gilded chairs, the pictures and some silver candlesticks, a small Sèvres clock and a pair of Meissen vases. It was a room that recalled vague memories, it struck the tone of another age, and as he stood before the fire, his hands clasped at his waist, he was touched by the thought of all that had gone before—his mother's pride and her lonely prayers, his own past innocence and the journey east through the woods, his father's dreams and his sense of human justice. It was a chamber suited to Allen's mood, for it seemed to argue against man's hope and against the fulfillment of desire, against love's consummation. Marcus Hendrick was seated near the hearth, his legs stretched out, the toes of his boots turned up. He was holding a brandy glass in his hand, his spectacles were pinched on the bridge of his nose. The ribbon that held them cast a shadow across his face in the dancing firelight. He was speaking of the election that was to come; he was torn between the issues and the expedients involved; he could not make up his mind whom he was going to vote for. He believed in the preservation of the Union, and yet, when he read the speeches of Bell, or heard his supporters talk of the compromise that would save the nation but perpetuate slavery, it seemed to him that a vote for the Constitutional Union Party was a vote for the one thing he abhorred most in all the world. But on the other hand, when he saw the addresses of Lincoln, he knew that the course of emancipation led to the country's dissolution and he felt that without the Union, freedom was as dross. He told Allen this, peering up through his spectacles, his thin face sallow and deeply lined. "I do not know how to mark my ballot," he said, his voice very tired. "I only know that trouble lies ahead."

Then he turned his gaze to the window, looked out at the quiet, sunlit street, at the lawn and the scattering of fallen leaves, and moved his eyes slowly back to the room once more.

"Do you know," he said, "that your friend, Houston Knott, is electioneering? He is speaking for Breckinridge. He is breathing fire."

Allen did know this.

"Yes, sir," he replied. "I was in town the other night and I heard him speak."

Allen had come to Gallatin to sign a draft at the bank, and he had had supper with the cashier, a Mr. Whitworth. He had gone out to Mr. Whitworth's house and met Mr. Whitworth's wife, and on the way home, when he had ridden by the square, he had seen a crowd of people on the courthouse lawn, and a speaker standing in the torch light on the landing. He started to pass on, rode halfway around the congested square, then looked again and recognized the speaker as Houston and got off his horse to hear what Houston Knott would say. There had been many people, most of them farmers, in leather and homespun and worn denim. The hitching rails were crowded with wagons and mules, and the cool breeze of the fall night stirred in the smell of tobacco and sweat, and the long, tanned, gaunt faces looked up toward the platform where the pine knots smoked and the boy in broadcloth pounded on the rostrum. The boy barely old enough to vote, with gold seals on his watch chain and a longing, yearning, hungry look in his eyes, spoke in a voice that seemed close to tears, a tone that rose and shouted in the cool night and then fell off to speak softly, just above a whisper.

"Let me tell you something," Houston Knott had said. "This is my home, the land I live in. We came here and cut the trees; we cleared the land and built our houses and plowed our furrows. And those people from the North, those cheating, lying, thieving, pot-gutted, nutmeg-selling Yankees, they went to Africa and came back with a shipload full of niggers and they brought those niggers to us and said let us sell you some niggers. That's what they said. 'Let us sell you some niggers. For we have been across the waters to the other side of the world, and we have got niggers to sell to help you build your fences.' They brought us niggers that couldn't even talk, that would grunt like a sow in farrowing time, and thought God was a snake or a bird in a tree, and would like as not kill and cook and make a meal of one another. They brought niggers out of a dark jungle and carried them over in the dark hold of a ship, and they sold them to us while the niggers were sick and starving, and they pocketed their profits and went back home up to the North. And what did we do?"

Here a pause; Allen remembered it clearly. Houston pointed now, his arm toward the crowd. "What did you do? You took that sick, hungry nigger that had never tasted greens or a sweet potato and taught him to talk and to worship God. And you gave him the lumber to build himself a home, and you gave him cloth to make clothes to cover his hide, and you called the doctor when he was sick, and your wives took care of the nigger children, and your preacher married the nigger women and men, and you told them the right and the Christian way, and you taught them to talk the language Christians talk and you made a place for them in your church and gave them a chance to go to heaven. And what did we ask? What did you require of them in return?" Another pause, so quiet now that the rustle and crack of the burning torch was audible. "Nothing but an honest day's work, the simple, honest sweat of the brow in return from the sons of Ham for assuming their burdens."

Houston stepped forward, the hand raised, the long arm covered in black broadcloth, the white, tapering fingers, the slender wrist. "All you ask for civilization, for the gifts out of your bounty, in full measure given, are fidelity and the performance of simple duty. And the Yankees with your gold jingling in their pockets—your gold from the original sale of the slaves, your gold from high tariffs, and high shipping charges, gold from your tobacco that they carried on their cars, gold from the plow points and trace chains they have sold you—these Yankees tell you to set the nigger free. Let the nigger run loose among your wives and children, while the Yankee sits on his haunches and smacks his chops.

"Let me tell you something. You may think all this doesn't make any difference to you. You may say, I'm not a rich man. I don't own any niggers. What difference will it make to me if the niggers are free? The other night when I had finished speaking, a gentleman came to me here on the steps of your courthouse, and he said, 'Houston, I'm a poor man. Oh,' he said, 'I own me a little place and I work it and make my mite off of it for the woman and the mouths of the chaps I have to feed, but it's not a fine place and I don't own no niggers and I never aim to. But,' he said, 'what a man owns he owns and he's got a right to it and ne'er man has a right to take what he owns away.' That was what that gentleman said to me, but now I want to tell you of another right—the right of our people to act as they choose, to govern themselves as the constitution of this nation guarantees, the right to protect themselves from the threat of emancipated niggers running the country, loose and free. Vote for Breckinridge, the *Southern* Democrat. Vote for your rights, and we with God's help will prevail."

Standing there in the parlor in front of the fire, Allen saw the scene in all its bright detail, heard the words that Houston Knott had uttered, heard the rising inflections, the rolling, pleading tones, the fall that sometimes came at the end of a sentence. He saw once more in his recollection the lean and noncommittal faces, listening, watching the courthouse steps with narrow eyes. There in the room where his mother kept the things that she loved, where the porcelain clock ticked on the chimney piece and the firelight brightened the gilded rounds of the chairs, he felt suddenly that the sun had turned back on itself, rushed back through the turning corridor of time, and his old memories rose, not in fragments now, but all of a piece, a unity, a span of years. He had never felt this before. On the night that he had heard Houston speak, he had remembered the boy and the boy's ambitious dreams, but these had then seemed somehow segregated from the rest of life. Now, under the spell of his mother's house, where the pain of his heartbreak, his loss of Kate was always poignant, the amalgamation of the past became suddenly complete, and he knew as much as he would ever know of the integrity of life, of all the world's fateful and curious ramifications. For whom did Houston talk against? Against Bell, of course, who stood for moderation. But more than against Bell, he was against Lincoln, whose name was not even on the Tennessee ballot, and all that he represented and all who supported him in the North. And Houston spoke, too, against Allen Hendrick, who was part Negro, and against Lucy, who was more Negro than Allen, and against Marcus Hendrick, who believed in the freedom of all men. And yet, if slavery were abolished, Allen Hendrick would lose one hundred people while Houston, personally, stood to lose only two or three. If Mr. Lincoln were elected and the Negro given manumission, then all the hard years Lucy had spent in Memphis would have been wasted and all her hopes for a planter son would have come to naught. And if, as Houston seemed to wish, the country were divided, then Marcus Hendrick would lose the one thing he loved more than justice: the Union whose flag he had fought for in 1812.

Houston did not hate the Negro. Allen knew this. Not personally, not man to man. He did not, Allen suspected, even feel very strongly about slavery. For him the whole question of abolition was a point to talk against, like the time Joe Henry Witherspoon ran from the crippled bull, or the way Joe Henry's upper teeth protruded. But if Allen's love were still alive, if there remained some possibility that he might marry Kate, this sort of talk, more than anything else, would hurt his chances. Houston did not speak for the old Whigs, for the men like General Hendrick, who had loved the land; nor for the men of science like Anse Weaver, who fretted about the secret part of the brain, that factor, that motive force that they could not touch. He did not speak for Kate, nor for Dr. Cox at the Female Academy, nor for Mrs. Richardson in her house on Vine Street, nor for Ben Hill, who dealt in Negroes, nor for Valeria, who had been raised in Mississippi, nor in the end even for Captain Rutledge, who would not let his daughter marry a man who had Negro blood.

Houston spoke for no one; but from the first night that Allen had come into Gallatin, riding with his father in the buggy, the brass-bound rifle heavy on his knee, Houston had been a part of his life, and what Houston had said had affected Allen. And not only Houston. Call any name, and that name was important. For the person who bore that name had shaped Allen's life. If Lucy had not been ambitious, if Marcus Hendrick had not been an expert in money, if Ben Hill had not distrusted Marcus, what would Allen's life have been then? Or if John Hendrick had not died of yellow fever, or if on that first day at Cedarcrest, that first, hot afternoon when they sat in the parlor, the Negro boy had not come and exposed the general's duplicity by shouting at the door, or if Allen had not mentioned the name of General Jackson, where would they all be now? His mind raced on, tracing the labyrinth of all the days he had lived through, and for the first time since he had said good-by to Kate his heart misgave him and the tears rose to his eyes. For had he done what his mother and father would have wished? Had he been precisely fair to Kate? He did not know. He would never know the answers.

But he understood now, as he had not understood before, the lesson that his father once had tried to teach him. On that morning in spring, in the dining room, when Marcus Hendrick had at last finished his story, the long tale of his own, Marcus', past, and of his marriage in New Orleans, to Lucy—then, hearing the cock crow, seeing the candles' flame grow dim in the light of the morning, Allen had thought only that his father spoke of the past, passed on the traditions and the family lore, as he would repeat a grandmother's maiden name or give the date when the first Hendrick crossed the waters. Allen saw now that his father had meant to do more than this and that the recollection must have cost Marcus some pain. What Marcus Hendrick had tried to convey was the simple fact of the continuity of life, the single thread that is never cut but which goes on generation unto generation to the end of time. The simple truth that the future and the past are a part of the same passage, and the present not even a mark on the map, but a point, a position without length or width, without dimension. So, Allen saw, man goes on, living in the shadow of a history that he does not comprehend, acting on the grounds of expediency, as expediency makes itself known, for, as Marcus Hendrick had told him on another night, no man can be certain of his own motives. Houston Knott spoke of the sons of Ham, and Allen said good-by to Kate on the garden walk, and Lucy remembered New Orleans and Poitiers, and Marcus Hendrick brooded over the election. And caught between the future and the long, long past, they molded, shaped the fortunes of each other. Houston spoke for no one and yet he spoke for all. Few who listened to him hated or even feared the Negro, and yet most of them would fight to keep the Negro a slave. Or nearer home, Lucy Hendrick had prayed for a son to ransom her misery; and Allen in his pride and anger at Captain Rutledge had turned his own chance of happiness away.

"Father," Allen said, breaking the silence that had fallen between them, "don't worry about Houston. Not many people will listen to him. He does not even mean a lot of the things he says."

"No," Marcus Hendrick replied. "He cannot do much harm. He can neither save nor break the nation." Marcus removed his spectacles and held them in front of his chest, let them dangle on the ribbon from his fingers. "But I do not like to hear him. The words he speaks are poison to my ears."

For a moment then he made no sound. He stared at the fireplace, but his eyes appeared to see nothing; his eyelids were narrowed, and he seemed to peer off into the distance, as if his gaze were sharp enough to pierce the wall.

"My boy," he said at last, "I have lived a long time. I am sixty-five and I have lived through many things. Father is dead now, and Cedarcrest is yours, and Lucy loves you very much, Allen, and you have made her happy. Happier than I have ever made her, happier than she has ever been before in her life. But she is lonely here, and I think sometimes of taking her away. I think, we will go when Allen is married, or we will go when the election is over and when we know what the country is going to do. I tell myself, we will go at this time or that time when this issue or that one is finally settled. But I am old enough to know that the issue is never settled, and so old that I don't know what to wish for any more."

"You are only sixty-five, Father," Allen said softly. "Grandfather was almost ninety when he died."

"Years," Marcus Hendrick replied gently. He spoke with infinite patience in his voice. "You speak in terms of years and numbers, but they mean very little when enough of them have gone. Once," he went on, "there was much to be believed in, much to be worked for, though the cause was often hard. There was a time when I might speak with what I considered to be the voice of truth. But what can I say to your friend, Houston, now? What can I say to your lady, Katherine, or to her father who was my father's friend, or even to you, who might listen to what I advised you? It seems that one virtue cancels out another, and that the good of the world is warring with itself."

He rose and walked to the table. Then he replaced his glasses on his slender nose, the movement of the hand slow, the hand trembling.

"I do not know," he said simply. "I cannot tell what to hope for any more."

They sat in the parlor and talked some more that afternoon, spoke of crops and investments which were perilous now, while the sun went down in a red October twilight and the autumn sky grew dark as the night came on. But when he remembered it later, it seemed to Allen that these were the last words he had heard his father speak. He saw Marcus Hendrick many times after this. He even heard Marcus Hendrick discuss politics, heard him wish fervently for Mr. Lincoln's success, heard him voice the hope that the country might hold together. But it appeared to Allen when it was over and done, when Marcus was dead and buried at Cedarcrest beside the general, that never after this day had he spoken from the heart. The things he said had been uttered as if by rote, like lessons retained but not understood, like lines learned at night to be repeated in the morning.

Two months later, when the campaign was over and Mr. Lincoln was preparing to take Mr. Buchanan's place, Vernon rode out to Cedarcrest with a message for Allen. It was a Friday morning, the twenty-first of December, four days before Christmas, and the weather was damp and cold. Throughout the night a little snow had been falling, clinging for a while in the boughs of the cedar trees, then melting, dripping to the sodden ground. The creek and the river were running high, and at daylight, when the snow changed to rain, the roads were heavy to travel and deep with mud. For an hour after breakfast Allen had been in the Cedarcrest office, sitting by the fire and smoking and waiting for the mail to be brought out from town. From time to time he would go to the window, rub a clear place on the misted glass, and look out at the drive and the cold, gray day for some sign of the groom who had gone to Gallatin on one of the mules. This was the reason that he saw Vernon ride down the drive, caught sight of him just as he crested the hill, and he recognized him by the fact that he rode a horse. Or rather, he knew that it was not his own boy coming with the letters and the morning papers, and as the rider moved closer, down toward the creek, and then up between the wet, green trees toward the mounting block, he remembered the familiar tilt of the head, the long legs, the tightly buttoned duster. Vernon rode across the lawn and around the house, entered without knocking through the side door, and Allen heard him talking to Uncle Aaron in the hallway. But they were not arguing, not even bantering; the sounds of their voices were soft, almost friendly, and in a moment there came a rap on the office door.

"Come in, Vernon," Allen said. "Come on in here and get warm by the fire."

Vernon entered, his oilcloth duster dripping, his hat off and it dripping too, marking a trail as he walked across the floor. He came and stood in front of Allen's chair, in silence, unable or unwilling to speak, his face impassive except for his eyes which moved, darted about the room, his body motionless except for his fingers, which tugged and pulled and clutched at the wet hat brim.

"What is it?" Allen said.

And Vernon said nothing.

After a moment Allen repeated, "What is it, Vernon?"

"It is Mr. Marcus," Vernon said. "He passed away."

He got it out at last in a voice that was weak, and tears came to his eyes and he took out a handkerchief and blew his nose. He would not say much more, except that the end had come suddenly, that Marcus Hendrick had risen from the breakfast table, taken a step toward the dining room door, and had fallen and never regained consciousness again. Vernon had got on his horse and ridden to get Anse Weaver, but Marcus Hendrick had died before Anse had arrived. Now that he had delivered his message, Vernon turned away. He was going back to Gallatin to help lay out the corpse.

So they rode back to Gallatin together, Allen and Vernon, through the cold, wet day, splashing and slipping through the puddles and the mud, their breaths turning to mist, their horses steaming. It took them a long time to get there, for the horses were wary; it was one o'clock when they passed the courthouse square.

Vernon did not get to help prepare the body. When he and Allen got to the house, Anse and Judge Knott had already bathed the corpse, shaved it and dressed it and combed the hair, and Marcus Hendrick lay upstairs on a tester bed, small and neat with his hands crossed at his waist. Judge Knott had gone home, but Anse was still there and Valeria had come too, and she sat next to Lucy. She had got to make her visit at last; she had come at last to the house to see Allen's mother. Lucy had been crying. Her eyes were red, and there were wrinkles on her cheeks that Allen had not noticed there before, that seemed new as if the tears themselves had left them. She wept a little more when Allen took her hand, but for most of the time she kept a stern composure.

"Mother," Allen began, but there was nothing to say. With all that she must have remembered out of their past love and grief, what word of his could assuage her pain or add to her comfort?

For a little while she let him hold her hand, and they sat together, looking at his father's body, at the high forehead and the delicate, pale lips, the cheeks creased and almost sunken, the closed eyelids. Two little depressions remained on the bridge of his nose, to show where in life he had worn his spectacles; the glasses were in his pocket now, attached to his coat lapel by the thin black ribbon. In the middle of the afternoon Allen went downstairs to talk to Anse.

"I do not know whether I could have foretold it," Anse said, "even if he had been my patient, which he was not."

"I know," Allen said. "He would never go to a doctor."

"Young Hendrick," Anse said, crossing the parlor, moving toward the chair where Allen sat, placing his hand lightly on Allen's arm. "I am very sorry. I wish there were something I could do to soften the blow."

"You are very kind," Allen said. He paused for a moment with his mouth shut tight. Then he asked, "What did Father die of?"

"Apoplexy," Anse replied. "I cannot be sure, but I think he had a stroke. It happened fast. It was over quickly."

Allen made no reply. This was Friday, and on Sunday, when he had seen his father last, Marcus Hendrick's health had seemed as good as usual. He had seemed old and tired, but he had not been sick, not ailing.

"But what brought it on?" Allen asked. "Why today? Why this morning?"

Anse stood with his eyes tilted up and bit his lip and frowned as if he were thinking.

Then he said, "It is only a suspicion, young Hendrick, but I will guess at the answer."

He moved a step or two to rest against the mantelpiece. "I have known Major Hendrick a long time," he said. "And I know what he believed in. I remember hearing about him all my life, and he was my friend, just as you are my friend, and that is why I presume to speculate about what he was thinking. He was gone when I got here, and while I was waiting for Judge Knott to come, I walked down to the dining room where Major Hendrick had fallen. The room had not been cleaned, the table had not been cleared away. The dishes were still there, just as he had left them. Let me show you what I found beside his plate."

Anse walked to a table in the corner of the room, picked up a newspaper, and folded it in the middle, and came back and handed it to Allen Hendrick.

It was a morning edition, brought up from Nashville on the train, and on the front page, surrounded by advertisements, was a single-column story in heavy type.

IMPORTANT FROM CHARLESTON

SECESSION
of South Carolina
Passed unanimously at 1.15 o'clock P.M.,
December 20th, 1860

AN ORDINANCE

To dissolve the Union between the State of South Carolina and other States united with her under the compact entitled "The Constitution of the United States of America."

CONVENTION DECLARES

the

UNION

is

DISSOLVED

There was a story under these headings, the text of the ordinance, quotations from some of the delegates to the convention, some speculation about the secession of other states. Allen glanced at this but he did not read it. And he wondered how much of it Marcus Hendrick had read, how far down the column his eyes had gone before he pushed back his chair and tried to leave the table. What had he thought of in that instant before his death? His boyhood trek through the wilderness, his movement with the army through Indiana, north along the Maumee toward the Michigan snow? Or his nights in the office at Cedarcrest, with Jackson, who had intended to be President, and Oliver, who traced empires on the blank space of a map, and Winchester, who spoke like a professor of Latin and Greek? Or had he remembered Memphis and the flatboat men? Or Arkansas and Mrs. O'Connor? Or the New Orleans heat and the house on the Ramparts? Or the house in Memphis, where Lucy had prayed for a son? Or the trip back to Middle Tennessee with Allen riding beside him? Or all of these things? Or something else, something Allen himself had never heard of?

Marcus Hendrick had seen a good deal of what there was to see in the nation: he had been to college in New Jersey. He had been taken prisoner at the River Raison and transported to Canada by the British and exchanged at Buffalo and sent back home. He had been down the Cumberland River, through Tennessee and Kentucky, and the Ohio as it wound past Illinois. He had been down the Mississippi and from the gingerbread packet deck, he had seen the banks and the green country, the fields and the trees and the pasture and the cotton and the corn. Somehow, Allen knew, he had carried the image of it: the picture of a whole nation he had kept in his mind. And now . . . the black type on the cheap paper, the ordinance passed at one-fifteen o'clock.

"Young Hendrick," Anse said softly, "it may have been for the best. There will be more news like this before we have seen the last."

"Yes," Allen replied. "You may be right about that too."

The body remained in the house in Gallatin until noon on Saturday; it was left in the bedroom, and Lucy sat there with it, sat up through the long night in a straight-backed chair. It was not according to custom that the widow should watch with the corpse, and there were others who would have stayed with her if she had been willing for them to stay. But she was not willing, and she kept the vigil unattended, except for Allen, who looked in on her from time to time. She sat by the bed, a small woman in a black crepe dress, her head erect, her skirt smooth over her knees, her feet close together. She had her beads clutched in her hands, and Allen supposed that she was saying prayers and he believed that this was why she wanted no one with her. Her eyes were dry, and the expression on her face was not completely sad, though her lips seemed particularly thin and her eyes looked weary. Her eyes were red and deeply circled, and at the corners there were wrinkles in the flesh. From time to time as the night wore on, Allen went in to sit for a moment or merely to stand beside her chair, and after midnight, when the house grew damp and cold, he brought a shawl and placed it on her shoulders. The next day the body was put in a casket and the casket removed to Cedarcrest.

This was the way Lucy wanted it. She believed that Marcus Hendrick should be buried on the grounds of the house where he had been born, and she wanted his old friends to have a chance to see him. So it turned out that she was not only praying when she sat alone with him through the winter night; she was saying good-by, she was looking for the last time at his slender face. But Allen did not recognize this at first. He assumed that for a day she might stay away from the house out of a sense of consideration for those who might not wish to see her; but it did not occur to him that she would stay away from the burial too. Only when the hearse had already come and the casket was being carried down the wide stairs—only then did he guess the truth.

They were standing in the door to the parlor, and when the coffin had gone by them—carried by six Negroes: Vernon and Aaron and four others who had remembered Marcus Hendrick from their youth —when the pallbearers had gone past them and out onto the porch, Lucy turned away and moved back toward the parlor fire. Allen followed her, across the carpet, past the chairs and the piano to the corner of the hearth where he stopped and put his arm around her waist.

"Mother," Allen said, "I will send for you tonight. I will send the carriage and you can sleep out there and we will have the services tomorrow."

She did not say anything, but she shook her head.

Still he did not understand her. He believed that she must be objecting to the time of the funeral or to the hour he had named to come for her.

"When, then?" he said, "when do you want to come?"

"No," she replied. "I am not coming. I will not be there."

"Ma'am?" he said, for he could not have caught her meaning. She could not have spoken the words that he thought he heard.

"I am not coming," she repeated. "Go on now. They are waiting to drive away."

"Mother," he said, "it is Father. It is not they who are waiting, or me, it is Father. Father who is waiting out there in the hearse, and Father who will be buried tomorrow or Monday or whenever you want to bury him, but you are his wife, Mother, his widow, and you have got to come."

"Allen," she said softly. "Please go with them, Allen. Don't make them tarry for you out there in the cold."

"Mother," Allen said, "you can come to Cedarcrest. It was you who wanted to bury Father there, and you can come there and stay for the rest of your life; you could have come there to live at any time since I have owned it."

She turned and moved to the other end of the fireplace. She seemed to tremble slightly, her shoulders seemed to jerk beneath her dress, but the movement was quick, almost imperceptible, and in the poor light of the parlor Allen could not be sure.

Then she said, "I do not want to come to Cedarcrest. Can't you understand that?"

And for a moment he thought that he did understand. To his great surprise and somewhat to his sorrow he thought she was proud.

"It is not for me," he said, noting an edge of testiness to his voice. "It is not simply to come to Cedarcrest. It is to attend Father's funeral."

Another pause, another almost imperceptible movement of her body, and then slowly, quietly, she said, "He is gone. He is gone, and I have prayed and looked upon his face, and I will keep on praying for him till God comes for me too."

Her voice was soft and even, but the tears were coming now, gathering in her eyes and running down staining her cheeks, staining the ivory-colored flesh that was newly wrinkled.

"Oh," she said, "he gave me his life. He gave me his life and the fair hope of his days, and now in death I can give him back his dignity."

She was returning him to the position he had relinquished for her, she was restoring him now to the glory of his birthright.

"Mother," Allen said, and he swallowed hard and bit his lip before he could continue. "Valeria will come and stay with you. Would you like that? She could sleep here with you."

She shook her head once more. "No," she replied. "No, my dear, she is kind, but I do not want that either."

◊ 21 ◊

SO ALLEN WENT without his mother to Cedarcrest, where Marcus Hendrick was buried, and the next afternoon he returned to Gallatin with Valeria and Anse. Or rather, they began their journey in the afternoon, the three of them riding together in the same carriage, but the roads were muddy and very slow, and they did not get to the town limits until after nightfall. In the first full darkness of the December evening they rode across the square, past the lighted inn, the shuttered stores, and on to the rented house, where the carriage stopped and the three of them got out. For Anse and Valeria were going in with him: Valeria to seek to comfort Lucy, to visit with her and do whatever women did—Allen Hendrick did not know what; and Anse to sit with Allen for a while in the parlor.

When they got to the house they found it dark. Because it was winter and night and the air was damp and cold, Allen knew that the shutters were most likely fastened; but there was no hint of light, no trace of the lamp's glow at the edge of the window frames, no glimmer to be seen through the cracks of the shutters. It occurred to Allen that his mother, weary from her sorrow, was probably resting, and with Anse and Valeria at his side he moved quietly up the walk and quietly turned the knob and opened the door into the hallway.

The house was cold. The inside darkness was very still, the air was motionless and a little musty. Anse Weaver struck a lucifer match, and when it flared Allen could see that the door to the parlor stood ajar, but no fire burned in the parlor fireplace.

[243]

Allen called out, "Mother."

Anse touched Allen's arm.

"Wait," Anse Weaver said. "She may be asleep. Let's light a lamp and then you can go and look for her."

But he did not have to go and look, for in the sitting room they found the note. A pink Sèvres clock sat on the mantel, and leaning against it was an envelope addressed to Allen, and he took it and broke the seal and read the letter.

My dear son,

I do not know how to begin to say what I want to tell you, or among all the things that I must say, which to say first. But to speak first of what I intend to do, at five hours after noon I shall go to Nashville on the cars, and I shall depart on a boat for New Orleans on Sunday morning. From there I shall go to live with my brother on his plantation. So when you see this, I shall have been for a day on the water.

Oh, my dear, is it an untruth, is it a falsehood for me to say that I leave not only for myself, but as well for you? I remember a night not long ago—though it will seem long to you, for some years have marched by since then—a night in summer when a bird sang to the moon and from my room I could hear you and your father talking. You were discussing that free man, that Negro Ben Hill, and in the course of your talk your father spoke of human motives. He said that no one could be sure of why he acted as he did, that man's motivation was never pure, never altruistic, never completely a function of love, and perhaps in abandoning you I am being only selfish.

But, oh, my darling, what could we do, the two of us alone in the great world? Where would we live? How would we pass our hours? I leave now wondering why you have not yet married, not knowing your case or how your romance stands, but hoping still, praying still for your heart's fulfillment. Were I to come to live with you, were I to move to Cedarcrest, what dreams of yours would be broken then, what chance for happiness would vanish. Nor could you live here in better state, for my presence in the same house with you would impose stern conditions. I cannot tell you how your father suffered—though you know something of it— nor can I show you how I suffered, knowing his pain was for me.

And that brings me to the heart of what I want to say. I come close to the truth now to speak of my own poor frailty. I cannot endure it all again, I cannot live with your suffering or with my own loneliness. Not for another twenty years, or ten or even one, if no more are left to me. Understand. Comprehend and forgive my weakness. My love for you and for your father remains unimpaired though the flesh be weak and the spirit broken. If I could help you by remaining with you, I would search for strength to stay. I would pray for fortitude as I pray now for your forgiveness and for your happiness and for a happy ending to your love. But my staying could bring only misery to us both. And I shall welcome a friend to talk to once more, and a house where I can visit.

My dear, will you come to see me? Someday, not soon, but when your affairs have crystallized, can you spare a few weeks to visit me in Louisiana? I love you as much as I loved your father. Both of you, I love better than I love myself. May God bless you and may He bless his soul.

And this was all, except for her signature and a postscript saying that she had taken Marcus Hendrick's gold.

He did not know how long it took him to read his mother's letter. But apparently he took a long time, or perhaps he read it more than once, for when he finished, he saw that Anse had built a fire. He looked down and saw the kindling beginning to flame, and later he remembered watching how the fire spread, how it curled around the logs and singed the bark, and how tiny sparks broke free and rose up the chimney. He stood looking down at the fireplace, feeling nothing. It was as if his mind had stopped—or more than this: as if by some spell of the night and the empty house his physical processes, the beat of his heart and the flow of his blood, had been suspended. Then, slowly, he came to himself, and he tried to fold the letter and replace it in the envelope, and for a moment or two he could not do this because his hands were trembling. The paper shook, rustled slightly in the quiet room. Then he did get it folded and put away, and, moving very deliberately, he took off his coat and sat down in a chair near Valeria. His head felt very warm and light, and there was a pain in his shoulders and in his chest, an ache in his throat and in his temples.

"Allen," Valeria said. And he was conscious that she had spoken to him, called his name once or twice before, and he had not answered.

He turned toward her. "Yes," he replied.

"Is the letter from your mother?" Valeria asked.

"Yes," he said.

Then he handed her the envelope and said, "You read it. Read it out loud so Anse can hear it. Read it loud enough for me to hear it again."

But when Valeria took the letter and began to read, Allen did not listen. His mind went beyond the sound of Valeria's voice, beyond the words that Lucy Hendrick had written, and in his fancy he saw how it must have been; his mind's eye peered backward in time to his mother's departure.... She had taken Marcus Hendrick's gold, and to get it she must have gone to his office: she had walked out on the streets of Gallatin for the first time in her life. After all her years of staying at home, she had ventured at last beyond her own gate; and in his imagination Allen saw how she must have looked—the slim and uncertain figure that crossed the rain-swept square and moved from door to door in search of her husband's office.

For she would not have known where the office was, or being told the name of the street it was on, she still could not have gone directly to it. Except for the house in which she lived, she knew the location of no address in all of Gallatin. So she must have looked for the inscription on the glass, the sign nailed up beside the door and found this—*Marcus Brutus Hendrick, Attorney at Law*—and the wood of the sign beginning to crack, the gilt of the old letters peeling. But the gilt, the sign, had held out long enough; they had lasted beyond the man himself, beyond the flesh and the beat of the heart, beyond the old weariness and love and disappointment. Recollecting her husband suddenly, as one recollects the newly dead, had she trembled and felt her knees grow weak, had she raised her handkerchief toward the face that was hidden beneath the parasol?

He did not know. But he knew that she had gone on, up the penumbral stairway to the narrow, dingy landing; she had unlocked the door and stepped into the office. And what had she thought of the clutter and the dust, she who had always been so neat, who had lived so immaculately? She had seen the table strewn with papers, the desk where the ledger books were piled, and the decanter of brandy and the glasses and the ashes on the hearth and a pair of old carpet slippers beside a chair. And what had gone through her woman's mind, which at other times had always cherished neatness?

What shock at the sight of the unswept floor? What grief on seeing the room her husband had worked in?

Oh, Allen Hendrick thought, she did not have to leave. Oh, he thought, she should not have gone. She should have stayed with me, because I love her.

"Allen," Valeria said. She had finished reading the letter, and she reached out now and took Allen Hendrick's hand.

"My dear," she said. "My dear, I am so sorry."

He did not answer at once. He rose and walked up and down before the hearth, then stopped and stood with his back to the chimney piece.

"It is my fault," he said, speaking bitterly. "If I had told her about Katherine, she would not have gone."

"No, no," Valeria replied gently. "It is not your fault. Don't say such things, Allen."

"It is, by God!" Allen said. "If I had told Mother that Kate will not marry me, that she will never marry me, then Mother would not have gone back to Louisiana."

He paused. Then he said, "Don't you understand? She knew I wanted to marry, and she thought that by leaving here she would be helping me."

"No," Valeria replied. "I'm afraid I don't understand. Not about you and Katherine or about Katherine and your mother. Not any of it."

"Then listen and I will explain it to you," Allen said testily. "You listen too, Anse. Kate will not marry me, because I am a nigger."

In the silence that came when he had stopped speaking, Allen could hear beyond the house the creak and keen of the wind against the outside shutters and the faint drip of the rain upon the ground. Anse rose and went to the dining room and came back with some brandy. He poured two drinks and handed one of them to Allen.

At last Allen said, "No, that is not exactly right. Kate will not marry me because her father will not let her. He is the one who objects to my being a nigger."

Allen hesitated. Then he went on, "But it's the same thing. I am a nigger, and she cannot marry a nigger. And that is the way it has always been. I have been a nigger every day of my Goddamned life."

"Hush," Valeria said. "Hush, Allen. My dear, you must not talk that way."

"Hush, hell!" Allen Hendrick said. Then more softly, "I'm sorry, Valeria, but it's true."

Valeria looked down at her lap for a moment. "Then Katherine told you that she could never marry you, that her father objected, and that she would have to stop seeing you?"

"No," Allen said. "Not exactly. I stopped seeing her."

"My God, young Hendrick," Anse Weaver said. "I'm damned if I follow you."

"All right," Allen replied, "it was this way. Captain Rutledge is the oldest man in the world. He is shriveled up and feeble and his blood has turned to water, and he sits around cold and shivering all day, and he doesn't even know where he is. Half the time he thinks he is back in the East, and he believes things are the same as when he was a boy. He thinks the Indians are still running loose and free, or he fancies he sees people he knew when he was young, or he is convinced that he is still a soldier fighting up in Michigan. He is feeble and senile, and he would not recollect my face if he were to see it. And yet he knows the name of Allen Hendrick. And he remembers Mother. Beyond all other things, he remembers us. Oh," Allen Hendrick said, and the sound was almost a groan, "I cannot tell you just how much I hate him!"

"No, Allen," Valeria said. "He is only doing what he thinks is right. You must not speak of him that way, my dear."

"Doing what he thinks is right?" Allen said incredulously.

He was very angry, and for a moment he was unable to speak. He opened his lips, then closed them, and his hand tightened around the brandy glass.

"Doing what he thinks is right?" he repeated. "I suppose that's what everybody has been doing to me for the last twenty years— and to Mother, too, for longer than that. What they thought was right! God damn what the world thinks is right! Let me tell you something. The way I found out I was a nigger, the very first I ever knew of it, I was in Father's store in Memphis, and a dirty-bearded old man came in out of the canebrake and said, 'Son, you're a nigger, ain't you?' and I guess he was just bound to do that because he thought it was the right thing to do. It was his bounden duty to keep the record straight. Damn him and his duty. He took his coffee or whatever he'd bought and went back to Arkansas or wherever he had come from; but for years after that I used to lie awake at night, thinking how someday, when I was grown, I would hunt him down and kill him. And I'd do it yet. If I could find the son of a bitch I would damn sure kill him!"

"And what would that change?" Anse Weaver asked softly. "Would that make you look any prettier or smell any sweeter?"

"Nothing!" Allen Hendrick replied sharply. "All right! It would change nothing! Except it would make me feel a whole lot better."

There was a pause while Allen took out a cigar, lighted it, and threw the match into the fire. His hands were trembling, but his voice, when he began to speak again, was even and steady.

"When we left Memphis, Mother and Father and I, and first came to Gallatin, I thought maybe no one would know about me—and about Mother, about who we were. But when we got here that first night, Uncle Aaron was waiting, and I knew he knew about us, and I wished that night that I could kill him too. But I didn't have time to stay out there on the veranda and plot the murder. Mother called me in here. The chairs were still covered against the dust, and outside in the hall Vernon was still moving back and forth, bringing in the trunks and the furniture, and Mother made me stand here while she told me a story. That's right. We had been on the road for God knows how many days, and we had been sleeping and eating catch as catch can, and here we were in a house with a sound roof and servants and clean sheets and it was late at night; but instead of going to bed, Mother told me about my uncle, about her brother who was a free man of color and who fought with General Jackson at Chalmette. And after that for a long time I thought only that she wanted me to know about her people too. That she wanted me to know that along with the stain there was something of courage in the Martineau blood—something to be proud of. And maybe that's all she meant to tell me, but the story, the example, has meant more than that to me. For my uncle was a nigger and he knew what it meant to be a nigger. And he knew that what Anse said just a minute ago is true. That it doesn't make you look or feel or smell any better to kill somebody else. It doesn't help, because there are too damn many other people left who know you are a nigger and who treat you like a nigger, and you can't kill them all. You can't kill the whole damned world.

"You can't kill the world," he repeated thoughtfully, the tone of his voice almost bemused. "Do you see? There is something about you, something that makes everybody else insult you and vilify you, and if there were only one or two or a dozen people treating you badly, you could go to them and challenge them, you could make them answer. But this way, the way it is with me, there is no enemy, nobody that I can single out, no flesh and blood to fight against to get satisfaction. So I always thought about my uncle: at least one time in his life he knew where he was. He knew that the people in the red coats were trying to kill him and that he was trying to kill them, and the reasons may not have made any sense, but everything was nice and clear, the issues were laid out and they were beautiful and simple."

There was a pause and he puffed his cigar.

"By God," he said, "I have had enough. Father is dead and Mother is gone, and Kate is not going to marry me. And all the time up until now, all the world has been against me, so there was no single adversary, but maybe there is one now. At least for some of what's happened I can blame Captain Rutledge."

Valeria and Anse said nothing.

"If he weren't so old," Allen said. "If Captain Rutledge weren't so decrepit, I'd twist his nose. I'd grab him by the snout and ring his neck like I would a rooster's."

And still there was silence, but no reply was necessary. In spite of his anger Allen was aware that his talk had come full circle. He had arrived back at the point where he had started.

"I still haven't explained it, have I?" Allen said ironically. "Well, Captain Rutledge told Kate she could not marry me. And I could not stand that, could not endure what he was doing to Mother and, I admit it, what he was doing to my pride. Because I have some, by God! Even a nigger boy like me has some pride. So it's my fault that Mother left. I should have told her that I would never marry. But damned if it isn't his fault too. It's Captain Rutledge's fault, too, that she's gone, and he will have to answer for it."

There was one more silence, this one longer than the ones which had gone before it, and at last Valeria got up and took a step toward Allen. It was as if she had been waiting to make certain he had finished. She looked up at him, peered intently at his face.

"My dear," she said gently, "you have suffered much, you and your mother. But listen to me. Believe me. Not only you. Not you alone, to suffer while the rest of the world lived in happiness and fine contentment.

"Allen," she said, and her voice was full of infinite tenderness, "I would not minimize what you have endured, what you will have to endure for the rest of your life. I know only too well that I have been a part of the world that has treated you unjustly. But, Allen, think of your grandfather. Think of your father. Think even of Captain Rutledge himself, or of Katherine, who loved you, who loves you now. I know she does. Think of this whole world of people that you love and hate, and try to consider what they have endured. For them, too, it has not been easy.

"Oh," Valeria said, "I will not equate your sorrow with that of others. I will not tell you that there is anything quite so bad as what you go through, for from my own experience I know nothing of it. But every man has his own particular grief. We all feel some pain for which no single man or woman can be blamed. Oh, my dear, the human heart is made for breaking."

She stopped. Her voice that had been filled with emotion came to a halt. And for a moment Allen Hendrick was almost convinced, he almost believed her. He looked at her face, at the pale forehead, the arched eyebrows, and beneath them the eyes serious and wide and around the eyes the very first signs of age, the first barely perceptible lines, and these had formed too early. For she was young yet; she was only twenty-four.

Suddenly, in his fancy, the past came rushing back. He remembered the first time he had ever seen Valeria, and how on that sun-drenched, summer afternoon they had stood in the cemetery at Cedarcrest, stood in the shade of the maple trees, and looked at the fresh-cut stone above the grave of John Hendrick. And he recollected the weary set of her face during General Hendrick's last illness, and the lonely note that had crept into her voice when she had said, "Now, when I marry, you will have to give me away."

Here in the living room of the rented house in Gallatin, she was standing motionless, gazing up at him; and he felt great affection for Valeria, great sympathy for all that she had gone through, for all the losses life had made her suffer.

"Love," Valeria said. "Think of Katherine and of your mother, whom you love. Be patient and you and Kate will marry someday.

Forget about hate and the wrongs that have been done to you. Forget about vengeance."

It lasted a moment longer, this spell she had cast. It was as if humanity itself, the fate, the common lot of man, had been evoked by the words she had used, and lay almost palpable over the room, encompassing the three of them. Anse, who longed to know the physical truth, who yearned to know the secret that the dead brain withheld, the fact that refused to disclose itself to the dissecting knife. And Valeria with all the old sadness beginning to show in her face. And Allen himself momentarily at rest from the heart's dark anger.

"Believe me, Allen," Valeria said.

And Anse said, "Yes. She is right, Allen."

But at the sound of their voices the mood was broken.

"I don't know," Allen replied. "You talk about other people. But other people are not like me. I am Allen Hendrick."

Valeria started slightly, as if she meant to reply. But she did not reply. She said nothing.

She broke the silence only to say good night, and Anse said good night, and they left.

Allen Hendrick was alone in the house in Gallatin.

❖ 22 ❖

THE NEXT DAY, the twenty-fourth of December, he returned to Cedarcrest, and when the Christmas holiday was over and the slaves were back at work, he bought two hundred acres that adjoined his land on the south and put his people to work pulling the stumps and cutting the timber. Every morning he went himself to the field to see how the clearing of the land was coming on, and after noon, after he had had his dinner and his nap, he spent several hours in the office reading newspapers. His father had left some currency issued by a Kentucky bank and a few shares of stock in a South Carolina railroad. Lucy had not wanted these—she would not have known what to do with them if she had taken them with

[252]

her—and starting with this little bit of paper, Allen began to speculate with the Nashville banks. He was not as good as Marcus Hendrick had been; his wits were not as sharp, he did not know as much. But through the month of January he was able to increase his holdings six hundred dollars, and a part of this he changed into gold. Occasionally, when he thought of it, it seemed foolish to work so hard just to make money. But watching the slaves and reading the papers took his mind off Kate.

While he worked in an effort to forget Katherine, the Federal Union continued to break apart. Mississippi, Florida, and Alabama left the nation. Then Georgia and Louisiana and Texas voted to secede. There was a convention in Montgomery to form a Confederacy, but still there was talk of compromise and there was no war. The end of February came and the first flowers: the jonquils and blue crocuses along the garden paths, to be cut and put into vases and placed in the cemetery. There was no grass as yet on the grave of Marcus Hendrick. The earth was still bare and raw as it had been in December; the newly chiseled stones were clean and white. There were leaves showing on the maple trees; the days were often cold, the wind blew strong and there were clouds to hide the sun and often there was rainfall. But spring was coming nonetheless, and it was of spring that he spoke when he wrote his mother.

Last week [he wrote to her near the middle of March] I rode into Gallatin to do some business at the bank and when my errand was concluded there, I rode out to examine the house where you used to live with Father. I still pay the rent on it, you see, for there is more furniture there than I can accommodate at Cedarcrest, unless I should put it in a barn or an outhouse where it would be likely to ruin. Sarah, your old cook, still lives on the place. She dusts and sweeps and builds fires to dry the rooms; and she is pitiful for being free. She has few friends, and now that you are gone she seldom has anyone to talk to.

It was very cheerful at the house. It is spring here in Tennessee and the blue flags that you had Vernon put out along the fence are well up, though as yet they have not blossomed. I went up to your sewing room where so often we used to sit, and I took your chair and looked down at the street and the sun was bright and the day was very beautiful. Some children came by, capering along the walk, dancing as if to celebrate the pretty weather. I should like to know how you are down there. I know that the days are different there and that the people most likely eat different foods and that the flowers that grow there are not the same as the ones in the Cedarcrest garden. Indeed, we are in separate nations now, though I expect that sooner or later Tennessee, too, will join the Confederacy.

You asked me about Vernon. He has gone to Nashville. I gave him some money and he went to the city and got a job.

She answered his letters. She was living not in New Orleans but on a plantation in Ascension Parish with her brother and her brother's wife and their children. She told him how the house was built—square, or oblong rather, with upper and lower verandas, and with an outside stairway the only connection between the two floors. Once she sent him a picture of the place where she lived, a drawing she had made in pencil on a piece of white paper. Behind some large trees that were draped with moss the great box of a house was completely surrounded by columns—smaller columns than Allen saw in Tennessee and extending lower, extending down to the very ground, with a spoked railing around the upper balcony and the lower porch open and very wide. She had put an X on one of the windows to show the room where she slept and he was glad that she was living so well and that she was so comfortable. *"Mon cher,"* she wrote, "I doubt that you could accustom yourself to the climate here. But the land is black and we grow sugar cane and rice and a little cotton. In the fields my brother's people go without their shoes most of the time."

Allen tried to think of it, now that it was almost April—a group of Negroes with their bare toes on the cold, damp earth. But he could imagine only Tennessee, and there in Louisiana the earth would not be cold. There the spring would almost be gone. It would almost be summer.

So the days passed and he corresponded with his mother, and he thought of Katherine and of her father sometimes and he went about his business of farming and of trading notes. Then on the morning of the thirteenth of April, a Saturday full of sunlight, and in the orchard the fruit trees in full bloom, he read in his paper of the firing on Fort Sumter, and two days later President Lincoln called for volunteers. It had begun now. There would be a war. And what would Tennessee do when the shooting began? Secede probably. And then would Allen Hendrick fight too? Would he support secession?

In the days that followed, he reached no decision. He left off trading banknotes and turned his attention to his land. Another week or two and it would be setting time, and the ground was not quite ready yet, though the plants were maturing. Each morning after breakfast he consulted with Mr. Finch. He went to the fields as soon as the people did, and stayed to watch their progress till the bell called them to dinner. I will let it go, he said to himself, I will let time slide. I will wait to see what Tennessee does before I make my decision.

But one day, one afternoon when he was at the house, he had a visitor from Gallatin. He was sitting in the garden, on a bench by the lake, and perhaps because the birds were singing and there were sounds to be heard from the children playing in the quarter lot, he did not catch the noise of hoofbeats, and Houston Knott spoke to him before he knew that Houston Knott was there.

"It is a good life," he said, his tone bantering. "Pastoral leisure suits a gentleman down to the ground."

Allen rose and greeted Houston and shook his hand, and they sat down together on the bench, and Allen sent a boy to the house to bring them some whisky. Then when they were settled with their drinks in their hands, the cups sweating in the fine warmth of the day, the ice diluting the fine warmth of the whisky, Houston crossed his legs and said:

"The time has come now, Allen. Our state will have to decide now. And I believe that Tennessee will go with the Confederacy."

Allen nodded. The editorials in the newspapers that he read seemed to indicate that what Houston said was true.

"I reckon," Allen said, "but I don't know much about it."

"We will go," Houston said with emphasis. "You can take my word for it."

He turned away from Allen and looked out for a moment at the lake, this short, barrel-chested boy who had come to the full flesh of manhood. He was wearing broadcloth, his politicians' clothes, with a pearl pin in his wide cravat and pearl studs to hold his shirt together. He seemed to be a little warm; there was perspiration on his upper lip and perspiration on the backs of his hands that were fat and hirsute.

"I have a commission," Houston said at last. "Governor Harris believes we will leave the Union too, and he has given me a commission to raise a company of militia."

Allen did not answer.

But Houston did not seem to expect an answer. Not yet anyway, for he went on:

"I want you to join it, Allen. I want to put your name on the rolls. We will be ready then when the war begins and we won't miss the fighting."

"Houston," Allen said.

"Wait," Houston interrupted him. "I have the commission, but I do not have to be captain. You can be captain or Frank Armstrong can be captain. We can elect our officers, and it will not matter who is at our head, for we will be a select company, a company of gentlemen. I am not going to take just anybody. I am going about this quietly and asking only those I can trust, asking only men of breeding who can be depended on."

Again Allen said nothing.

"Well?" Houston finally asked. "Can I enroll you, Allen?"

Allen got up and took a step out toward the lake, toward the waters where the swans went preening by, their long necks arched, their feathers glistening. Then, turning back to Houston, he said:

"I don't know. I don't know what I am going to do yet. I will have to tell you later."

Houston rose too now and took Allen's arm.

"I need you, Allen," he said. "If you were somebody else, if you were Joe Henry Witherspoon, you could wait until Tennessee had declared war, you could take your time to make up your mind and it would not matter. But you are different. You are a big man, Allen. Look"—and Houston swung his free hand in an arc—"all this land belongs to you. That is your house. Those people working yonder are your people. You are a Hendrick and you own Cedarcrest and the public will all be watching you. They will want to see which way you jump. They will want to know your sentiments."

These were the words that Houston spoke, and hearing them, Allen felt as if he were about to fall, as if the firm earth were spinning beneath his feet, as if the lake were rising bright toward the yellow sunlight. But quickly the dizziness, the attack of vertigo, passed and his feet were firm again and his ears heard the silence.

Watching. Indeed, they would all be watching. Not only the Douglases and the Witherspoons, but the Rutledges would be watching too, Kate and her aunt in Nashville and her father. Suddenly he realized how his mind had been cheating itself, how his heart had been clinging fast to the old ambition. Even with their last quarrel unresolved and with thirty miles and a lonely winter between them, the hope of marriage had continued in his breast; hidden away, it had lived on in secret.

Then thinking of Captain Rutledge, Allen remembered not so much the marks of time—the trembling head, the sunken cheeks—but rather the military tone that the old man's life had kept, the title of rank he had held to, the memories of war and service he had cherished. . . . And there was Katherine's brother, too, the boy in the picture that hung on the Roseneath wall. Percy Rutledge, too, was a soldier.

If I do not go, Allen Hendrick thought, if I stay at home while a war is fought, then truly for me and Kate it will all be over. But was it not over now, irrevocably finished?

Once more in the sun-bright afternoon his head turned round. It was as if he could feel the spin of the world, the shudder of the globe beneath the gravel of the path, and he believed then that if a chance were left he would have to take it. For he loved Kate. And he hated the captain. And he would have to keep on trying to possess one and confound the other.

And as for the Yankees, they did not matter very much. But he supposed that he could learn to hate them too, at least enough to fight.

For only a moment longer did he hold back. He looked beyond the paths and the road to the quarters, beyond the smokehouse and the low stone wall, to the cemetery where his father and the general slept beneath the maples. Father, he thought, what would you say to this? But he knew the answer, had known it before he framed the question in his mind, and the only thing left to wonder about was whether Marcus and General Hendrick would forgive him. Whether on the resurrection day, if, indeed, resurrection day ever came, they would speak to him and take his hand before God's angels.

And no answer to this either. So, then, there was only his mother left to think of. She will understand, he thought. Or more than that. She would be proud of him, as she had been proud of his namesake, Allen Martineau, her brother.

"Allen," Houston Knott said softly. "You will come, won't you, Allen? I know you. You will not hold back. You will be the man."

Allen Hendrick breathed deeply of the sweet April air. Then he said:

"Yes, I will come. I will join your company."

◈ 23 ◈

THROUGH MAY and the first weeks of June the company drilled in a field south of Gallatin, a level piece of ground that once had been a pasture. Every morning except Sunday, Houston appeared dressed in a gray uniform and a bright gold sash; he took his position in front of the men who were drawn up in squadrons, and he would consult his book and the drill would commence. Or at least that is the way it was in the beginning, before Houston had had time to learn the various commands. For the first few days he rode with the tactics book open, the pages fluttering in the breeze of the horse's movement, the print shaking before him to the jar of the gait. Once he lost his place, and another time he dropped the book and two squadrons passed over it, and once he gave the wrong command and marched the company into a creek. But under the tuition of a pair of his lieutenants—Frank Armstrong and Raphael Carter, who had been educated at military schools—Houston improved rapidly and he soon became for his audience an object more of admiration than of mirth.

And there was always an audience. Sometimes it was small and there were only a few people, three or four of the town loafers who had got tired of spitting at the mockingbirds on the courthouse lawn. And sometimes in the morning there would only be children watching the company, little boys who were out of school now and had nothing else to do. But there was always somebody and sometimes in the afternoons the crowd would be large. The road would be lined with conveyances and people, with buggies and wagons and tethered mules and horses, and grown men and women would look on while the cavalry raised the dust.

One day when there was a good crowd, late in May when Houston had learned his commands and signals and the company had learned to obey fairly well and hold a fairly straight line—one afternoon Allen saw a familiar carriage come down the road and stop. It was the Rutledge rockaway and it moved down the pike very slowly, and Allen saw that a chair had been tied on its top. The company was standing at ease, and from his place in the formation Allen watched John Noble come down off the box and bring the chair with him, and the crowd gave way for John Noble to bring the rocking chair onto the field. Then the Negro went back and opened the door to the carriage and helped Captain Rutledge make a shaky descent to the ground.

The old man was dressed in carpet slippers, black trousers, and a green roundabout and a shawl and a wool hat on his head. In the bright, late-spring heat he was dressed as if for winter, but even with all the clothes that he wore, he looked very thin and his shadow fell thin and long on the grass of the field. His head trembling, his walk slow and shuffling, he leaned heavily on John Noble's arm and moved to the rocking chair and sat down and the slave covered his legs with a lap robe.

Allen looked at the frailty that the old man's life had reached, the pain and weariness his years had brought him, and for a moment he almost pitied Captain Rutledge. But not for long. Because to Allen the captain's feebleness was a matter of irony and Allen Hendrick himself was the butt of the joke. Captain Rutledge was very old; his teeth were gone and his head shook and he could not even walk without help and he lost the thread of his own thoughts and he grieved over dying. He was the weakest thing a man could be without being dead, but he was strong enough to keep Allen Hendrick from marrying Katherine.

From the back of his horse Houston bowed to the old man, and Captain Rutledge raised his hand in a half-salute to return the greeting. Then Houston formed the company in a column of fours and they went at a gallop up to the end of the field and turned there and came back again with the guidon flying. They kept their lines straight and rode back down, rode hard back through their own dust and Houston drew his sword and it flashed in the sunlight. When the company passed Captain Rutledge they turned their eyes right, and Allen saw the old man try to rise in his chair. He half lifted himself and his mouth opened wide, but Allen could not hear his shout for the sound of the horses. And when they came back to form in line in the middle of the field, Captain Rutledge was weeping. The tears were bright on his sunken cheeks. They streamed down his face and dripped off his chin. He lifted his hand as if he were trying once more to salute, but he could not make his head stop its violent trembling.

Next to Allen in the line was a long-nosed, redheaded country boy named Harry Venable. "Look," he said to Allen. "Look a-yonder at old Captain, and him a-crying. Him an old man, and a-shedding tears for a fact."

Allen said nothing.

"Hit's because of us," Venable went on in a whisper. "Hit is because we ai're soldiers. And he were a soldier too. And that in the olden time and him proud to remember."

But still Allen did not reply, for he was looking at the captain, watching the shake of the feeble head and the course of tears from the red-rimmed eyes, and the legs as slender as sticks beneath the lap robe. Once more he felt a surge of pity, a moment almost of affection for the old man that came quick and sharp like the prick of a pin and was as soon finished. And in its place the bitter recollection, the memory of nights in the garden with Kate, and the captain's refusal to let them wed, and his insult to Allen Hendrick and to Lucy. At this moment the palsied head tilted and the hat fell off, exposing the thin gray hair and below it the parchment-thin flesh of the forehead. Behind that flesh and the brittle bone the forgetful mind raged on and formed in conjunction with Allen's name the word *nigger*. But not now. He would not even be thinking of Allen now, and he could not see well enough to recognize the men in the company. It occurred to Allen that in another year the captain, if he lived, would not even remember that Kate had wanted to marry him. Indeed, he perhaps did not even recollect it now—except at times when his mind was clear—and he had never known anything of Allen's pain and anguish. Or had he known and been indifferent? Allen could not say.

But in the fierce rush of his blood, the pound of the vessels at his throat that made his breath come short, he turned to Venable and whispered.

"What?" he said peremptorily. "What did you say?"

"He is a-weeping and hit is because of us," Venable repeated. "Hit is like a woman and her moved unto tears. We ai're soldiers and that is why. He is a-crying for us and the joy he takes to see us."

Still looking at Captain Rutledge, Allen Hendrick slowly, thoughtfully nodded his head.

That night, when he was alone at Cedarcrest, he sat in the office for a long time and smoked a cigar and thought of Captain Rutledge. He sat and remembered how the old man had tried to salute, and how he had shouted when the troops rode by, and how the tears had run down his face at the sight of soldiers. And it occurred to Allen Hendrick that maybe at last he had found the way, the key to the fulfillment of his love, the ground on which he might defeat his enemy. So two days later he got leave from drill and caught the cars and went to Nashville. He checked in at the hotel and then went back down Church Street and arrived at the academy just at teatime, just at the softest part of the afternoon when the sunlight came golden through the high parlor windows and the sound of voices was as soft as the clink of the cups.

He was admitted by a maid who took his cane and hat, and he found his own way through the dim hall to the door that opened into the parlor, and from the door he got his first sight of Katherine. She was not looking in his direction. He saw her in profile, in silhouette really, framed against the bright glass of the window, and he noticed first that she had changed the way she fixed her hair. The curls that once had hung down her neck were gone, and in their place was a flat chignon, and the effect was to make Katherine's neck look longer and somehow more graceful and more beautiful and more mature. It was a minute change, and otherwise she looked no different, but it was alteration enough to touch his heart. It was a shift, a mutation in her beauty that he had not expected nor prepared himself to see, and he paused in his course through the doorway and felt his throat tighten, and his flesh grow cold.

This was his only moment of weakness, the only instant when his resolution almost failed. For later, when they were alone together, or as alone as people could ever be in the academy parlor—Miss Clayton, the teacher, sat near the door, two other couples sat in other corners—when he and Katherine were seated near one of the hearths, with the sun gone from the windows now and the day fading into the first early twilight, he knew that he could not return to the old way of courtship, the old business of loving her and waiting, longing for a time that had not been named, a date that remained unset. This had been his temptation, when he had first entered the room and had seen her beauty again after long abstinence and had felt so poignantly the enormous force of his love.

Now he had regained his composure. And as he sat with his legs crossed, his hands on the chair arms, his fingers rubbing gently the polished walnut frames; as he sat through a drawn-out silence with Katherine, he saw himself and his love in their proper relationship and focus, and in his mind's eye he saw the face of Kate's father whom he hated so much. It was, Allen Hendrick thought, ironic that one might use his enemy, play upon his enemy's weakness to gain the cherished ambition, and with it to gain revenge. Or not revenge really. Rather, his marriage, if he could accomplish it, would only set right the wrong Captain Rutledge had done him and his mother and father—for he had begun now to include Marcus in his grievance—and if the old captain wept, and this time wept in pain, then so much sooner would the balance be achieved.

Looking at Katherine, who wore a yellow dress that became her and an amethyst and seed-pearl brooch at her throat, he said:

"Darling, I am sorry about that night, about losing my temper. I regret these months that we have been apart."

She did not answer at once. Then she said, "I know. I am sorry too."

"Kate," he said. "I did not mean to say those things about your father." He was splitting the letter of the truth here. "I said them because I loved you. I still love you. I have never stopped."

He paused a moment, then went on, "If I could get your father's permission, would you marry me now? If I went to him and asked him, and he said yes? Would you then? Do you still love me enough for that?"

"Yes," she said, "yes. But, my dear, it has not changed. His mind is no different now than it was last summer."

"I have changed," Allen Hendrick replied. "I know more now than I did then. Give me a chance, Kate. Let me try it."

"Darling," she said, "I will help you if I can. I want this as much as you do. But you will have to tell me how to act. You will have to tell me how you mean to go at Father."

"My dear," he said, leaning toward her. "Of course I will tell you. I could not do it without you. You will have to come home to Roseneath and help me."

There in the Female Academy parlor he told her what he intended to do, or rather did not tell her, told her only of the surface plan and not of the motive, nor of the advantage that he meant to take of the old man's tears. But while he was in Nashville he bought a new uniform, a jacket of gray flannel faced in yellow, and blue trousers and high boots and a wide leather belt, and a sword to go on the belt and a new pistol. He went home with all his finery, and on the following Sunday morning he rose and put on the uniform, even the saber, even the Navy revolver, and he mounted his horse that had been carefully groomed, and he rode to see Captain Rutledge. He turned into the Roseneath driveway with the horse trotting and spraying gravel and the plume in his hat quivering and catching the sunlight, and the sun bright on the polished boots and the polished holster. And luck was with him, for the old man was sitting on the porch.

Captain Rutledge was alone on the wide veranda, the same black wool hat on his head, the same lap robe across his legs, and he appeared to be watching Allen in his progress up the driveway.

I should have brought a flag, Allen Hendrick thought ironically. I should have brought a squadron along, and a bugler; but he reflected that the business he had with Captain Rutledge was too private for that. He dismounted and hitched his horse. He took off his gauntlets and straightened his shoulders and stood for an instant looking down into the old man's face.

Then he said, "Captain Rutledge."

"Yes, sir," the old man replied. "I was a captain. I was a soldier once, but that was long ago."

"I know that, sir," Allen said. "I know you well. I am Allen Hendrick."

In the silence that followed, Allen looked at the teetering old head, at the paper-thin skin with the veins showing behind it, and the blood vessels themselves marking the slow beat of the pulse. And he thought, I will have to be braced for it now. I will have to be ready. I must not lose my temper, whatever he says.

But the reply, when it came, was not in anger. It was merely a little sad, a little surprised.

"You, young man?" Captain Rutledge said. "You are Allen Hendrick?"

"Yes, sir," Allen said.

"Then lean down here," the captain replied. "Put your head down into the sunlight and let me see you."

Allen stooped until his head was out of the shadow, until his face was not far from that of Captain Rutledge, and the old man examined him for a long time. The captain let his gaze play deliberately over Allen's features. The red-rimmed eyes, like the eyes of some day-blind bird, strained and blinked and peered out from the trembling sockets.

Then Captain Rutledge said, "Yes. You are Allen Hendrick. I can see the favor. I can tell it in your face."

A pause, and then, "Sit down, Mr. Hendrick. Your grandfather was my dear friend, sir. I loved him deeply."

And because the old man's voice was kind, it caught Allen Hendrick unawares, for kindness was the one thing he had not counted on. Earlier that morning, before he had left Cedarcrest, he had girded himself, steeled himself against a show of anger. He had gone out onto the veranda and breathed deeply in the damp, early air. He had calmed himself as a man calms a horse or a puppy and for a little while he had laid the bitterness; for a little while he had contained it in his heart.

But he had not prepared for hospitality and the soft word. And because he had not, the pity came, suddenly as it had that other day on the drill field, and once more very sharply felt. For an instant Allen's sorrow for the captain's feebleness and age was palpable in the sinews of his neck, in the nerves that ran through his breast and through his temples. He groped his way into a chair. He sat in silence to recover himself, to get back his anger and the purpose that went with it, and these came when he recollected what he had come here to do.

"Captain Rutledge," Allen said softly, "I am going to fight the

Yankees. Did you know that? This is a Confederate uniform I am wearing. It is the uniform of the South."

The captain was holding a walking stick, and he pounded it twice on the floor now, and he shifted his teeth in his mouth before he answered.

Then he said, "I will never see it. I am going to die, and I'll be better off dead than watching a war the likes of this, better off than staying alive to see the Yankees destroy our nation."

He paused and in the fullness of his emotion he tapped the floor again with his stick.

"General Hendrick is better off in the cemetery than living. I used to regret his passing, but I don't any more.

"Young man, we have got to whip the Yankees! We have got to drive them out of our nation! We must beat them home!"

With the exertion of talking, the old face had grown very red. The captain seemed to be having trouble breathing, and he panted and wheezed and puffed out his cheeks.

Allen was watching him carefully, and he waited for a little while. He let some of the color leave the captain's face. He could not allow the old man to have apoplexy; the old man's time might conveniently come later, but not yet. Allen could not yet afford to have him die.

When Captain Rutledge seemed calmer, Allen said for the second time, "I am going, sir. I am going to fight the Yankees."

Like a stump speaker, a politician, he repeated his own words for emphasis. Then he moved his new sword from its scabbard and held it out toward the old man. There on the porch, in the broad, open daylight, Allen Hendrick drew the sword and held the glittering hilt toward Captain Rutledge. And for the first time that day he felt, not ashamed, but a little embarrassed, a little self-conscious. He glanced about quickly, half afraid that someone might be watching him.

Then he said, "Look, sir, this is my sword that I mean to carry against them." And there he paused.

Captain Rutledge looked at the weapon.

"Let me see it," he said. "Let me hold it in my hand."

Very gently Allen pushed the hilt toward him, and slowly the old fingers closed around it and they held it, momentarily, in a shaky grasp. Captain Rutledge tried to lift the sword. With the blade waving erratically, he raised the saber almost to his eye level. Then his strength gave way, and the sword fell and clattered flashing through the sunlight and came to rest new and shiny on the edge of the porch.

In the silence that followed, Captain Rutledge began to cry.

Tears came to his eyes and spilled over onto his cheeks, and in a voice fraught with sorrow and disappointment he said:

"Too old. Too weak even to hold it. Too old to fight now when men are needed. I am too old for everything but to die."

Allen delayed for an instant. He swallowed once and then bit his lip lightly until he was sure of the tone of his voice and of his words.

Finally he laid his hand on the old man's forearm, and speaking almost in a whisper, soothingly, and with great tenderness, he said:

"No, sir, not too old. It is your time to stay at home, Captain Rutledge, and watch us and advise us. It is your wisdom that we need, sir, not your strength."

Allen paused and Captain Rutledge continued to cry and he shook his head and wiped his nose with the edge of his finger.

"Listen," Allen said, "I will go for you. If you will allow it, I will represent you in this war. I will carry that sword in your name when I go into battle."

Though a few tears still rose to his eyes, Captain Rutledge seemed nonetheless to have brightened. Once more he was peering down at the sword.

"I have Percy, sir," he replied. "You are kind, but Percy is coming home now. I will have him."

"You will have both of us," Allen Hendrick said softly, "if you will permit it."

He hesitated once more.

"Captain Rutledge," he went on, "I am Allen Hendrick. And you knew my grandfather. You knew him for a soldier and for a man. And I am a soldier too, now, and I want you to think that I fight for you. For I respect you, sir . . .

"And I want to marry Katherine."

There was a long silence, and the old man's lips moved, puckered, and drew back over the ill-fitting teeth.

"No, no," he said at last. "No, no."

"Captain Rutledge," Allen said, his voice sharper now and louder. "Look at me, sir."

He stood up and smoothed the cavalry jacket.

"Look at me," he repeated. "I am a Hendrick and a soldier, and I am going out to fight. And I want to fight for you and for Katherine. Look at me and tell me what you see in my disfavor."

"No," the old man said, crying once more, almost sobbing. "No," he said and he pounded his stick on the floor.

"Katherine loves me," Allen Hendrick said. "Ask her if she does not love me. She is here. Call her and ask her."

The captain made no answer.

"Captain Rutledge," Allen said, "do you remember when you went to Michigan with my grandfather and with my father? They fought with you, sir. They were your comrades, your friends."

Captain Rutledge looked up at Allen and nodded shakily. "I recollect it. . . . That was a long time ago. . . . They are all dead."

"Yes, sir," Allen said. "They are gone now. But they loved you. And I am their son and grandson. Would you turn me away?"

"Your mother," Captain Rutledge said but said it weakly, and the voice trailed off, died in the quiet day.

And Allen knew at last that he had touched the captain, he had found the key.

"Call Katherine," Allen said, and before the old man could answer, he said, "I will call her."

He stepped to the door to do so, but she was already there. She was standing just inside the hallway, just out of sight in the shadows, and he did not know how long she had been there or how much she had heard.

"Now," he whispered to her urgently. "Tell him you love me. Tell him you want to marry me. Now."

She did not move.

"Allen," she said. "Oh, Allen."

He caught her wrist and pulled her gently out into the sunlight. "Now," he said, the whisper louder. "Tell him. Now."

Captain Rutledge was looking at them.

"Kate," he said, "this boy. Do you know who he is?"

And now there were tears in Katherine's eyes, and she stooped and put her arm around her father's shoulder and said, "Yes, Papa. I do know him."

Then a pause while she pressed her lips tight together.

"Yes, Papa. And I do love him, Papa. I do want to be his wife."

"Kate," the captain replied sorrowfully. "His mother, Kate."

"She is gone, Papa," Kate said. "And he is a Hendrick. Try to remember that."

"Too old," the old man said. "Too old. I should have died ten years ago. Or before that. I should have died in Michigan before you were born."

"Papa," Kate said. "Don't talk that way, Papa."

He did not seem to hear. He looked at Allen, scrutinized him carefully, and said, "You look white. You could pass for white if people didn't know who you were."

But they always know, Allen Hendrick thought bitterly, for this was a line he had heard before.

"People know I am a Hendrick," Allen said. "They know I am a soldier. When the war is over they will know I have been there. They will know that I fought."

"When the war is over then!" the old man shouted. "Come back then, and if you are really a soldier, if you have done your duty and we have won the war . . ."

"We may marry?" Allen said.

Captain Rutledge did not answer Allen.

"Kate," he said quietly, "let him prove himself first. Let him go away and show what he is, and maybe before this is over you can forget him."

"Oh, Papa," she said, and her voice broke. "I cannot forget him. Even if I tried, I could not. I love him."

"No," he said sadly. "No. But you will wait. And then if you must. If you think you must. Then, if he is really a soldier, really a Hendrick. And if we have won the war."

Here he hesitated.

"Then, even if I should live that long, I will not prevent you."

24

ON TUESDAY, two mornings after he had visited Captain Rutledge, Allen himself had a visitor at Cedarcrest. It was just after breakfast on the day before Houston's company was due to leave for Nashville, and Allen was in the office smoking a cigar and checking over the equipment he meant to take. He was squatting on the floor in the midst of his paraphernalia, the cooking utensils and saddlebags, the blankets and oil cloths and bullet molds and penstaffs, when he heard the sound of a horse on the drive and he rose and looked out the window and saw Percy Rutledge.

He saw Percy and knew him beyond all doubt, recognized him from the picture that hung on the Roseneath wall, though the face of the man who was now moving toward the house was more mature than that of the boy in the portrait, and the costume, the clothes were different. On this morning Percy was wearing a black hunting coat, high boots, and corduroy trousers, and a high-crowned straw hat, and he was carrying a large crop with a leather thong on the end of it. Allen noticed this, before his eyes returned to the features, to the short nose that turned up at the end, and the small blue eyes and the wide forehead. Often in the past, when he had looked at Percy's picture, Allen had been struck with the similarity between Katherine and her brother, and this family resemblance was apparent to him now. But he also saw something that he had not seen before—that Percy, and Katherine too, looked like the captain. There was something about the line of the mouth, and the long, slightly hollow plane of the cheek that gave the three of them a mark, a stamp of kinship. It would be better, Allen thought, if he looked like only his father. But this way it would balance out: whatever disposition Allen might have in his favor because he looked like Kate, would be canceled by his likeness to Captain Rutledge.

Then the knock came, and Allen hastened to the door and opened it and bowed and conducted Percy Rutledge into the parlor.

He stood aside that Percy might precede him into the quiet, formal room, which was dim now with the windows shuttered, and cool at this hour of the day. Then, before he would be seated, Percy introduced himself to Allen; he nodded slightly, almost imperceptibly and said:

"I am Percy Rutledge. I am Katherine's brother."

Allen smiled broadly and bowed once again.

"I know, sir," he answered. "I recognized you from your picture. Won't you have a seat?"

He had overdone it. He had made a travesty of manners, a burlesque of good breeding by the width of his grin and the low sweep of his comic-opera bow and his slow drawl that was impudently obsequious.

He had done this deliberately to insult Percy Rutledge, for inadequate as they were, words and gestures were his only weapons for vengeance, and his only defense against all of white mankind. He could not say, *My mother is not a nigger,* because she was and everyone knew she was; and as long as the world wanted to look down on niggers, there was not much he could do but curse and vilify the world in return. Because of this, and because he knew that Percy had come to tell him that he could not marry Katherine, he hated Percy Rutledge—whom he had never seen before today, who to him was a stranger. Strongly touched as he was by his own anger, he was able, nonetheless, to remain relatively calm. Above the heat of his passion a part of his brain remained aloof and cold, and coldly he began to bait and torment Percy Rutledge.

"I know you, sir," Allen said again, his voice parodying his normal accents, "but you could not know me. I am Allen Hendrick, and I welcome you to Cedarcrest."

For a moment there was silence, and Percy's face grew red. He had almost consented to take a chair; he was almost in the act of sitting down near the fireplace. He grew rigid and then straightened up.

"Go ahead and be seated, sir," Allen said sarcastically. "Be seated, Mr. Rutledge. I will not have you stand, sir. I could not bear that."

Percy Rutledge took a step toward Allen. He was breathing heavily, and his hands were thrust deep in his pockets. He took them out and took the crop from under his arm and clenched them around its heavy handle. He was silent, apparently in an effort to subdue his anger, for his face had continued to grow red and a vein stood out beneath the skin of his forehead. Looking lower, Allen could see a twitch in his neck.

"Listen," Percy Rutledge said, speaking the single word quietly. Then much louder he said, "God damn you, you listen to me!"

And Allen, secure in his own control of himself, overplayed his hand now; he went too far. He was elated to see Percy so miserably angry, and he felt that by insulting Percy he was having a kind of vicarious revenge over Captain Rutledge too. So he said:

"Take care, Mr. Rutledge. Take care, sir. It is dangerous to speak hastily."

"Not to a nigger," Percy Rutledge replied coldly. "It is safe enough when you are talking to a black son of a bitch."

Allen's head grew light above his shoulders. There was a moment of numbness while the joy, the elation, died. It was an instant of stasis, as if the world hung still, as if the globe had paused for a few seconds before it resumed its spin and its orbit with a sickening rush. And in that short pause he saw his mother. With his mind's eye he looked upon her face. He saw the delicate wave of her hair, the light wrinkles that crossed her forehead, and the full lips and the ivory-colored skin. But she faded too as the world picked up once more, and Allen Hendrick ground his teeth together.

He cast about for a weapon, for something with which to hit Percy, and his eye fell on the poker that stood beside the hearth. He lunged to grab it; he moved quickly with his hand outstretched, and he had almost reached the poker when Percy hit him. He felt the blow fall just above his ear, and for a moment it seemed to hang there, the lick itself round and palpable and growing larger. It seemed to swell like the knot it would leave, and then there was only pain and the flashing blindness, and he became aware that he was sitting on the floor.

Allen's ears were ringing, but gradually he heard a noise beyond his own skull; there was a sound beyond him somewhere in the room, but he could not decipher it. Then as his vision cleared, he saw Percy Rutledge looking down at him, and Percy's lips were moving. But still Allen could not understand him. Still there was only the pain, and through the hurting that was constant, the burning surge of his pulse, the throb with each pump of his heart, and his heart was racing. He felt his head, lifted his fingers gently, and felt blood, and he wondered vaguely what Percy had hit him with. He looked and saw Percy holding the crop, gripping it wrong end up by the switch, and he knew that doubtless the handle was heavily weighted.

Percy spoke again, and now he could make out the words.

"I didn't come to do that," Percy Rutledge said. "But I didn't mind it either."

Allen did not reply. The pain in his head was so severe that he could think of nothing to say. At that moment he could not even fully comprehend what Percy was saying.

Percy Rutledge went on.

"Listen," he said, "you are not going to marry Katherine. I know what you did to Papa. You bullied and tricked an old man. But you are up against something else now. You cannot bully me. Understand that. It doesn't make any difference to me what promises Papa might have made to you. I haven't promised you a damned thing. But I make you one now. If you even try to see Katherine again I'll kill you."

Percy turned and took a step or two toward the door, then swung back again to face Allen.

"You son of a bitch," he said. "I ought to go on and kill you now. If I did I'd be doing the community a service."

He paused, looking at Allen.

Then he said, "You black son of a black nigger bitch."

Allen struggled. His hand moved ever so slowly. He watched his own arm, his own fingers that were smeared with blood tremble toward the poker. It was as if the pain that coursed through his head shut him off, segregated his mind from all the rest of his body. With a feeling almost of detachment he saw his fist close around the brass handle. Then he took a deep breath and tried to rise. He pushed with his legs and his legs shook beneath him. He fell forward and his cheek rubbed into the pile of the rug.

"I was pulling for you," Percy Rutledge said softly. "I was hoping you would make it. I was anticipating the chance to knock you down again."

Then Allen heard Percy's footsteps move away.

After a while he was able to rise, and he went up to his room and washed his face. He washed the place where Percy had hit him, and he lay down on the bed.

On the Sunday that followed, he saw Katherine for the last time until the war ended. On Wednesday he had come down to Nashville. He had left all that he possessed in the hands of Anse Weaver: he had given Anse most of his money to keep, and had signed over to him a power of attorney. Free of his old responsibilities, he had marched away from Gallatin with Houston Knott's troops. They had moved away from the courthouse with a band playing and flags waving and women waving their handkerchiefs and saying good-by. But Allen had a headache from the blow Percy had struck him, and he knew that Kate was in Nashville and he would see her when he got there and this farewell was neither sad nor final to him. He simply shook hands with Anse and kissed Valeria and got on his horse that was laden with equipment and rode away.

But on the last day that Kate would be in Nashville, on Sunday in the Female Academy parlor, it was good-by with nothing but the war to look forward to, and a great sadness took possession of his heart. He moved through the academy hallway and into the parlor, and when Katherine was with him they sat down near the windows and drank a cup of tea. She was all in white with green trimmings, minute green bows sprigged onto her skirt, a cameo hung around her neck with a green ribbon. She was very beautiful, and when she spoke she leaned very close so he could feel the warmth of her breath against his ear. Allen felt an urgent necessity, an obligation, since he would soon be leaving, to settle every question that lay between them, to speak on all subjects with finality, but he could think of no unresolved question, and there was nothing really serious for him to say.

"I love you," he said, taking her hand, feeling the warmth of her flesh against his fingers.

And she replied very softly, "Oh, darling, I love you too."

They were silent for a moment and then he rose, moved to put his teacup on the table. Up until this time his face had been in shadow. Now when he turned she saw the knot on the side of his head.

"Allen," she said with alarm, "what happened to you?"

He looked at her. He did not immediately know what she meant.

"Darling," she said, "you are hurt. What happened to your head?"

For a moment he weighed the alternatives. He hovered between some falsehood and the truth. He looked at Kate's face, which showed considerable concern. Her eyes were open wide and the flesh around them was wrinkled. He was touched at this instant by her vast loveliness, the lightness of her skin, the evenness of her features, and touched, too, by this display of her affection for him. He was tempted to let it go, to spare her. But in the end he could not pass up this chance for revenge.

It was almost as if the other scene were happening again, so fresh, so bright did his memory recreate it. He saw Percy Rutledge, his complexion growing red, the veins in his neck swelling. And he heard Percy's voice saying *nigger son of a bitch*. Then his own voice said:

"It was your brother. Percy hit me."

Her mouth dropped open in surprise. Her lips parted, and her face grew paler still, leaving her eyebrows dark against the utter whiteness of her forehead.

"No," she said. "Oh, no."

She reached out as if she were going to touch the place, the wound that was beginning to heal, the protuberance that was receding. But her hand seemed suddenly devoid of strength. It grew limp and she let it fall to the love seat beside her.

"Oh," she said, "how could he have done it? Oh, Allen, what did you do to make him so mad?"

"I invited him to sit down," Allen replied evenly.

Then he said, "He was mad when he got there. It didn't take much after he caught sight of me."

"Allen," Katherine said. There were tears in her eyes, tears spilling over and running down her cheeks. "He was mad when he got where?"

She paused. Then she grasped the cuff of his jacket and pulled on it, jerked on it to emphasize her words.

"Where?" she demanded. "Tell me about it. I have got to know."

"Be quiet," he said. "Lower your voice, Kate. Listen to me. It was at Cedarcrest. He came there Tuesday morning to tell me that we must not marry. . . ."

He hesitated, tempted once more to spare her.

But again he went on, "And to tell me that he would kill me if I saw you again."

"He is a fool," she said angrily, but with her voice softer now, under better control. "He did not mean that. That was just talk. But, darling, why did he hit you? What did he hit you with?"

"With a crop," Allen replied. "It had a weighted handle."

"Oh," she said, pounding her fist in her lap, "the idiot! But why?"

"I told you," Allen replied testily. "Because he did not want me to marry you."

"But, Allen," Kate said, "he did not have to strike you just to say that. What led up to it? What was said or done that made him angry enough to hit?"

"Confound it!" Allen replied, "I told you he was mad when he got there. I don't remember every single word that was said."

She put her hand over her mouth and turned her face away from him. He sat silent and stared at the window and bit the corner of his lip.

He sat and felt the blood rush warm to his face, and knew that he was blushing in anger and in embarrassment: he had not foreseen that their conversation would end like this. He had not dreamed that she would question him so sharply or that she would show what seemed to him reluctance to saddle her brother with any blame. But he reasoned that that would come later, her anger at Percy, and even now, while she sat with her features averted, he could not be sorry he had told her—he hated Percy so much.

At last in a voice that was calmer but very sad she said, "Oh, Allen, Allen. Will there never be an end to trouble? Oh, will there never be peace?"

He put his hand on hers, feeling again what he had lost momentarily, the old tenderness, the old familiar racing of the heart.

"Don't worry," he said. "It will be all right. Don't worry."

As he spoke the clock struck and visiting hours came to an end.

"I have to go," he said. "Walk with me to the door."

She accompanied him through the dim hall, and Miss Clayton came too, following after them. He could not even embrace her. They could not even kiss.

"Do you have to go back?" he said. "Can't you stay a few days with Mrs. Richardson?"

"My dear," she replied, "after what has happened? Percy is at home waiting for a commission to come through from Montgomery. He is there convenient to tell Papa what I am up to if I should stay down here."

Allen nodded. "All right," he said. "Good-by."

She was crying. "Allen," she said. "Allen."

He waited. Then as if it were an afterthought, his voice casual as he could make it, he said, "I would not mention this other business to Percy. It is best to say nothing about it, I think. Just let it drop."

"I won't," she whispered.

Then she said, "Oh, darling, hurry back to me."

He managed a grin.

"I will," he said. "I will attend to the Yankees. I will make it quick."

◆ 25 ◆

Allen Hendrick was in the army for four years, and during that time he learned many things and he saw many sights and he traveled to many places. He began his career in Gallatin, Tennessee, in May of 1861, and he went from there to Nashville, and then to East Tennessee, and across into Kentucky to Fishing Creek, where there was a battle. Then, with Houston Knott's company, he came south again, skirted Nashville and went into Mississippi and was engaged at Shiloh and a little later at Corinth. After this there were many raids and skirmishes, brushes with the enemy at crossings and villages that had what seemed to Allen curious names. There was fighting at Iuka and Palo Alto and Tupelo, at Okolona and Baldwyn and at a town called Rienzi, and then it was the autumn of 1863. On the sixteenth of November, Forrest arrived to take command of some of the cavalry in Mississippi, and for those who were included in his charge—and Allen Hendrick was one of these—it was then that the war began in earnest. Skirmishing became a pastime now, a kind of grim jollification to amuse the troops and keep them slim between the real set-tos. Between Fort Pillow and Brice's Cross Roads, between Memphis and the Johnsonville Expedition. And in the fall of 1864, fighting with the infantry once more now, as a part of Hood's army, Forrest's cavalry moved again into Middle Tennessee.

These were the places that Allen went, these were the routes that, years later, he would be able to trace on a map and point to and use as a motive for a tale, a reminiscence. But at the time one place was not much different from another except insofar as the food and the water supplies were concerned, and the character of the terrain did not matter either unless it was a battle ground.

When Allen first left Nashville, he thought almost continually of Kate; or rather, he thought almost continually about the Rutledges. For when her face mounted before his mind's eye, it seemed always to be flanked by those of her father and her brother. Indeed, he often had difficulty separating the emotions that he felt, and there were times when his most tender recollection would be defaced by the sudden flash and stab of hate. He would think of her as she had stood in the Roseneath garden, her face lifted, her hands clasped at her waist, and crowding, intruding into his consciousness, would come the memory of her father, who had remained in the house. Or he would see her as she had been at the Female Academy, Kate wearing a summer dress, yellow batiste or a very light brocade, and then without willing it, he would think of Percy.

His imagination was fearful in its intensity, and it would not be curbed. Once on an afternoon when he was very tired, when he had been for a long time without sleep, the march halted for a few moments, and he dismounted and lay down beneath a tree. While he was thinking of Katherine, he dozed off, and in a dream he was standing in the door to the Rutledge living room. He saw the parlor with great clearness, in colors more brilliant than the actuality would present, and the captain was sitting in a rocking chair, staring at Allen. But there were other discrepancies beyond the brightness of the room; there were the figure and the face of Captain Rutledge. The body that Allen saw was that of a young man, the hands were brown and strong and covered with stiff black hairs, the shoulders were broad and the thighs were heavy beneath the pants legs. But the face above a youthful neck was very, very old, and the only difference here was that the head did not shake, there was no palsy.

In the dream Captain Rutledge peered at Allen for what seemed a long time. Then he turned and beckoned to the portrait that hung above the mantel, and the figure stepped out of the portrait, Percy stepped out and came down into the room and stood there in the room beside his father. He put his hand on the back of the captain's chair, and, dressed in the Yankee uniform that he had once worn, in the blue jacket with the gold buttons and the blue trousers with the gold stripe—dressed in those Yankee clothes, he smiled and Captain Rutledge smiled at Allen.

It was a curious dream, and Allen Hendrick did not understand it.

But the war he understood. It was his war to win for Katherine, to win for himself and he longed for the ultimate moment to come, the moment of victory. In his fancy he saw himself returning from a war the South had won, and mounting the steps to the Roseneath porch, where Katherine and Percy and their father would be waiting. He would go to claim the prize that would then be his, he would go in search of the revenge he would have earned. It was for this that he was waging war, it was for this he was fighting.

One night when the war was still young, or if not quite young, not hopeless yet either, one night in spring he was sitting around a fire, talking to three or four dirty, bearded men who were Forrest's veterans. Or rather he was listening to them talk, and one of them said, "Hit ai're a war con-cerning the niggers, I reckon, and I never owned 'ere one. I never worked 'ere nigger, but I never countenanced settin' 'ere nigger loose."

And another one, whose face was still smeared with the powder from the cartridges he had been biting that afternoon: "It is niggers and it ain't. For the Yankees it is niggers, maybe, but for me it is Yankees. They come, and I said, 'Right shore, now, I will jist go out and meet 'em and let 'em know I'm still a-livin' here.'"

And the third one spat in the fire and said, "Hit is something like that. Hit is jist two nations and them a-fightin'."

Then the first man turned to Allen and said, "You ai're wealthy to own land and people, and you can read the print in a book and cipher figures. Ain't it niggers? Ain't that why you ai're fightin'? Ain't that why you ai're here?"

Allen leaned toward them across the circle of firelight. He looked at them one after another. He gazed into their eyes. Then, very softly, his voice gentle and firm, but at the same time somehow pleading, he said, "Listen. There are a lot of reasons. There are a lot of good reasons. And one reason is as good as another as long as we win."

His voice rose. "We have got to win! Do you hear me? We have got to fight the sons of bitches until we have won!"

There was a short silence.

Then the first man said again, "But why ai're you fightin'?"

"Like you said," Allen replied smoothly, deferentially. "Because of the niggers. Like you said, because of the Yankees."

Then he thought, I have told them a lie. And thought this without compunction, without regret.

And then, By God, I will lie to them again. I will lie to them every day before breakfast if I have to. They have got to keep on fighting. We have got to win.

So he kept secret the reason he was fighting the war, and he lied when he thought lying would help, and as time went on and war went badly, he developed an instinct for morale. He could sense a coming desertion, he could almost read the minds of the young boys, weary from the long marches, sore from the saddle and scared of the sough and rumble of the guns. He could see defection brewing in the eyes of middle-aged men, at night or during a lull in military action, or in spring when the ground was ready for the plow. When Allen thought a man was planning to desert the army, he would go to him and ask him to remain. He would go over to the man's mess and call him aside, and they would walk to the edge of the camp and Allen would talk. He had a regular speech that was as good as any Houston Knott could deliver, and in his speech he referred to the Yankees as invaders, and he spoke of defending Southern homes and mothers and sweethearts, and sometimes with his tawdry eloquence he would make grown men weep. He would see men thirty and forty years old with tears running down their cheeks, and in spite of the seriousness of what he was doing, in spite of the necessity to keep men in the army, there were moments when he had to turn away to hide his smile.

God damn them, Allen Hendrick said to himself, they have got to fight. We have got to have them to win the war. God damn them, why shouldn't they hate the Yankees?

There was in Houston's company a young recruit, a boy named Darrell Halliburton, who had run away from his home in Southern

Mississippi and joined the army when he was sixteen years old. He was a blond boy with a long, sad face and thin lips and very pretty teeth; and one afternoon just at twilight, at that soft, deliquescent moment when the last light is fading into dark, Allen saw Halliburton walking away from camp. He was moving furtively. He would go a few steps toward a line of woods along a hilltop, pause and look back, and go forward rapidly again.

Allen ran after Halliburton, caught him by the arm, and stopped him and made the speech and waited for the tears. He spoke of the invader and Southern womanhood, and he searched Halliburton's face for a sign of contrition, but none was there. Halliburton simply returned his gaze, and the blue eyes, the thin lips showed nothing.

Then at last the boy said, "Yeah. That is good to talk about. What you said is what I heard at home and what I read in the paper. But about them Yankees, it is different now that I have been here, now that I have seen them."

"How?" Allen said impatiently. "How is it different?"

"Why, they are men," Halliburton said. "Except for their suits they look much like you and me do."

"Look!" Allen said loudly. "God damn the way they look! They are Yankees and you have got to stay and fight them."

"No," Halliburton said. "I have seen them now. I don't crave any longer to kill a Yankee."

"You bastard," Allen said. "You yellow bastard. You're afraid they'll kill you."

The boy nodded, the movement barely perceptible in the dusk.

"Yes," he said. "I am afraid. I acknowledge that."

"Then you had better be afraid to desert too," Allen Hendrick said. "Because if you leave I'll tell the provost marshal. If you desert I'll help him run you down. I'll see you shot."

This time it looked as if Halliburton would cry. For an instant his chin trembled, then the line of his mouth grew firm, and he turned and walked back toward the camp.

So the war went on, and Allen Hendrick did his duty, and sometimes did a little more than his duty, not only in the camp but in the field. He was commissioned after the action at Fort Pillow—for killing niggers, he thought ironically. He was made a lieutenant for being at the head of a charge against the colored troops. By the fall of 1864 Houston Knott was a colonel and Allen was a captain in command of a company, and that is why on a day in November he was sitting on his horse on a bank of Duck River, covering the crossing for part of Hood's infantry who were heading north into Middle Tennessee.

It was a bright day but cold, with the chill of winter: there was a wind out of the north and the air was damp and the ground was damp and soft from a recent rain. Allen had deployed his company, still mounted, in a rough perimeter that was anchored on the river, and he had stationed himself in the middle of a cornfield that looked down on the muddy highway and on the slope of the river bank and the pontoon bridge. He watched the soldiers as they moved across, jostling each other on the swaying bridge floor, slipping on the incline, fanning out when they reached the highway. They kept no formation. In their rags and tatters, they did not even look like soldiers; dressed as they were in a hundred different cuts and hues of clothing, they looked like a posse gathered from among the very poor, or like a backwoods militia that had been mustered quickly and ordered quickly to the front. Those who were lucky had captured clothing, Yankee coats and hats and pants and boots. There were others in hunting shirts of homespun plaid or linsey-woolsey, and there were some with strips of blanket tied to their feet and some with russet shoes. They wore beards, they were dirty, they were uncouth and noisy; they sang and yelled taunts at staff officers on horses, and they yelled at Allen Hendrick as they went by.

One of them—a short, red-faced man with a long nose—pointed at Allen and called, "Look yonder, boys, hit's a statue in that 'ere cornfield. Them cavalry boys done struck a mon-u-ment to theyselves."

Allen turned his head to look at the speaker, and there was a great cry on the road beneath him, a hullabaloo of mock surprise.

"Whoa, now, whoa," a voice shouted. "It's moving, boys. I seen it twist around."

And another said, "Run, men, the pretty thing's a-shaking. The head is a-cracking off and it's bound to fall."

They told him they had found his mule, they ordered him to come out from under his hat, they sang the song about joining the cavalry and having fun. But he did not care; it did not matter what they said to him. What mattered was the way they handled the Yankees, how they performed in the battles that were to come.

"Go it, you dirt eaters," he yelled back. "Go it, you bastards, but you'd better make haste. We'll have the bluebirds whipped before you get there."

The soldiers filed by, man after man, company after company across the bridge, and then Allen noticed an officer make the crossing on a horse. Or rather, it was not the officer but the animal that caught Allen's attention—a big, black plantation horse grown a little lean but still straight-backed and apparently sound of bone, and still very handsome. And then Allen looked idly at the man who sat very straight on his beautiful horse and who wore the three stars of a full colonel. The uniform was old but meticulously patched; the blue facing of the blouse was faded, the blue stripes on the trousers were frayed. The cloth was clean and the boots were blacked; and the man seemed clean and worn, too: he was a match for the uniform he went about in. There was a scar on his forehead. Three fingers were missing from his left hand. Like almost everyone else, he had grown a beard and a set of mustaches. But there was no mistaking the short nose, the high cheekbones, the small eyes. The colonel on the pretty horse was Percy Rutledge.

Seeing him so suddenly, Allen could not say what he felt, though the physical sensation was plain enough, the prickle of the hairs at the back of his neck, the chill down his spine, the numbness in his stomach. It was the old anger, but it was something more than that, and something beyond mere surprise at the fact of their meeting. There was, in his deep emotion, a tinge of disappointment. For the man he saw before him now, the colonel in the tattered uniform with a scar on his forehead and three fingers gone from his hand, was not the Percy Rutledge whom Allen had pictured in his dreams. For more than three years, while he had plotted his revenge, Allen had called up before his mind's eye the vision of a boy with a smooth face who sat on a sunlit veranda with his father and his sister. Now, on a day in November, on the banks of Duck River, with the ragged Army of Tennessee marching by, the face appeared in truth, in the flesh, and, oh, how the flesh had changed, how the face had altered.

"Colonel," Allen said, but the word came out softly and cracked on the last syllable and was swallowed by the wind.

Then he called again, "Colonel. Colonel Rutledge."

This time it was loud enough for Percy to hear.

He turned and looked at Allen and for a second or two his eyes gave no sign, no hint of recognition. Then the lids narrowed and the wrinkles on the sides of his face and on his forehead deepened, and he rode up into the cornfield, rode up to Allen and extended his hand.

It was wrong, this gesture; it was so far from what Allen had expected that at first he did not even reach down to remove his glove.

"I am Allen Hendrick," he said. "Do you remember me? Do you know who I am?"

Percy nodded and left the hand extended.

"Yes," he said softly. "I know you. I knew you right after you spoke to me, down there on the road."

He had no right to do this, no right to pretend friendship, no right to offer it, after what had happened that afternoon at Cedarcrest. Allen felt his skin grow warm, and his tongue felt dry inside his mouth, but he clamped his teeth together and took off his gauntlet. He had no choice that he could see except to shake Percy Rutledge's hand.

"I have wondered about you sometimes," Percy said. "I knew you were in the cavalry, but I lost track of your regiment. I didn't know whether you were with Forrest, or maybe with us, with General Wheeler, or maybe even in Virginia with Hampton or with Stuart or one of the Lees."

And what could Allen Hendrick say to this? This pleasantry which was wrong too? Or more than pleasantry, this apparent interest in how he had fared and where he had been. But he would not be tricked. Allen made up his mind to this. The softness of Percy's words would not be subterfuge enough to fool him; they would not lure him into believing that Percy no longer hated him.

So he said shortly, "I am with General Forrest. Houston Knott's regiment. General Bell's brigade."

Percy Rutledge nodded. "I see," he said.

He paused and glanced down at the road, where the troops were still passing. "God knows, I'm glad you all are with us. God knows how much we are going to need your help."

A long silence this time, while they both watched the infantry and listened to the steady sound of the marching, the feet against earth and the drone of voices and the occasional command.

Then Allen Hendrick thought, I will try him now. I will see how sweet he can dance to another tune.

He took a deep breath and said, "Percy, what do you hear from Gallatin? What have you heard about Kate?"

Percy turned his head quickly and looked hard into Allen's eyes. His face grew rigid for a moment; his lips pressed together and his jaw muscles gathered, tightened beneath the skin. But this flash of anger—if it was anger—passed quickly. Percy seemed to relax.

"Allen," he said softly, almost dreamily, "it has been a long time, hasn't it? It has been three years, three and a half years since either one of us has been there. And out here——" He waved his arm to include all the fields, all the brown and evergreen hills, the bridge and the muddy river and the men of the army. "Out here so much has happened to us, to change us, you and me, and to change the whole country. And it must be that way at home too, everything changed and different there——"

"No, by God!" Allen interrupted. "I have not changed. I acknowledge no difference."

"Allen," Percy Rutledge said, his voice still soft, "why don't you give it up? About Kate, I mean. Why don't you give up the idea of marrying her?"

"Listen," Allen said harshly, "I cannot make you tell me what you know. If you really have heard from home. If you have something you could tell me. But I'll be damned if I have to listen to your foolishness either. I mean to marry Kate. She has said she will marry me. She has given me her promise. And Captain Rutledge, he promised too. I made a bargain with him and I mean to keep it."

The hard look, the rigid lines returned to Percy's face: beneath the tanned skin the muscles hardened. Then once more after a second or two the tension had passed.

"Allen," he said, "Father is gone. He passed away two years ago."

"Gone?" Allen said, and his voice was harsh. The word was loud and rasping. "Gone?" he shouted.

"Yes," Percy Rutledge replied. "My father is dead."

"No!" Allen insisted. "I say he is not! I say he is not dead! Damn you, you don't know! You are lying!"

For it could not be. Allen could not let it be. Not now, after all the anguish of the war; not now, after all his hopes and dreams of vengeance.

And then he thought he understood it. This was the reason behind Percy's soft words, the motive behind his show of friendship. He had been leading up to this trick all along; it was this deception he had set himself to practice. It was obvious that Percy believed he could stop the marriage by convincing Allen that the old man was dead.

So Allen said, "How do you know? You haven't been back there. The Yankees are in Gallatin. You can't even hear from them through the mail."

"Go to hell!" Percy Rutledge said, his eyes flashing.

"Tell me," Allen shouted. "How do you know?"

In the silence that followed, Allen saw Percy Rutledge clench his good hand above the saddle, saw the fist tremble and the knuckles grow pale. He saw, as he had seen once before, the vein showing through the skin on Percy's forehead, and the scar there like the knuckles had turned very white. Now the anger endured considerably longer, but for the third time that day Percy kept his temper in control. The color gradually faded from his face, his body relaxed, and he shook his head as if to clear it.

Then he said, "I learned it from a prisoner we took at Chickamauga. He was a man I knew in the old army, and he had been garrisoned for a while at Gallatin. He visited Father three or four times before he died."

He hesitated, and almost as an afterthought he said sadly, "Father had been gone almost a year by the time I found out about it. He died early in September of '62."

Allen shook his head. "No," he said but without conviction. "No," he said, but he knew that it was true.

It had the ring of authenticity; it was too simple, too plausible in its coincidence, to have been made up. But how could it have happened? How could fate have cheated him so bitterly? Why had time so completely deprived him of his revenge?

And the denial, the deprivation of time had been complete. Or almost so, so vast was the world's alteration. For, oh, the face that he looked at now was not the face that he had seen before, the voice was no longer the voice that had called him a nigger. Even the spirit, the heart of Percy Rutledge had changed; he had learned to subdue the bright glow of his anger. But however he had modified, he was Percy Rutledge still, and whatever kind of man was left, Allen Hendrick could hate him.

"Damn you," Allen said, "you had no right to do this. Neither of you did. He should not have died. And you should not have changed. I say you had no right to become so different!"

"Allen," Percy said, and he seemed more calm than at any time throughout their talk. "Allen."

"Damn you!" Allen Hendrick said. "God damn you!"

Softly Percy Rutledge called his name again. "Allen. I am almost sorry that I told you. I did not know that you hated him so much."

"Damn you!" Allen said.

But Percy was leaving. He turned his horse and moved back onto the road.

"By God, it is just you now!" Allen Hendrick shouted after him, but he did not know whether Percy had heard him, and if so, whether he understood what Allen meant.

So he said to himself, It is only him now. Only him to pay for all that both of them have done. He felt his anger reach a sudden pitch. It surged through his flesh with a steady beat. It coursed like his blood to reach his extremities. Then he thought of Katherine and his anger died.

He had not even asked about her again, and surely Percy had known. After he had heard that Captain Rutledge was dead he had not even thought of her, and Percy would have had news of her, too, from the same prisoner.

But he would have told me, Allen Hendrick thought desperately. She must be just the same. If anything were wrong, if anything were changed, he would have told me.

He looked off up the road and saw Percy Rutledge. He was far away now at the top of a hill, and his figure was very straight against the skyline.

"I hate you," Allen said under his breath.

Then he said it aloud, "You son of a bitch, I hate you!"

But what he felt was not really hate, not the pure hate that he had known for so long and cherished for so long—for all the years since he had left Gallatin. Rather, there was disappointment and a keen sense of loss: and in the chambers of his heart a great vacancy.

26

ALLEN HENDRICK did not take part in the Battle of Franklin: along with Stephen Lee's Corps and most of the army's artillery, he was late in getting to the field.

After he left the crossing at Duck River, he was caught in a fire fight with a Federal patrol, and it was very late before he could disengage completely and bury his dead and pick up his wounded and start north again. So he did not arrive at the hills south of Franklin until four in the afternoon, and by then the infantry was already in line, already moving out against the Yankee fortifications. There was cavalry too, in support of the foot soldiers on both flanks, but from a distance, from the high ground where he had halted, Allen could not tell one division from another, and he did not know where he was likely to find his own brigade.

He sent out couriers in search of a command post or a general officer who knew the plan of battle, and who would be willing to tell Allen where his company ought to go. And while he waited for his messengers to return, he watched the charge of the two corps of infantry, the long line spread out across the brown valley. With their guidons and flags and battle pennants flapping, catching the breeze, and flashing in the sunlight; with the bayonets fixed and flashing, and the movement steady, they flushed the game out of the grass they walked through, and they followed the quail and the rabbit toward the Yankee guns. For one moment, though undoubtedly there was noise in the valley, the hilltop was quiet beyond the sound of any animal, beyond the sough and keen of the wind or the song of a bird. Allen Hendrick heard no sound beyond his own heartbeat, the thrill and surge of his own excited pulse. Then a moment more and no faltering, the troops below moving well still, and moving unheard on the hilltop, with the officers on horseback, not shouting yet, not waving yet or flashing their hats or their sabers, and no death yet; but death there, death beyond in the Yankee earthworks and the fallen trees and the abatis. Oh, Allen Hendrick knew this moment, remembered it well from out of the past, the terror before the first shot was fired, the fear that accompanied the silence at the beginning of the charge, when you knew they were there, and you knew they could see you, but they were holding off till you came in range.

Allen leaned forward in the saddle, peered forward across the neck of his horse, and now from a greater distance the line looked very thin over the wide field; but it was straight yet and it moved on yet, and still there was quietness.

Oh, Lord, Allen Hendrick thought, let it begin.

And then he thought, When it does begin, the Lord will have to help them.

An instant more, and it seemed to Allen that he could see the progress of the sun, that he had caught it in its retreat toward night and darkness. But he could not be sure, for the quietness and the waiting were like part of a spell, a kind of morbid enchantment cast over the universe. And in his great pity for the men who walked toward death he felt his head grow light.

Then, suddenly, it came.

A single gun at first, and then the rest of the artillery joined in, firing canister and firing fast; the shot cut the grass and raised the dust, and the smoke from the muzzle blast gathered in clouds and rolled and billowed across the field toward the moving rank that had begun to close up again.

For a moment the artillery fire had breached it. Allen had seen the first of the men fall, and he noted how from a distance the dead looked very much alike, though they did not look alike when you got up close to them. He knew that on the field when you were walking or lying or crawling among them, you would notice how they had fallen in different positions and stiffened in different positions and how their faces and even their uniforms were dissimilar in the extreme. But seen from the hilltop, they lay like marks on the grass, and no one looked much bigger or smaller or more pitiful than the other.

Allen thought this, and he saw the line begin to disappear. It was blocked from his view by the rising smoke and the sound increased with the first small arms that began when the Confederate center hit the first redoubt.

"By God," Allen said, turning to one of his lieutenants, a tall, black-haired man who was mounted on a lean, gray mare. "By God," he said, "we have got to move into it."

"Yes," the man said, "we ought to do something. But where'll we go, Captain? Where's our regiment at?"

"I don't know," Allen replied. "We will have to take a chance on finding them. Let's go toward the river. Let's move to the right."

So he made the correct guess and moved to his right, and he led his company across the Columbia turnpike, just at the middle of the field where the battle had started, where Cleburne and Brown had overrun the Federal outpost. With the guns still firing sharply along the Yankee fortification—the artillery heavier, the small arms more rapid than any he had ever heard before—he rode past the dead that he had seen first from the hill, the corpses that from a distance had looked so much the same. They lay in every conceivable posture and this did not surprise him; there were many of them, and this he had expected too. Or rather, he had not expected it: he had known there would be a large number of casualties, but not so large a number as he looked at now. In some places there had not been room enough for them to fall. They lay across each other, on top of each other, one man's arm on another man's breast, one's feet turned up on another's stomach. And, oh, they looked poor, they looked very poor. Their faces were thin to show the bone, and their clothes were ragged and torn and patched—one's jacket was slit all the way down the back, and the flesh looked very white in the late sunlight.

He had known, of course, that they were going hungry, for there were times when even in the cavalry you did not get anything to eat; and always there was too little forage for the horses. And in the cavalry, too, there was always the worry about clothes, and how long it would be before you could capture some boots or a set of blankets. And Allen Hendrick had known that it was worse in the infantry. That the foot soldiers were hungrier and raggeder and that sometimes their battles were bigger and bloodier, but he had never dreamed that it would be like this. Not since Shiloh, where he had been out of the battle really, stuck away on one of the flanks, had he fought with any large body of walking soldiers, and now on the front, along the wide arc of the main Federal positions, it was like the world had split apart and all hell was coming through. He knew that musketry sounded like the clatter of lumber, but what he now heard was one great and continuous roar. He knew that usually through the smoke you could see a muzzle blast, but this front seemed to burn with an even, steady glow.

Allen glanced at the lieutenant who rode beside him, and the black-haired lieutenant had turned pale. He looked back at the ragged, impoverished corpses, and for an instant their death and their poverty seemed somehow to be a reproach to him, as if he had had something to do with keeping them poor or getting them shot at. There was an instant when, riding under the gaze of the dead, he almost felt guilt and the grim responsibility.

But I didn't do it, he said to himself. I did not know, I did not know. How could I know what they had been going through and how many would perish?

Then he thought, And anyway they had their own reasons for coming. They had something they wanted to fight for, and whatever it was, it was their business. It was not mine. It had nothing to do with me.

Then he said aloud, "It is not my fault. I did not make them come. I did not do it."

But with the noise of the battle no one had heard him speak.

When he found Houston Knott, it was full dark and the cavalry was pulling back to go into bivouac, but in the center the infantry fought on. They met on the banks of the Harpeth River, Allen and his men on horseback and facing toward the front, and Houston was on horseback too. But the men had been fighting, as usual, dismounted, and they were moving away from the battle line, back down the stream to where they had left their mounts.

"I'm sorry," Allen said, beginning this way without saying hello or saluting. "We got caught at Columbia. We just got up."

"It's all right," Houston said. His face was dirty and it looked very tired. He was eating a cracker and little crumbs were caught in the hairs of his beard. "We have been in it, but we didn't do much."

"Listen," Allen said, leaning over and catching Houston's sleeve. "Send us up. We are fresh. We are ready."

Houston shook his head. "No," he replied. "You come on with us. We're going to draw forage and feed and eat."

They had been shouting at each other, their heads very close, that they might be heard above the sound of gunfire. Now the activity in the center increased. They were mostly small arms but they were firing rapidly, and it looked to Allen as if at least a division was engaged.

"But the fight," Allen said excitedly. "It isn't over yet. We have got to win it. We have got to win the war."

"It is over for us," Houston said. "For a while anyway. We have got our orders. Old Bedford is across the river with Jackson's division, but he's coming back too."

"But listen," Allen insisted, pointing, swinging his arm toward the noise of the battle. "It is still going on and we could help." His voice rose shrilly. "I want to win. Don't you understand that? Not only for my sake but for all the rest of them. We have got to win after what the infantry has been through today."

And for that other reason that never left his mind, for Kate and for his ultimate triumph over Percy and for—but he remembered with a renewal of disappointment that the old man, Captain Rutledge was dead.

"By God," he said to Houston Knott, "we have got to win."

Houston looked down at the rest of his regiment, at the dismounted cavalry that moved away from the Yankees, walking wearily, their weapons slung. They moved around and between Allen's company that still sat on horseback, and occasionally one of them would pat a horse on the rump.

"Be sensible," Houston said, his voice firm but a little indulgent. "We all want to win. You know that. But to do it we have to follow orders. Lord knows you've been in the army long enough to learn that."

In the center of the line the firing went on sporadically until after nine o'clock, until after Allen had eaten his scanty supper and fed his horse and unsaddled and lay down by the fire. The shooting would stop, play out, and then start up suddenly again, build to a climax and drop off and once more there would be silence. Or rather, not silence, but a different, softer kind of sound, the murmur, the rising cries of the wounded. This was something that Allen had seldom heard before, for in the cavalry, or at least with Forrest, you did not often hang around a battlefield. When the fighting was over, you picked up your own people, or left somebody to pick them up, and got your mount from the horse holder and moved on. He had seldom heard the call of the wounded, and never had he heard so many of them, never heard the cry rise in such magnitude, such despair. The sound was like a continuous groan in the night: it seemed to rise out of the cold, damp earth, and to hang there, almost miasmic, almost palpable. Oh, Allen Hendrick thought again, I did not do it. I did not make them come. It is their war too, and they brought themselves into it.

He turned his mind away from the wounded and the noise that they made, and he thought of the battle that he had watched that day, and he wondered how many men had died and who had won it. He had not been able to see, to ascertain the victor, before he left his hilltop; he had asked Houston and Houston did not know.

"I don't know," Houston had said, "but there is one thing I can tell you. On our end of the line the Yankees did not run."

Now, Allen lay by an old fire and looked up at the dark and cloudless sky and at all the stars that glittered there: at Orion, who stood with his sword at his side, and above Orion were the Gemini, the brave brothers. He lay and thought of all that had happened in the last three years, the miles he had marched, the distance he had come since he left Gallatin. And he thought of the past and of the people he had loved: he thought of General Hendrick and of Marcus Hendrick, of Lucy, who was in Louisiana now, and of Anse and Valeria. And he thought of Katherine, and bitterly he thought of her father, who had escaped any scourging of spirit or flesh, who had passed away.

There beneath the stars, with the swelling chorus of the wounded sounding around him, he turned his eyes to the distant, the painful, past. And looking back, he saw a hundred crossroads, a score of contingencies, that might have changed his life. If he had not loved Katherine, would he be here now, on the cold November ground south of Franklin? Or if Katherine had been willing to disobey her father and marry, or if Lucy Hendrick had gone to live with Allen at Cedarcrest, would he then have joined Houston Knott and ridden off to war? Or to go back even further, if Marcus Hendrick had survived the shock of the news of secession, might he have prevailed upon Allen to avoid the conflict and remain at home?

He did not know. He could not answer these questions. And at last he decided that the answers did not matter very much. He was here and he loved Katherine and he had hated her father. With this conclusion in his mind he went to sleep.

But he did not sleep for long. When Houston woke him the stars had hardly changed their positions in the sky.

"Allen," Houston said, "Percy Rutledge has been wounded. He was here today with the infantry, and he was hit and he wants to see you."

"Me?" Allen asked incredulously.

But already he was pulling on his boots. He made a quick roll of his blankets and saddled and mounted and set out with the courier who had come to find him and to show him the way.

"Hurry," Allen said to the man who rode beside him.

But the courier kept on at a slow trot, picking his way carefully through the heavy traffic, the wagons and limbers and hospital details that moved everywhere now that the shooting had stopped.

"God damn it!" Allen Hendrick shouted. "Hurry! I have got to get there! Don't you understand that? I can't let him die!"

"Are you 'ere doctor, Cap'in?" the corporal asked.

"Hurry, you son of a bitch!" Allen Hendrick replied.

But if he had been a doctor, he could not have saved Percy Rutledge, and he knew that as soon as he entered Percy's tent. In the yellow glow of the lantern that hung from the center pole Percy appeared very pale except for a streak of dirt on one of his cheekbones, or perhaps it was a bruise where he had fallen from his horse. He breathed. His chest rose and fell laboriously beneath the cover, and Allen could hear the sound of his wind through his lungs and throat. Otherwise there was no movement, no flicker of eyelid or lifted finger to show that he had heard Allen's footstep or that he was aware that Allen was with him now in the tent.

"Percy," Allen said, and his voice was completely flat. It was even, without rancor or sympathy, without regret. "I am here," Allen Hendrick said. "It is Allen, Percy."

Then Percy opened his eyes and said, "Yes, sir, I see."

There was a silence with only the sound of Percy's breathing.

And then Percy Rutledge said, "I am glad. I had hoped you would get here. I had prayed that I would get to see you before I died."

"No," Allen said. "No, you are not going to die." But it was not very convincing; his denial was no comfort to either one of them, and Percy did not bother to make a reply.

"Listen," Percy Rutledge said. "I want you to promise me something. When you get home I want you to leave Katherine alone."

"Leave her alone?" Allen Hendrick echoed. "Leave her alone?"

"Yes," Percy replied, softly, calmly. "She will have worry enough now, sorrow enough with me and Papa gone."

Allen Hendrick looked down at the pale face, at the scar across the pale forehead and the eyes that had grown weak and bloodshot, and the dark bruise that stained the thin, white cheek.

He is going to die, Allen thought. He is going to die and leave me alone, with no one to fight against any more, with no one to pay for what he and his father have done to me. Allen thought of the death of Percy Rutledge with a sense almost of bereavement; and then the bereavement changed to a quick, urgent anger, and he said:

"No, damn you, I have promised you enough. I made a bargain with your father, and I aim to keep it."

Percy almost smiled. In spite of his apparent pain the slender lips almost turned upward.

"Your bargain," he said with mild scorn. "What is it worth to you now? After what happened here this afternoon, what chance do you think you have of fulfilling its conditions?"

"I am going to keep it!" Allen Hendrick shouted. "You are wrong! We are going to win this war! By God, we have got to!"

"Ah," Percy Rutledge said, "you are that kind of a fool. But the war, who wins the war doesn't really matter, does it?"

"Of course it matters," Allen Hendrick said. "It matters more than anything else in the world. There can be no question of losing! We have got to win it!"

"Let that pass," Percy said wearily. "Assume we do win. It is still all over for you. Don't you understand that?"

"I made a bargain," Allen said stubbornly. "Your father made a promise."

"Then I release you from the bargain," Percy replied impatiently. "Forget your talk with Papa for an instant and try to understand me."

He paused, breathing heavily, grimacing.

"When I saw you yesterday," Percy said, "at Duck River, and I saw how you had hated Papa, then I knew."

Allen waited a moment.

"Knew what?" he asked.

"That you would never marry Katherine. That hating Papa and me the way you did, you could not love her, not enough, not any more."

"God damn you!" Allen Hendrick said. "You lie! You are a liar, and you tell lies from your deathbed, so for me there can be no recourse, no chance to right the wrong. No opportunity to push the lie back down the throat that spoke it."

"Allen," Percy said softly, "I speak the truth."

"You lie," Allen said again, talking very rapidly. "If what you say is true, why did you call me over here? Why did you try to convince me that we were going to lose the war? Why did you ask me to promise that I would not marry Kate?"

"You don't really understand it, do you?" Percy asked. His voice was surprised and slightly tinged with pity. "Not even after three years of war. Not even after what you saw out there today."

"I understand that I am going to marry Katherine," Allen Hendrick said.

"No, you aren't," Percy replied. "Whoever wins the war, she will not have you. I have released you from the bargain you made with Papa; but you will not even want to marry her when I am dead."

"Then why did you send for me?" Allen asked furiously.

And Percy replied, "Because I wanted you to see it with your own eyes and know the truth of it. I wanted to be certain that you knew that I was dead."

There was a pause. Then Percy raised his hand a little way off the blanket. "If you please, sir," he said.

"Yes," Allen replied. "I will go."

He lifted the flap of the tent and went out into the night, out into the chill of November and the glitter of the cold November stars. Oh, he thought, whom can I turn to now? Who could pay now for the wrongs he had suffered? For his own thwarted marriage? For Lucy's exile? For all the heartbreak and the ruined dreams, the confounded ambitions? Oh, who indeed? And who was his enemy now? He did not know; he could not answer.

He went to his horse and mounted and rode back the way he had come.

Never in his life before had he been so lonely.

◊ 27 ◊

SIX MONTHS LATER the war was over and he was paroled from the Confederate service, and he rode north to Nashville in search of Katherine. Now that Captain Rutledge and Percy were dead, he believed that she would most likely be living with her aunt, Mrs. Richardson, and when he reached the city, he went directly to the house on Vine Street and rang the bell. He was wearing his uniform which was old and soiled and tattered; he had a beard, and his hair grew down over his ears, and even the horse that he had left at the hitching rail was gaunt and dirty. It occurred to him that he might better have gone home first and cleaned himself up, but after four years he could not spare another day or two away from Kate. If I can just see her, he thought, just look at her for a little while, then I can go on to Cedarcrest and get some money from Anse and buy myself a new costume.

So, fresh from the war and the long journey home, stained by the road and a little tired and a little hungry, he rang the bell and the door opened, and a man in a Yankee major's uniform looked at him curiously, questioningly and said:

"Yes?"

For a moment he believed that he had the wrong house.

"I beg your pardon," Allen said. "It has been four years."

While the Yankee major stood with his hand on the doorknob, Allen glanced around to get his bearings. He looked out at the street where there were people passing by, peered right and then left down the long porch, and lifted his gaze to see the wide, familiar fanlight. Beyond the major, in the dimness of the hall, even the carpet was as he remembered it, and the chandelier of red glass and the curving stairway. He was not lost. This was the house Mrs. Richardson had lived in.

"I beg your pardon," Allen said again. "I thought this was the residence of Mrs. Richardson."

"Not any more," the Yankee major said. "I live here."

Allen waited, but the major offered no further explanation.

"Do you know where I could find Mrs. Richardson?" Allen Hendrick asked.

"No," the Yankee said impatiently. "I don't have any idea." And he shut the door.

But where had Mrs. Richardson gone, he wondered, and how would he go about finding her? He had no notion where he might begin, and standing there on the porch where long ago he had come to visit Katherine, he felt suddenly alien and the city seemed strange. He noticed, not for the first time but with a new sense of helplessness, how the streets were crowded with blue uniforms and with well-dressed civilians whom Allen did not know, and with Negroes who had once been slaves but who now were free. In every block there was a new building, a new house, or a new place of business and a new proprietor's name above the door.

Allen could think only of the Female Academy. There they would undoubtedly remember Katherine. Someone there might even know where she was.

He mounted his horse and rode to Church Street and turned left and moved toward the depot and there on the corner were the buildings and the wall and the iron gates which were closed and tightly locked.

And though the bell pull remained outside the wall, this time there was no reason even to ring, so plain were the marks of vacancy and desuetude. The windows were shuttered; the grass was uncut. The covered portico which had been kept so neat and clean was strewn with leaves and scraps of paper and there was a pile, a drift of leaves, by the main door. The statuary had been removed from the yard. There were weeds coming up between the bricks of the walks. The gates themselves were beginning to rust and the paint was flaking.

He had not known that it would be this way, though he had set himself to find some alteration. He had prepared himself for change, but not for so complete a change as this, and he held to the bars and looked in at the abandoned academy. He peered into the sunlit court where the puffballs of dandelions swayed with the gentle breeze, and his heart seemed to slow and he felt a great tiredness. For, oh, he remembered how once it had been; for an instant his fancy brought it back again, and he saw it, saw himself in his tailored clothes, in his beaver hat and his polished boots, and he moved with a light step and tapped his cane on the sidewalk. For a moment, too, his heart turned back, returned to the old innocence for this little space of time, and he felt the old love, the old ambition. He saw on the walk beside the boy who was himself, the girl who was Kate, who had been Kate four years ago, and she smiled and spoke and he heard her voice, trembling, whispering, full of infinite mystery, but he could not understand what she was saying.

Then a voice from out of the real world spoke and said, "It is closed, young man. When the war commenced, Dr. Cox was forced to close it."

He turned to see an old lady, or rather not old, only middle-aged, but pale and worn and wearing full mourning. Her hat, her veil, her dress were black; she wore black gloves and shoes and she carried a black parasol with an ebony handle. Only the face was white and it was very white, though through the veil Allen saw it but dimly.

"Dr. Cox had to close it," she said once more.

Then she said, "You're a soldier, aren't you? You just got back and you didn't know that."

"Yes, ma'am," he replied. "I didn't know. I thank you for telling me."

"It is a shame," the lady said. "It was a good school. In the old days it was always full of girls. And it was gay here, too, then. The boys used to come and serenade the girls. They would stand here and sing to them."

"Yes, ma'am," Allen said. "I remember."

"Oh," she replied. "Maybe you did it too. Maybe you were one of them."

"No, ma'am," he said. "I never sang, but I used to listen."

There was a silence.

Then at last she said, "There are so many things that are different now. There are so many new things we will have to get used to."

So he knew of nothing to do except go on to Gallatin now and see if perhaps Kate was there after all, or if someone there could tell him where to find her. He crossed the river on a ferry and rode through Edgefield; he moved out the pike through the slow spring afternoon and on into the cool May darkness. The stars came out, and a little later the moon, and the tired horse held his pace, and at midnight Allen was at the town square looking at the courthouse. He stopped here as he had stopped at the Female Academy, sat and looked for a while at the familiar landmarks, then started on the last miles to Cedarcrest.

Two more hours and he had come to his own drive. In the moonlight he turned and rode between the cedars, mounted the hill that would bring him in sight of the creek bed and the bridge across it and the next rise of ground and the old stone house. He felt the thrill of coming home, the pleasure so sharp it was almost like fear, the sensation sharp in his breast and in his stomach. It was almost like the first time he had come there with his father, so greatly was he moved after four years of absence; and that other time, he remembered, the general and Valeria had waited at the end of the sidewalk.

But now in the moonlight there was no one to be seen. No living soul, and no house either. Only a ruin. A shell of four jagged walls.

He knew what had happened. This was a sight that he had seen before, through Mississippi and Alabama and part of Tennessee—wherever the Yankees had come and used the torch. The roof of the Cedarcrest house was gone. The vacant windows shone with the white glow of the moon. He could see a scattering of fallen stones in what had been the garden.

He knew what had occurred, but he did not know why. Why they had burned his house and left all others standing. Gallatin, when he had gone through, had been the same as it had been before the war. Along the road between Cedarcrest and Nashville he had seen no damage.

Why me? he thought. Why did they do this to me?

"God damn them!" he said aloud. "We should not have stopped. We should have kept on fighting."

But he could not go back now. There was no army, no Forrest's cavalry to return to. So he clucked to his horse and rode down the hill and then up again to the mounting block and got down there and went up to the very edge of the ruin, to the main doorway.

Inside, some of the walls, the interior walls that were made of brick, were still standing. But the plaster had cracked off, and the floors were gone, and there was a great hole where the cellars used to be, and it was filled with rubble and the charred remains of the giant timbers. Over everything, over the ruins and the yard and the loose, fallen stones, there was a dusting, a fine powdering of ashes.

He turned away, unable to look any longer, unable, for a while at least, to stare any more at the ruins. It occurred to him that he would never know who had done him this way—never see the figure of the man who had burned his house. Oh, he thought, if I could only find him! If only for one minute I could meet him face to face!

In his great anger, his great pain, he could not stand still. He moved rapidly around the house, picked his way among the stones, and crossed the garden, and the fury kept gathering like a pressure that was palpable in his breast; it clutched his heart; it exerted a force against his windpipe.

He went between the locust trees into the quarter lot, stood in the bare space between the rows of darkened cabins, for the cabins had not been destroyed. They were dilapidated. They needed care. But they remained. To leave the quarters unharmed was ironic—though perhaps unintendedly so—and Allen's anger grew even more and the pressure in his breast became stronger and at last he called out in defiance to the empty night.

"Come out!" he shouted. "Come out, you son of a bitch! Come out into the moonlight where I can see you!"

A great silence followed the noise of his voice. There was a hiatus in the sounds of the night. Then a whipporwill took up again, and an owl, and a dog barked in the distance.

And to Allen's amazement a light showed through the open door of one of the cabins.

There was a flare as if of a lucifer match, then the glow of a lantern, and the lantern moved across the narrow porch, and swung slowly down the steps and into the lot, and an old, old voice said,

"Who dere? Who meddlin' round the premises?"

"By God," Allen Hendrick shouted in reply, "it's me!"

The lantern lifted shakily to cast its light on Allen's face, and the movement, the moment itself was a redundance in the smooth flow of time. It had happened before a long time ago in front of the rented house in Gallatin. Then, when Allen Hendrick was only fourteen, old Aaron had raised the light and looked in his face, and he looked in Allen's face now with the same mild surprise, the same curiosity. It was as if the progress of the world had come full circle and were now turning back upon itself. Then the old man spoke and the spell was broken.

"It is," he said softly, his voice gentle and kind and tinged with relief. "It is you, and I had give you up and give up the idea that you would ever come, that I would ever see you."

"You," Allen said without attempting to disguise his disappointment. "And I reckon you're all that is left out of a hundred people."

"Yes, sir, Young Master," Aaron replied. "They is all gone. Only me now and I here alone. I the only one that prove faithful."

"Master," Allen Hendrick replied. "I'm not your master."

He paused.

Then he said, "Why don't you leave too? You're free too. Why don't you go like the rest of them?"

"Go where?" Aaron asked. "I got no place to go. I too old to start out anywhere and expect to get there."

Then there was another pause and finally Aaron said, "You want me to go? I old and I live in that cabin all the years. You ask me now to leave and go way from this land and from Old Master?"

"No," Allen said wearily, "you stay if you want to. Just tell me about the house, why the Yankees burned it."

"They never," Aaron replied. "I never see no Yankees. I here all this time and the war go on and I never see one."

"Wait a minute," Allen said angrily. "They had to burn it. It didn't burn up by itself. Lightning didn't strike it."

"No, sir," Aaron said, shaking his head. "Not Yankees."

"Then, damn it, who?" Allen Hendrick shouted. "Who the hell did burn it if the Yankees didn't?"

"That nigger," old Aaron replied. "That trash nigger. The one yo' daddy taken a fancy to when he was alive."

He felt as if he had been struck a blow, so painfully did the memory rush upon him. The name echoed in the crevices of his brain: *Ben Hill, Ben Hill*. And in his mind's eye the man took shape—the small eyes set close together, the smooth, wide, handsome face, the golden watch chain and the diamond stud, the broadcloth coat and the ring on the fleshy finger. Once Ben Hill had stood in the door to Marcus Hendrick's office and looked at Allen, smiled down at him, as if he had never heard the song about Jim Crow and never passed a tobacco field at setting time. And later he had come into the same office with a valise full of money which he dumped on the table, and the ring and chain and diamond stickpin gone. And he had said, *You never showed me the trick, and me honest.* And later, in Nashville, he had stood outside the bank and gazed inscrutably at Allen Hendrick and fingered a package of banknotes, and his voice had been harsh. *Times change. Folks change . . . the fleas don't bite on the same dog's ass all the time.*

And now . . . now when Allen spoke, his own voice was soft, so sharp was his pain, so great his consternation.

"When?" he said, "why?"

"Uncle Aaron, you're going to have to tell me about it."

They went into Aaron's cabin, where there were a table and a chair, a rocking chair, a bed, a chest, and some cooking utensils. Allen sat down and the old Negro took a seat across from him, and he told Allen how the Yankees came and the slaves left. The word spread that the Union Army was in Gallatin, and the Negroes went into town to be fed by the Yankees or simply took to the road to see some more of the world. So there was only Aaron left and Mr. Finch, the overseer, and then Mr. Finch packed up and left too, and the old Negro man alone remained. He managed to feed a few of the chickens, to keep up with a few of the cows and the pigs, and he worked a garden. From time to time Anse Weaver would visit him. Indeed, Anse attempted to hire free labor to work the land, but free labor was hard to find and unreliable. So Anse simply brought staples out from town to old Aaron, inspected the house, and instructed the Negro when to build fires and when to open the windows and give it an airing. Things went on this way through part of '62, through all of '63 and '64 and a few months of '65. Then, toward the end of April, on a morning four weeks or so before this very night on which Aaron sat in the cabin and told Allen his story, Aaron saw three strangers ride over the crest of the hill and move on down the driveway.

Or rather, he saw three horsemen silhouetted against the blue April sky, and at first he assumed that they would turn out to be Anse and two of his acquaintances, two friends who had come out with him from Gallatin for the ride. It was not until they got to the creek that Aaron saw they were Negroes. They were at the house before he recognized one of them as Ben Hill.

The war was over now, but Aaron did not know this. Beyond

Anse, he had no communication with the outside world. But as he told Allen, even if he had known, he could not have guessed what Ben had come for. It was true that he did not like Ben. He looked down on Ben as he did on every other Negro, slave or free, who had not been the chief factotum in General Hendrick's household. And he particularly disliked Ben because Ben traded in people.

This, however, Ben had apparently forgotten or had never known.

Ben Hill was wearing his old costume. He had on the broadcloth coat and the golden watch chain, and there was an expensive repeater on one end of the chain and a set of jeweled lodge seals on the other. The men with him were dressed the same way, but as Aaron described it to Allen, they were not accustomed to such finery. They looked uncomfortable and their cravats were clumsily knotted. One of them—a man whom Ben referred to as Jim, a giant Negro with a bullet head and a scar on his face and two teeth missing— Jim kept pulling on the tails of his coat and stretching his arms as if the seams of the sleeves were binding him. The other man was called Murray and he was short and ugly. His eyes were bloodshot and he had a habit of twisting his fingers together and cracking his knuckles. They were all armed. Each had a pistol in his belt, and all of them had rifles strapped to their saddles.

Ben Hill looked around, scanned the landscape in every direction before he dismounted.

Then to Aaron he said, "Has he come?"

"Who?" Aaron replied.

"Allen Hendrick," Ben Hill said. "Is he home yet? Is he in the house? Is he at the stables?"

"You know he ain't," Aaron said. "He off to the war. He gone to fit the Yankees."

"The Yankees fit him," Ben Hill replied. "The Yankees have outfit him and all the balance of them. The South has been whipped. The war is over."

There was a long silence, and at last the tall man, Jim, said:

"You gine wait?"

"I come to wait," Ben Hill replied. "I aimed to get here first. I done hated this boy and his daddy for a good part of my life. This is the only opportunity I ever had. It is the only one I'm ever likely to get. I don't aim to skip it."

"Then," Jim said, "if we gine wait, we might jist as live search for the gold while we is waiting."

Aaron did not understand this talk, though they were making no obvious effort to shield their meaning. He thought over what he had heard and decided that they had come to plunder the place before Allen got home; he believed they were looking for jewels or for silverware or money. Through the next few days it appeared that he was right.

They questioned Aaron sternly; they questioned him several times; once or twice they threatened to whip him or burn his feet or shoot him. They wanted him to tell them where Allen had hidden his gold, but in the end they concluded that Allen had not confided in Aaron.

"If he knowed," Ben Hill said, "he would not be here now. He would have taken the money and taken to the road. A man may get old, and that for a fact. But a man, he don't get too old for stealing."

So the three Negroes searched for what they could find, and Aaron continued to assume they did what they came for. It was true that they kept a lookout night and day, a man stationed in the bell tower watching the long driveway and a stretch of the pike. But that was a sensible, an ordinary thieves' precaution, and throughout the day they dug in the garden and in the lawn, and they used divining rods all around the house and the stable. At night they looked for hollow places in the walls. They tore out paneling and slit open chairs and emptied mattresses. And all the while they kept their eyes on Aaron, and Aaron prayed that Allen or Anse Weaver would come.

Then he discovered the primary purpose of Ben Hill's visit to Cedarcrest, and the fear that his prayers might be answered made his heart turn cold. Ben was waiting at Cedarcrest to kill Allen Hendrick.

Aaron did not guess this. Ben Hill told him. Ben had given orders immediately after his arrival that Aaron should stay with him and his henchmen in the big house at night, fearing, of course, that Aaron might go for help, to a neighboring plantation, perhaps, or to the provost marshal at Gallatin. Most of the time Aaron was simply locked in an upstairs room, left without a light to spend the evening alone, while the other three Negroes tore up the furniture and beat on the plaster.

Then one afternoon the small man, Murray, came upon a demijohn of whisky. Mr. Finch had left it behind when he moved—had forgotten it probably, for it was in the overseer's house in one corner of the cellar—and Murray brought it back to the big house, and he and Jim got drunk. They were both unconscious by nightfall, and when Aaron came in to be locked up, he saw them sprawled out on the dining room floor, their broadcloth coats removed and Jim's shirt torn. There were several broken glasses in the corner near the door to the hall, and one of the men had vomited beneath the sideboard.

Perhaps Ben could not endure a night alone, watching from the bell tower without someone to talk to; or maybe, as Aaron grudgingly suspected, he was disgusted with the company he had been keeping, outdone with the behavior of what Aaron called the "field niggers" who were asleep downstairs. At any rate, while he sat in in the tower and watched the road, he made Aaron sit beneath him on the ladder and talk to him. That night he told Aaron that he meant to kill Allen.

While Aaron sat in the darkness, cramped in the small space and uncomfortable on the rungs of the ladder, Ben Hill started at the beginning, not of his life, but of his relationship with Marcus Hendrick. He told how he had traveled for Marcus and made money. He remembered particular transactions that he had made, how much Union Planters he had traded for how much Natchez and how much profit he had made on this or that individual trip. Not all the trades, of course, or all the journeys, but he could recall the ones on which he had had the most success. And he remembered how he had gone to Nashville—oh, how well he remembered that!—and his money had grown as if by magic and then, as if by magic, it had all disappeared.

"It was like waking up one morning," he said, "and finding that thieves has come a-visiting you in the night, and has taken all you possess and all your substance."

He was silent for a while.

"It is worse," he went on. "For they is a chance you might catch a thief and get back some of what he taken. And then no thief can cart off all you own and all your people."

At that time Ben Hill was fifty years old, and he told Aaron that he walked out of Marcus Hendrick's office with less than five dollars in his pocket and only the clothes that he had upon his back.

"It was a long time to come," Ben Hill said, "and a hard road to pull along, but I kept a-goin'. I never knowed nothing but people, slaves, and how to trade them to make money, and me a nigger myself, too, and born to go round to the back door, and remove my hat and step aside fo' the white man. And a war coming on, and nobody want people, no market to begin with and it dropping, and I never learn about that other business, about that paper.

"I aware," he said, "that they must be a way, but I could not discover it. I have taken up a bill and examined the picture there, and it would be a train, maybe, or a woman in a loose and undone kind of dress, and I could not see it. I looked and I could not see, and whatever it was that give a man the sense to tell, I never knowed, for Major Hendrick never teach me. I did not know the good from the bad and what would be good in the days to come. I had good money and I lost it all because the major he would not share his learning with me.

"He wanted me to lose it," Ben Hill said. "He was cunning, and that was his way of settling with me. He craved for me to lose. That was his design."

Then at last Aaron spoke. From the ladder where he sat with his legs cramping and the wooden rungs cutting into his hips and pressing his back, he said, "He never done that. Major Marcus, he love the black man. He a fool about a nigger. That why he consort with you."

"Shut up!" Ben Hill shouted, and his voice was loud in the confines of the tower. "I know what he did."

Ben hesitated, and when he went on his voice was filled with scorn. "You been a slave all your life. I ought not to talk to you about it. You cain't never understand it."

Aaron took another tack. "Major Marcus, he dead," Aaron said softly. "This boy you wants to kill never done nothing to you."

"He was in it too," Ben Hill replied sharply. "Once on the street, down in the city, I showed him some paper, put the paper into his hand and said, 'What must I do with this and me poor and needing money?' And he say, 'I don't know.' And I ask him again, and he say, 'I don't know,' again, and he will not tell me.

"Old Major dead," Ben Hill said, "and I cannot get to him. But that boy, he was in it too. And he come back, and it be night or day, he ride down yonder pike, and I aim to kill him."

That is what he said that night in the tower; that is what he told old Aaron.

But Allen Hendrick did not come riding down the highway until Ben Hill had gone. A few days after he talked to Aaron in the tower, Ben Hill apparently came to the conclusion that Allen was already dead. Or rather, he weighed the likelihoods, the probabilities. His position, Ben's position, was growing dangerous now. The roads were full of returning soldiers, men who had been fighting four years to keep the Negro in slavery and who were touchy on the subject of black freedom, and who were, for the most part, hell on bushwhackers and plunderers, and who would have killed Ben if they had known what he was doing to Allen's house. Already some of them had come to Cedarcrest to beg for food. At these times Ben took off his jewelry and posed as the faithful slave, the loyal butler; but sooner or later he and his cohorts were bound to be discovered, and the longer they stayed, the more certain their discovery became. On the other hand, each day that Allen Hendrick did not return was one more reason for believing that he had been killed during the fighting, and so the moment came when it seemed expedient to Ben to leave. There was a morning in May when the danger he was facing must have seemed to him all out of proportion to the possibility of Allen's ever showing up again at Cedarcrest, and he and the men with him packed their gear and saddled their horses and Ben sent for Aaron.

"He is dead already," Ben said to Aaron. He was very insistent on this point, very certain. His voice was loud. "Allen Hendrick. He ain't coming back."

Ben paused.

Then he said, "He dead, and I am sorry. All these years I study what I do to him and his daddy, how I make them pay for the suffering they cause me. I think of them, and the way I get mine back. I think it, and I keep it locked in here."

With his fist he tapped himself on his full round chest.

"Now," he said, "they gone. Now somebody else done beat me to it."

Once more there was a silence.

"But I gine do one thing," Ben went on at last. "I gine burn this house. And you watch me do it and you watch it burn. And if I wrong, and Allen Hendrick do come back, you say to him, 'Ben Hill, he burn your house. I stand and look on while he light the torch. Ben Hill, he burn your house, because he hate you.'"

There in the cabin, Aaron's voice stopped: his story was finished.

Allen waited a moment without speaking, and his head throbbed with the heavy beat of his pulse, and he clenched his hands and they were wet with perspiration.

"Where did he go?" Allen said at last.

"They ride away," Aaron replied. "That all I know. They get on they horses and I see them go out the driveway."

"When?" Allen demanded. "How long ago?"

"Four days, five, a week," Aaron said. "I don't rightly remember."

He could catch them. If he hunted long enough. With a fresh horse and a supply of food, and money in his pocket to see him down the road, he could run them to earth and kill Ben Hill and kill Ben Hill's two henchmen. There was a moment of excitement when he thought how it might be done. He could ask at every crossroad, every house that he passed, and they would have been noticed, wherever they had gone—three niggers in broadcloth coats and diamond stickpins.

He got up to do this, to set out after them. He got up and put on his pistol and stepped out into the day, for it was day now. It was the first light of morning.

He crossed the quarter lot and went up through the garden, walking fast and panting, grunting with each suck of his rapid breath. He pounded the earth with the heels of his boots; as he moved he kept ramming the palm of his hand with his fist.

Kill, he thought, kill. I will kill the bastard.

"I will kill them!" he said, hitting his palm again. "I will kill them all!"

Then the burned house came into view, the cracked and hideous remnant of the house he had loved.

All at once the anger faded and he knew he would not chase them. He did not know why, but he knew he would not, and he felt very weak and very sad; there was a numbness, a lethargy, that accompanied his sorrow.

He sat down on a stone and looked at the ruined wall, looked through a window at the ashes inside, then shut his eyes to block out the sight, and looked again and shut his eyes again, and looked still once more and this time he could stand it. He would have to stand it, for the house was gone. As long as he lived, it would never be rebuilt, and if he meant to live, he would have to learn to look at it.

Seventy years ago General Hendrick had been a young man, and he had come out from Maryland and built this house, and Marcus Hendrick had been born here. And the general had died here and left the house to Allen, and Valeria had married here, and Marcus Hendrick's funeral had been held in the parlor, and he was buried in the graveyard.

Oh, Allen thought, I did not harm Ben Hill. And Father did not harm him either. Why did he hate us so? Why did he do this to us, when we did not harm him?

He let these questions lie for a while in his mind, and the sun came up over the green hills and the birds came out to feed in what once had been the garden.

He cast his mind back over the story that Aaron had told; he thought of it, recollected it scene by scene, and he remembered how Ben had said to Aaron, *He dead and I am sorry. All these years I study what I do to him and his daddy, how I make them pay for the suffering they cause me. I think of them, and the way I get mine back. I think it, and I keep it locked in here.*

And he had smote himself above his old, corrupted heart.

Suddenly, sharper than the pain of his loss, the meaning of Ben Hill's words took possession of Allen.

Like me, he thought. Oh! he was like me! In his mind he had carried a picture of his vengeance.

But just as earlier in the day he had not been able to look at the house, Allen could not now turn his thoughts on himself; he could not bear to recollect his own thirst for revenge, his own hatred.

So he pondered the case of Ben Hill. And after a moment he said to himself, Ben did it because he was a nigger.

But this was not quite right, it was something more than that, something about the way Ben had seen the world and seen himself, and the way he had viewed the accident of his own blackness. Being a Negro, he had believed that no white man could respect him, and maybe he had had good reason to believe this. But good reason or not, this belief had been the source of Ben Hill's destruction. If he had trusted Marcus Hendrick, he would never have grown poor, and he would never have had to burn Cedarcrest, and he would not have to be living now with his heart full of hate, with his poor heart torn by the burden of hate's unfulfillment.

If he had only seen, Allen Hendrick thought.

And the words clung for a moment in his mind and repeated themselves with a slight variation.

If I had only seen. If I had only known. If I had only listened to what all my life people tried to tell me.

His mother, who had told him of her brother at Chalmette and who had left him finally in a last effort to reform him; General Hendrick, who had willed him Cedarcrest, given him money and power and advised him to stay with the land; his father, who had told him the story of his, Marcus', love, how he had courted Lucy and admired her beauty and the strength of her spirit; and Anse Weaver, who had spoken to him of patience; and Valeria, who had spoken to him of forbearance; and in the end, even his enemy, even Percy Rutledge, who had tried to show him the destructive quality of revenge. Each of them had tried to teach him to have a little more respect for himself. They had all attempted to instruct him in his own human value.

They had all tried to help him. And if he had not been content to listen to their words, he might at least have profited by their examples. They had not all been happy; they had not all even been fortunate. (Allen remembered how his father had once defined these words, repeating the definitions from Herodotus.) They had suffered, and many of them were dead, but in their lives they had found something of reason, something of glory.

All of them, Allen thought: Father in his marriage to Mother; Mother in her love for me; Grandfather in his reconciliation with Father; and Valeria and Anse in their marriage; and old Captain Rutledge by once having fought for his nation; and Percy by, at the end, forgiving me.

But what they had shown him he had not seen. What they had told him he had not heard. None of them had been able to make him understand. Not even Katherine.

Oh, he thought, what I have thrown away. Oh, what my pride and my foolishness have cost me.

He heard a noise at his side and he looked up and saw Aaron and saw that Aaron was gazing at him, and he did not know how long Aaron had been standing there. He moved over to the edge of the rock he was sitting on.

"Have a seat, Uncle Aaron," he said, patting the stone beside him. "You look tired."

The old man hesitated, and then he did sit down, and for a long time they sat and looked at the house in silence.

"They was no call for it," Uncle Aaron said at last. "He never needed to come here and burn that house. Burning it, that never helped him any."

No, Allen thought, no earthly call. No reason under God's sun, but Ben had done it. Ben Hill had done what he had done. And Allen Hendrick had done what he had done. And there was no turning back now. There was no undoing.

"No," Allen said. "But most likely he doesn't know that yet."

Then he said, "Poor old Ben. He doesn't even know it."

They sat for a while longer, and Allen turned his thoughts to Kate; he thought of her and he knew what he would have to do, and he felt some hurry now, some urgency.

He thought of Katherine and the memory came flooding back, the recollection of her as she had been in the old days at the academy before they had begun to argue in the Roseneath garden. He was struck with how clear the memory seemed, how sharply the details of her face came through to lodge before his mind's eye in all their beauty. The turned-up nose, the high cheekbones, the full lips, the blue eyes, the wide forehead. In his memory he had not seen her this way in more years than he could accurately calculate; and for a longer time than he knew the memory of her had not touched him so: it had not, as it did now, set his heart to beating. At Duck River, south of Franklin, he had not even pressed Percy to find out how she was, so full was his brain of the hate he bore her father.

So he said again, "No. There was no call for what Ben did. But a man will do many a thing that there is no call for."

Later in the morning he cleaned himself up as best he could, and he got his hat and crop and mounted his horse and went to Roseneath. He rode up the drive where he had gone on a Sunday morning four years ago, and though this day was not Sunday, and this time there was no one on the porch, no old man with a palsied head to greet him—the two mornings were very much alike, soft and sweet with spring and bright with sunshine. He hitched his horse and went up on the porch. At the door he stood for a moment, not quite willing to knock yet, not quite willing to begin. Then he did knock, and in a moment she was standing there before him.

She was in mourning. She was wearing a plain black muslin dress, black shoes, a small black apron. She had her sleeves rolled up to show her wrists, and a little strand of her hair hung loose, and there were minute beads of perspiration on her forehead. She had been working, cleaning house or cooking or washing dishes, he did not know what. And it did not matter, not what she had on or what her task had been, she was so beautiful. The love that he felt for her rushed over him for the second time that day, the love that came back after four years, stronger than any memory, any recollection. And perhaps he had thrown it away, destroyed it with his hate for her father and her brother.

"Allen," she said, and her voice was the same soft voice, the voice that lingered always on the verge of a breathless whisper. "You have come back. My dear, I am so glad. I am so glad to see you."

She gave him her hands and he held them for a moment, the touch of her flesh, more thrilling, more painful than the sound of her voice. For an instant they stood in the doorway, and then she turned and led him into the parlor.

She led him into the room that was clean now, no longer cluttered as it had been in the time of Captain Rutledge. It was neater than Allen had ever seen it, and because of this more formal: there was a symmetry to the arrangement of the chairs. She made him wait while she went for tea—he suspected that she needed a few moments to compose herself—and while he was alone, he stood before the hearth and looked up at the portrait of Percy Rutledge. With his hand on his sword and his eyes gazing off into space, the blue eyes peering far, far into the distance, he was very handsome—he was fair as youth itself, and the youthful dream of the world, the golden vision.

Then Kate returned, and he shifted his attention to her. Unlike the boy in the picture, she had changed, and the change was beyond time's simple alteration. She was older, but she was still so young age could not count for much. It was as if the flesh had been rearranged to show the heart's sense of loss. Her sorrow was evident in the corners of her mouth and in the delicate, barely discernible lines across her forehead.

"I looked for you," Allen said when they were seated. "I stopped in Nashville, at your aunt's house, but there was a Yankee living there."

Kate smiled faintly.

"Yes," she said, "they have gone. He was a railroad man, you remember. He took a job in Philadelphia."

"But you?" Allen said. "Did they just go off and leave you?"

"They invited me to go with them," she replied. "But I couldn't. I don't blame them, but I just couldn't."

"You have been alone here?" he asked.

She smiled. "No," she said. "Some of the people are still here. The old ones mostly."

"You came back to help them, to take care of them," Allen said. It was not a question.

"No," she replied. "I came because I wanted to. Because I love Roseneath."

Then she said, "For us back here it has been easy. Except for the loss of Papa and Percy, it has been nothing. I have just been here trying to work the land."

They fell silent then, and Allen sat for a while in the cool and shadowy room and tried to get up enough courage to tell her about Percy. At last he took a deep breath and said:

"I saw Percy, Kate. I was with him in Franklin. At night . . . after he was wounded."

"Oh?" she said. It was a gasp, a sharp intake of air that conveyed her surprise and the pain of her recollection.

"Yes," Allen said, and his voice was softer than he had meant it to be, "I visited him in his tent. I talked to him."

He told her how Percy had sent for him, and he repeated everything that Percy had said; and without sparing himself or attempting to make his own case less black, he told her all the things he had said to Percy. He related that Percy had relieved him of the conditions of his bargain with Captain Rutledge, and he told her how Percy had predicted that she would not marry him.

While he talked, she wept; there was another long pause while she sat and stared out of the window and raised her handkerchief from time to time and wiped her eyes.

Finally she said, "Allen, what is our responsibility in all this? Oh, I know we did not kill Percy. I know that if you and I had never existed, he would still have been at Franklin last year, and being brave, he would have led the charge and regardless of us, he would have died there. But when I think that he had to speak of us —of you and me—at the last hour that he was alive, I wonder how long he had worried about us and what a burden our selfishness must have imposed on him."

She dried her eyes once more. "I remember Papa," she went on. "Poor, old, unhappy man. He should have been allowed to finish his life in peace. But I would not leave him alone. I continued to annoy him."

"I know," Allen Hendrick said softly. "But it was I who plagued him."

"Both of us," she replied. "And all he wanted us to leave him was his dream. All he required was for us to let him keep the old notion, his idea of what the future would be, and his hope of fulfillment after all his years of labor. You know, the trouble with my marrying you was mostly just that he hadn't counted on it. That it fell beyond the limits of what all his life he had conceived the future course of his family to be. That is the way with life. That is what makes simply being here, simply living, such a great curiosity. It is never like you think it is going to be. No matter how closely you stick to a plan, no matter how successful you happen to be, the future always brings a surprise, a difference. Sometimes we need a little while to adjust, to get accustomed to the unexpected. I think now that was the way with Father. If we had left him alone, he would perhaps have finally allowed us to marry. And his last days would have been passed in considerably more peace."

"Maybe so," Allen Hendrick said. "But it's hard to believe. It's hard to believe that he would have ever wanted me for a son-in-law."

"But we should have waited nonetheless," she replied. "When you are young, you can afford to wait—even for justice."

He did not answer. There was a time when he would have said, *Yes, but what about me?* and felt then the anger swelling through his blood, and the sense of wrong tingling in the fissures of his brain, and the flesh itself tightening, the muscles drawing together, to strike out—if they could—against the world's profound inequities. But not now. For him the time of hate was over.

So he said, "And Percy?"

"I don't know," Katherine replied. "I don't know. He was wrong to interfere with us, wrong to strike you that day with his crop. But at the end he had changed, he understood things better. At the end he still objected to our marriage, but not for the old reason. He objected to you, to what you had become, and not to"—she hesitated—"your mother."

"I guess that's right too," he said.

He rose and walked to the fireplace and stood there with his hands clasped behind his back.

Then he said, "I was wrong. Maybe everybody else in the world was wrong too, but I am not going to worry about that. I am just going to confess my own mistake and not concern myself about the others. But time has gone on and the past is over now, and there is nothing I can do to change what has already happened. I cannot go to your father or to Percy and say I am sorry, though I am sorry and I will say it freely to you. Maybe now——" His words stopped and he looked down for a moment at the carpet. Then he raised his eyes and went on, "I mean, I still love you, Kate. Or perhaps what I want to say is I love you again, like I used to love you before . . . before I began to think too much about your father and Percy. I love you better than I did then, Kate. I still want to marry you."

She spoke very softly. "Allen."

"I know what Percy said," he went on, "but it is different now. I have changed. I, too, have altered."

"Allen," she said once more, and that was all that she needed to say. For the tone of her voice was very sad, and her eyes were closed and she was crying again, and the flesh of her cheeks seemed very hollow beneath the high cheekbones.

But after a while she did go on. "No. Not now. Too much has happened, no matter whose fault it was or what the reason. Oh, we cannot ignore the past. We cannot simply forget the old guilt and the old agony."

He understood this in a way. He knew that they had to right the old wrongs for their own sakes—his and hers—that even in a sad and unjust world the end of life was not redress but expiation. This was what his brain was able to comprehend, but in his heart there was the old emptiness, the old longing. He felt as alone as he had felt after the death of Percy, and now he lifted his hands slowly and folded them idly in front of him, and then unclasped them and let them fall at his sides.

More to prolong the moment than anything else, to delay the instant when he would have to turn away and move through the hall and out into the sunlight, he said:

"Ben Hill burned my house. Did you know that?"

"Burned it?" she asked in consternation.

"Yes," Allen replied.

"Oh, no," she said, "I did not know that. Oh, Allen, what a horrible thing to do."

"I guess so," Allen said. "He was like me in a way. I expect since then he's probably been pretty lonesome."

Now he would have to leave her and he looked long at her face, at the rounded chin and the full lips and the high forehead.

"Maybe next year," he said. "Maybe two years from now. Maybe sometime."

"I don't know," she replied, and in her tone there was a note almost of desperation. "I cannot tell about the hereafter. I know only about the present."

"Yes," he said.

Then he said, "Kate," and the sound of her name seemed to drift, hang for a moment in the air between them. "Good-by, Kate."

"Good-by," she said, and then she opened her lips again as if she meant to say something else, but she did not. She closed her mouth without speaking. Her chin began to quiver and she gazed down at the floor.

Allen Hendrick walked out of the room. He went out on the porch and hesitated there, stood there for a while looking out at the sunlit morning. He looked out at the quiet and sun-drenched world, at the fields and the line of green hills, and no man or beast or bird broke the bright silence. He tapped the leg of his boot with his crop, waited a moment, and tapped the boot once more. Then he walked down the steps and got on his horse and rode out the driveway.

Voices of the South

Hamilton Basso
  The View from Pompey's Head
Richard Bausch
  Real Presence
  Take Me Back
Robert Bausch
  On the Way Home
Doris Betts
  The Astronomer and Other Stories
  The Gentle Insurrection and Other Stories
Sheila Bosworth
  Almost Innocent
  Slow Poison
David Bottoms
  Easter Weekend
Erskine Caldwell
  Poor Fool
Fred Chappell
  Dagon
  The Gaudy Place
  The Inkling
  It Is Time, Lord
Kelly Cherry
  Augusta Played
Vicki Covington
  Bird of Paradise
Elizabeth Cox
  The Ragged Way People Fall Out of Love
R. H. W. Dillard
  The Book of Changes
Ellen Douglas
  A Family's Affairs
  A Lifetime Burning
  The Rock Cried Out
  Where the Dreams Cross
Percival Everett
  Cutting Lisa
  Suder
Peter Feibleman
  The Daughters of Necessity
  A Place Without Twilight
Candace Flynt
  Mother Love

William Price Fox
  Dixiana Moon
George Garrett
  An Evening Performance
  Do, Lord, Remember Me
  The Magic Striptease
  The Finished Man
Reginald Gibbons
  Sweetbitter
Ellen Gilchrist
  The Annunciation
  In the Land of Dreamy Dreams
Marianne Gingher
  Bobby Rex's Greatest Hit
Shirley Ann Grau
  The Hard Blue Sky
  The House on Coliseum Street
  The Keepers of the House
  Roadwalkers
Ben Greer
  Slammer
Barry Hannah
  The Tennis Handsome
Donald Hays
  The Dixie Association
William Humphrey
  Home from the Hill
  The Ordways
Mac Hyman
  No Time For Sergeants
Madison Jones
  A Cry of Absence
Nancy Lemann
  Lives of the Saints
  Sportsman's Paradise
Beverly Lowry
  Come Back, Lolly Ray
Clarence Major
  Such Was the Season
Valerie Martin
  A Recent Martyr
  Set in Motion
Willie Morris
  The Last of the Southern Girls
Padgett Powell
  Mrs. Hollingsworth's Men

Louis D. Rubin, Jr.
  The Golden Weather
Evelyn Scott
  The Wave
Lee Smith
  The Last Day the Dogbushes Bloomed
Elizabeth Spencer
  Landscapes of the Heart
  The Night Travellers
  The Salt Line
  This Crooked Way
  The Voice at the Back Door
Max Steele
  Debby
Virgil Suárez
  Latin Jazz
Walter Sullivan
  The Long, Long Love
  Sojourn of a Stranger
Allen Tate
  The Fathers
Peter Taylor
  In the Miro District and Other Stories
  The Widows of Thornton
Robert Penn Warren
  Band of Angels
  Brother to Dragons
  Flood
  World Enough and Time
Walter White
  Flight
James Wilcox
  Miss Undine's Living Room
  North Gladiola
Joan Williams
  The Morning and the Evening
  The Wintering
Christine Wiltz
  Glass House
Thomas Wolfe
  The Hills Beyond
  The Web and the Rock